Sacrifice the One

Barbara Williams

Sacrifice the One

Monica P. Carter

URBAN
CHRISTIAN

www.urbanchristianonline.net

URBAN CHRISTIAN is published by

Urban Books
10 Brennan Place
Deer Park, NY 11729

ISBN-13: 978-1-893196-94-0
ISBN-10: 1-893196-94-1

First Printing April 2007
Printed in the United States of America

10 9 8 7 6 5 4 3 2 1

This is a work of fiction. Any references or similarities to actual events, real people, living, or dead, or to real locales are intended to give the novel a sense of reality. Any similarity in other names, characters, places, and incidents is entirely coincidental.

Submit Wholesale Orders to:
Kensington Publishing Corp.
C/O Penguin Group (USA) Inc.
Attention: Order Processing
405 Murray Hill Parkway
East Rutherford, NJ 07073-2316
Phone: 1-800-526-0275
Fax: 1-800-227-9604

ACKNOWLEDGMENTS

I most humbly first give thanks to God for allowing this gift to travel through my pen. I appreciate the ability to craft words into stories that touch lives.

Of course, I could not move forward without thanking my mother who, through her example and love, gives me the strength and courage to always press forward.

To those others close to my heart, I thank you for being there: My sisters, my friends—you know who you are.

I want to thank the book clubs and booksellers who gave this book a chance when it was first self published—a few, I must mention by name: The Jackson Mississippi Readers Club, RAWSISTAZ, Sistahs Book Club, Sistahs of Reading Club, Sistah Circle Book Club 2. Booksellers include Black Images, Jokaes, Shrine of the Black Madonna, Pyramid, Black Classic Books, Muddie Waters, and the chains—Borders, B. Dalton, Barnes and Noble, Walden. I must give a special acknowledgment to Coastal bookstores and their owners who were so generous to me in my early career, but who suffered Hurricane Katrina—Afro American Book Stop and Community Books in New Orleans and Book Ends in Mississippi. You are forever in my heart.

Thanks to my original editor, Carla Dean, who worked with me on the self-published project; and a tremendous thanks to my current editor, Joylynn Jossel, who helped me grow under this new Christian imprint.

To my agent, Dr. Maxine Thompson, you make miracles happen.

To so many writer friends, I can't begin to name you, but I must call out two: Michelle McGriff, who puts up with my late-night online musings, and Toschia, who doesn't mind if I call fifty/eleven times a day.

And to the one who walks with me each day, Anubhav. I love you.

DEDICATION

To the people at the Afro American Bookstop and Community Books in New Orleans and Book Ends on the Mississippi Gulf Coast, not even a hurricane can wipe away the print you made in my heart. Your mark will always be there.

Prologue

"You like that?" Robert asked, his dark eyes seeking Rose's.

Rose moaned and nodded, shifting her body ever slightly under the soft stroke of her husband's hand. "Yes, baby," she said, and saw his face light up under her approval.

Rose usually relished the feel of her husband's hand on her caramel skin as he expertly awakened her to his touch. He was tender and took care always to put her needs above his. But tonight, that wasn't enough.

The sigh escaped her lips before she could swallow it back. Robert instantly froze. "What's wrong?"

Rose shook her head. "Nothing, baby," she said, and touched Robert's face.

He was unconvinced. "Why did you sigh? Am I doing something wrong?" Anxiety creased his brow.

"No, you're great," Rose said. "Everything is fine."

"You sure?"

"Yes," Rose said and pulled on her best smile for her husband. She rolled over and kissed him, letting her tongue play with his lower lip.

"I love you," Robert whispered into her neck.

"I love you too," Rose whispered back.

"You're all I need," Robert said, "all I'll ever need."

Rose couldn't repeat the words, so she kissed him again instead, hoping her husband hadn't noticed that she did not repeat the words. She knew they would be a lie. She needed something else.

Rose closed her eyes, let herself fall back onto the bed, under the weight of her husband. She lay there, for how long, she didn't know. She opened her eyes when she realized the room was quiet. Robert was staring down at her.

"What's wrong?" he quizzed.

"What do you mean?"

"You're not saying anything," Robert said. "You're just lying there. Are you sick? Do you have a headache?"

Rose thought to pretend, but she took in a deep breath and let it slowly escape through her nose. She sat up in the bed, pulling her knees to her chest and wrapping her arms around her legs.

Robert sat up next to her, concern marking his face. "Do you need something?" he asked. "If it's your head, I can get you something for it. Or if it's me, if I was doing something wrong, just tell me and I'll make it better."

Rose smiled softly. Oh, Robert. He just didn't get it. "I really want a baby," she said, the words but a whisper in the room.

Robert froze.

"Baby, I just think we should try one more time," Rose said in a soft voice.

"Is that what's been bothering you?" Robert shot back. "Here I was, thinking something was wrong."

"But it is," Rose pleaded. "Something is wrong. If we could just—"

"Rose, we've already decided," Robert cut her off.

"I know, but you just don't underst—"

"Drop it, Rose!" Robert moved from the bed and pulled on his pants.

"Robert, come back here!"

But he was gone.

Rose let her head fall back against the headboard. The ecstasy of nights together like this was nice, but she wanted more. She needed more. What she craved from all this was a baby, a little being who would call her Mama and look at her with eyes wide and full of wonder. Somebody she could dress up in barrettes and cute, puffy socks.

Each time she thought a baby would be hers, her heart sang and she positively felt as if she were floating. She hummed and couldn't wipe the smile from her full lips. She could almost feel the baby's breath on her cheeks, could almost hear the gurgles and coos. But each time life dashed those hopes. The last time this had happened, she had lain in bed for weeks, unable to see how she could possibly get over another miscarriage. Her heart constricted and bunched up in a wad of hurt that tied her stomach in disappointed, bitter knots. She refused to speak to anyone, even Robert. Her eyes stared listlessly at the wall and she twisted between her fingers a tiny cap she had knitted for the girl she had been sure God had finally given her.

I was so mad at God, she recalled now, the last miscarriage on her mind. Robert had watched her in twisted pain, his own faith already shaky. "God doesn't care about us," he had said, his voice hard with anger.

She knew she had to be strong for Robert, had to defend God, to remind her husband of the Lord's mercy, but with her own feelings so raw, she had said nothing.

"That's why I don't go to church," Robert had continued. "Why? All God does is make bad things happen. What did we ever do to him?"

"We can't blame God," she finally said. Her life had to be

the example to help him see his way, finally, fully, to the Lord. So she had pulled herself from the depths of depression.

But secretly, she battled, even now as the moonlight cast a pale glow over the bed, the spot now cold where her husband had lain only minutes before.

I don't know how much more I can take. How do I have faith when You keep taking away from me the one thing I want most? I'm not a bad person. What about all those who do really bad things and you bless them still? Why do you do this to me, Lord?

She shook her head to clear it of those thoughts. She tried to focus on the good in her life. *I am blessed. I love my life. I am married to a wonderful man. I have my health. I have—*

She couldn't finish the thought.

The one thing she was missing overshadowed all she had. And if she didn't get it, she knew she would die. If she didn't have a baby, she'd simply die.

A baby was something Robert could take or leave. But he knew how desperately his wife longed for a child. He sat on the hood of the car under the carport, the sounds of the Texas night his only company. Well, the sounds and his thoughts. Sometimes, in the still of the night when the feelings of inadequacy would haunt him for not being able to give her the one thing she craved more than anything else, he wondered why it mattered to her so much. *Am I not enough?* Wasn't their life all right, even without a child? Didn't he shower her with affection and surprise her with gifts? Wasn't he all she needed?

But he knew the answer. He hadn't missed the fact that she hadn't repeated his words when they were in bed. When he told her she was all he needed, she hadn't been able to say the same in return.

"I try as hard as I can!" he spat the words out in frustration, jabbing his fist in the air. "No matter what I do, it'll never be enough. Not unless I give her a baby."

But he squeezed those thoughts from his mind. "Stop thinking like that," he told himself. "Everything is all right. Everything will be all right."

Chapter 1

Robert remembered the first time he saw Rose. She was the new kid in school—all shy like—her sandy hair pulled back into a tight ponytail, her knees shiny from too much baby oil. She was tall and slender, a dream in a flowered, pink cotton dress that the wind flirted with in the slightest way. She dropped her books as she seemed to float up the steps to the building, and unknowingly into his heart. He stopped to help her pick them up.

From that moment, on the stone steps of Clear Love Colored High School on a blue-sky day in 1954, he was hooked.

It seemed unreal sometimes that they had been together since that day, when he was in the tenth grade and she was in the ninth. How quickly twenty years had passed. They hadn't started out as an item, a couple. No, he wouldn't have dared approach her like that—not him. Not with . . . well.

Robert shook his head to clear the thoughts. Reminiscing wouldn't get him through this two-inch thick stack of overdue freshman research papers. But as he tried to get his mind back to grading, a tiny smile tugged at the corners of his lips.

He had to admit he was getting excited about the baby they were soon to have. Just think, they would finally get to hear the pitter-patter of little feet running through the house. Rose, his Rose, would have her precious baby. A baby he had finally been able to give her. It had taken all these years, and just when they had vowed not to try anymore, their time had arrived. Twenty years of being together, and they would now have a new member to their family. Come spring, they would have a baby.

He picked up the phone and dialed.

"Hello?"

"Hi, honey," he said into the receiver after Rose answered.

The sound of the voice on the other end produced an all-out grin. He imagined what she looked like right at that moment. Her reddish brown hair would be in a long braid, hanging straight down her back, and she would be wearing pink, fluffy slippers. The gentle curve of her stomach made her walk with a wobbly gait.

"I was just checking on you," he said. "How do you feel?"

Rose giggled. "Will you stop it? This is the tenth time you've called since lunch."

Robert grinned sheepishly. "No, maybe the eighth time."

Rose rolled her eyes. "Well, for the eighth time, I'm fine and the baby is fine. How are you going to get any work done if you're always on the phone with me?"

Robert looked at the papers on the desk in front of him. "I guess you're right. I do have a few things that need my attention before coming home." He paused. The slightest edge of worry seeped into his voice. "You sure you're okay?"

"Robert, get off the phone and do some work," she said

sternly. Her voice softened. "By the way, I'm fixing your favorite dinner."

Robert glanced at the black clock on the gray wall. The sun had disappeared behind the Randall Stout administration building on the other side of the State Line College campus. It was quarter past five. "I'll be home by six-thirty," he said.

"I know. You told me that the last time we talked," Rose said. "I love you."

"I love you too," he said. "Bye."

"Bye, honey."

When Robert placed the phone back in the cradle, he tried to concentrate on the students' words on the pages, but his mind wouldn't let him. His heart still raced sometimes when he heard Rose's voice, or felt the touch of her hand. He didn't know what he would ever do without her.

As Rose hung up the mustard yellow phone, she smiled. Robert, he was such a worrier. She told him time and time again that everything was fine; that the baby was fine. Unlike the other times, this time, she *would* be a mommy. She wouldn't lose this one. She shifted her weight in an attempt to relieve that recurring faint feeling of heaviness down below. In a moment, it was gone. She touched the roundness that was her stomach.

Rose wished she could take something for the elephants that were stomping around her skull, but she didn't dare. She would do nothing to jeopardize her baby, not even by just taking a headache powder. She rubbed her eyes. That blurring was there again. She blinked, trying to remove anything that could be in her eyes.

Her rings no longer fit and her face, naturally thin with high cheekbones, had evolved into puffy cheeks. Slippers were now her only comfort, as other shoes seemed to strain to get around her feet.

Her hoop earrings jingled. She wore a polyester shift dress in tan, black-and-white print. She might be pregnant, but that was no reason to look unkempt or sloppy like so many women did when they were with child. She couldn't wear many of the fashions of the mid-1970s right now, but one day she knew she'd be back to knit dresses, cute skirts, and tight-waist bell-bottomed jeans. And she would dress her little girl just like her. They'd be twins.

Rose hobbled to the kitchen and turned off the stove. She loved cooking for Robert, but not when she was hurting. She balled her fists, planted them in the small of her back and stretched. She breathed slowly in and out, trying to get some relief from the low, dull pain in her back. She craved this baby. She would be glad to be free of the heavy feeling in her stomach and the aches, though. *I won't miss this swelling one bit,* Rose thought as she smiled wryly.

The day she passed her twentieth week, she collapsed on the bed and cried. She had made it past the risk of miscarrying. None of the other pregnancies had grown this far. She could finally relax. God would finally grant her request.

After that, the quivery, nervous feeling in her stomach that she had tried for months to ignore eased and Rose, for the first time, grabbed Robert and drove to a hardware store to pick out paint for the room that would be the nursery. She allowed herself to think of the possibility of naming the child. Her mother tried to tell her she would have a boy, but Rose knew in her heart that the baby would be a girl. And Rose had only one name that would work. Joy. Her baby would be her joy. That was the only name she could have—Joy.

Rose spent much of her time reading about babies—what they needed in their first few months, at what age they began to walk and talk, how to tell if the child was gifted.

She knew everything there was to know about a child's development after birth.

Dr. Duran confirmed that she was fine. *Well, that isn't exactly true,* she thought guiltily. Dr. Duran had said she was doing as well as could be expected, but he told her to use good judgment and pay attention to this pregnancy.

Actually, he had forbidden her to get pregnant. But she didn't tell Robert. She had, in fact, told him her doctor said she was all right to try to get pregnant again. *Well, obviously, I was all right. I'm pregnant. And the baby is fine.*

It was the first lie of her marriage.

See how much Dr. Duran knew.

Dr. Duran had actually gotten angry with her when they found out she was pregnant again. He said a woman in her mid-thirties had a greater risk of having problems with a pregnancy, and that, combined with her history of miscarriages, made him shake his head at the idea. "Rose, a baby is just not something I would recommend," Dr. Duran said many months ago after Rose had gone to see him following a conversation with Robert. She had tried to talk with Robert about conceiving and he had gotten out of bed and stormed off—something he rarely did, but when he did, she knew there was no convincing him.

The next day, she had tried to broach the subject again, but Robert wouldn't have it. He made her promise to go to the doctor to "get this taken care of," as he put it. He wanted Rose to see the doctor to permanently remove her ability to even conceive, the memory of the last miscarriage still fresh. She did go to the doctor.

But not to end her ability to have a baby. She had tried to see if perhaps something had changed with her health, if maybe Dr. Duran would now give her permission to carry a child, so she could run back to Robert with the doctor's blessing. She knew that would be the only way he would agree to try.

She had failed to gain the blessing, but she had succeeded in getting pregnant.

She had never kept secrets from her husband, but this time was an exception. She pretended to be surprised when they found out she had conceived.

Rose hadn't told Robert that Dr. Duran warned of the possibility she may need to be on total bed rest toward the end of the pregnancy. She also didn't tell Robert that Dr. Duran said she would have to see a specialist, a physician who worked with what Dr. Duran referred to as high-risk pregnancies, later if problems developed. She didn't feel the need to tell Robert because she didn't want to worry him, especially since she felt fine. *That's not entirely true. You're not concerned about worrying him. You just don't want him to be angry.* She shrugged off the nagging voice.

I want this baby.

And she knew she wouldn't lose this one. She just felt it in her bones. God had finally answered her prayers.

He had given her Joy.

The phone in Robert's office rang, interrupting his conversation with a student. He held up a hand, asking the student to give him a moment. "English department," he said.

"Sweetheart," Rose's voice was soft.

He smiled. "Oh, so now you're calling me back," he said in a playful tone. "Just a minute ago you—"

"Robert!" Rose's voice was barely audible in the phone, urgency now making the word taunt.

Robert bolted straight up in his chair. "Sweetheart, what's wrong?" Panic laced his voice when he heard the way she gasped his name.

"Robert, it's the baby! Something is wrong with my baby! Help me!" Rose's voice was shaking. Her words came out in a sharp, run-on sentence.

Robert shooed the student out of his office and clutched

the receiver to his mouth, his fists folded so tightly that the indentations of the tendons were plain to see. He tried to speak in an even tone. "Okay, just calm down. Tell me what happened," he said.

"Robert, I don't know." Her voice was breathless and strained. "It hurts! Something is not right." The phone fell from her hand and clanked to the floor.

"Rose! Rose!" Robert called into the phone. "Rose! Rose! Answer me."

He knew she couldn't hear him and that time was running out. He slammed down the phone and then hurriedly dialed emergency services, rattling off the address to his home, before dashing out the door. He pressed in Dr. Duran's number and gave a breathless recap of the conversation with Rose. He bumped into the dean, but couldn't even make an apology at the surprised look on the man's face. There was no time for explaining.

Robert headed home, but saw the ambulance wheeling away from his house, so he followed it, not caring if he ran a light or annoyed other drivers. He sprang from the car as paramedics wheeled Rose from the ambulance. She looked so small on the stretcher, strangers talking excitedly around her. He elbowed through the small bunch of emergency staff. "That's my wife!"

"I'm sorry, sir, but you'll have to move—"

"Don't tell me to move! That's my wife you have there!" He shoved the startled-looking paramedic who had spoken. "Rose, Rose, can you hear me?"

Someone pulled at his arm. "Sir, please, we've got to get her inside. You shouldn't even be back here," he heard a female voice say as he stumbled against the stretcher as paramedics wheeled Rose into the emergency area.

He jerked away, but allowed reason to sink into his consciousness. He turned to the woman. "Where are they taking her?"

"Sir, the doctor will be out in a little while to answer your questions. Let me show you where you can wait." The woman's voice was firm, as if she talked to crazed husbands every day. She waited for him to acknowledge the words that she had just spoken, and then turned to show him to the waiting area. Without a word, he followed.

Three hours later, Robert was at Rose's bedside. She smiled faintly. Wet strands of hair were plastered to her forehead. "I'm sorry," she said.

"Shhhh, be quiet." Robert put his finger to her lips. "Save your strength. We'll talk later."

Dr. Duran rushed to the hospital after hearing of Rose's emergency. Now, hours later, he reappeared. He stepped into the room and closed the door. Smiling, he pulled up a chair and grabbed Rose's hand between his two.

"Rose, you gave us quite a scare," Dr. Duran said.

She waved him off with her other hand. "Well, you know I like to make it interesting around here. I'll do anything for attention," she joked.

Her attempt at levity didn't do anything to lift the mood. Dr. Duran looked at Robert, then back at Rose. The doctor cleared his throat and stood. "Rose, you know I told you this would be a difficult pregnancy. I even questioned whether it was the best thing."

A bewildered look crossed Robert's face. "What do you mean? I thought you said we had a good chance, that this pregnancy was the best we'd had," he questioned.

Dr. Duran nodded and looked directly at Robert. "Well, that's true. None of the others progressed this far. This pregnancy has been going remarkably well—remarkably well considering the fact that there is still significant risk. This is why I told you not to—"

"Dr. Duran, can we not talk about all that," Rose cut him off and offered a shaky smile, her eyes cutting quickly to

Robert. "Let's focus on the good thing. And that's the fact that a baby will be born."

"Well, before we can get to that, we have to get you all right," Dr. Duran insisted.

Robert's brow furrowed as the doctor's words fell on his ears, explaining how Rose's blood pressure had skyrocketed into some condition that posed a severe risk. For a brief moment, Robert's years of education and teaching at college meant nothing. His mind couldn't comprehend the words: preeclampsia, seizure, danger. Robert stepped closer to the bed, as if he could somehow shield his wife from the doctor's words.

Dr. Duran decided that Rose would have to stay in the hospital for the next few days. And that meant Robert too. Robert left her side only to grab some clothes and a few magazines and books he thought would interest his wife. He almost hated to step away from her bed to go to the bathroom. That's how much he was afraid.

He spent time sitting in the chair next to Rose's bed, sometimes talking to her, sometimes staring out the window without seeing the skyline of the city that was dressed up for Christmas with red, green, and white lights draped across buildings.

Rose drifted in and out of consciousness the first couple of days. Tubes were her source of food, and machines were her lifelines.

Robert gritted his teeth when Rose's parents rushed into the room that first day. He wanted them to leave, to leave them alone. This was private time, a time for Rose and him, not company.

"Oh, Lord, we come to you humbly asking for your blessings," Rose's mother prayed, leaning close to her daughter and touching her sunken cheek. "We thank you for the baby you're giving us. . . ."

The words grated on Robert's ears. *We don't thank God for anything! It's His fault my wife is in pain like this.*

". . . in Jesus' name, amen," Rose's mother finished the prayer and kissed her daughter's forehead. She turned to her husband. "Well, I am trusting God for a miracle. He is the source of all strength."

"Yeah, if He's so powerful, why is she even in the hospital in the first place?" Robert shot back. He had never been close to God, and so many things had happened in his life to cause him to be angry with a maker who would take so much from him. What God would let a young boy suffer at the hands of bullies? And who would cause a woman as loving as Rose to struggle to hold onto a baby when that's what she wanted most?

Barbara cut her eyes at Robert, but spoke to her husband. "I knew Rose shouldn't have married him. I told her, all those years ago, you can't be unequally yoked. But no, she had to up and—"

"Sweetheart," Phillip said the one word and Barbara bit back her words.

They stood awkwardly about the bed, Rose's parents on one side, and her husband on the other. Robert tried to force himself to be cordial to the intruders, but insisted they leave in the evening.

Barbara resisted at first, but was finally led away by Phillip.

Rose's sister came the second day to comb her hair. Robert could have done it himself, but she arrived while he was in the bathroom and had her fingers in Rose's wavy tresses when he stepped back into the room.

Once again, he gritted his teeth to keep from saying anything. *Why can't these people see we don't need their intrusions?* he thought to himself.

After a few hours, as if sensing that her presence was not welcomed, his wife's sister finally went home.

* * *

Dr. Duran gave no hope that Rose would be able to carry the baby to term. He said the best hope right now was that, with bed rest and treatment, she would be able to maintain the pregnancy for a few more weeks. However, if her condition worsened, Dr. Duran said they would have to take the baby. He also mentioned something about bringing in another doctor. Dr. Duran reassured Robert that with modern technology, babies born early had wonderful chances for survival. The only chance for survival Robert cared about was Rose's.

Robert was ready to give permission to induce labor, to take the baby, to do whatever they needed in order to make sure his wife would be all right, but the doctor said they could wait a few more days for Rose to come around so she could have a say in the matter.

On the third day, Rose stayed awake longer, allowing Robert the chance to feed her and discuss what the doctor had said.

"I'm so tired," she said weakly with her head sunken into the pillow, her body barely making a dent in the narrow bed.

"Hey, listen," Robert said, brushing her hair off her forehead. "Dr. Duran thinks the baby may have to come soon. He said medical advances make survival rates for babies—"

"Rob, I can't let my baby be born at thirty weeks!" She looked at him with eyes wide with dismay. "Her lungs, her heart, they're all developing. Don't you know the health problems she could have?"

"But, baby, don't you know the health problems *you* could have?" Robert insisted. He tried to keep his agitation in check.

"I would give anything to have this baby. Anything."

"Sweetheart, I know, but we have got to listen to the doctor. He is the professional here and knows about the probability for survival based on his expertise and depth of knowledge. We cannot ignore reason and prudence."

"You don't understand. I can't risk my baby."

Robert could see the lines changing into a frenzied display on the monitor attached to his wife. He knew the conversation was upsetting her. So, he decided to let it go—for now.

He leaned in, kissing her cheek. "Okay, we'll talk to the doctor again. We'll do whatever you want. Get some rest."

But before he finished his sentence, she was already asleep.

Rose was adamant about carrying the baby to term. Dr. Duran again outlined the possible problems. Her blood pressure had increased, and she was swelling. She was at risk of having a seizure, or possibly dying.

Dr. Duran brought in another physician, Dr. Stokes, who discovered an underlying heart condition. Rose knew she had an irregular heartbeat that in the past hadn't been any cause for concern to her or any of her doctors. However, the other doctor said somehow her rhythm was now off and her heart was working feverishly to pump blood to her and her baby. Because of this finding, Dr. Duran forbade her from getting out of the bed to do anything, even to go to the bathroom.

When Dr. Duran and Dr. Stokes explained the suggested course of treatment involving the use of a drug combination, Rose looked at them with narrowed eyes. She demanded to know what risk the medicine would pose to the baby. In an even tone, Dr. Duran told her that it was the safest choice she had, especially if she wanted to maintain the pregnancy any longer.

"Sweetheart, the doctor makes some good points," Robert said, eyeing Dr. Duran, who nodded, even as Rose shook her head. "These are extenuating circumstances, and we should acquiesce. Dr. Duran and Dr. Stokes know what's the most advantageous and expedient course of treatment, given the direness of the situation."

Rose didn't want to hear anymore. Her baby needed to stay inside her for six or seven more weeks, and that was that. She started to argue, but Dr. Duran interrupted, telling her that they could watch the condition as long as she did as he advised. Then, he glanced at Dr. Stokes and wrote something on his notepad. Dr. Duran said they would try to wait for the thirty-fifth week if her condition did not worsen, but that's as much as he would agree to at this moment—and only if she followed all of his instructions.

Dr. Duran's eyes darted to his watch. He would continue the conversation later, after Rose and her husband had a chance to talk. Dr. Duran had experience with mothers who couldn't see the big picture—that their lives were in danger—and knew that maybe she needed a little time to come to terms. If not, he would have to use his best medical judgment. But for now, he would wait. He told Rose and Robert that he would leave them alone for a while and come back, then he left with Dr. Stokes.

Rose watched them leave, then turned her head toward Robert. The baby had to have that time. Her baby would have the best chance, no matter what.

But Robert wasn't so sure.

"Sweetheart, let's think about what the doctor is saying," he pleaded.

"Rob, there is nothing to talk about," Rose said. She only called him Rob when she was trying to get a point across. "I would do anything for my baby, make any sacrifice."

"But you're not listening!" Robert's frustration made his words come out in clipped tones. "What kind of life would you give the baby if you're not there? You could die if you do this."

Rose smiled softly. Didn't Robert know God had given

them this baby? Didn't he know there was nothing she wouldn't do to make sure her baby was fine, especially after all these years of waiting, after all the tears of miscarriages? Didn't he know she would die if she *didn't* have this baby?

"Rob, if I knew there was more I could give my baby, my Joy, and I didn't do it, don't you know how that would kill me? Don't you know if I decided to have this baby now knowing her chances of survival—of having a normal life—were slim, I would never forgive myself? Can't you see that?"

"And can't you see that I don't want anything to happen to you? Can't *you* see that? Your obstinate pursuit of this foolhardy plan is analogous to a pilot who still insists on flying even though the mechanic tells him that there isn't enough fuel to make the journey. It is unthinkable and lacks foresight." Robert jerked his hand away from his wife and abruptly stood. *She is being so unreasonable. But then again, she is always like that. She always has to have her way.* And usually, he let her; however, not when it came to this. "Rose, I am not going to let you—"

Rose's voice became stronger than it had been in weeks. "Let me? Tell me, Robert, what are you not going to *let* me do?"

"Look, I'm not going to argue about this." Robert glared at her. "You're being completely irrational and simply are not thinking."

"Oh, I'm thinking, Robert. I'm thinking about my baby. You're the one not thinking. You never wanted this child anyway! And stop using your 'professor' tone with me. I'm not one of your students."

Robert strode back to her bedside. "Okay, fine, you're right. I didn't care anything about having a baby. All I wanted was you. Always have. Always will. But no, you just had to have a baby. So, when I found out we were going to have one, I said fine. I figured if that's what it took to make you happy, I could go along with it, since *I* obviously wasn't enough."

"Oh, don't play the victim here," Rose shot back. "It's not about you. It's about wanting to have a complete family. I would think you would understand that."

Robert shook his head. She was impossible. "Look, I was all for that idea. We tried, Rose. We tried. But we agreed not to try anymore because it didn't look like a baby would be in our future. I said if having a baby was that big of a deal, we could adopt. But you didn't want to do that. Again, because everything had to be your way.

"I didn't want you to get pregnant again. I didn't know if you could stand another miscarriage. That's why I was surprised when we found out you were pregnant this last time. And I tried to be happy. In fact, I was. But none of this is worth it if something happens to you."

Rose opened her mouth and then quickly closed it. She grabbed her midsection. "Oh, Rob—"

Robert immediately began pushing the buzzer to get the nurse. "Help! Help!" He ran to the door and started yelling down the hall. "Somebody come quickly! My wife!"

It took an hour to stabilize Rose. Dr. Duran said the excitement wasn't good for her but that she was no worse for it. He cast a chastising glance at Robert, yet spoke with affection to Rose.

Robert sat quietly in a chair next to the bed and held his wife's hand. The two were silent, each in thought.

The night before, Rose had a talk with God. It seemed a cruel joke that God had played on her. He had let her get so close to being a mommy, but still her baby's life hung in limbo. It was so unfair. Her mama had taught her never to question God, but she couldn't help it.

"Why are You doing this to me?" Rose had asked God,

screaming in her mind, careful not to let Robert see her angst. "It's so unfair!"

In the silence of the room, she tried to breathe deeply to calm her emotions. Her anger turned to desperation. Rose bargained with God. *If You will just protect my child, I wouldn't ask for anything else.* But she was scared.

Rose turned to Robert and squeezed his hand. "Robbie, can you ask Augusta to come in here for a minute?" she asked.

Robert didn't want to step outside the door. Rose saw his hesitation and waved her hand in a motion that told him to go ahead. "Robbie, please. I need to talk to my sister."

A tense muscle flexed in his jaw, but he did as requested. Robert glanced back at his wife before closing the door behind him. He didn't want to be away from her for a second. The emergency from a few hours before had scared him. He could remember the way his heart seemed to jump into his throat—where it felt like it was still sitting.

Moments later, Augusta was at her sister's side. "Yes, baby?" Augusta cradled her older sister's face and rubbed her forehead. Augusta's eyes searched the visage of the sister who used to hold her in her lap and rock her to sleep at night after a bad dream. "What do you need?"

Rose looked at Robert and tried to clear her throat. She spoke so weakly that he and Augusta had to lean in to hear what she was saying. "Robbie, can you excuse us for a second?"

"Huh?" Robert was caught by surprise. They had no secrets.

"Robbie, I need to talk to my sister. Alone," Rose said, her voice barely a whisper. She was getting tired.

Augusta stared at Robert, then eased closer to her big sister and waited for him to leave. She knew he didn't like this, but what could he do? Augusta folded her arms across her chest and glanced pointedly at Robert. Not wanting to upset his wife, Robert shoved his hands in his pockets and shrugged.

"Okay," he said as he leaned forward and kissed Rose on the forehead. "Call me when you're finished. I'll be just right outside."

The two waited for Robert to close the door. Then, Rose turned to Augusta. "I need you to do something for me," Rose said, grasping her sister's hand.

Dr. Duran allayed Rose's fears. He said there was a good chance both mother and baby would be fine. Rose took a deep breath and looked skyward. "Thank you," she mouthed to God. He'd let her be a mother after all.

Robert castigated himself for the earlier argument. How could he have let it get out of hand like that? How?

"Love, I'm sorry about earlier," he told her, opening the shades to let the sunlight inside.

Rose took another steadying breath. "I am too. I know you're just concerned."

"So, what did you and Augusta talk about?" he asked. He tried to sound casual, but the curiosity was eating away at him.

Rose smiled wanly. "Just girl stuff." Before he could ask another question, she added, "Come here." She patted the bed next to her. "Come talk to me."

The bed sank under Robert's weight. Rose placed her hand on his leg.

"I'd like to carry the baby until at least the thirty-fifth week. By then, she'll have completely developed lungs and weigh about five or six pounds. She might still need oxygen, but she would be out of danger."

Robert was ready to do whatever he needed to keep her happy. He almost choked on the words, but managed to get them out. "All right."

He leaned in and held her close.

Chapter 2

The baby arrived in the thirty-fourth week. She came in the middle of the night, wailing and tiny. Nurses barely let Rose kiss her before whisking the baby off to some faraway room. Suddenly, the baby wasn't the cause of worry. It was the mother. Something had gone terribly wrong. Rose's heart raced and her eyes dilated. Doctors could not control her blood pressure—or the heavy bleeding.

Robert paced back and forth in the waiting room. It was January 1975 and his whole world was reeling. He couldn't see how everyone else just walked about as if nothing had changed. A magazine on the table reminded him the Pittsburgh Steelers had just beaten the Minnesota Vikings to win their first Super Bowl. He could hear the faint sounds of the Jackson 5's song, "Dancing Machine", coming from someone's audio cassette player. Everyone walked around as if today was any other day, as if his wife was in no danger.

Robert had never been close to God—especially since it seemed God hadn't answered many of his childhood prayers—but now he talked to his maker as if he did so every day. Robert spoke in quiet, urgent tones, making deals as quickly as they came to mind.

"Just make her all right," he said, hiding in the bathroom, away from scrutiny. "Please let Rose be fine."

It seemed as if Robert had aged ten years overnight, as he twisted his hands in nervous anticipation of what the doctors would say as he regained his seat. Each time someone entered the room, he looked up, a question in his eyes. His heart pounded so hard in his chest that he felt certain anyone around could hear the thump-thump of worry and fear.

God owed him this.

"If you just let her live, I promise I will never let any other harm come to her," he whispered, fingering a worn Bible he found on a table. "If you just let her be okay . . ." His lips were parched and his stomach in knots.

Phillip and Barbara, Rose's parents, who were sitting in the waiting room, glanced at each other. Rose's father coughed to clear his throat. "Robert, Robert. God will take care of her. "

Rose's father strode across the room and rested his hand on the shoulder of his son-in-law. Robert didn't hear nor feel the man. His eyes were fixated on the doorway. Why were they taking so long? Why?

After what seemed like hours, they let Robert in to see Rose. At first, he couldn't tell if she was even breathing, she was so still. He swooped down, the salt of his tears mixing with that of the sweat on her forehead. Something fluttered on his cheek. Her eyelashes danced next to his skin. Relief flowed through him. Maybe God had finally answered one of his prayers.

"Oh, sweetheart, I'm so glad you are okay." The lump in his throat dissolved.

Rose struggled to get the words to escape her mouth. Robert had to lean in to hear her.

"How is my Joy?" Rose whispered. Her lips were cracked.

Sandy hair darkened with sweat lay slick against her fore-head. Her eyelashes were clumped together with moisture from tears or sweat; Robert couldn't tell which.

"Huh?" Robert said. Oh, the baby. "Oh, she's fine," he answered in an attempt to ease his wife's worries. In all honesty, he didn't know. He had actually forgotten about the baby in his concern for his wife. But he felt sure the baby was all right. Otherwise, wouldn't someone have said something?

Rose smiled, a funny expression crossing her face. "I'm so glad. You know, they only let me touch her, not hold her. Can you bring her here to me?"

Robert hesitated, not wanting to leave her side. "She's probably sleeping."

Rose shook her head. "Have them bring her to me." Her voice shook and her breathing was shallow. She struggled to find the air to form the words. "I . . . need . . . to . . . see . . . my . . . baby."

An eerie feeling came over Robert. "Okay."

He called a nurse to the room and told her about Rose's request. The nurse left, but in a moment, she was back holding the baby.

Rose struggled to sit up, but didn't have the strength. Robert gently grabbed her underneath her shoulders in order to lift her to a sitting position. Her breath came in short, low bursts. The nurse carefully placed the baby in Rose's arms. Rose swallowed. Her eyes were starry with emotion when she looked up at Robert.

"Isn't . . . she . . . beautiful?" Rose said, gazing down at the baby.

Robert nodded.

Rose tilted her head slightly, motioning for Robert to come closer. He moved so close that his leg touched the bed. Rose reached for his hand and placed it on her shoulder.

"Thank you," she said softly.

"For what?" Robert asked.

"For letting me know what it feels like to be a mother," she said. The faint freckles on the bridge of her nose shone under the harsh light.

"Robert, I'm really tired. And I'm not sure that I'm going to make it out of here."

Robert jerked away. "Stop talking like that. Stop talking like you're insane!"

The tears that had glistened in her eyes a moment ago seeped out of the corners and down her cheeks. "Just in case something happens to me, you've got to take care of my baby. You have to raise her and tell her that her mommy loved her. You've got to make sure she knows."

Robert didn't want to hear any more of this foolishness. He knew it must be the medication making her talk like this, but something in her voice told him it wasn't. The hairs on the back of his neck stood on end. He shook his head. "No. You're going to be fine. And you're coming home. You're going to tell her yourself!"

"Rob, Robbie, please. Just . . . listen . . . to . . . me."

He could tell it was taking all of her energy to speak. "Shhh. We can talk in the morning when you wake up. And then, in a few days, we'll all go home."

Rose started to say something, but didn't. She stroked her baby's head and kissed her. Then she tugged on her husband's hand. He knelt next to the bed and she managed to lean in to kiss him.

"You know, being your wife has been my greatest joy. That and being her mother." She wanted to get the words out—just in case. Rose had promised God a lot of things in the past couple of weeks, had even said that He could take her if He just let her child be okay. The thought of leaving made her heart hurt. She wanted to be here with the family she had fought so hard to have. Surely, God wouldn't hold her to her end of a desperate bargain. Would he?

Chapter 3

They buried Rose on a Tuesday.

Robert purchased a casket in a color called blush. He insisted that Rose's hair was styled with it floating around her shoulders and that she wore her favorite dress, the pink one with the scooped neckline.

Robert stared straight ahead while clutching the child to his chest and rocking slightly. The black suit hung loosely from his narrow, bony frame. He was too numb to notice the people who filled the church to come pay respects to his wife for the last time. The song played, unnoticed. The eulogy read, unheard. The only sound Robert was aware of was the pounding in his ears as the blood rushed through his head and pulsated in his temples. He couldn't believe she was gone, that she had left him.

Barbara had suggested that it wouldn't be good to take the baby outside just yet, with her only being a few days old, but Robert waved her off. This was his child, and she was going to her mother's funeral. After all, she hadn't even gotten a chance to spend much time with the mother who had died the same day the child was born. He had dressed the baby in a pink dress similar to Rose's and wrapped her in a blanket to protect her against the wintry air. It would be her last time in the presence of such a beautiful woman. Robert wished Rose could just hold the baby. Hold the baby for whom she had prayed. But since she couldn't, he did.

Leaden legs carried Robert toward the casket. His breath was caught in his throat as he looked down at his sleeping wife. He touched her hair and leaned closer. He held the baby out as if Rose could kiss her. "Here she is," he whispered.

Robert's shoulders started shaking, and from behind, it looked like he was laughing, big, huge guffaws. The silence gave way to a low moan, and then a cry that grew louder. Coming from somewhere deep, was the sound of a sorrow-soaked soul.

In a moment, the ushers had closed in on Robert, tearing at him like hungry folk fighting for free food. They elbowed each other, each wanting to be the one to comfort the bereaved husband. Robert jerked away.

"I'm not leaving her. I'm not," he said, eyes wide and one hand holding onto the edge of the casket, the other clutching the baby.

"Let me talk to him. Let me," Barbara said as she elbowed her way through the sea of black-clad women. He would have to pull himself together.

The ushers parted as if for Moses and his rod. Barbara faced Robert. "Robert, please, I know you hate to see her go, but she's gone. Come on. Let me help you to your seat," she said.

"No!" Robert jerked away, sending Barbara stumbling backward into the ushers who caught her.

The ushers looked at each other, from one to the other. They had seen distraught people before, but this was something else. Brenda Lewis, the youngest of the five, cast a quick glance into the audience and then toward her older sister, Lola, as if to say, "This fool is crazy." But she quickly wiped the expression from her face at the somber look her sister gave her. Barbara heaved herself up, her bosom rising and falling in quick, short bursts.

The pastor touched Robert on the shoulder. "Brother Robert," Pastor Johnson said in a low, even voice. "It's all right. It's all right. Your wife will be with you forever. In here." He touched his own chest, and then pointed to Robert's. "Nobody can ever take that away from you. She'll be with you. And she'll be with this beautiful baby. But right now, what she needs you to do is to honor her memory and your love by letting her go to rest."

The congregation seemed to wait. No one breathed. All eyes were on the man whose heart cried before them.

It was something about the pastor's words that spoke to Robert. His sobs dried and he wiped the wet from his nose with the back of his hand. The pastor handed him a neatly folded and embroidered handkerchief, which Robert used to blow his nose and then gave back.

He looked toward his wife once more, and with trembling lips, kissed her good-bye.

His eyes found the pastor's. Pastor Johnson extended his hand.

Robert took it.

All too shortly, they were outside standing beside a heaping mound of winter-wet dirt, ready to lower his Rose into her resting place. Robert gulped to swallow words he'd never again get to say to her. Tears blurred his vision for a moment, causing the scene before him to float just beyond clear sight. He wrapped his arms around the baby even tighter.

The January brisk cold turned the baby's nose red.

Robert pulled the knit cap lower over her head to cover her ears and much of her face. She didn't make a single sound as her father stood next to her mother's grave. It was as if she could sense the seriousness of the moment. Even as others cried, she remained silent.

A gray sky, the color of steel, underscored the sadness of the day. No birds flew overhead. No flowers bloomed. Naked trees swayed in jagged bursts of energy as the wind whipped them back and forth. The funeralgoers clutched their coats about their waists, bending toward the ground to shield themselves from the bone-chilling air that bit their cheeks. Their eyes stung as much from the wind as from the thought of letting go of one of their own.

After a few brief words from Pastor Johnson, the crowd turned back toward the road. Brown and gray leaves crackled beneath their shoes as they walked in slow, heavy strides away from the grave just outside Mount Bethel Baptist Church Number Two.

After the meal, the guests finally cleared out of the house, all except for Rose's parents and sister. Robert clutched the baby to his chest, standing in the middle of the bedroom that not too long ago he had shared with his beloved. Now, she was gone, and in her place were these strangers, trying to take what little of her he had left.

Augusta wanted to take the baby. But Robert declined. For a moment, he wondered what it was that Rose had told Augusta that day at the hospital. Rose's mother and father had also said they would take care of the baby for him. But again, he shook his head. No, this baby was all he had left of his Rose. And nobody—nobody—was going to take her away from him, not even for a minute.

"Robert, it's no trouble, really," Barbara insisted, glancing toward her own husband, who looked at Robert. "We don't mind taking the baby for a while."

Barbara's eyes settled briefly on the white, flowered spread neatly arranged on the bed. Pillows perched atop the covers, like so many soldiers standing at attention. A single framed picture stood next to a lamp on the nightstand. Nothing else was there. The fragrance of Chanel No. 5 haunted the senses.

"I said no." Robert's eyes left no room for argument. He kissed the baby.

Barbara swallowed hard. "Okay, well, tell us what you want us to do," she said, "and we'll do it."

Her eyes watered. They had just buried under damp, red dirt, the daughter she had given birth to way too short a time ago. Her heart ached, but Barbara wasn't a woman to shed tears in public, so she choked them back. Barbara touched the baby's head softly.

"So, have you settled on a name?" she asked.

Robert had put off choosing a name. Rose had decided on the name Joy because this baby would symbolize her joy. But his heart couldn't grasp joy at this moment, not when he felt lost and oh so sad. Therefore, he settled on the only name he could think of for what remained of his Rose here in his arms. He looked at Barbara.

"Her name is Rosetta. Rosetta Love." He chose the name Love because she was all he had left of his true love.

Barbara's breath caught in her throat. She put her hand to her mouth, biting on her knuckle. "Rosetta Love."

When Rose's family left, Robert slowly lowered himself onto the bed. The baby was sleeping. He lay her down and just stared. Only two days ago, the doctors had allowed her to come home. They seemed to be amazed that she was doing well and gaining weight. They said babies born as early as she was often had to struggle to survive. But Rosetta had none of the breathing problems and other maladies they had feared.

After a while, her image became blurry as tears welled. He wiped them away. "Rosetta Love."

He picked up Rose's picture from the nightstand.

"You are so beautiful," he said. This photo was of Rose only, dressed in a white, lacy dress, her hair piled atop her head, with tendrils cascading down the sides. He slowly traced his finger around the outline of her face. Her image smiled back at him.

Robert recalled their wedding. They had gotten married the day after Rose graduated from high school. Barbara and Phillip had forbidden Rose to wed while she was still a student, so Rose set the date for after graduation. Barbara pleaded, threatened and cajoled Rose. She threw out ominous predictions that if Rose went through with this wedding at such a young age, she would never do anything else with her life.

In 1958, getting married at the age of eighteen wasn't considered all that young, Rose had argued. However, Barbara had hopes of her daughter actually going on to college—a major feat for a young, colored girl. Doors were opening that had not been available to her back when she was Rose's age, Barbara retorted. But Rose had looked at her, with angelic eyes, and explained that the only door she wanted was the one that led to a life with Robert.

And that's the door Rose chose.

Barbara swore not a dime of her money would go toward paying for the wedding that she felt was robbing her daughter of the chance at a life better than her own.

So the two teenagers—Rose fresh out of high school and Robert going into his second year at the university—pulled together the money to make their union lawful.

Barbara threatened to boycott the wedding, but Phillip put his foot down. She attended the wedding—albeit unhappily. She had shed tears, just like other guests, but hers were not ones of joy, Robert knew with bitter certainty.

Rose wore a simple white dress with wisps of lace around the neckline. It was little more than a church dress. Robert knew it wasn't the billowing creation she would have liked, but it was all they could afford. And in it, she looked radiant.

Robert looked down at the sleeping child.

"This is your mommy. The best mommy you could ever want. The best wife I could ever have."

He lay on the bed, placing the baby next to him. And in his arms, he cradled his dead wife's picture. He fell asleep with his back to his child and his wife's smile in his eyes.

And so that's how Robert started and ended each day. He would say a few words to the picture of Rose in the morning and at night, do the same. He talked to her about the baby, about his day, about life. He talked to her and cradled her close. And when he wasn't talking to her, he was talking to Rosetta Love, telling her what a special child she was and what a special mother she had. He wouldn't let anyone else keep her, though he did allow Barbara and Phillip to visit. He was not letting this precious baby out of his sight. Even if he wanted to, he felt that he'd be letting Rose down if he handed over the care of her daughter to someone else.

Robert didn't know what he would do when he had to return to work at the university. He didn't want to leave Rosetta Love.

"We'll be happy to take care of the baby," Barbara said repeatedly.

"Barbara, thank you, but we're fine," Robert said as he tested the warmth of the baby formula on his hand, making certain that it wasn't too hot. He hoisted Rosetta into his arms and crooned to her. "Hey, precious baby," he said, kissing her on the cheek. He gently put the glass bottle to

Rosetta Love's mouth and faced Barbara. "Tell your grandma we're fine. Just the two of us."

Barbara turned to the refrigerator. "Okay, well, at least let me fix you dinner. What would you like?"

She knew it would be pointless to talk to him now.

"Oh, I'm not hungry," he said. His tan slacks sagged on his already skinny six-foot-tall frame, even though he had pulled the rawhide belt as tight as it would go. Robert remembered the last good meal he had eaten. It had been before Rose had gone into the hospital. She had fixed gravy and chicken.

Meals since then had become a blur. Since the funeral, he had eaten just barely enough to survive. Food had no taste. Old favorites held no allure.

Barbara ignored him and proceeded to look in the cabinets. She'd cook something anyway. Cooking was always her antidote for a sad or tiring day. Though today, she doubted if even that would take her mind from the daughter who had gone away far too soon.

She hummed "Swing Low, Sweet Chariot" softly as she turned the fire up under the pot of water to boil spaghetti and plunked down a skillet and browned ground beef for Robert. While she busily moved about the kitchen, neither attempted conversation.

The space between Barbara's brown eyes creased as she recalled the day her baby told her she wanted to get married to the man who now sat before her. Bile seemed to rise in her throat as she thought about what her daughter's life could have been if she had just not married this man. *She was always so hardheaded*, Barbara thought. Her fleshy forearms shook as she forcefully stirred a batch of corn bread.

Barbara knew she had to dismiss these sinful thoughts if she was to see her child in heaven one day. She drew in a deep and steadying breath and finished cooking.

She carefully placed a plate in front of Robert, who smiled politely. "Thank you, Barbara."

"I was happy to do it," she said flatly. She rubbed her hands on her apron, which she had found in one of Rose's closets. Barbara had given it to her daughter as a wedding gift—a wedding she wasn't happy to support but knew she had to if she wanted to preserve the relationship she had with her child. "Why don't I hold the baby while you eat?" She stood over him expectantly.

After a moment of awkward silence, Robert cleared his throat and slowly handed over Rosetta Love to her grand-mother.

Chapter 4

Barbara took to coming over in the evenings to fix dinner—a dinner that Robert would play over. Barbara's newfound interest in Robert wasn't so much because she wanted to make sure her deceased daughter's husband was eating. It was more so because those times seemed like her only opportunities to hold her precious child's baby. And if that meant fixing a meal for Robert, then she would bite her tongue and do it.

"I'll take her," Barbara firmly but carefully pulled the baby from Robert's arms. She held the baby close to her chest and walked to the window. Just outside, a tree Rose had planted years before twisted in the wind.

Tears caught in Barbara's throat as she thought, *My daughter's life could have been so different if she hadn't married that man.* Barbara's lips stretched into a thin, hard line.

She turned away from the window and struggled to pull on a smile. "I hope you enjoy your food," she said. "I'm going to wash the baby."

After nearly two months on leave, Robert returned to

work. Barbara had been anticipating his return to the university. She knew then he would be forced to allow her to help with the baby more often. But Robert took Rosetta Love to class with him. Barbara swallowed her disappointment behind angry words. "He is just being selfish," she said to herself. "Rather than let me spend time with the baby—*my* grandbaby—he'd rather take her to work all day. I know he's doing it to spite me."

But Robert's thoughts had nothing to do with Barbara. Being near his daughter made him feel close to his wife.

Coworkers stopped by to coo to the baby and to bring her toys—toys that Robert would sterilize before giving to her. He had heard horror stories of how germs could be transferred from adults to babies.

"She is so cute," said Jackie Amos, a fellow English professor. "I remember when my baby was this tiny."

Jackie had been the one who brought lasagna by the house after the funeral and had called to see if Robert needed any help with the baby. He had known Jackie for ten years.

Jackie kissed Rosetta Love on the forehead and played with her tiny fingers. The baby cooed in response. As Jackie handed the baby back to him, Robert dug deep in the diaper bag for a wipe. He then took to carefully swabbing each of Rosetta Love's fingers as Jackie stood by watching silently. Robert was so consumed with sanitizing her fingers that he didn't notice Jackie's raised eyebrow.

His smile was almost a grimace as coworker after coworker paraded by, kissing and touching Rosetta Love. Genevieve, who cooed way too loudly, and James, who constantly offered child-rearing tips—though he had no children, were just a few of the many who made it a point to stop by Robert's office and take a peek at his pride and joy. And then there was Marla.

Marla taught English across the hall. On this day, she lumbered into his office during a break. Rosetta Love was lying in her stroller, though not sleeping.

Marla's shoes made sliding noises as she only halfway picked her feet up while moving across the tile floor. Marla was one of Robert's favorite coworkers. She was funny and always had a good joke—and snack—to share. Throughout the years, she had filled in for him numerous times whenever he was absent.

Marla was forever asking him to fix her up with one of his male friends, but he always had to remind her that she knew the same people he did, the other professors. She wondered why she could never attract a decent date. Robert, however, didn't have the heart to tell her the reason may have had something to do with the fact that she smelled like sweaty gym clothes that had stayed too long in the duffel bag, mixed with stale cigarettes.

"Hey, li-ttle gi-rl," Marla said in a singsong voice while waving pudgy fingers in the air in a motion to tickle. "Come give me some sugar."

Robert didn't know what came over him, but something propelled him from his seat behind his desk. In two steps, he was standing between his child and Marla, a can of disinfectant spray raised in midair.

"What are you doing?" Marla asked, oblivious to Robert's intent. Marla moved to step around Robert, but Robert stepped with her, blocking her movements.

Marla looked momentarily confused, before realizing he didn't want her to touch the baby. She took an involuntary step backward, swallowing. "Oh, I–" She didn't know what to say.

Robert saw the hurt in her face and felt a bit guilty, but the fear of her exposing his child to her germs was stronger. He made no apologies. "Perhaps you can come back and see her at another time."

Marla cleared her throat. "Oh. Sure. I probably need to get back to my office anyway. Plenty of work."

She backed out the door.

The dean said nothing at first, but after a week of Robert bringing the infant to class, stopped by Robert's office and declared Rosetta Love couldn't be in the classroom on a daily basis—she was a distraction.

"But, Dean, she's as quiet as any child I've ever seen," Robert said, packing up for a trip down the hall to class. The baby's diaper bag slid down his arm. Rosetta Love was sleeping in her stroller. "I promise she won't interfere with the instruction I give to my students."

The dean took in Robert's office. A bottle served as a paperweight for a stack of student essays, while a rattle lay just at the edge of the desk, sure to fall to the floor at any moment. Books of Chaucer and Angelou propped next to a pink baby blanket.

The dean shook his head, his glasses sliding down the bridge of his nose. "Everyone feels sorry for your loss, truly," he said. "But, really, this has gone on way too long. You have to pull yourself together and conduct yourself like a real professor, not a babysitter."

Robert gritted his teeth. He shifted his weight from one leg to the other, and then back again. "I am not acting like a babysitter," he said. "I'm acting like a father."

The dean waved off his words. "Of course, of course," he said. "I'm a father too, and I tell you, I would never have even thought about bringing my children to class."

"But, Dean—" Robert began.

"There is no 'but,' Robert," the dean said. He glanced at his watch. "The baby goes. Now if you'll please excuse me." The dean stepped away from the desk, cleared his throat and waved a hand over the clutter on Robert's desk. "Please, clean this stuff up."

Robert fumed as he pushed Rosetta Love's stroller to the

car. He walked slowly, a slight limp giving the rolling
stroller an odd rhythm. The dean just didn't understand.
Nobody did. Nobody understood why he had to do this,
why he had to take the best care of his—Rose's—daughter.
They didn't understand that this baby was his lifeblood.
And if something happened to her, he'd just die.

Faced with no other choice, he reluctantly gave in to Barbara's request to keep the baby during the day. He would
wake up, talk to Rose, get the baby dressed, and take her to
Barbara and Phillip's. As he drove off each day, he felt like
he was somehow leaving behind the last of his Rose.

Barbara wrapped the little girl in her arms. The child's
eyes gazed into her own, seemingly in wonderment. An
overwhelming feeling of love welled in Barbara's heart.
The baby, even at only a few months old, reminded her of
her Rose. She could see why Robert never wanted to let
Rosetta out of his sight, because neither did she. It was almost like having a piece of Rose still here with her.

The baby's eyes were hazel, just as Rose's had been. Her
skin was about a shade or two darker though. Not like that
color they called peach in the box of crayons, but more like
those tiny caramels that Rose loved to pop into her mouth.
Already, the baby had a full head of slick, black hair. Black,
like her father's, not sandy and coppery like Rose's.

Barbara sat in Phillip's big recliner, cradling the baby to
her chest. The soft smell of powder and lotion enveloped
her. Tears blurred Barbara's vision for a moment as she
reminisced about bringing her own baby home thirty-five
short years before. Bringing her home and loving her.

The same as she would love this baby. Her baby's baby.

Barbara had held many dreams for her girls, Rose and
Augusta. They wouldn't make the same mistakes she did.
They wouldn't get married because it was expected of
them. They wouldn't forfeit their educations and their own

lives just because tradition said they should. They would be doctors and lawyers. They would be important people.

The thought of her girls doing something amazing had propelled Barbara through each day. It wasn't that she didn't love Phillip—she had grown to love him—but she wanted more. Back in her day, though, more wasn't possible. Little girls grew up to become nothing more than wives.

So she had.

The ringing of the phone snapped Barbara out of her reverie. Rosetta Love jumped, and then smiled. "You like that? You like the telephone?" Barbara said to her.

Barbara made funny faces at the baby as she made her way to answer the summoning phone. "Hello?"

It was someone from church asking about choir rehearsal. Barbara answered the question, ending the call as quickly as possible, and returned her attention to her grandchild.

The day seemed to go by much too fast for Barbara. She knew Robert would be there soon to take away the highlight of her day—he always seemed to come too early. As she predicted, the doorbell rang at a quarter till five.

She twisted the knob and he walked in. Without a word, Robert's eyes immediately searched the room for his baby girl.

Barbara dusted the flour from her hands and turned the heat down under the rice on the stove. "The baby is sleeping," she answered to the unuttered question.

Robert visibly relaxed. Barbara bristled slightly—what did he think, that she would leave the baby somewhere or harm her own grandchild? She wanted to scream that she would take care of the baby like her own, but Barbara held her tongue. She had to remind herself this was a man grieving.

For a moment, the old anger returned. Barbara hadn't spoken to Robert for the first two years of his marriage to her daughter, so upset was she that Rose had chosen to marry at such a young age and throw away her future. It had all been Robert's fault. If he hadn't been there—if he hadn't been so eager to snatch up her Rose—who knew where she would have ended up? She surely would have gone to college and become the doctor she had wanted to be all the way through high school. That is, if she hadn't gotten tied down with a husband.

Barbara cleared her throat and blinked away those thoughts. That was years ago and she had forgiven him. Her lips smiled; her eyes did not. "So, Robert, how was your day? Would you like to stay for dinner?"

Robert was already on his way to the back bedroom where he knew he would find the baby. "Maybe next time," he called from the other room. "I just want to get Rosetta Love home and spend some time with her."

"Oh, of course," Barbara said. She had known he wouldn't stay. She wouldn't have known what to do if he had accepted. She turned back to her cooking.

A moment later, Robert returned to the kitchen, the baby's bag over his shoulder and Rosetta Love cradled in his arms. "Thank you, Barbara, for watching her today."

Barbara continued to peel the small, green apples in short, hard strokes. "It was my pleasure." For a moment, the only sound was the swish of the knife next to the apple's surface. The skin on Barbara's hands was wet with the juice of the fruit. "I'll see you in the morning."

Robert nodded. "Yes, well, good night."

Outside, Robert paused and stared at the closed door behind him. After all this time, something about Barbara still made him feel uneasy. She had been pleasant enough in the weeks, even these months, following his Rose's death, but the coldness was there just below the surface.

He knew she blamed him for the life Rose had chosen. That Rose chose marriage and family over a career was a black mark against him in Barbara's book, he knew.

He shook his head as he turned to go to his car. He favored his leg a little, an almost imperceptible limp making his gait slightly awkward. Robert couldn't understand how Barbara could blame him, after all this time, for the choice Rose had made. It didn't make sense.

Barbara placed the plate of rice and gravy and chicken in front of Phillip. The apple pie baked in the oven.

"When Robert came, you would have sworn I had stolen the baby. When he walked into the door, his expression was like, 'where is she?'" Barbara said as she poured Phillip some tea. "He acts like nobody can take care of that child but him. He acts like it pains him to leave her here every morning."

Phillip tasted the chicken and closed his eyes, breathing deeply. "This sure is good," he said, and Barbara's expression softened as Phillip continued. "You have to remember, he is a man who is still grieving. That's all. Losing your wife and the mother of your child is not an easy thing to come to grips with. I'd probably be the same way if I lost you. I would hold anything or anybody that reminded me of you close to my heart."

For a moment, Phillip thought back. There had been a time when it felt like he had lost her. But that was a lifetime ago.

Barbara opened her mouth to add another comment, but Phillip raised his finger to his lips. "Shhhh, I don't want to talk about that. I just want to talk about you. How was your day?"

Barbara closed her mouth. She leaned down to kiss her husband. "You old, sly devil, you don't want to hear about my day. You just don't want to hear me talk about Robert."

Phillip touched her hand. "Did I tell you today how blessed I am to have you in my life?"

Barbara's eyes softened and she smiled back at her husband.

"I swear, just the sound of his voice irritates me," Barbara said as she was sitting in the choir stand, waiting for Sister Irby to begin rehearsal. Nettie was perched next to her. Barbara was still fuming over the treatment Robert had given her. "He acts like he's too good to sit a spell and eat."

Nettie grinned. "It's a wonder Robert lets you fix him anything to eat at all," she said. "I know I wouldn't. I'd be scared you would put a little something extra in my plate."

Barbara grunted and wiped imaginary lint off her skirt. "Don't think I haven't thought about it." She smiled. Her friend of nearly fifteen years always made her smile.

But Nettie hadn't started out as her friend. No, the first time Barbara saw Nettie—the summer of '61—her stomach churned with dislike as the woman sashayed across the church yard with a plate of golden fried chicken in her hands, smiling like she was the queen of the world.

Nettie and her husband had just moved to town, and the colored newspaper had done a big write-up on her. The writer hailed all of her accomplishments as the founding member of some organization up north that awarded scholarships to colored children. Barbara imagined the woman lived the life she herself longed to live—educated and making a difference.

That was enough to make the housewife loathe the career woman. And then, here she was, bringing a plate of beautiful chicken. Didn't this woman know Barbara was the best cook in the church?

No, Barbara had not taken a liking to her.

The new woman had called out to Barbara, "Hello, Sister. I'm Natalie Bradshaw. How do you do?"

Barbara had shifted her eyes quickly, pretending she didn't

see or hear the woman. But Natalie wasn't deterred. "Sister, can you tell me where the kitchen is?"

Barbara grunted a response and did a half gesture with her hand. "That away."

Natalie had breezed by her, taking her perfectly browned chicken with her.

Barbara turned on her heel to follow the woman. She was going to set this interloper straight about who ran the kitchen in this church. Certainly not some high and mighty soul from up north.

But before Barbara got a chance to take her position in the kitchen, Natalie handed her a plate. "Here you go, sister."

Barbara tried to hide her surprise. She didn't want the plate but didn't want to cause a scene. "Thank you, Nettie."

The woman smiled. "Actually, it's Natalie."

Barbara smiled back, tightly. "Thank you, Nettie."

The other woman's smile didn't dim. She handed Barbara a napkin and eased her toward a table. "Here, take this seat. Try my chicken first."

"No, I'm not that hungry," Barbara demurred. She would die before she would allow this woman to serve her. She wasn't going to let this woman come in and take control.

"Please, sister, try it," Natalie said. "I'm so proud of it. This is my first social at this church. I just wanted to bring something so I could make a contribution. "

Before Barbara could comment, a strangled cry erupted from the person next to her. She looked over to see a horrified Rev. Johnson staring at a perfectly brown chicken leg. It was bleeding from the inside out. Barbara stifled a grin.

Natalie gasped. "Oh, pastor!" she grabbed the plate and tried to dab the blood off the chicken with a towel. Her lip quivered. "I'm so sorry!"

Barbara pursed her lips to keep from laughing outright. So, Miss Perfect wasn't so perfect after all.

Barbara took over. "Here, let me have that." She took the plate.

Natalie followed her, wringing her hands. "I tried so hard. I don't know what happened. It was so pretty on the outside, so I thought it was done. I should just give up. I can't cook. It never turns out right."

Suddenly, Barbara didn't dislike the woman after all. She put her hand to Natalie's elbow, carrying the offending plate with the other. "Come on, dear, let's go fix some other plates. I brought some chicken too. It's right over here."

Nettie elbowed Barbara to bring her back to the present. "I see Sister Irby coming now," she said, straightening up in her seat. She whispered, referencing the earlier conversation, "I will say this now, last time I saw that Robert, he looked like a sack of bones, poor thing. Maybe you *should* try to fix him something to eat—with nothing extra in it, though, now."

Barbara waved off her friend's comments and stood with the rest of the choir to praise the Lord.

The morning's sunlight awakened Robert. He looked over at the clock, which read six A.M. Rose should be just about ready to come in from her morning run. *I'll surprise her and have breakfast waiting,* Robert thought to himself. He moved to climb out of bed, but a sharp pain in his chest reminded him that his beloved wasn't out running and that she wouldn't be coming home ever again. He slumped back onto the bed.

Robert had heard enough people—some strangers, some close family—talk about his grief. "It will get easier with each day. Time heals all wounds. God doesn't give us more than we can bear."

If he heard another empty platitude, he felt that he would reach out and squeeze the person's neck until the words died.

They all sounded so smug, like they knew the answers to his grief. They all made it sound as if his heartache was just a passing phase. That after a few nights of sleeping with it, he would become accustomed to it and leave Rose and the memories he held in the past.

But it wasn't getting easier, and time wasn't healing any wounds. He sure didn't have any faith in what God would do, since it seemed that He had ignored every one of Robert's pleas. No, God wasn't listening. And whatever interest He had in talking to God died that day in the hospital.

He wondered each morning how he would get through the day, how he would go on. It was like a physical thing. His chest felt tight, and his skin clammy. The pain in his stomach felt like someone was sticking him with a hot iron. The despair burned in his gut.

Then the tears would come.

Every day.

Time hadn't made it easier.

Fortunately, the thought of his little Rosetta Love helped to ease the churning in his stomach. It was thoughts of her that prompted him to slowly climb out of bed each morning, cradle Rose's picture close, say a few words to her, and then face another day.

Robert wondered if his grief would ever leave. It was as if no matter where he went, it followed.

Neighbors and coworkers who had at first brought over covered dishes and offered soft words, now seemed to avoid eye contact with him. No one stopped by his office to coo or to hold the baby. No one offered any new toys. No one talked about how cute she was.

As he entered the English department office, an immediate silence came over the room. "Oh, don't let me stop you," he said, annoyed. He knew they had been talking about him.

The fact that they thought he didn't know or that he was too stupid to figure it out incensed him.

"Oh, nobody was talking," said Genevieve, who cast an anxious glance at Darlene, the administrative assistant who stood next to the copier.

"Yeah, I was just. . . . making these copies for her," said Darlene, jerking her Afro toward Genevieve. Darlene's bracelets jingled in the air, her carefully painted nails flashed in the shine of the light coming in the window.

Robert ignored them and went to retrieve the mail from his box. They were such small-minded people.

Out of the main area of the office and out of earshot—or so they must have thought—Robert heard the conversation pick back up. "He's lost so much weight," came one whisper.

"Yes, and he wasn't all that big to begin with. Now he's just one tall sack of skin and bones. I hear he has a strange fixation on that baby too," another shot back.

"Well, I really think he needs some kind of mental help," said the first voice. "It's not right for a man to be acting the way he does. I've never seen a man so attached to a baby. It's not natural."

Robert cleared his throat loudly as he reentered the area. A guilty silence greeted him. Neither Darlene nor Genevieve would meet his eyes.

He cast them both withering looks and slammed the door.

Outside of the office and away from their voices, the words played over in his head. They thought he needed mental help? Well, how was he supposed to act? His wife had died less than a year ago. Surely, he was allowed to grieve. And what about the way he cared for their child? Shouldn't all parents take special care with their children? Robert didn't understand. But that was quite all right. He would pay them no mind. He had other important things to concern himself with, such as going to talk with Rose.

He stopped by the florist and got a dozen of her namesake flowers, pink ones. Then he drove to the cemetery and parked his car on the side of the road.

He gathered the flowers and the most recent pictures of Rosetta Love.

Robert sat on the ground next to Rose's grave. The flowers from last week were still there.

"Hi, sweetheart," he said. He lightly touched the headstone. "I brought you something."

He put the flowers next to the grave and pulled the pictures from their envelope.

He held up the first one. "This is your Rosetta Love three weeks ago. See how she's growing. She's getting big now. Well, long. The doctor says she will be tall. But she isn't really putting on any weight, just like her mother."

Next, he pulled out the picture of a smiling Rosetta Love gazing at a storybook character. "And this is her at the library reading time last week. I almost didn't take her because I didn't want her to catch any baby germs, but your mother insisted that it would be good for her."

Then he sat in silence. Robert took in a deep breath and held it before slowly letting it out. He thought if he breathed in deeply enough and held it, maybe he could recapture her scent. And in his mind's eye, maybe he did. But the memory was nothing like the reality.

He curved his hands into fists, the nails cutting into the palms of his hands. "Why?" He looked at the gray headstone next to him. "Why did you do it? Why did you have to leave me?"

The tears were wet on his cheeks. They trailed in straight lines down his face, curving under his chin. They dripped on his shirt and pooled on the top photo. "I miss you so much," he said, his voice raspy. "I miss you, and I need you." A bird settled on the headstone for a brief moment before Robert shooed it away. "I am so lost without you. I can't laugh. I can't open my eyes in the morning without seeing you and then missing you. I can't be happy. Why did you go away?"

He didn't get an answer. So he sat there in silence. He stared as an ant crawled on his pant leg, not bothering to wipe it away. He didn't care. Any other feeling would be better than this pain.

Robert let Barbara plan a small family gathering to celebrate Rosetta Love's first birthday. She made a fuss of ordering decorations and baking a cake. Rose's sister, Augusta, came over with her two children, Cecil, twelve, and Donald, fourteen. Cecil wanted to play with his older brother, but Donald sulked in a corner, pouting because he was forced to come to this dumb birthday party for a baby instead of getting to hang out with his friends.

Who has a birthday party for a one-year-old? It's not like she'll remember it, Donald thought, but knew his mother wouldn't hear of him skipping it.

Robert had even allowed Barbara to keep the baby overnight the day before, which was a first. He never let Rosetta Love be away from him overnight. However, he knew it would be best because he needed to be alone.

Yes, he needed to be alone on the eve that marked the one-year anniversary of the death of his wife.

He awoke that morning with a headache like he hadn't had in years. He rolled to his right, but stopped. Beer cans dotted the floor where he had fallen into a miserable sleep sometime in the wee hours of the morning. At his elbow were photo albums, all turned to pictures of a smiling Rose.

He opened his mouth, as if he could just exhale the stale

taste and stench of beer. He turned his neck gingerly. It ached like the rest of him. Yet, that brief moment of physical pain was welcomed. It almost made him forget the heartache that had him in his present state.

The ringing within his head made his eyes hurt. "God, make it stop," he said, forgetting for the moment that he was at odds with God. He slowly climbed to his knees in an effort to stand. The hardwood floor had made an imprint in his skin.

He furrowed his brow as he realized the ringing in his head was coming from somewhere off to his right—the telephone.

He didn't feel like answering it. There was nobody in the world he felt like talking to at that moment. Nobody besides the one person whose voice he could never again hear.

Robert had stood in the shower and let the cold water hit him hard in the face. He would make it through this day. He tried to convince himself that it was a day to celebrate. His daughter was turning a year old. Still, all his mind would let him think about was the fact that his wife was gone. And this day marked the anniversary of that day.

Adjusting the water to a warm temperature, Robert drew in a deep breath, as much to calm his thoughts as to hold the tears back. He was tired of crying. He just wanted one day where his eyes weren't wet with tears, just one day. He wondered if he'd ever have such a day again.

Nobody understands how close Rose and I were. They've never loved like that and they can't begin to imagine how I feel. I lost more than just a wife. He felt like he had lost the one person in the world who understood him, and who was there for him no matter what.

His mind went back to the night of his senior dance. Rose

had been excited about going. She had been a junior. They had planned for weeks what they would do. Her mother had purchased her a dress—pink, of course—and had taken her to the hairdresser. Rose's parents always made sure their children took some responsibility for their own purchases. Barbara said it taught them responsibility. And so Rose had saved a month's worth of allowances and babysat for five straight Saturday nights to save enough money for the shoes to go with the dress. She didn't mind however. It would all be worth it, just to walk into that dance.

Robert was supposed to arrive at her house an hour before the dance so Barbara could take pictures of the two of them. At a half hour till the start of the prom, his phone rang.

Even before he picked it up, he knew she would be on the other end. He finally lifted the receiver after the sixth ring.

"Hey, what's the holdup?" Rose's voice held excitement and irritation. "Come on."

The silence was her first indication that something was wrong. "Robbie?"

He drew a deep breath. He opened his mouth to say the words that he knew would ruin her evening, but nothing came out.

"Robbie, what's wrong?" Rose repeated.

Robert swallowed. "I don't have the tickets."

"What do you mean?" she asked. He couldn't quite tell what to make of her tone. "Did you lose them in your room or something? Did you look around? On your dresser?"

"No." He knew he would have to tell her. "I—I never bought the tickets."

"Robbie? What do you mean? We've been planning this for two months." Confused dismay entered her voice.

"I know." He felt small. The one thing she had been

counting on and he couldn't give it to her. She didn't ask for much, just a trip to his dance. Robert balled his fists and his nose flared. That blasted lowlife of a father.

"Robbie, tell me what happened." Her voice was stern. "Tell me before I come over there and wring your neck."

So he told her. He wasn't able to get the tickets because his mother needed to borrow his money so the lights would not be disconnected. She had promised to pay him back, but things kept coming up.

Robert hated to confess this family secret to Rose, whose family was so perfect with a mother who could stay at home, a father who worked—and never came home drunk—and a sister she actually got along with. Well, maybe *perfect* was the wrong word. Rose had told him about her parents' secret. So, they weren't perfect, but in Robert's eyes, they were as close to it as he had ever seen.

Rose knew some things about Robert's family as well. For instance, that Robert's father, Wilbert, had lost his third job in as many months because he couldn't stay sober long enough actually to do anything, and that Robert's brother made fun of the way he walked. Still, he hadn't wanted to tell her this latest humiliation.

If his revelation angered her, Rose never let it show. "Okay, well, I'll ask my mom for some money for the tickets," she said.

"Actually, it's not just the tickets," he confessed. "I don't have a tuxedo."

"Robert, were you just not planning on going to the prom at all?"

"It's not that," he said. His voice cracked as he delivered the news that the prom wasn't in their plans for the evening. "I . . . I . . . Someone was going to loan me theirs, but at the last minute, they decided they wanted to go to the prom after all."

In the silence, he imagined the anger that was sure to be in her hazel eyes.

"I'm sorry," he said. He felt incompetent and unworthy. He had let her down.

Her response forever sealed her in his heart: "That's okay. I didn't really want to go to some stinking prom anyway. Why don't you come over here and we can listen to records and eat ice cream? All I need is to be with you."

Robert knew she had dreamed of the prom. But here she was saying it didn't matter. That all she wanted to do was spend some time with him.

The cold water spraying from the showerhead pulled him back to the present. He had been in the shower so long that all the hot water had run out. It was just as well. He didn't need to be thinking about the past.

Nevertheless, as he turned the water off and his wet feet hit the linoleum floor, his heart felt heavy. In his mind's eye, he saw a smiling Rose. "All I need is to be with you."

Suddenly, he felt an overwhelming desire to be among her things. He padded, water dripping from his naked body, into their bedroom. Her clothes still hung in the closet and her shoes still lined the floor. He pushed aside her purses and found exactly what he was looking for, a box of love letters they had written each other over the years. She had kept every one of them.

Dust floated from the box as he tugged it from the high shelf. He blinked to keep from getting it into his eyes. A sneeze shook his shoulders. None of that mattered, though, as he cradled the box to his chest and took it and sat on the bed.

He removed the lid. The top letter was in a plain white envelope and read simply, "My dearest love," penned in a strong cursive that looked more like calligraphy than handwriting.

His brow furrowed. He didn't remember this letter, but

of course, he couldn't expect to remember all the envelopes she had given him over the years. He figured that it was as good as any to start reading. And so he opened it.

My dear Robbie,

If you're reading this letter, it must be that I'm no longer there with you. And if that is the case, I hope you forgive me. I hope you forgive the gamble I took to complete our family. But Robbie, you know how badly I wanted us to have a baby.

I wanted a miniature one of you running around. I wanted someone to dress in cute little clothes and take to the zoo. I wanted what other women have with ease. I wanted it for us.

You know how hard we tried all those years. I know the miscarriages hurt you just as they hurt me. I know you said you didn't care to have a child, that it didn't matter, but I felt terrible for not being able to give you a child, because I know that's what every man really wants deep down—something of his bloodline. And so I tried this one last time. I know we said we wouldn't try for babies anymore after the last miscarriage. We even talked of adopting.

The doctor told me the risk was too high to try to get pregnant again. He told me not to do it. I know I should have told you about the doctor's visits, but I couldn't. I know I lied to you and told you everything was all right, but I really thought I knew. I didn't mean to mislead you. Robbie, I hope you know I had to take that chance. I knew that if it paid off, our family would be complete.

But now, I've left a hole in it. And I'm sorry. I'm sorry I didn't listen to the doctor and wanted to do things my way. I'm sorry I didn't tell you how serious it was until it was too late. I'm sorry I kept this one secret. I'm sorry.

I wanted a baby for us, not just for me. Remember when we were young kids? We always talked about the children we would have. So I was just trying to give us what we both wanted. I've asked God to forgive me for doing things my way, and I hope you will too. Please don't be mad at me. Just take care of our baby.

> *Until we see each other again,*
> *Always your love,*
> *Rose.*

Robert sat speechless. The water had long since dried on his chocolate skin. He clutched the letter so tightly in his bony hand that his knuckles began to hurt. He understood the words that were on the pages, but he struggled as they sank into his consciousness.

He and Rose had talked about how dangerous it was to have a baby—three miscarriages were a pretty good indicator that any pregnancy would be difficult for her. So they had agreed not to try anymore. Rose said she was seeing to it that she wouldn't get pregnant again. When they found out she was this last time, Rose said it was an accident. But that it had been such a calculated gamble, he couldn't wrap his mind around that. She had lied.

The anger that welled inside his chest surprised him. He shook his heads against it, and he tried to swallow it down. He couldn't be angry with her, not his perfect, beloved Rose.

He couldn't be angry with her.

On the morning of the day everyone was ready to celebrate the birth of his daughter, something else was on Robert's mind. No, he couldn't blame his precious Rose. But somebody would have to pay.

So he turned his anger to the person he knew had taken her away from him.

Chapter 5

Nine years later

Seta raced across the yard and tore open the door. "Grammy, Grammy! Look!"

Barbara laughed as the girl crashed into her. "Hold on, child. Calm down. Now tell Grammy what has you so excited."

Seta proudly held out her report card, displaying all *A*'s.

Barbara tugged on the glasses around her neck and set them atop her nose. She moved the paper closer to her eyes, then held it at arm's length, and then a little closer. "Now, let's see here. Another beautiful grade card," she said, smiling proudly.

The silver braces didn't dampen the ten-year-old's wide smile. She hadn't made a *B* all school year.

Barbara took the girl's book bag. "Come on, this deserves a celebration," she said, gesturing with her hand for Seta to follow her.

Barbara opened the freezer and pulled out the strawberry ice cream. The girl's eyes widened. Grammy never allowed her to have ice cream before dinner. Barbara laughed at the girl's expression.

"There is more where that came from, if you keep doing so well." Barbara smiled.

Seta looked at the clock. It was almost four. "Grammy, do you think I can ride my bike down to my daddy's house and show him my report card when he gets off work? It won't be dark."

Barbara looked away from the child's eager expression. "No, baby, I don't think—"

"Come on, Grammy, please?" Seta's eyes begged. "Please. I just want to show my daddy."

Barbara's face softened. It was natural for the child to want to share her good news with her father. "Sure, baby. Now eat your ice cream."

Seta delved in with relish, while some dribbled down her chin. She giggled and wiped it away. She was happy.

At promptly five o'clock, Seta rolled her bicycle into her father's yard. She let the bike crash to the ground as she hopped off and rang the doorbell. After a moment, the door slowly opened.

"Hi, Daddy," she said when Robert answered the door. Her smile dimmed a little as he stood in the doorway.

Finally, after what seemed like a long moment, he stepped aside. The heavy, gray curtains in the living room were drawn shut, casting the room into a deep shadow. On the mantle over the fireplace was a wedding picture of a smiling couple, arm in arm.

"I wanted to show you this," Seta said, suddenly shy. She pulled her report card from her pocket and smoothed it with her hands. She handed it to him. After a moment, he reached for it and held it as if it were contaminated with something he didn't want to touch.

Her father glanced at the report card and thrust it back at her, his thumb and finger letting go of it as she reached to catch it. He turned to walk back to the kitchen. "I have something on the stove." His tone was curt.

She followed closely behind, took a deep breath and tried again. "See, Daddy, I made all *A*'s." She knew if he would just look, he would surely see her grades and be so proud of her.

He waved her off. "Don't you always get straight *A*'s?"

Her face crumpled for a second, but she managed to paste her smile back on. *He is just tired and busy,* she thought to herself. Then she had an idea. "Do you want me to finish cooking for you, Daddy? I can, you know? Grammy let me make rice the other day. And I can make macaroni too."

She could cook for her daddy. That would surely make him smile.

He waved her off, as if she was a fly buzzing in his ear.

"No, I have it handled here. Well, it's getting dark. Why don't you hop on your bike and get back home before nightfall comes." It was more of a statement than a question.

Seta looked around. Newspapers littered the counter and papers covered the kitchen table. Glasses, some half-full with brownish-colored liquid, were in the sink.

"I don't mind staying. I can clean up for you."

She took a deep breath and the words came out in a rush before she could lose her courage. "Daddy, I want to come live with you. I'll do whatever you say. I'll cook and clean. I'll fix you dinner every day."

Her eyes pleaded with him. *I just want to be with my daddy.* Her grandparents were nice, and she did love them, but she craved a relationship with her father.

The man continued stirring what was on the stove as if he didn't hear her. She tried once more. "Daddy, I could—"

"No!" Robert snapped, cutting off his daughter.

The word wasn't loud or forceful, but it was final.

"But, Daddy—"

The man whirled on the girl, pointing the spoon in her face. "I said *no!*'"

He felt a tiny twinge of something at the sight of the hurt in her eyes, but he shrugged the feeling off. He couldn't have her live with him. He wanted nothing to do with her, hadn't wanted anything to do with her since he stopped calling her by her name.

Seta looked down so he wouldn't see the threat of tears in her eyes. She sniffled and cleared her throat. *It's okay*, she told herself. *Daddy is just tired.* Her grandma had told her about how sad her daddy would get sometimes because he missed her mom so much, and she understood. She understood because she also knew how sad it was to miss someone. She looked up again.

"Okay, Daddy. Well, you have a good night." She stepped toward him and hugged him tightly around the waist. The movement seemed to catch him off guard. "I love you."

As Seta stepped outside, she knew she would have to hurry home. It was almost nightfall. Her grandma had told her to be back before it got dark, or to have her daddy drive her home if the sun went down. If she pedaled fast, she knew she could make it before dark.

Seta and her grandparents lived four blocks away from Seta's father. Seta's father lived in a neighborhood that had a mix of people. The majority were young couples with children, but some were middle-aged and childless, while a few were older. Some were black. A few were white.

As Seta pedaled back home, she heard rapid-fire Spanish coming from a yard where two dark-haired boys played with a dog. A woman in the house next to her father's had been on her knees, digging in a flower bed. The houses were old, wood-frame structures. Some were two-story, some one or split-levels. This was life in Clear Love, Texas on any given day.

Seta had to cross a major thoroughfare in order to get to her grandparents' street. Though the neighborhoods were relatively close, they were starkly different. There were no whites or Hispanics in her grandparents' neighborhood. It was an older, black community, made up mostly of retirees or middle-aged couples with neatly manicured lawns. A few seemed to be overdue for a trim though. The bricks were faded, and a few houses cried for new paint in their nakedness.

No children raced through the streets. A few people worked in their yards, but there was no buzz of activity like what she had seen on her father's street.

That was one reason why Seta wanted to live with her father. She longed to be around children her own age, not just at school. She sometimes sat with some of the other girls in her class at lunch, but she didn't have anyone she would consider a friend. She sometimes overheard the other girls talking about what they would do over the weekend, or talk about the latest movies, but they never invited her to join them. They sometimes frowned when she walked by, turning up their noses. "She thinks she looks good," they would say in stage whispers so she could hear.

Seta wanted to tell them that they were wrong about her, but she didn't want to be further rejected. Therefore, she did the only thing she could think to do. She would listen to her grandmother's voice in her head, telling her to stand straight and to walk with her shoulders back and her head held high. And so she did.

Maybe if she lived near them, they would like her.

She parked her bicycle in the carport of her grandparents' one-story, brick home. Mr. Spivey stood from the weeds he was pulling to look Seta's way. She waved to him before running into the house where her grandmother greeted her at the door.

"I was just about to call over there to see if you had left already," Barbara said as Seta walked into the door. "Wash your hands and we'll eat."

Seta did as she was told. A moment later, the three were settled around the table.

Barbara cast a glance at Phillip. "So, how was your father?" Barbara asked, pursing her lips.

"He's okay," Seta said. She knew her grandmother didn't like her father much, though she didn't know why. It was nothing Barbara ever said, but it was just in her tone. So Seta didn't want to tell Barbara that her father was in a bad mood.

Barbara searched the child's face, but let it pass. "That's good. So, was he happy to see your good grades?"

"Yes, very," Seta said, smiling broadly. "He told me he was very proud of me and that he might let me come and live with him."

Barbara raised her eyebrows. "Oh, did he now?"

"Yes, but I told him that I liked living with you, so I couldn't go." Seta took a sip of her milk and shoved a forkful of mashed potatoes in her mouth to end the conversation.

Barbara stared at the child for a moment and opened her mouth to say something. Instead, she closed it and smiled. "That's right. You know this is your home. Has been since you were one year old."

For a moment, no one said anything. Flashbacks to that day nine years ago, when Seta came to live with them, flooded Barbara's mind.

Robert had come over for Rosetta Love's birthday party, but he was distant—more distant than usual, if that were possible. Barbara half expected him to snatch the baby away from her, especially after having spent the night away from Rosetta Love. But he didn't. He didn't ask about her or go near her. He only said he needed to talk to Barbara.

Barbara had said sure and that she would talk to him after the party since people had already started to arrive—Augusta and her husband with the boys, a few neighbors, some people from church and Robert's sister.

He sat in a chair in the corner of the room and didn't budge during the entire party. People tiptoed around him, casting quizzical glances at Barbara. She shrugged her shoulders—she knew Rose must be on his mind. She was on all their minds. A smoldering anger welled in her chest as she glanced toward Robert.

Didn't he know he wasn't the only one who missed Rose? Why couldn't he put his own selfish feelings aside and try to have a good time, at least for the baby?

After the cutting of the cake, Robert tapped on Barbara's shoulder. "I have to talk to you now."

Barbara glanced toward the guests and then back at Robert. "Can't it wait? Just for a half hour?"

"No."

Barbara held the knife out to Augusta. "Hey, baby, can you come and serve everybody cake? I need to speak with Robert."

Augusta put down her glass. "Sure, Mama."

Barbara stepped to the other room with Robert. "What is it that can't wait?" she asked as she folded her arms across her chest. She frowned as if she smelled rotten eggs.

"I want you to have . . . the baby," Robert said.

Barbara's brows furrowed. "What do you mean?"

For the first time since Robert had arrived, she noticed the two bags that were on the floor next to his feet. He held one out to her. "These are some of her clothes. You can come get more whenever you need to. I just need to have some time to think."

"Didn't you have some time last night?" Barbara asked. *What is going on with him?*

Robert shook his head. He didn't want to elaborate. "I just require some time to ponder my current circumstance. And I cannot do that with her around."

There he was, sounding all stiff and formal. Barbara was puzzled at Robert's request, but nodded. Of course she could have her grandbaby come stay with her for a while. "Sure, Robert, whatever you need." Perhaps this would be the thing to help him get on with his recovery. Maybe the baby reminded him too much of Rose. Lord knows, she was looking more like her every day. "I'd love to have Rosetta Love come visit."

Robert held up his large hand. "And that's another thing. Don't call her Rosetta. And certainly not Love."

Now he has really lost it, Barbara thought. Her whisper was a hiss. "Robert, what kind of crazy mess are you talking?"

Robert spoke calmly, ignoring her tone. "She was named after her mother, but quite evidently, that was an egregious mistake. She is nothing like her mother. And Love? Well, I named her Love because she was born out of love, but . . . but I cannot bear to think of her in that way because she took away my love. And I want nothing more to do with her."

Barbara cast her eyes skyward. *Lord, help me to deal with this crazy fool,* she prayed. "Robert, we're all sad that Rose is gone. But that's it. She's gone. We can't bring her back. All we can do is protect and love the little girl she left us. That's all. That's what she would have wanted."

For the first time Robert's cool, controlled tone gave way to anger. "What she wanted? We want to talk about what Rose wanted? What she wanted was to have a child. That's what she wanted. She blatantly wanted to disregard the doctor's advice and go about having this child just because *she* wanted one. What she wanted was to take unnecessary risks with her life. What she wanted was to trade her life for that of a child. Well, she got what she wanted. Now she's gone, and I'm all alone."

"But, Robert, that's just it. You're not alone. You have a beautiful little girl in there that is having a birthday. She needs you." Barbara let out an exasperated sigh. Robert was acting as if he had taken leave of what little common sense he had.

"No, she doesn't need me, and I don't need her. I don't want her," he said. "Now, you can take her, or I can find somewhere else for her to go. But right now, I can't deal with seeing her every day, knowing that if it weren't for her, I'd still have my wife."

Barbara fluttered her hands. "Okay, okay, we will keep her for as long as you need us to. But remember, she needs you. And when you're ready to come get her, you do that. Rosetta L—"

"Don't call her that!" Robert said through clenched teeth. A vein pulsed in his neck. His eyes were shining pits of rage and resolve.

Barbara didn't agree with all this craziness, but she thought it best to go along with whatever Robert said—at least while he was in this state of mind. She would listen to his wishes, for now. She pursed her lips, but nodded. From that day forth, she called the baby Seta.

"Grammy, I'm not hungry," Barbara heard from somewhere to her right.

Phillip touched his wife's hand. "Dear, you all right?"

Barbara shook her head to bring herself back to the present. She smiled. "Yes, I'm fine." She turned to Seta. "Now, what did you say?"

"I'm not hungry."

One of Barbara's rules was that Seta was to eat all her food. Barbara opened her mouth to remind the girl, but Phillip jumped in. "That's okay, baby. Since you have done so well in your books, you can have your way tonight," he said. He glanced at Barbara.

Seta slid out of her seat and kissed her grandfather's cheek. "Thank you, Poppy."

When Seta was out of earshot, Barbara turned to Phillip.

"You can't keep spoiling that child! We can't just raise her to have her way whenever she feels like it. Besides, we don't have food to throw away around here, you know that."

"Barbara, just let the girl be," Phillip said around a mouthful of food. His tone had a touch of sternness to it.

Barbara jutted out her jaw. She sawed into her meat. "Fine."

They ate in icy silence.

After dinner, Barbara carefully wrapped the meat in aluminum foil and placed it in the refrigerator so she could serve it for dinner tomorrow. She and Phillip had never lived extravagantly—hadn't been able to afford to—but these last few years since his retirement meant they had to practice a new level of thrift. They weren't paupers by any means, but they had to watch their money. Everything was so expensive these days. Food was outrageous. And medicine, medicine could drive anybody to the poorhouse. Then there was the expense of bringing up a growing child. Raising Seta wasn't something Barbara would trade, mind you, but it was a consideration.

At least the house is paid for, she thought as she scraped the last of the potatoes into a plastic container. She wrapped Seta's plate and put it into the refrigerator. Somebody would eat it later. *No perfectly good food is going to waste around here.*

"Phillip, you let that child get away with way too much," Barbara grumbled, "letting her leave the table without eating her food." It was shameful the way he allowed that child to run him. But she smiled slightly. At least he loved the girl. That's all anyone could ask.

Barbara pulled out the broom and hummed a spiritual while she swept.

Chapter 6

Seta's pencil moved furiously across the lined notebook page. Her head was bent close to her desk and her ponytail dangled around her shoulder. Around her, classmates talked. She ignored them. She was working to finish her writing assignment, even though Mr. Booth said they could take it home if they didn't finish it in class.

Finally, she finished her work. She read back over it, erasing a misspelling. She dusted it off and pushed away from her desk. She walked to Mr. Booth's desk. "Mr. Booth, I'm finished."

Her teacher smiled at her. "Seta, I said you could have this evening to complete it."

She nodded. "I know. But I just wanted to turn it in to you now."

Mr. Booth took the girl's paper. Seta was clearly his best student. He wasn't surprised that she had completed her assignment early. He cast a disdainful glance at the class. Too bad more of them weren't like her. "Thank you, Seta."

She beamed and danced back to her seat. Mr. Booth was proud of her, she could tell.

Seta took her lunch tray and slowly looked around. She could sit by herself—she usually did—but today she didn't want to do that. It would be nice to have someone to talk to while she ate. Maybe she could eat with one of the girls from her class. She saw Tonya Tuffs sitting by herself, but that would never do. Sure, Tonya would welcome her, but Tonya was gross. She picked her nose and chewed with her mouth open. No one ever sat with Tonya.

Seta scoured the room some more and spotted a girl named Jessica sitting with some others, but she wouldn't dare sit there. They were popular. They'd laugh at her.

Seta slowly walked to an empty table in the back, sat down and opened her milk. And today, like all the other days, she ate alone.

Seta saw Mr. Spivey outside when she walked home from school. She stopped to chat with her neighbor for a second. Rumor had it that old man Spivey's wife had run off with a white man many, many years ago and he had gone a little crazy. He sometimes sat on his porch, chewing on a broom straw and staring into space.

Today, however, he was washing his car. He had on a thin, white T-shirt with no sleeves and shorts that stopped short of his knees. Black church socks came up to the middle of his calves and his church shoes were splattered with suds.

Yeah, he sure is crazy, Seta thought. *Who washes a car in church shoes?*

"Hey, Mr. Spivey," she called. He grinned a wide, toothless greeting and wiped his hands on his pants.

"Hey, Little Miss Muffet," he said. "Come let me give you some of this candy. You like candy?"

Seta ran to him. Mr. Spivey gave out the best candy. "It's in the house, come on," he said, gesturing with his head for her to follow him. She looked around quickly to make sure her grandmother was not looking out the window. Barbara didn't like her to go into other people's houses alone. Her concern was silly, Seta thought. Mr. Spivey was old and crazy, but he wasn't dangerous.

She followed him inside. Plastic covered the chairs and couches in the living room. Seta wondered how anyone could sit on that during the sizzling Texas summer. Hearing the rattle of the candy dish, her mind was quickly drawn back to her mission.

"Here." Mr. Spivey gave her a handful of hard candy and chocolates. He smiled. "Now, be good, ya hear?"

"I will, Mr. Spivey," Seta said around a mouthful of lemon drops.

He followed her back outside.

The family piled into the five-year-old blue-green Cutlass Supreme. Barbara pushed up the armrest and let Seta sit between her and Phillip. They were off to pick a pumpkin at the church's annual harvest festival. It would have suited Barbara just as well to grab a pumpkin from the corner store and bring it home to carve and make a pie. But Phillip insisted on taking the child to the festival so she could eat cotton candy. *Like she needs cotton candy*, Barbara fumed. *We're already paying a heap of money for these braces she's wearing. Those sweets can't be good for that child's mouth.* But she agreed.

"Grammy, do you think we can stop by the dunking booth this year?" Seta asked.

"Oh, no!" Barbara said as Phillip slowly pulled into the street. "I'm not letting you get near that dunking booth. You'll catch cold."

Seta frowned, her bottom lip sticking out in a sullen pout. "But Grammy, I won't catch cold. And it will be fun."

"No," Barbara said, turning her head to look out the window. The trees were dressed in fall's browns, grays, and pale greens. Soon, the holidays would be upon them. She didn't need Seta getting sick.

"Now, Barbara, what harm could it be?" Phillip asked, his eyes on the road. The child would be ten only once. She needed some fun in her life.

Barbara clenched her teeth. Phillip knew she hated when he disagreed with her in front of Seta. "It's a silly game, and it's one that could make her sick," she said.

Seta pleaded. "But, Grammy, I've been so good in school. You never let me do anything fun. I promise not to get sick."

Phillip eased the car onto the church parking lot. "Come on, Barbara, it'll just be a little bit of water. Not enough to hurt a fly."

Barbara threw her hands in the air. "Fine. But if she gets sick, I don't want to hear it!" She snatched open the door and climbed out.

A gleeful Seta crawled out after her.

Seta lay in bed that night listening to the silence. She smiled as the sound of Poppy's soft snoring drifted in from the next room. She wondered if her daddy snored. She imagined not.

Seta slipped her hand under her pillow and, without looking, fingered the picture that was there. She didn't dare turn on the light for fear her grandmother would see its glare under the door. But she didn't have to. The smiling face was etched in her memory. She knew the face by heart, the creamy skin with just a hint of brown, the freckles across the nose, the sandy ringlets that tumbled from her head. She even knew the teeth, the eyes and curvature of the neck.

It wasn't as if she felt like the woman was really her mother. Instead, she was a beautiful stranger that Seta longed to transform into physically. All she knew of her mother told her how much everyone liked the woman in the picture and how much they missed her. She prayed her usual prayer. "Dear God, if you just make me like her, I know everybody would be happy. My daddy won't be sad anymore. And me, well, I'd be so happy too. She looks so pretty. Make me beautiful and graceful and Creole-looking just like her.

"I don't ask for much," Seta touched the cross pendant on the necklace her grandmother had given her for her last birthday. The cross always made her feel somehow more at peace, even secure. She prayed took a deep breath, her hand feeling the familiar coolness of the crucifix. She prayed. "If you make me like this woman, I think maybe then my daddy would want me. Maybe he'd come for me. Or at least . . . maybe he'd like me. Maybe he'd let me be his daughter again. Please God, make my daddy want me."

The last of the prayer evaporated from her lips.

Lately she had started to think more about her parents, especially her father. She had a good time at the festival, but imagined she would have had even more fun if her mother and father had been there with her. She had lived with her grandparents for as long as she could remember. That was the only home she knew. And she was happy. Still, she longed for her father, though she wouldn't tell her grandparents because she didn't want to hurt their feelings.

Seta drifted into her favorite daydream.

She was doing homework at the kitchen table. Her grandmother burst into the house and beamed at her. "Seta, we have a wonderful surprise for you. Close your eyes."

And when she opened her eyes, her father was standing in front of her with his arms spread wide. "Will you please come and live with me?" He waited, holding his breath.

Seta looked at her father for a second and then to her grandmother. Her grandmother smiled and nodded her head in approval. "Of course, Daddy, I would love to live with you," Seta finally said, putting down her pencil. She ran to him, stepping into his arms.

Tears were in his eyes. "I've been waiting so long to hear you say that, sweetheart," he said.

Seta went to sleep with a smile on her lips.

"Seta, I swear, you're going to send us to the poorhouse," Barbara complained as she held up a pair of Seta's old pants to the girl's waist. The pants stopped shy of her ankles. "I can't keep buying you new clothes every other month. You are just like your mother, growing like a weed."

At ten, Seta was gangly and boyish. It seemed just as soon as she broke in one pair of jeans, she had to have a new pair. She was taller than the other girls in her class, and most of the boys too. They sometimes called her Big Bird.

Seta felt guilty about her growth spurts. She knew her grandparents didn't have a lot of money. Her grandmother had never worked outside the home and her grandfather was retired. She overheard them sometimes talking about money. She knew that if they didn't have to take care of her, they would have more of it. *They might even be rich, if it wasn't for me,* she thought.

"And stand up straight!" Barbara pushed her palm firmly into the small of the girl's back. Out of habit, Seta sometimes slumped to hide her height. Barbara's voice softened. "Look here, your height is a blessing. Many girls—and boys— would love to be as tall as you are. Don't walk about hiding it. Stand tall."

Barbara knew her granddaughter was sensitive. Barbara sometimes let her tongue get the best of her, especially when she thought of money.

Phillip had worked at a neighborhood grocery in the early years of their marriage, until the war when he and many of their neighbors had gone off to fight after the attack on Pearl Harbor. Fight, though, was the wrong word, Barbara knew. Phillip, like scores of other blacks, had worked in support detail during the war. Afterward, when he returned home, he toiled for the rail company, then as a bus driver, and later, at the automobile plant making car seats.

Eventually, the plant made him retire because his hands were too slow. *He gave them all those years and when he couldn't do the volume of work he used to, they put him out to pasture*, Barbara thought bitterly. Well, that was part of the reason. The other part had to do with the machines doing the work humans used to do.

Phillip had spent most of his life working. He and his brother both had left school in their middle-school years to scrounge around for work. It was the Great Depression, and the responsibility of helping to support the family fell upon their shoulders. Phillip had then married and never returned to school. His jobs were always decent and sometimes provided a good wage, but the retirement pay was a completely different story.

Barbara sighed for seemingly the thousandth time as she thought about how her life could have been so different if she hadn't been made to marry and give up her dreams of grandeur. She grew up idolizing the female writers and artists she read about who were a part of the Harlem Renaissance. They seemed to have so much style and resolve. They had hard times, true, but they lived to do what they loved. But it wasn't just them she had dreamed of emulating. She read voraciously any newspaper piece about Eleanor Roosevelt, who was the wife of the president in the 1930s. She was someone who stood up and talked with a nation listening to what she had to say about many things, including the unfair treatment of blacks.

Barbara shook her head, returning to the present. It would do no good to think about what could have been.

She had a child here who needed her. This girl would live the life she hadn't been able to. She would be free and she would go far.

Barbara and Phillip would just have to scrimp and scrape to make sure this girl had the resources to make her dreams come true. She would make sure this one made good use of her future.

Phillip's small pension and the Social Security weren't much, but they'd make them do. The money would come from somewhere. They would manage.

"I'll let out the hem in these pants and well, we'll go shopping this weekend," Barbara said between teeth clenched around sewing pins. A tape measure wrapped around her arm as she tried to see how much the girl had grown. "We'll get you a few things to tide you over. Hopefully, they'll last you a while. Now, go on. Go outside and play if you want. But don't get dirty or mess your clothes up."

Seta grabbed her basketball. "Can I go to the park?" she asked, excitement making her voice go up a notch.

Barbara took the pins out of her mouth and shook her finger. "*May* I. May I go to the park. How many times do I have to tell you to use proper English? You can't walk around here sounding like some uneducated ragamuffin."

Barbara nodded her assent to the girl's query. She hoped her only granddaughter would run into some nice young ladies and perhaps make some friends. Barbara ached for the loneliness she knew her granddaughter must feel. Seta had never been very outgoing. Barbara took that back, the girl had been as a young child, but that open spirit had slowly slipped away.

Barbara would sometimes catch Seta hungrily watching other children at church or at the park. Her hazel eyes—gray filled with flecks of green—would follow them until they were out of her line of vision. Barbara had often tried to help make introductions, but Seta would shyly turn away.

"Maybe you'll see some girls from school," Barbara prodded. Seta shrugged. Seta cast her eyes to the floor and turned to leave. Barbara called to her, "Shoulders back, stomach in! Stop walking like you're some common street child," she said, grabbing firmly to Seta's shoulders. "Remember, you are a lady, even if you do insist on playing basketball at every turn."

Seta sighed but did as she was told. She lifted her head and threw her shoulders back. A moment later, she was on her way to the park. She hoped she would find some boys playing basketball. She didn't mind inviting herself into a circle to play basketball. That was easier than inviting herself into a circle to make friends.

When she got to the park, she saw a pack of girls giggling and playing hopscotch. She thought for a moment about going to say hello and see if they would let her play. They glanced at her as she approached, then turned back to each other, laughing.

Seta bit her lip and tried to shrink into herself. Across the way, some guys were already playing a game. She sat down at the edge of the pavement to wait for their game to end, hoping they'd want to include her in the next.

The game was finally over. Seta stood; however, no one noticed her. The guys made calls for their next game, lining up their teams. She stepped forward.

"Hey, can I play?" She could hear her grandmother's voice in her head screaming "may I," but she ignored it.

The guys all turned and looked at her. "Nah," one said, and they all laughed. "We don't play like girls."

She stepped onto the court, planting her feet squarely and shot back: "I don't play like a girl either."

One of the guys let out a slow whistle. "So, what you saying? You want to take one of us on?" he asked.

She was nervous, but said resolutely, "Yeah."

The guy's chest puffed out and he stepped toward her.

"Little girl, do you know what you are doing? You might not want to play with us. Go back to the sandbox."

Seta's saucer eyes narrowed. "I don't play in the sandbox."

"Ohhhh, man, she told you!" said one of the guys standing in the background.

"She didn't tell me nuthin'," the guy said. He stood in front of her, inches from her face. "Man, I'm not going to waste my time playing with some little girl."

He waved his hand dismissively in her direction. Seta hated being made to feel like she was insignificant. "That's because you know I'll beat you," she taunted. Basketball gave her bravado. It was a bravery only felt on the court.

She stared him down. The other guys let out a slow whistle.

The boy wrinkled his nose, then nodded. "Okay, Miss Loudmouth, I'll play you."

Seta smiled. Finally, she'd get a chance. Then the guy paused. "So, what do you want to put on it?"

Seta frowned. "Put on what?"

"The game," the guy said. "If I win, what will I get? Don't you know, anytime you want to get something you got to give something?"

Seta had played basketball with plenty of boys but had never had this question before. She didn't know what to say. "I don't know," she said, slowly.

The guys looked from one to the other. The guy who challenged her pretended to think a long time about the wager. Then he waved his hand in the air. "Man, it don't even matter. I'll just play you for the fun. You're just a little girl."

The other guys backed off the court. The boy squared off against Seta. He blocked her first shot. The guys broke into raucous laughter. "Take it easy on her, Mike!" one yelled.

Seta ran to get the rebound. He beat her to it. She jumped to block his shot and fell. The other guys seemed not to be able to catch their breath. They were laughing so hard. From the sidelines, they taunted such things as, "So, Mike, where'd you get her, the day-care center?" "You need to stop babysitting." "Man, Mike, you need to give her a break. Let her go home to her mama."

Seta's face burned with embarrassment and frustration. It had been quite a long while since she had lost a basketball game. Seta had been playing basketball since she was old enough to carry one. She usually played with some of the boys from her class. These new guys were something else. Next to the boys in her class, she shone. Next to this guy, well, she could only wonder what went wrong.

Finally, the game was over.

The guy named Mike shook her hand and then tousled her hair. "Hey, kid, don't be mad. You actually played pretty good."

She shrugged. "Whatever."

She turned to walk away, but he held her by the shoulder. "No, really, you did a good job."

"What, for a girl?" she spat. She snatched up her basketball.

He shook his head. "No, for anybody. How old are you?"

"Ten."

His eyes widened. "Really? I would have put you at about twelve or thirteen; 'round our age."

The other guys gave each other high fives and gathered around Seta.

"Hey, man, she's just ten," said the guy named Mike. He stood taller than she, with big feet wrapped in even bigger sneakers. The sneakers were beat up with scuff marks on the top and strings that looked like a dog had chewed at them. "She was jamming for a ten-year-old, huh?"

The other guys nodded in assent. Mike turned back to her. "Hey, come by anytime you want to play. We're usually here on the weekend."

Seta began to feel a little better. She'd be back.

As she slowly walked home with her basketball wedged under her arm, she thought back over the game. She didn't like losing. She spit on the pavement. The rocks and twigs made crunching sounds under the soles of her off-brand sneakers.

She stopped at Ms. Lela's corner store. The steps were rickety and the screen door that was missing a spring easily flew open. Seta's eyes adjusted to the dimness.

"Hey there, child," Ms. Lela called to her from beside the counter. "You haven't been in here in a while. How come?"

Seta hadn't been there because she hadn't had any money. Even the penny candy had been too expensive. She didn't know why she stopped today, because she didn't have any money now either. "I just came by to see what you have new," she said, peering into the canister on the counter.

"The penny candy done gone up," Ms. Lela said, peering at the girl. "You can get two Now and Laters for a nickel. Here is a box of lemon drops for a dime."

Seta's mouth watered at the prospect of sucking on Now and Laters and lemon drops. But then she remembered she didn't have any money.

The phone rang. "S'cuse me, baby." Ms. Lela turned her back to Seta. No one was watching her. Seta's hand was already in the candy jar. Her fingers curled around a Now and Later. She started to lift her hand, but stopped. She had heard enough of Rev. Johnson's sermons to know that stealing was a sin worse than any other. Thieves got their hands cut off, at least in his sermons they did. And her grandmother had told her often enough that God didn't like someone who took what didn't belong to them.

Seta let the candy fall back into the jar, removed her hand and picked up her basketball.

Ms. Lela returned. "So, you decide on what you want?"

Seta shook her head. "No, I'm not going to get anything." She glanced at the candy jar. "I'll come back when I have some money. Anyway, I should be getting on home."

Ms. Lela sucked on her teeth. "Tell your grandma I said hi, ya hear?"

"Yes, ma'am," Seta said. She hated never having any money. All she wanted was a piece of candy, and she didn't even have the money for that. She stomped out the door and turned toward home.

She let her mind wander. She wondered if her daddy could show her some new basketball moves. The ones she had learned were some she picked up in gym class and in games with some of her classmates. But that guy Mike, well, he did a number on her. She tossed her head, "I bet my daddy could beat him," She mumbled to herself.

She had never actually seen her father play the game, but had full faith that he would know how and would be good. She would ask her daddy to teach what he knew. Her mind played around with that thought for the rest of her walk home. Yeah, her daddy would show her.

When Seta stepped into the door that opened into the kitchen, her grandmother's eyebrows shot up. She asked, "What in the world happened to your hair?" Barbara dried her soapy hands on her apron and tried in vain to wipe the girl's flyaway hair back into neatness.

Barbara shook her head. "I just don't understand why you'd go out there roughhousing every day," she said, turning back to the sink of dishes. Barbara was constantly demanding her to act like a lady and to look presentable at all times. Barbara couldn't understand why the girl insisted on horseplay and running around like a madwoman. *I don't know where she gets that wild streak.* Barbara knew Seta's mother had never been like that, that's for sure. *Must be that other side of her family*, Barbara thought with an audible grunt.

Seta took the cue from her grandmother and tried to

smooth her hair back into place with her hands, but it just fell in all directions around her shoulders. Barbara glanced back at the girl; the older woman's eyes narrowed when she saw Seta's pant leg.

"Go get my belt!" Barbara said, her eyes moving from the pants to Seta's face. "Didn't I just finish telling you not to mess up your clothes?"

For the first time, Seta looked down and noticed the rip in her pant leg and the blood that stained her knee. "But, Grammy . . ."

Barbara wasn't hearing it. "There is no but," she said. "Go on, go get my belt!"

Seta began to shake her head and held up her hands, inviting understanding. "Grammy, please, I didn't mean to," she pleaded, shaking her head. "I didn't even know."

Her face threatened to screw up into a cry, but Barbara held up her hand. "You better not. You better not let a single tear fall out that eye. You are too big to run around here crying at every turn. Now hush up!"

"But—"

Barbara's eyes lit with fire. "Don't talk back to me!"

Phillip walked into the kitchen, a worried expression on his face. "What's all this racket?"

"You see her tearing up her clothes? Good clothes we provide for her," Barbara said. She held Seta firmly by the shoulders and pivoted her around so Phillip could see the front of her pants. "I'm going to teach her a lesson yet. Now go on, go get my belt."

Phillip looked from the frightened eyes of Seta to the determined eyes of his wife. "Let's just hear the child out first, okay?"

"Poppy, I didn't even know." Seta's eyes were wide. "I was playing basketball and fell. I didn't even know my pants were torn."

"It's all right. Why don't you go change?" Phillip said.

Seta looked toward her grandmother. Barbara breathed deeply. The anger began to dissipate from her chest. It wasn't the girl's fault that she was so clumsy. Barbara gestured toward the hall. "Go on. You heard your grandfather. Take those pants off and get your bath. I'll see if I can sew them," she said.

Barbara glanced down the hall to make sure Seta had closed her door. She cut her eyes at Phillip. "I swear she gets more like that daddy of hers every day. You see how she came in here? Hair all over her head, clothes all messed up. Rose would never have walked around in public like that. But by God, if I don't do anything else before I leave this earth, I'm going to teach her to be a lady. Lord knows, I will, even if I have to beat the tomboy out of her."

Phillip opened the refrigerator. "Barb, just let the girl be. You're too hard on her. Much as you would like, you can't turn her into Rose."

"I'm not trying to turn her into anybody!" Barbara's voice rose. She knew good and well that Seta was not Rose.

Phillip took a soda out of the refrigerator. Barbara took it from him, wiped the top and poured it into a glass. She handed it to her husband.

Phillip kissed her on her forehead. "You're a good woman."

Barbara sat at the piano in the living room and slowly let her fingers glide over the keys. A spiritual song wafted up from the keys. A moment later, she smiled, as she felt someone sit down next to her.

"You like that?" she asked, and Seta smiled.

Seta plucked a few keys and they played together. It was one of their favorite things to do when Seta was younger, though they rarely played much these days. Barbara's fingers weren't as limber as they once were.

"Grammy, why are some people mean to others?" Seta asked.

Barbara took a deep breath. "What do you mean?"

"Well, I was just wondering," Seta said. "Sometimes, the kids at school, and those on the playground, are so mean and rude to me. They call me names and nobody likes to play with me. And even my daddy, well, I wish he would just smile at me sometimes. Am I that ugly?"

Barbara struggled against the burst of emotion that overcame her. She stopped playing the piano and put her hand on Seta's. "Look, in this life, some people just don't have the love of the Lord in them. They are hateful, but it has nothing to do with you. It's about their souls."

"So you're saying my daddy has a hateful soul?" Seta was concerned. "Will he go to hell?"

Barbara detected the girl's alarm. She tried to assure her. "Well, it's not as easy as that," she said. "Your daddy's feelings are just hurting right now. We'll just keep praying for him. We'll pray that God touches his heart and allows him to see the blessing that you are."

That old scoundrel couldn't see a blessing if it stared him in the face, Barbara thought to herself.

"But I've been praying and I don't think it's working," Seta said.

"Well, the Lord always answers prayer," Barbara said.

"Always?" Seta wanted to know.

"Always," Barbara said. "He sits high and looks low and He will never leave you or forsake you."

"What is *forsake?*"

"He won't let you down," Barbara said, and Seta's eyes lit up.

"Okay," the girl said, and stroked the crucifix that hung around her neck.

Chapter 7

Seta ended the school year at the top of her fifth-grade class. The school was going to hold an awards program to recognize achievers, and Barbara said she could have a new dress for the occasion. But Seta wanted something more.

"Do you think my daddy will come?"

Something flickered over Barbara's face. Just as quickly, it was gone. "I'm sure he wouldn't miss it, baby," she said.

Seta smiled, satisfied.

The next day, Barbara paid Robert a visit. She rang the doorbell. She didn't hear any movement inside, but saw Robert's car in the driveway. She leaned on the bell.

A moment later, the door creaked open. He paused for a minute, then moved aside.

She stepped into the house and blinked. Her eyes had to adjust to the darkness. *Why is this man sitting in here in the dark*, she wondered. Her eyes went immediately to the photo of a smiling couple in a wedding photo. That seemed so long ago. As her eyes went back to Robert, the contrast was stark. Dark circles had taken up residence around Robert's eyes, and his shoulders were stooped. His forehead shone where hair had once been.

"Good afternoon, Robert," Barbara said, frowning with an air of superiority. *The place could use a good cleaning.* Even in the dark, she could see that.

"Hello, Barbara," he said, pushing his glasses up on his nose. The years hadn't been kind to his mother-in-law. Most of her hair had turned a light gray. Her skin was sallow, with cheeks that had sunken in slightly. Barbara was round, with thick ankles. She still had that feisty spirit though.

"I just came by to let you know that your daughter will be expecting you at her school's awards program next week," she said, looking around with disdain.

Robert shook his head. "I'll be busy."

Barbara frowned. "You don't even know when it is."

"Well, next week is just a busy week, period." Robert was busy pretending to straighten the pillows on the couch. He didn't feel like having this conversation. Ever so often, Barbara would take it upon herself to try to bully him into some involvement in that child's life.

You'd think after all this time, the woman would have learned, Robert thought. He had closed off that part of his life all those years ago. No birthday visits, no holiday gifts, and not this. He just wasn't interested. But Barbara wasn't the brightest one on God's planet.

Barbara rolled her eyes skyward. "Robert, I don't know what goes on in that head of yours, but you have a child who needs you. It will take all of an hour out of your precious day. And besides, do you think you're the only one who still misses Rose? But you've got to snap out of this. You've got to stop acting this way."

Robert had gotten used to wearing his grief. In the first few years following Rose's death, it was like a palpable thing. It had gotten easier though sometime after he sent the baby away. Still, after all these years, he missed his wife. *They still don't understand. And they don't care. They don't care that Rose was my soul mate, that she was my best friend, my advocate, my very life force. People talk about love, but they don't understand what it means. How can I get over loving my wife?* Rose had accepted him when no one else did. She looked at him with eyes filled with nothing but love. It didn't matter that he came from a no-count family. It didn't matter that he hadn't been like the other boys. None of it mattered to her. She was the only person in the world who allowed him to be just Robert.

He missed her and he blamed that child. *If that girl hadn't ever been born, I'd still have my wife. We'd be happy. We'd be traveling the world, watching the sun set from exotic locations. Doing all the things we had only dreamed of doing. And now, I have none of that. Just memories.*

There was no way he was going anywhere to celebrate something Seta had done. After all, hadn't she done enough?

Aloud, he said simply, "I'm not going, period. Doesn't matter what you say." He knew he sounded childish, but he didn't care. Barbara wasn't going to make him go to some ridiculous program for some child he had divorced himself from years ago.

Barbara jabbed her finger into his back. He stood and turned toward her. "What are you doing?" he asked.

"Robert, you are the most selfish human being I know," Barbara said. All the old feelings of animosity resurfaced. "First, you stole my baby from me. And now, you have the nerve—the nerve—to turn your back on your own. Lord knows what Rose ever saw in your sorry self. I wish you could have been the one who died!"

Seta wore a pink-and-white dress—her grandmother's choice—to the awards ceremony. Her ankle socks gave way

to skinny calves, shiny with cooking oil Barbara had insisted on slathering on her skin to make it gleam. Her hair
was pulled back in a tight ponytail, the rest of it cascading
down her back.

"You look just like your mama," Barbara had told Seta
when she kissed the girl before they left the house that
morning.

The auditorium was hot, but Seta didn't notice. She
watched the doorway the entire time. Every time a latecomer
arrived, she looked up hopefully. Then her face would always fall when she saw it was not her father.

Barbara touched Phillip's arm. "I can't stand him," she
said, her fingers digging into her husband's arm. Phillip
knew of whom she spoke. "He's a hateful, hateful human
being!"

"Sweetheart, don't you think you're being a bit harsh?"
Phillip asked.

"Harsh!" Barbara hissed. "That scoundrel is just the
most—"

"It's not for us to sit in judgment," Phillip said. "You of
all people should know that. You sing in the choir and
praise the Lord as loudly as anybody, but you can say some
really bad things yourself."

"Are you saying I'm not acting right?" Barbara huffed.
"Look, I take food up to the shelter every chance I get. And
I donate clothes to the mission. And I—"

Phillip patted her hand. "All I'm saying is that we can't
judge him when sometimes our own actions aren't as pure
as they should be." Barbara drew herself taller in her seat
and turned her head the other way. Phillip felt the stiffness
and rubbed her hand. "Let's just enjoy the day," he said.

Barbara poked out her jaw, but finally nodded, though
she wasn't ready to let go of the original subject. "I don't
know why he does this to that child."

"I know, sweetheart, I know." Phillip patted her hand again and looked toward the stage where Seta sat.

When the program ended, Barbara and Phillip walked to Seta. Phillip handed her a bouquet of flowers. "We are so proud of you," he whispered when he kissed her cheek.

Barbara nodded. "Your mama would have been so proud."

Seta swallowed. "Thank you," she said, looking at the flowers. She smiled to conceal the sadness in her heart.

That night, Seta sat on her bed with her Bible on her knee. She had looked up that word *forsake* that her grandmother had mentioned before. Her grandmother had been right. The Bible really did say God would not forsake her, that He wouldn't leave her or let her down.

"Well, God, I prayed really hard for my daddy to come to my program," Seta said, closing the Bible. "I thought You said all I had to do was pray."

"Turn the light off and go to bed," Barbara said, sticking her head into the bedroom. She saw the Bible on the girl's lap and smiled.

"That's good," Barbara said. "I've taught you well. You always spend time with the Lord. Every day."

"Well, I seem to spend a lot of time, but it's not doing anything," Seta said.

Barbara's eyes narrowed. "Child, what are you talking about?"

"God," Seta said. "I prayed to Him and He didn't answer. I don't think He likes me."

"Girl, stop talking like that!" Barbara said. "You can't talk about God like that. And maybe He didn't answer your prayer—whatever it is—because you weren't acting right. If you're not doing what He says, He won't answer you. He'll turn a deaf ear to you. Don't you know everything we get from God, we have to earn it? That's why we live according to His commandments. That's why I try so hard to teach you to be good. If you're not good to Him, God won't be good to you. You have to earn your blessings."

Seta frowned. *Oh, it's like that. I should have known. God is just like everybody else. He wants something first before He'll do something for you.*

She put the Bible on the nightstand in disappointment and clicked off the light.

"Good night," she told her grandmother. Why couldn't God just answer her prayer? What did she have to give Him first?

"You know that scoundrel didn't even come to the baby's program at school," Barbara said to Nettie, who sat at the table in Barbara's kitchen.

Nettie scowled. "You didn't think he would, did you?"

"No, but . . ."

"Well, why are you still talking about it?" Nettie breathed in the aroma of the still-warm cake Barbara was frosting with a knife. Nettie rubbed her finger along the edge of the dessert, in a comfortable gesture born of years of friendship. She licked the icing off her finger. "So, you going to let me take some of that cake home?"

Barbara held the knife in midair and cast a sidelong glance at her friend. "I thought I gave you a recipe years ago, for a very simple cake."

Nettie was fifty-eight years old and still didn't know her way around a kitchen. She would often beg Barbara to make her a cake for the holidays, and sometimes just on regular days. Nettie pursed her lips and let out a light laugh. "Girl, you know I can't bake no cake," she said. "Stop trying to shame me."

Barbara shook her head, a tiny smile on her lips. After all this time, Nettie's ineptitude in the kitchen was a running joke between them. Barbara didn't mind fixing food for her friend. "Well, actually, I baked this one for you anyway. I know poor Charles must be starving over there. Tell him I'll fix him some good stew next week."

After Nettie's cake-baking experience ended with her broiling instead of baking a chocolate cake one holiday years ago, her husband, Charles, pleaded with his wife not to try anymore homemade dishes.

"Well, I'm sure he'll want to kiss you," Nettie said. "You know we've been eating sandwiches all week. We're going out to eat tonight because he said he can't stand to eat another piece of meat between two slices of bread. I say, good. I was tired of sandwiches too."

Nettie leaned over to see what was on the stove. "You know, if you really want to do something for us, you can just send me home with a few plates of whatever you have over there."

Barbara shook her head in mock disgust. "Girl, you are a mess."

Nettie shrugged. At least she had taken her friend's mind off Robert and his ways.

The deep grief that Robert had felt for years had subsided into a dull ache. He could laugh, sometimes, and even managed to focus on work. He took a yearlong sabbatical after giving the baby away. He came back to work refocused and determined to do something that would make Rose proud.

It had always been their goal that he would make dean, and maybe even provost. Within a few years, he became the chairperson of his department at the college. He now occasionally even attended the church where they had been members. He wasn't sure why he went, but sometimes he felt drawn to that place. Church and God had always given Rose so much peace. Maybe he went there searching for that same feeling, or maybe he just wanted to do something that reminded him of her.

However, that didn't mean things were back to normal. His home was still a shrine to his wife, and he sometimes closed himself in the house all weekend to think and remember. And to sometimes cry.

The outsiders had never understood the special bond he and his Rose had shared.

He recalled the first time she saw him naked, their wedding night. He had been willing to have sex before they got God's blessing, but she had not. Even that young, her relationship with God had been strong. That had often annoyed Robert, because she would seem to throw God's name into everything. What did God have to do with their relationship?

He had asked her once as they listened to records on the porch as her mother prepared dinner inside: "Do you really think God cares what we do in our lives?"

She had looked at him, aghast at his question. "Of course He cares!"

"Don't you think He's too busy way up there to be bothered with whether we have sex or anything else we do?" Robert asked.

"Oh, Robert," Rose said. "God cares so much for us. He cares about everything that concerns us, down to the hairs on our heads. He wants us to live good lives and to be happy."

Derision laced Robert's voice. "Well, seems that He has failed a lot if He wants this to be a happy world," Robert said. "Why does he cause so many problems if he wants us to be happy? Wars, famines, diseases—"

"God doesn't make bad things happen," Rose said, drawing from her Sunday school lessons. "He gives us choices. And sometimes He allows bad things to happen because He gives us free will and we make bad choices."

"Some God," Robert said, unconvinced. His voice dropped.

"Well, I say, we should spend a little less time worried about Him and more time worried about each other. I love you. I want to make love to you."

He touched her lightly on the thigh but Rose brushed his hand away, giggling as she glanced around to be certain her mother hadn't spied her through the front door. Barbara had told Rose that good girls didn't take their clothes off for men who weren't their husbands, and this is what Rose had repeated to Robert. Occasionally, they would exchange a kiss under a tree, but that's as far as it got. "God sees us at all times," Rose had told him then, smiling so sweetly he had forgotten his annoyance at God for prohibiting sex.

On their wedding night, Robert had so looked forward to at last holding her close. He had wanted to turn off the light before climbing into bed, but she insisted he keep it on. He squirmed, but finally knew there was no way of getting around it. He slowly pulled down his pants. He hesitated, without looking at her, before letting them fall to the floor. He took off his right sock and stopped. His hand slowly moved to roll down his left one. He hung his head in shame.

Rose giggled, and his heart stopped. He snatched his sock back up. He was crushed that she would laugh.

"Come on, silly!" she said, brushing his hands away. She snatched down his sock and threw it aside. "You're being a slowpoke. This is what we've been waiting for. Now, come help me get undressed."

Robert's trepidation dissolved. She hadn't been laughing at him. And, seeing his withered leg at such a close vantage point, she never let on that it bothered her or that anything was wrong.

Robert had been afraid Rose would laugh or stare as everyone else did when they first saw his leg. The muscles never developed to be strong and firm like the ones in his other leg. A bout with polio when he was a young child had left its mark. His mother said he should be glad to be alive, but that was easy for her to say. She didn't have to walk around with a deformity.

In the instance when Rose pulled him to her even after seeing that, he knew she was the one person in the world who would never judge him. And that's why it was so hard to let her go.

The thought of dating another woman had crossed his mind. He knew he'd never love another again, but he did feel lonely. He wanted a companion to share the house with, to take care of him. There was a woman at church who had shown interest in him and had even cooked him a meal from time to time. She had dropped by a time or two with a covered food dish. "We've been missing you at church," she would say if he missed a month or two.

"I haven't had a chance to get by there lately," he would say, or something similar. It felt almost blasphemous to him that this woman would talk about church with him. Church was Rose's thing. But the woman sure knew how to cook some chicken.

Robert frowned as he looked around his bedroom. It had always been so neat when Rose was alive—she hated clutter. Those days, though, were long gone. It seemed that every pair of shoes he owned was strewn across the floor. The white sheets had darkened to the color of an eggshell, reminding him he hadn't changed them in months. He had started sleeping on top of the flat sheet because the fitted sheet had begun to smell.

Maybe he could find someone to keep his house clean and to talk to him when the walls seemed to close in on him, a companion of a sort. He shook his head though and ran his hand over his face to clear the thoughts. He inwardly apologized to Rose for thinking such a disloyal thing.

* * *

Seta took to playing basketball with Mike and the other boys on the weekends. Barbara allowed her to go, though she always admonished Seta to watch out for the boys.

"Don't let some little scoundrel play in your pants," Barbara said to her.

Playing in her pants had something to do with boys touching Seta "down there." Seta didn't know why her grandmother always said that. Why would she let some boy play in her pants? It was silly. But she always nodded and said, "Yes, ma'am."

"I might not be able to see everything you do, but God does," Barbara admonished. "And He will strike you down dead in your steps if you do something wrong, I promise you He will. You remember the Old Testament. He turned that woman into a pillar of salt—you don't want to turn into a pillar of salt, do you? And I know you remember those ungrateful children of Israel, when He gave them their manna and they complained and He turned it into bugs? And I know you remember when he burned up all that stuff when His people started not paying attention to Him? Well, you just remember that. He can do the same to you, if you stop listening to Him. Remember, you can't hide from God."

Seta's head was spinning. She loved God, but He was scary too. "I know," she told her grandmother. "I will be good. I don't want to turn into a pillar of salt."

"Good," Barbara said.

At first the boys sometimes gave her a hard time because most of them were twelve and thirteen, and she was only ten. She thought the teasing would stop when she turned eleven, but it did not. Eleven only brought her more of the same.

"Seta, why don't you go and play with the other girls?" Joe asked, throwing the ball at her, hard. She caught it with a loud clap.

"Because I want to play with you," she said. Besides, the girls probably wouldn't let her play with them anyway. They didn't want to be her friend. She looked down at the ground.

"Well, you can't always come up here playing with the big guys," he said, to a few snickers from the other guys. "This is for grown folks."

Seta knew they were all looking at her. She drew a circle in the dirt with the toe of her shoe and tried to shrink. She didn't know what to say. Why wouldn't they just play the game?

"What, cat got your tongue?" Joe prodded. He strode over to her and snatched the ball from her hand. "Gimme that ball."

She wished she could sink into the ground. All she wanted was to play a game of ball with them. They confused her. Sometime they were so nice, but other times . . .

"Knock it off, Joe," a voice came from her back. She turned around. It was Mike.

Relief coursed over her face. She hadn't heard him approaching.

"Man, I was just kidding with her," Joe said with a dismissive wave. "She knows I'm just kidding with her." He chucked her under the chin. "Ain't that right, lil' mama?"

"Uh, yeah, I know." She let out a nervous laugh.

Mike gestured. "Come on," he said to Seta. He then turned to Joe and said, "Pick your teammate. We'll play you." Within a minute, the exchange was forgotten. Seta took the ball out and threw it to Mike. With her back to Joe, she dashed onto the court. Mike passed her the ball. She took a shot. It dropped into the bald rim.

"Niiiiiice," Mike said approvingly.

Joe frowned. The game progressed.

Seta stole the ball from Joe and threw it to Mike. He

dunked easily. "Aw man, y'all are gone get drug!" said someone on the edge of the court.

"Shut up!" Joe said. He moved to guard Seta. His voice was low, "You wanna play with the big guys, huh? Well, I'll treat you like one." He bumped her. She didn't fall, but stumbled.

"Foul!" someone said from the sidelines.

"Man, that wasn't no foul!" Joe said.

Mike eyed Seta. He shook his head. She nodded. She wasn't going to worry about it.

Seta drove to the hoop. Joe was at her back. She lifted the ball in the air, cocking her wrist to aim for the goal. Joe chopped at her arm, sending her careening to the ground. She landed palms first. Her head slammed on the pavement.

Immediately, a crowd surrounded her. "Seta, Seta." She could hear her name in the distance, but couldn't open her eyes. Her head felt like horses were stomping on her temple. Her palm felt like she had stuck it in a bucket of scalding hot water and held it there. She wanted just to lie there until the aching stopped, but she envisioned Joe's sneering face in her mind's eye. So, with everything she had inside of her, she willed her eyes to open.

"I'm okay," she said, rolling to her knees. Someone grabbed her by her shoulder and helped her up. Once in a standing position, she looked down at her hand. Blood, grass, and dirt mingled in the raw white meat of her palm. She tried to shake off the piercing sting of the cuts.

"Man, that was dirty!" Mike said to Joe. Mike squared off, toe to toe, with Joe. Joe stepped back.

"Man, I was just going for the ball," Joe said, looking around for support. Nobody met his eyes.

Seta spit on her raw palm to dislodge some of the grass and dirt. She wiped her hand on her pants and cleared her throat. "Hey, it's okay," she said. "Let's finish the game."

She saw the guys on the sidelines nodding with approval and grudging respect. "Man, that girl is all right."

The game ended with Seta and Mike winning, though not by as wide of a margin as they were leading by before the foul. Seta missed two shots but managed to steal a pass meant for Joe.

Mike gave her a high five at the end of the game. Her hand still stung, and she struggled not to grimace. Mike smiled. "You did all right, kid." He pinched her cheek. He gathered his backpack and looked around for her. "C'mon. I'll walk you home."

He never let her walk alone whenever it was almost nightfall. If he couldn't walk her home, he'd deputize one of his friends.

"You did all right back there. You showed them," Mike said to Seta.

Seta looked down and smiled. Her friend Mike was proud of her. They walked in silence for a while. Mike gestured toward Ms. Lela's store. "You want something to drink?"

Seta shrugged and shook her head. "No, that's okay," she said shyly. She didn't have any money.

Mike walked up the steps. "Come on. I know you have to be thirsty. I'll get us something." He went in and grabbed a few things, paid and stepped back outside. "Here," he said, tossing a soda at Seta. She caught it.

She smiled gratefully. "Thanks."

Seta opened the can. It fizzed over, spilling onto her hands. The soda stung her open cuts, but she didn't mind. Mike jumped out of the way of the spewing soda. Seta quickly held it away from her so it wouldn't get on her clothes. She giggled. Mike laughed. "Sorry 'bout that," Mike said.

They sat on the steps of the store, eating moon pies and drinking RC colas.

* * *

Seta tried to sneak into the house so she would have time to wash her hands before her grandmother saw them, but Barbara called out to her. "Come give Grammy a kiss."

She trudged into the kitchen, trying to hide the palms of her hands against the side of her pants. "Hi, Grammy," she said and hastily kissed Barbara. She turned to retreat, but Barbara's voice halted her.

"What's the rush? You don't have time to talk to your old grandma?"

Seta tried to escape. "I think I'll go wash my hands and get ready for dinner."

Barbara looked at her granddaughter quizzically. Seta would never offer to go wash her hands. "You all right? You must have bumped your head or something," she said and laughed.

Her laugh died in her throat, though, as she got her first good look at Seta. Dried blood dotted the girl's hairline.

"What in the world?!" Barbara's slippers hissed as she slid across the floor to examine the child's head.

Seta held her breath. She knew she was going to get it now.

"Baby, what happened?" Barbara dusted her hands on her apron before tilting Seta's head to one side to catch the light.

"I fell."

"How did you fall?"

"Playing . . . basketball." Seta grimaced and waited for the onslaught of words.

Barbara sighed. This child was going to kill herself over that blasted game. However, Barbara didn't dwell on it, which surprised Seta. Barbara had matters that were more pressing. "Well, come sit on my lap so I can see how bad it is."

Barbara sat in a kitchen chair and hoisted the girl onto

her lap. That is when she noticed Seta's hands. Still, it would do no good to fuss.

Instead, she bathed Seta's head and hands.

From then on, Barbara said nothing about Seta's insistence on playing basketball. When Seta passed to the eighth grade at age thirteen, Barbara allowed the girl to try out for the basketball team because she remembered what it was like to be thirteen with a dream.

"Well, if you're going to do this thing, you might as well be the best at it that you can." Barbara was resigned. She would have liked Seta's passion to be something nice, and demure—and ladylike—but if this was her choice, so be it. Barbara had begun to slow down and not allow herself to become so worked up by much these days. At sixty-two, she was beginning to feel weary.

Barbara went shopping for basketball shoes and shorts for Seta. She had Phillip and Augusta's husband put up a basketball goal in the backyard next to the vegetable garden. Whenever Seta finished her homework, Barbara allowed her to go outside and practice lay-ups and free throws.

Phillip appreciated his granddaughter's dedication to her passion but wondered if her time would be better spent learning life's lessons. "Shouldn't Seta be in the kitchen with you, learning how to fix a meal or bake a dessert?" he asked Barbara one afternoon.

Barbara paused from stirring the cake batter, her arms white with flour. Her heavy bosom heaved. She drew her eyebrows together and narrowed her eyes, creasing the space between her brows. "No. That child is not going to spend her whole life in a kitchen cooking for some man or cleaning up behind him. She can hire somebody to cook or clean. She can't hire anybody to make passes or get rebounds."

Phillip shook his head. "Sweetheart, don't you think

you're going a bit overboard with this? Basketball is a good hobby, but girls don't grow up to play basketball. They grow up to have nice families. She needs to learn how to take care of herself and a family."

Barbara was adamant. Her eyes shot fire and her tone was steely. "She *is* taking care of herself. She is following her dream. And until her dream is no longer playing basketball in high school or maybe even college, then that's exactly what she will do. I will not let her throw away her dreams over a stove!"

The unspoken words *not like I did* hung in the air between them. Phillip swallowed. He knew Barbara held hostility at the dreams she thought she had given up by marrying him. Even now, after all these years, he saw she held onto some long ago notion. "My Rose never got a chance to follow her dreams. I'm not going to let her baby do the same."

Phillip shook his head. "Rose did follow her dream. Her dream was getting married and having a baby."

Barbara refused to accept it. She shook her head. "That's ridiculous! He made her think that's what she wanted. But I'm not going to argue. I don't care if Seta never learns how to boil water. That's all right. As long as she becomes the best basketball player that she can be, that's her right."

Phillip stared at his wife but knew further conversation was no use. Not when she was like this. He turned on his heel and walked into the living room. After a long day of stacking fruits and vegetables at his new part-time job at the supermarket, he was tired and just wanted to rest his weary bones. He sank into his easy chair and flipped on the television, while in the distance he could hear the thump, thump of a bouncing basketball.

Chapter 8

Robert traced the frame that held a picture of a smiling bride. Her eyes seemed to invite him to remember. He closed his eyes. Rose was the first and only woman who made him feel worth something. She was the one who had accepted him.

The first girl Robert had ever liked was Sylvia Best. She was pretty and smelled nice. At recess one day, he finally got up the courage to limp over to her as she played patty-cake with her girlfriends.

"Hi." He could still remember the nervousness in his nine-year-old stomach.

She stopped what she was doing and looked at him with a question. He handed her a bag of cookies he had begged his mother to bake. She took the bag, holding it gingerly, as if it held a disease and not a dessert. A few of the cookies' edges had crumbled, but he hoped pretty Sylvia wouldn't notice.

"What's this for?" she asked, her tight pigtails pulling her eyebrows up in sharp angles.

Robert's mouth was dry, but he managed to find the

words. "This is for you," he said. He shoved his hands in his pockets to hide his nervousness.

"For what?" she asked, glancing first at her friends, and then back at the skinny boy who stood before her.

"B—because," his tongue tripped over his words and he could say no more.

One of Sylvia's companions scowled and then burst out in a laugh that still echoed in Robert's brain.

"Gimpy Leg likes Sylvia! Gimpy Leg likes Sylvia!" the girl crowed as she ran across the playground.

Sylvia looked horrified. "No he doesn't!"

Sylvia threw the cookies down on the ground and raced after her friend as the others followed, laughing.

Robert was crushed. Sylvia had always seemed nice to him. He hadn't thought she would make fun of his leg or that she had noticed it, really. He instantly felt small and worthless.

He never approached another girl like that again. Even in high school, when other boys teased him about never having gone on a date, he refused. He feigned disinterest, but in all actuality, he was terrified of rejection, not to mention angry. Angry that his life had been reduced to ridicule in people's eyes.

Once, he had gotten up the courage to approach a girl, Susie Goode, but he choked back his words and froze under her withering stare. Robert had convinced himself no woman would ever want him. That was until his Rose walked into his life. He didn't approach her for a date, but they somehow became friends after that day he helped her pick her books up off the steps.

He had been skeptical; refusing to believe someone so beautiful could want to be with him. Then, one day, she shyly kissed him on the cheek and he was speechless. She immediately apologized, saying proper ladies shouldn't behave in such a way.

However, it wasn't her apology that stayed with him. It was the idea that maybe she could want to be with him. That maybe, just maybe, she could find him attractive.

From then on, things were different.

"So, you want to come to my sleepover?" Jessica asked, flipping her ponytail.

Seta was bent over tying her shoe. She started to walk when she straightened to a standing position, but Jessica was blocking her path.

"So?" Jessica was digging in her purse. She pulled out a glittery lip gloss and slathered it on her lips.

Seta's eyes widened. Jessica was talking to her?

"So, do you want to come to my sleepover or not?" Jessica dropped the lip gloss back into her bag. Her skin was a deep, chocolate brown that was smooth and free of the usual pimples girls had at her age. The gloss made her teeth look even straighter and whiter than they were. She carried an expensive bag and name-brand jeans clung to her narrow hips.

"Uhm, sure!" Seta smiled. No one had ever invited her to a sleepover before.

"Okay, cool," Jessica said. She turned to leave the locker room. "It's tomorrow night."

With that, she was gone. Diana Kimbrough flounced behind her, as did Amy Greer. Seta sat on the bench, rested her elbows on her knees and smiled at the floor. Maybe Jessica wanted to be her friend after all.

When Seta walked into the house, her grandmother was sitting in Poppy's overstuffed armchair. "Hi, Grammy," Seta sang. Barbara didn't say anything.

Seta cast a quick glance in her grandmother's direction and then grabbed a milk carton from the refrigerator and poured some into a glass, then drank it, sticking the carton back into the refrigerator.

"Grammy, guess what?" Seta put the glass into the sink. She pulled the bottom of her shirt up and wiped the evidence from her top lip.

Barbara's voice was soft. "What, baby?"

Her grandmother didn't look quite right. Her eyes were closed and her hands hung loosely over the arms of the chair. Seta stood in front of her grandmother. "Grammy, what's wrong?"

Barbara patted her lap. "Nothing, baby. Come sit on Grammy's knee and tell her about your day."

Seta, already taller than her grandmother and nearly as tall as her father, giggled and perched on Barbara's lap. Barbara grunted as air escaped her lungs and held the girl close.

"Now, what had you so excited a minute ago?" Barbara asked.

Seta forgot about her grandmother's tired voice and rattled off her news. "This girl named Jessica invited me to a sleepover tomorrow night."

Barbara's lips curved upward and she nodded. "That's good."

Seta looked at her grandmother. She had thought the woman would have been more excited. "I'm kind of excited, but nervous too, because I've never been to one before. Do they stay up and talk all night? Or watch movies? That's what they usually do on TV anyway," Seta rambled on.

Barbara shifted in the chair. "Yeah, they just do silly girl stuff, talk and then go to sleep."

Barbara touched Seta's cheek and turned the girl's face toward hers. "Now, don't let those girls get you into devilment. If they want you to do something silly, you tell them that your grandma said you couldn't. Don't let them get you into them drugs and don't let them have you up all night talking about mannish boys."

Seta rolled her eyes. Her grandmother wouldn't let her watch certain shows on television, banned the "devil's music," and had a whole host of other rules aimed at keeping Seta away from what she said were the "ways of the world." Seta had heard Barbara's lectures about drugs and boys a hundred times. "Oh, Grammy, you know I don't care about boys and I don't take drugs." She smiled widely to show off the teeth that had long ago shed their braces. "I'm too smart to take drugs."

Barbara nodded, and then shifted to relieve the dull ache in her chest. "Just remember that."

That night, Seta lay in bed thinking about the slumber party. She wished in a way that she had a mother to tell about it. Lots of folks sometimes apologized to her when they heard that her mother had died, but she never really knew why they were apologizing.

It wasn't like they had done anything wrong. If anyone had, it had been her. After all, she was the reason her mother wasn't there. Why was it that out of all the billion little girls in the world, she had to be the one whose mother had died and left her and whose father acted as if he didn't want anything to do with her? She must have done something really bad for God to punish her like this. She didn't think she was a bad girl, really, she didn't. But she must be.

She stared at the reflections of car lights that danced against the wall. After a moment, she flicked on the tiny lamp next to her bed and lifted her pillow. She pulled from under it a Polaroid whose edges were tattered with countless nights of daydreaming. As was her habit, Seta traced the outline of the smiling face. Everybody told her that one day she would look like the beautiful woman in the picture. Somehow, she found that hard to believe.

"Dear God, please—" but she stopped. Who was she kidding? God wasn't paying attention to her.

Seta recalled her grandmother's words. *I have to try harder. I have to be good so I can pray to God and He will hear me.* She stroked the crucifix around her neck and resolved to be perfect.

Seta then pulled the covers up to her chin and squeezed her eyes tight. She tried to envision what it must be like to have a mother and a father to love you and to live with you. She imagined that her mother would bake her cookies for school and wake her up with kisses. She imagined that her daddy would show her cool basketball tricks and scare away those big guys who roughed her up on the court.

Yes, her daddy would protect her. She knew he would.

She wanted to talk to her father.

She wanted to talk to him now.

Seta rolled slowly to the edge of the bed so it wouldn't make a sound. As she got up, it let out a long, low moan. She stood still to see if she had disturbed Phillip and Barbara. Then she moved to her bedroom door and leaned on it. There was no sound coming from the other side.

She slowly opened it. She was grateful for her grandparents' habit of sleeping with the door closed. She tiptoed past their door and into the kitchen. She didn't turn on the light, but instead, picked up the telephone and dialed Robert's number with the help of the lighted keypad.

On the fifth ring, she heard a gruff, "Hello?"

Her hand flew to her mouth. What should she say? Her eyes searched the room, as if for answers.

"Hello?" The voice had a slight edge to it.

She found her voice. "Uh, hi, Daddy."

"Who is this?"

A chill rippled from her head to her feet. He didn't know her voice. Her mouth was dry when she answered. "It's me, Seta." She twisted the phone cord around her forefinger.

"Seta?"

"Yes, your daughter." She could cut out her tongue for

calling. What had she been thinking? He would think she was crazy to call so late.

"I know who Seta is," he said, irritation making his voice sound loud in her ear. "Why are you calling?"

"I—I, Daddy, I want to come home." She hadn't uttered those words in three years, but they were as true now as they were when she was ten years old. She wanted to be with her father.

"You are home, Seta," he said.

"But, Daddy, I'm not," she said. "I want to be with you. I should be with you."

She heard the sigh. "Seta, it's midnight. Go to bed."

"But, Daddy—"

"Seta, there is no but. Go to bed."

She opened her mouth to say something else, but the phone went dead. Her eyes felt like a thousand porcupines were jabbing at them. She sniffed hard to stifle the tears. Although she wanted to call him back, she placed the phone back in the cradle.

She wished she knew what she had done that was so bad so she could fix it.

Robert had hung up before he realized what he had done. He grimaced; knowing the girl on the other end must be hurt. "Well, that's not my concern," he said, trying to ease the guilt at hanging up so quickly.

He didn't want to talk to her. That her feelings might have been hurt was of no consequence to him.

Robert sat on the bar stool, leaned his head against the wall and closed his eyes. He knew the child desired to be with him and may even need him, but he didn't know how to respond to her. He had spent so many years, twelve to be exact, resenting and maybe hating her a little.

It was true he didn't want her around. On the other hand, though, some part of him was starting to feel that perhaps he should be a bigger part of her life. He had taken to following her basketball career in the paper where they sometimes included junior high game scores. But that's all he could offer her right now. He couldn't be a father to her. It would be too hard.

Seta knocked on Jessica's door at ten minutes till seven o'clock. The door swung open immediately and there Jessica stood, blowing a big, pink bubble. "Oh, you are early," she said, pulling Seta by the arm. "Come on in."

Seta tried not to gawk at the living room but knew her face must have revealed her awe. She had never been in a house that was so nice. What seemed like miles of carpet rolled out in front of her, carpet that fluffed up around her shoes, it was so thick. Figurines decorated the shelves and green plants snaked around the tables and mantle. A large entertainment center took up the far wall.

Jessica pointed to a stand next to the door. "Hey, put your shoes right there. My mom doesn't like people to walk across the floor in their shoes."

"Oh, I'm sorry." Seta said, immediately taking off her sneakers. She silently thanked God for reminding her to wear some clean, hole-free socks. She looked down at Jessica's bare feet and then decided to take off her own socks. She wiggled her toes. The carpet strands were longer than some folks' hair.

Seta followed Jessica to the back of the house. "Here is my room. This is where we will be," Jessica said. Jessica's bedroom was the size of two of Seta's bedrooms. A canopied bed was in the center of the room and an entertainment system with a television and stereo was on the facing wall. Seta had never seen a television so big.

A poster of a man standing with his hands in his pockets with the words BOBBY BROWN scrawled in bold letters was next to the door.

The doorbell rang. "Make yourself comfortable," Jessica said. She handed Seta a glass. "Here, taste this."

As Jessica left the room, Seta took a sip of what was in the glass and almost spit it back. It stung her tongue and left it tingling slightly. She smacked her lips together. *What is this?*

A moment later, Amy and Diana entered the room, laughing loudly. Diana looked Seta up and down and then turned back to laugh at something Jessica said. Amy waved to her and said, "Hey."

Seta smiled back and held the glass. She wasn't sure where to put it—certainly not on that nice dresser. She felt like she was on the outside of an inside joke as the three friends exchanged a comment and then laughed together again.

Jessica must have noticed Seta's expression because she walked over to her. "Hey, guys, Seta was here *on time*," she said, looking pointedly at her other girlfriends. "Not like some folks."

Amy giggled. "We were trying to get here, but Miss Hot Stuff had to stop and talk to some guys."

"Some fiiiiine guys!" Diana said and started laughing.

Seta smiled awkwardly.

"Well, they did look good." Amy nodded.

Jessica waved her hand dismissively. "Never mind all that. Let's get this party started." She turned to Seta. "Did you like the drink?"

Seta frowned slightly, but said, "Yeah, it was okay."

"Okay? That's all?" Jessica asked, hands on hips.

"What was it?" Seta asked timidly.

Jessica laughed. "Oh, you are so green." She looked around and then moved to close her door. She opened her closet and pulled a bottle out of a bag. "It's wine."

Seta almost dropped the glass. Wine? Her grandmother

would kill her. "Oh, I don't drink," Seta said, shaking her head.

"Neither do I," Jessica said. "It's just a little something to wind down. We can't drink it now though. I have to hide the evidence for a minute. We have to wait until my mom comes in here to check on us. She'll be in here in a few minutes to make sure we're cool, and then she won't bother us for the rest of the night."

Seta looked with wide-eyed wonderment at the other girls. Jessica had turned to put the bottle back into her bag. Diana busied herself by picking at her fingernails. Amy shrugged her shoulders.

Jessica turned on the stereo. The girls immediately hopped up and started dancing, everyone except for Seta, anyway. Jessica beckoned her to join them. "Come on. Don't you like Al B. Sure?"

Seta grinned nervously. She didn't know who he was, but didn't want to look stupid. "Yes, he's cool," she said, bobbing her head a little. Her grandmother didn't let her listen to this type of music. It was the devil's music. And this wine, this drinking, well, that was the devil's drink. Seta tried to shake her grandmother's voice from her mind, but she couldn't get over the fact that God was watching.

She cleared her throat. *Maybe I shouldn't be here.*

Diana rolled her eyes. "Cool? That's all you have to say? He is way more than cool. He is so fiiiine!" She snapped her fingers, bringing Seta's mind away from God and back to the prospect of being accepted by her new friends.

"Yeah, Al B . . . um . . . Sure is fine," she said, scrambling to agree so her friends wouldn't find out she didn't know who he was or what he looked like.

"Did you see that new picture of him in the magazine?" Diana asked.

A knock at the door saved Seta from having to answer.

"May I come in?" a voice said from just on the other side of the door.

"Sure, Mom," Jessica sang, turning Al B. Sure down to a low croon. The girls settled on the floor, the plush carpet flirting with their toes. Jessica sat next to Seta. Jessica smiled sweetly, her hands clasped in her lap.

Jessica's mom slowly opened the door. She wheeled in a cart. She was tiny, with hair that trailed down her back. Her pants were tight and her silver high heels seemed to wobble as they disappeared in the carpet. She smelled like the perfume counter at a department store.

"Hello, ladies," she said as she wheeled in a stainless steel cart. "I brought you some snacks."

Seta's eyes gobbled up the sight of her friend's mom. She looked just perfect and smelled like a thousand flowers and spices.

Jessica rolled her eyes in exaggerated annoyance. "Oh, Mother, you know we can't eat all that. We have to watch our weight."

Jessica's mother shook her head. "Well, just don't worry about it for one night. Tomorrow, I'll go shopping for fat-free and diet foods."

Seta turned enviously away from the mother and quickly looked from one girl's face to the other. She knew they couldn't be on diets. Who went on a diet at thirteen and fourteen? She laughed, but cleared her throat as no one laughed with her.

"Well, enjoy!"

Jessica's mother said as she tiptoed from the room, her heels wobbling as she closed the door. Seta guessed the rule about no shoes must only apply to the children.

Once she had exited the room, the girls pounced on the tray. Cookies and cupcakes, corn dogs and potato chips loaded the stainless steel tray, as well as a bowl of chocolate candy and fruit punch.

"Well, I don't know about you, but I'm going to pig out," Amy said, shoving her hand into the potato chips. Her bracelet tinkled on the rim of the bowl.

"Me too," Diana said. "Besides, if Coach Bailey says one more thing to me, I am quitting the team. She gets on my nerves."

"That's because you have a smart mouth," Jessica said, nudging Seta. "I know you hear how she talks to Coach in practice." Jessica's voice raised an octave as she mimicked her friend. "'No Coach, we don't want to do it like that,'" she said. Amy laughed. "'No Coach, my daddy said we should shoot like this.' I would cuss you out too."

Seta smiled, but Diana cut her off. "What are you smiling at?"

Seta's smile died. "Nothing."

"Leave her alone," Jessica said.

Before Diana could say anything, Jessica stood and locked her bedroom door and asked, "You ready for some drink?"

Diana's head bobbed up and down in short, rapid jerks. Amy looked uncertain, but nodded also. All eyes then turned toward Seta.

"Oh, no," she said, quickly, holding her hand out, palm facing Jessica.

Diana snorted. "Don't be such a Goody Two-shoes."

Seta had to make a quick decision. She wanted these girls to like her, to accept her. She wondered if maybe God would forgive this one time, if she drank the devil's drink. She was not in the mood to be rejected, yet again.

She then held out her hand. "Are you kidding? Bring it on."

"All right!" Jessica rubbed her hands together.

The pink liquid bubbled slightly as Jessica poured it into a glass for Seta. Seta hoped her friends didn't notice the shaking of her hand as she held on. She could hear her grandmother's voice quoting a verse from the Bible that said, "Wine is a mocker."

Maybe she shouldn't drink it. She looked around for a spot to place her glass, but didn't dare place it on the floor.

"Okay, let's toast!" Diana said when everyone's glass was full.

"Shhh," Jessica frowned. "My mom might hear!"

She held up her glass. Diana lifted hers, then Amy.

"Come on!" Diana bumped Seta's arm.

Seta swallowed, then lifted her glass to meet the others.

"So, how was the sleepover?" Barbara asked, unpacking Seta's dirty clothes. Seta sat on her own bed, her legs crossed under her hips.

"It was great," she said, her eyes not quite meeting her grandmother's.

Barbara smiled. "So?" she said. "Tell me all about it."

Barbara's eyes sparkled with the excitement. She had anxiously awaited Seta's arrival, ready to hear that the girls were finally accepting her baby. She had often wondered if she should press the child more to go and seek out friends. But she hesitated because she didn't want Seta to feel the pain of another rejection. The disapproval that Seta endured from her father was enough. At least if the girl didn't try to make friends, no one could turn their back on her.

"Well, it was me, a girl named Amy, this other one named Diana, and, of course, Jessica."

Barbara rubbed her hands together with anticipation. "So, the other girls, they all liked you?"

Seta thought about telling her that Diana was rude to her and seemed not to like her at all, but she saw the hope replace the tiredness in her grandmother's face. "Yes, Grammy, they all loved me," she said.

Barbara sent up a silent prayer. "That is wonderful."

Chapter 9

Barbara looked at the rectangular piece of paper that lay on the kitchen table. It was Phillip's paycheck from the grocery store. As he had done during all the working years of their marriage, he handed over his check to Barbara so she could do with it as she pleased. *Phillip probably couldn't tell you how much he even makes,* Barbara thought. She handled all the finances. She would pay what bills she could, and maybe give him a little spending money for the week.

Barbara closed her eyes and rested her chin in her arthritic hand for a second. "Lord, I need your help," she prayed, her heart heavy. "I know you gave us this child and she is a blessing, I'm not saying she isn't, but it's hard. Seems that the month always lasts longer than the money, and right now, this month we need some more money. I need good food for her. My medications need to be refilled. Phillip is wearing worn-out work shirts. And I've got to find a way to get this child some new shoes; she just grows so fast. Lord. They're going to cut off the phone if we don't pay soon. And I really want to pay into the church building fund. I just don't know what we're going to do. I need You to show me the way."

Barbara wrote out the bills and their amounts. Her prayer was answered. She had enough money to pay for most things—those things that were really important, anyway. She could get the baby some cheap shoes and get Phillip a new work shirt. She would pay some portion of the phone bill tomorrow.

The last choice came down to the building fund and her prescription.

She'd have to put off getting her prescription until later.

Robert gathered the empty bottles into the plastic bag and walked to the outside trash bin. He looked around quickly and placed them in the bottom. He situated a few newspapers on top so if anyone were to look inside, they would only see paper, not beer bottles.

Drinking was a habit he took up in the years following his wife's death. He would never have dared have any kind of alcohol while Rose was alive. She thought spirits—any kind of alcoholic beverages—were evil; thoughts her mother had put into her head, no doubt. And now, Robert didn't know why he even bothered to hide the bottles, but Lola was coming over.

Lola, the woman from church who sometimes brought food over, had begun to drop by more often. And she would push him to come to church. He resented the contact at first, but had acquiesced under her kindness. He was beginning to attend church more than the occasional visit of the past few years. Religion for Robert meant disappointment—the God he knew hadn't answered any of his prayers as a boy with an infirmity. And in the years immediately following Rose's death, the two objects of his anger—God and that child—had clouded his thinking. But somehow, he found himself back at the church of his deceased wife on a regular basis. *I'm still not all gung-ho on this "God" business, but a few songs never hurt.*

Robert knew Lola from church and the two often sat in the same pew, though not directly next to each other when he would decide to attend. She had taken to bringing him a plate every couple of days, and lately, he started inviting her to stay for a cup of coffee. He didn't do much straightening, but he did try to hide the alcohol.

He hadn't paid much attention to Lola until the last few months. It seemed like she always seemed to show up wherever he happened to be.

She appeared to be a nice enough woman, large and soft. She smelled like cinnamon and peppermint. She often quoted Bible scriptures and always had a nice word for him. He could do without all the scriptures, but she was nice to have around. Robert looked at her as a bit of sunshine to his dark, cloudy days.

The Monday after the sleepover ,Jessica beckoned Seta over to her table at lunch. Seta looked around, making sure Jessica was indeed talking to her. When she saw that she was, she bit the inside of her cheeks to keep from grinning. She didn't want to appear too eager for Jessica's acceptance.

When Seta sat down, Jessica asked, "You didn't want to sit with us? The basketball girls should hang together."

The four of them—Jessica, Amy, Diana, and Seta commanded half a table. "Well, we all hang, except for Sophia," Amy said with a disdainful shrug.

Blond and blue-eyed Amy was the only white starter to socialize with the three black girls. Sophia, also blond, but with green eyes, preferred to spend time with the tennis team.

Jessica waved Amy off. "Oh, well, that's her business.

We're the real team, anyway. We should make sure *we* stick together."

Seta nodded. "Yeah, sure," she said, trying to sound confident. "You're right. We should hang together."

Seta tried to be prim and proper when she bit into her sandwich. She extended her pinkies straight out and dabbed at her lips with her napkin to remove any crumbs. She chewed slowly. She didn't want her new friends to think she didn't have any manners.

"Girl, what's wrong with your hands?" Diana asked, pointing.

Seta's eyes widened. "What do you mean?" She was trying to mimic the sophistication of women she saw on *Dallas*, the only story her grandmother watched on television.

Diana elbowed Amy and mimicked Seta's hand motions. "Look at her, holding her hands like those white girls in those movies. Looking like her finger got broke!" Diana laughed at her own joke. Amy let out a nervous giggle but quieted when she looked at Seta. Amy shifted her eyes away.

Seta put her sandwich down. She was embarrassed. She looked at Jessica, who waved Diana off with an annoyed motion. "Girl, just ignore her," she whispered to Seta but loud enough for Diana to hear.

"She's just mad because she eats like a cow, wasting stuff all over the place," Jessica said. As if to prove her friend's words true, Diana's hand knocked over her milk carton as she reached for the salt. The table erupted into laughter.

Diana grabbed a pile of napkins and angrily sopped up the white mess. She stood to go put the soggy pile into the trash, bumping into Seta, hard. Seta bit her lip, but didn't say anything.

The following Sunday night, Jessica telephoned Seta. "Hey, girl," Jessica said.

Seta's eyes widened. She held the phone a little tighter and stood straight. "Jessica?"

"Yeah, it's me."

"Oh, hi." Seta's mind raced for something to say. She was nervous. What if she said the wrong thing? She really wanted Jessica to like her.

"So, I was thinking that after Thursday's game, we could all go hang out for a while," she said. "I already called Diana and left her a message, and Amy is right here."

"Hey, Seta!" she heard Amy call from the background.

Seta smiled. "Tell Amy I said hey. And yeah, sure, we can hang out after the game."

She actually didn't know if she could hang out or not. Her grandparents attended all her games and usually they would go get ice cream afterward. It was a family ritual. She loved the certainty of knowing that no matter how the game turned out, her grandparents were there to take her out and tell her what a good game she played. But she wanted friends more.

After the game, Seta saw Jessica striding toward her out of the corner of her eye. She hadn't broached the subject of an outing with her grandparents before because she hadn't known what to say, but now she knew she had to hurry and ask permission before her friend came over.

"Grammy, do you think I can go out with Jessica?" she asked.

Barbara's eyes widened. *Seta wants to go out? With friends?* Before she could say yes, Phillip interrupted.

"But we always go out, Seta," he said, looking at his watch.

Seta's shoulders slumped. She bit her thumb. "Oh, Poppy, please?"

Phillip didn't like the idea of her going off with people he didn't know. There was so much devilment going on, and she was at that age where she was impressionable. Besides, this was their little special ritual. Seta knew they always went somewhere after her games. He looked to Barbara. Barbara nodded. "Let the child go," her eyes said.

Phillip was surprised. He would have expected his wife to be even more against the idea.

Jessica approached and stood next to Seta. "So, you ready?" she asked.

Seta wanted to say yes, but she wasn't quite sure. Barbara's eyes raked over the young girl, who was almost as tall as Seta. Jessica had changed out of her game clothes and was wearing a shirt that was cropped at the waist and jeans that fit snugly around her narrow hips. Pink lip gloss glistened on lips that blew bubbles with gum.

A boy walked up to Jessica and tapped her on her rear. She giggled. Barbara's eyebrow rose. She wanted her baby to have friends, but not those types of friends. *Fast tail*, Barbara thought.

Seta held her breath. Maybe they hadn't seen that. But a glance at her grandmother's face told her they had.

"So, you ready?" Jessica repeated.

Barbara cleared her throat. "I'm Seta's grandmother. And you are . . ."

Jessica started to roll her eyes, but thought better of it. She stuck out her hand. "I'm Jessica, Seta's friend," she said sweetly. "Is it all right if Seta goes with us? My mom will bring her home."

Barbara and Phillip exchanged a look. Neither wanted Seta to go, for different reasons, but Barbara gave a half-nod. "Yes, but I'd like to meet your mother."

Seta was happy and embarrassed at the same time. She was glad she would get a chance to go, but why did they have to embarrass her? Why did they have to act as if they didn't trust Jessica? Why did they need to meet her parents? They always treated her like a child. She couldn't stand when they did that.

I bet my daddy wouldn't treat me like a child, she thought.

Jessica had to think quickly. "Oh, my mom had to, uh, go meet with one of my teachers right quick," she said. "She's upstairs in the classroom. But I'll be glad to go get her for you."

"Jessica, come on!" someone yelled from across the room. It was Amy.

Seta jumped in. "Grammy, Poppy, can—may—I please go? They're about to go," she pleaded. "I promise I won't be late. It'll just be an hour, just long enough to get a burger."

Barbara took in a deep breath and let it out slowly. She didn't want to smother her. She had to give the child a chance to make friends. "Fine, but only an hour," she said, digging into her bra and sliding Seta two neatly folded dollar bills. She opened her arms wide. "Now, come give me a kiss."

Seta looked around. She quickly stepped to the older woman and planted a kiss on her cheek. Why must they humiliate her like this? But she bit her tongue. After all, they were allowing her to go.

As she turned to leave, Phillip cleared his throat. She hastily planted a kiss on his cheek as well. "Now, you heard your grandma," he said, gruffly. "Make sure you're home in an hour."

Phillip and Barbara stood arm in arm as Seta ran across the gym floor with Jessica. Phillip was disappointed that their routine had been broken. Barbara was too, but at least the baby would have some friends.

"You still want to go out to eat?" Phillip asked Barbara.

Barbara absently rubbed her hands together. "No, we can go eat sandwiches at the house. We don't need to spend the money."

Phillip patted his wallet in his back pocket. "Yeah, I suppose you're right."

* * *

Out of the eyesight of Seta's grandparents, Jessica gestured back to Phillip and Barbara. "Girl, your folks were really acting up," she said.

Seta shrugged her shoulders. She didn't want to talk about it. "They don't mean any harm," she said defensively.

Jessica held her hands up. "It's okay, it's okay," she said. "I was just saying. It's cool."

Diana strode up. "So, we ready?" Her eyes raked over Seta. She sucked her teeth. "So, you going too?"

Seta looked uncertain for a moment. She glanced instinctively at Jessica.

Jessica nodded. "Yeah, now let's get out of here."

Diana let out a short sigh and rolled her eyes, but didn't say anything else.

Seta didn't know if she should ask where they were going. She hesitated, then finally asked as they walked down the street, "Where are we going?"

Jessica laughed. "We're just going to go meet my boyfriend for a minute," she said. "He has some friends. We can all crash at his place for a minute."

Seta didn't know if she liked this. She thought they would go get something to eat, maybe a burger. She knew her grandmother wouldn't like this. "Is his mom going to be there?"

Jessica laughed. "Girl, no!"

Seta tried to breathe away the feeling of dread in her stomach. She was just going to hang out with her new friends. That's all. *I shouldn't feel bad about it,* she told herself. Besides, everything would be fine. She'd hang for a while and then head home.

The guy who had earlier smacked Jessica on the rear opened the door and stepped aside. The three girls walked inside the house. Seta had to blink so her eyes could adjust to the darkness. In a corner, she saw an older guy standing, raising a bottle of some kind to his lips.

Jessica grabbed her by the hand and dragged her to a boy in another corner. "This is my friend Seta," she said, smiling. "I think you two would make a cute couple."

Seta's eyes widened in surprise. The boy smiled, revealing a gold tooth. "Hey, baby," he said. He had to be at least fifteen years old. She shrank away from him.

Diana pushed her toward the guy. "Don't be a baby," she hissed. Then, she turned and kissed a guy who sidled up next to her. "We're going to party tonight."

Seta wanted to shake her head, but she couldn't move. Nothing came from her mouth. It didn't matter, though, because her friends had disappeared, leaving her alone in the corner with the guy. "So, lil' mama, what's your name?"

"Seta." It came out in a whisper. Her stomach was a quivery mess of gelatin. She leaned a steadying hand on her abdomen.

"Yeah, uh huh." He wasn't listening. He put a cigarette to his mouth, and then held it out for her. "Want some?"

"Oh, no," she said, turning her head away.

The boy's smile was crooked. "You are cute, you know that?"

Seta looked around for a way to extricate herself from the conversation. Where had her friends gone?

The boy blew smoke in her face. She coughed.

"Hey, I saw you play ball tonight," he said. "You scored about sixteen, seventeen points, huh?"

Seta immediately relaxed. If he wanted to talk basketball, she could do that. "Actually, twenty points and two assists," she said.

"Yeah, I knew it was something like that," he said. "You don't play like no girl though."

She looked down. The compliment made her shy. "I do all right."

The boy stepped an inch closer to her. He touched her arm. She shrugged away. "What's wrong, with you?" he asked, lowering his voice. "So, you want to go to the back?"

Somewhere behind her, she heard a door open and close. For a brief moment, she caught a clear glimpse of the guy standing before her. His eyes were red and he had a scar above his right eye. His hair was neatly cut, though, and a gold necklace glistened around his neck.

"Uh, no, I don't think so," she said, but he was already touching her. He tried to kiss her, and she quickly turned her head away. His hand groped for her tiny breast. She shoved him, but he closed in on her again, this time grabbing her between the legs. He attempted to grind his front into her body.

"Come on, baby, you know you want it," he said, his hot, stale breath hitting her in the face. He put down his cigarette.

Seta pushed him, hard. He stumbled backward. "Girl, what's your problem?" he yelped. He jerked her to him.

"What's the problem, man?" a voice came from somewhere over her shoulder.

A light flicked on, flooding onto the guy. Someone next to them mumbled, "Turn that light off."

Seta's eyes went to the face of her savior. Her mouth fell open. It was Mike, her basketball partner. Relief coursed through her body. However, it only lasted a moment before shame took over. She pulled her shirttail down, as if to cover herself. She fidgeted under his stare. He must think she was so stupid, to let this boy touch her in her pants like that.

The guy straightened himself up. "Ain't no problem, man, ain't no problem," he said. "I was just about to leave this crazy girl alone."

"I thought so," Mike said as the guy jerked himself

straight and stomped off. Mike turned toward Seta, his eyes narrowing. "What are you doing here?"

"I don't know," she said, not quite looking at him.

Mike looked around. "This is no place for you. You're just thirteen. These folks are fifteen, sixteen, and seventeen years old."

Seta found her voice. "So," she said defiantly. He couldn't tell her where she could hang out.

"Come on," he said, grabbing her arm. "I'll walk you home."

She jerked away. "Who said I'm ready to go? I'm not on the basketball court. You can't tell me what to do," she said.

"Get your stuff," he said sternly.

Seta didn't like his heavy-handed approach, but she had to admit she was ready to go. She was still shaken over the encounter with that other guy. She shoved her hands into her pockets so Mike wouldn't see them shake.

Seta looked around for her friends. As if on cue, Jessica materialized. "Hey, you having fun?" she asked. She had a beer in her hand.

"I think I'm going to leave," Seta said, glancing at Mike.

Jessica's eyes widened. She gestured for Diana to come over. "Seta is about to leave," she said, "with *him.*"

Her eyes were approving.

Seta shook her head. "It's not even like that," she said. "He's my friend."

"That's all right, Seta. I knew you had it in you," Diana said with admiration. For the first time since they had met, it actually sounded like Diana liked Seta.

"It's not like that," Seta insisted.

Mike tugged on her arm. "Come on," he said. "It's getting late. Let's go."

Jessica and Diana looked at each other and giggled.

Seta fiddled with her hands as she left with Mike. She

didn't know what to say to him. She wanted his approval, but knew he must be disgusted to have seen her in such a vulnerable position. As she inched closer to home, her thoughts shifted to another concern. She had let a boy touch her in her pants. What would happen to her now? Would a baby get in her stomach? Her grandmother always told her that only "fast tail" girls let boys touch them in their pants. And when they did, they would get babies.

Each step that brought her closer to home was leaden with dread. *Oh, God, please don't let a baby get in my stomach,* she prayed. *I will be good. I promise I will. Please.*

Mike didn't say much to her, except for good night. "You need to be more careful next time," he added as he pulled his baseball cap low over his ears and turned to walk away.

Seta chewed her lip. "I will," she said, touching her stomach lightly. *Oh, God, please.*

The living room light flicked on the second she opened the door. Barbara sat on the couch, and Phillip was in his old, overstuffed chair. With a grunt, Barbara sprang immediately to her feet.

The plastic runner crinkled under her feet as she walked across the living room.

No one said a word.

Finally, Seta swallowed. "Hello." She tried to act like it was no big deal, but she could see by the clock on the wall that it was a full hour past the time she was supposed to be home.

She looked at Phillip. His eyes held a deep disappointment. She looked away and glanced at her grandmother, who shook her head and crossed her arms across her bosom.

"You are not going to disrespect this house, if you think you're going to come up in here all hours of the night," Barbara said, her lower lip trembling with pent-up emotion.

"Now, this is the only home you've known, and you're going to treat it as such. I can't believe you are showing so much disregard. You were supposed to be home an hour ago. An hour, Seta!"

Seta jumped at the force in her grandmother's voice. She opened her mouth to protest, but Barbara cut her off. "I'm going to tell you now," her grandmother fussed, a growl in her voice. The words seemed to rattle from her chest. "When you think you're grown, you can get out and go make your own rules. Until then, you will show your grandfather and me some respect."

"But, Grammy—"

"Don't talk back to me!" Barbara's nose flared. Her breath caught in her chest as a pain shot through, but in a moment, she was fine. "I promise you, I will beat the devil out of you, girl."

Seta had no way of knowing that the harsh tone was born of fear. Barbara and Phillip had begun to entertain the possibility that something had happened to Seta. It wasn't like her to be late. When it was a full hour after her expected arrival, Barbara had begun to pace. At the sight of a safe Seta, her worry then turned to anger.

"But, Grammy, I didn't mean to—"

Barbara stepped closer to her granddaughter. "Girl, you have one more time to talk back! Now, go to your room. And you won't be seeing that fast tail Jessica for a while."

"But, Gra—"

The slap came before Seta could get the word out. She looked up, surprise widening her eyes. Her cheek stung.

Barbara was instantly sorry. Her hand just seemed to connect with Seta's face before she could even think about what she was doing. Seta wasn't waiting around for an apology though. The girl ran toward the door, anger causing her voice to break.

"I'm going to live with my daddy!" Seta said, casting angry eyes at the woman who raised her. "I'm going to tell him what you did."

Seta snatched open the door, not heeding the calls of Barbara and Phillip.

Seta didn't stop running until she reached Robert's door. Her hair, accompanied by tears, was in her eyes. She breathed hard, as much from anger and disbelief as from the run. She banged on the door. A porch light flicked on to chase away the pitch-black night.

A woman jerked the door open. "Yes?" the woman asked with a puzzled look on her face.

Seta didn't acknowledge the woman, but shoved past her into the house and shouted, "Daddy!"

The woman frowned. "Are you looking for Robert?"

Seta ignored her. "Daddy!"

Robert walked into the living room. "Seta, what are you doing here?" Surprise was evident in his eyes. He looked quickly from the child's face to the woman.

Seta fell into him, hugging him tightly. All the fears, anger, confusion of the evening seemed to pour out. She was scared that she had a baby in her stomach. Her friend Mike had seen her let a boy touch her in her pants. Her grandmother had slapped her. It was too much. She wailed as if her heart had broken. She knew she must look ugly, but she couldn't help it. She tried in vain to stop crying, but she only made more snot. She tried to wipe it away with the back of her hand, although all she succeeded in doing was getting it on her fingers and hands.

The woman gingerly handed her a paper towel. Robert awkwardly patted Seta's head. Finally, Seta's cries stopped. She drew in ragged breaths that came short and fast.

The phone rang, and the woman went to answer it. A moment later, she was back. "It's her grandmother," she said, looking at Seta. Seta shook her head. There was no way she was ever going to speak to her grandmother again. No, not after what she had just done.

"Lola," Robert said to the woman after reading the expression on Seta's face. "Take a message."

He turned back to the distraught girl. "Seta, what is wrong with you?" Robert looked around. This was not a good time. Lola stared at him, and so did the girl and boy who now stood at her side.

"Daddy, I want to come live with you," Seta said. She hadn't planned to say that, but the words just tumbled from her mouth. She wanted to live with her daddy because he wouldn't hit her. He wouldn't slap her and he wouldn't yell at her. He would just be her daddy and take care of her.

Robert caught Lola's eye above Seta's head.

He cleared his throat. "Seta, you can't come live with me."

"Why not, Daddy?" All she wanted was to live there with him. Why couldn't she make him see that she would be no trouble? She wouldn't eat a lot—just a little bit, here and there. She wouldn't get in his way. She wouldn't even ask for anything for Christmas. "Daddy, I promise I won't be bad," she pleaded, turning her face to his. Her eyes searched his face for acceptance, for an answer of yes. Seta grabbed at the front of her father's shirt, her palms grabbing tight wads of fabric and skin. Robert moved to extricate himself from the grasp, carefully prying the slender fingers from his shirt. He took a step backward.

Robert didn't feel like having this conversation. He cleared his throat. Lola gathered the children to her. "Come on, let's go get your baths," she said, shooing them out the room.

For the first time, Seta wondered who they were. She found a dry spot on her shirt and dabbed at her eyes. "Daddy, who is that lady?"

Robert knew he couldn't avoid it any longer. He cleared his throat again. "That's my wife . . . and her children."

Seta felt faint. She had to sit down. The words sounded like they were coming from somewhere very far away. *What did he say? His wife? Children?* She put her hand to her head to stop the sudden ache that seemed to squeeze her brain.

"Huh?" was all she managed to muster.

Robert plunged into the explanation. "I got married a few days ago."

The words didn't make sense to Seta. How could he have gotten married? She had just talked to him a few days, barely a week ago. And she had seen him . . . When had she last seen him?

How could he have gotten married? How could he have gotten a new family? A new daughter? He already had a daughter.

"I don't understand," Seta said. Her stomach was doing flip-flops, causing a huge feeling of nausea to wash over her. The room was moving. She held out her hand to steady herself.

Robert absently touched the glasses on his nose. He rubbed the stubble on his chin and shifted his weight from one foot to the other. A pang of guilt shot through him. He had intended to tell her, really, he had. He had actually thought the grandparents might have told her. From her reaction, however, he could see they had not.

Even now, Robert wasn't sure how he had ended up married again. Yet, one look down at the band on his finger proved it true. Lola had been the one making all those meals, cleaning the house and talking to him. She said that she needed a father for her children, and he needed a woman in his house.

The idea at first had seemed foreign to him, but the more he thought about it, the more he grew used to it. The thought of having another woman besides Rose in his home had first come some years ago. At that time, his guilt had pushed the idea from his consciousness. He knew he was betraying his deceased wife's memory.

But somehow, here he was.

He didn't like fixing his own meals, and he didn't like cleaning—not that he did much of that anyway.

And Lola did make good chicken.

So, the two went to the justice of the peace and had a small ceremony, just him, her, the minister, her children, a coworker and one of the women from the usher board at church.

He had crossed his fingers as he promised to love and honor her, knowing he could never do that. But he could let her take care of him and maybe provide some companionship. He hoped her voice and laughter would chase away the demons that lurked in the still of the house. He was tired of being angry, tired of being bitter, tired of being alone. In this marriage of convenience, he wanted to find his heart again. He had thought that perhaps the only way to finally move on and try to fill his hollow heart was to get a new wife, a new family. So, he had asked Lola to marry him. And she had said yes.

Seta's eyes searched Robert's face. Why was he standing there, looking down, rubbing his face? Why wasn't he looking at her? With a mouth dry with dread, she tried to speak around the lump in her throat. "Daddy, you have a new family?" Seta asked.

She prayed that she had misunderstood him, that he would break out laughing and tell her he was joking. He didn't.

Seta's face crumbled. Her hazel eyes melted into pools of water that plastered her black tendrils to the side of her face. She shook her head and buried her face in her hands. She could hear her grandmother's voice in the back of her mind telling her to hush it up, but the hushing would not come.

Robert sighed. He felt awkward. For the first time since that first year of his daughter's life, he felt something toward her other than resentment. He knew she didn't understand why he was doing this. He could tell by the shrill sounds of her cries that she hurt at a place that was deep and could only be touched by him. He wanted to reach out to her and hug her, but there had been too many years since he had last done that.

He didn't know what to do. So, he did the only thing he could think to do. He waved his hand dismissively. "Stop all that crying," he said. "Now, go wash your face and I'll get my keys and drive you back home."

Chapter 10

Barbara's heart leapt the moment Robert's car turned into the driveway. She quickly pulled on slippers and tugged her robe tight around her waist. She shuffled to the door. The stiffness in her knees made it painful to walk; yet she barely noticed. Her baby was home.

She flicked on the porch light and opened the door. Swatting at the bugs drawn to the light, she waited.

The driver's side door opened and Robert emerged. A moment later, the passenger side slowly opened. Seta climbed out haltingly. Even in the dark, Barbara could see she had been crying. She whispered a quick prayer and hoped what she feared wasn't so. One look at Robert, though, and her fear was confirmed.

Barbara had begged Robert to tell Seta about his marriage, but he had brushed her off. He said he would get around to it. If it was so important, she could tell Seta herself, he had told Barbara flippantly.

Barbara hadn't. She hadn't been able to find the words to tell this child that her father had gotten a new family. Especially when she knew how much Seta wanted him to embrace her. And now, she had found out on her own.

Anger flashed briefly in Barbara's eyes as she thought how selfish Robert had been; however, that feeling dissolved into protection as she wondered how she would make this hurt go away. She held open her arms for Seta.

So many things swirled around Seta's head. Her grandmother had slapped her. Her daddy had found a new daughter and a new son. She might have a baby in her stomach. She saw Barbara's outstretched arms but shoved past her and pushed into the house. She was still angry and not ready to let Barbara make it up to her.

Barbara opened her mouth to chastise Seta for stepping past her, then caught herself. She would let the child be. She turned her attention to Robert.

"I told you to tell her," she said through clenched teeth, shaking her head. All the old feelings of dislike for this man, who had first ruined her daughter's life and was now ruining her granddaughter's life, resurfaced. He was a pitiful excuse for a man and now, instead of taking care of and protecting this child of his, he was causing further hurt.

Barbara could see by the light of the porch that strands of gray were beginning to replace Robert's once jet-black hair. His reddish brown skin wasn't taut as it once had been and sad lines etched permanently around his mouth. He should be about forty-nine or fifty, Barbara guessed.

"Barbara, she just burst in and started talking," Robert said. "It wasn't like anybody invited her there."

"That's just it, Robert! She is your child. She shouldn't have to be *invited* to your home!" Barbara stopped talking for a moment. Gas pains shot through her chest. She took a steadying breath. "And another thing, it's about high time you came off your pity trip and stopped blaming that child for something she had no control over! It's been thirteen years! Thirteen years, Robert, that Rose has been gone. Let it go!"

Guilt and acknowledgement of the truth in Barbara's words made Robert lash out. "You don't know anything about me or what's going on in my head," he said, sneering. "You are a fine person to give advice, you with your own skeletons."

Barbara recoiled as if struck. Her eyes narrowed. "You can turn around and get off my property. Now!" she said through clenched teeth.

Robert didn't need urging. He turned on his heel and stomped back to his car. He didn't need that old contrarian telling him what to do and judging him. The nerve of her, she must have forgotten that he knew her secret. He wasn't the only one with baggage.

Barbara closed the door behind Robert and clicked off the porch light. She went to find her grandbaby. She walked down the short hall. Phillip was sitting at the foot of Seta's bed. Seta lay across it, her chin to hands.

"Poppy, I just don't understand why he had to go get some more children," she said. "I tried everything to make him like me. I make straight A's, and I never get in trouble. I try never to be any trouble because I want him to know just how good I can be. I want him to be proud of me. I don't even ask for anything for my birthday or Christmas. But nothing works."

Phillip slowly stroked his chin. He didn't have much formal education and had done manual labor all his life. Still, some things you knew, even without learning from a book.

"Baby girl, sometimes, it don't matter what you do. Some folks will like you, some won't," Phillip said. "You can't live your life trying to please everybody, even if that everybody is your own daddy."

He patted his leg, and Seta climbed into his lap. "Now, you hear me, and hear me good. You are the prettiest thing around here. You are the smartest thing around here. The only person you have to live for is the one you see in the mirror," he said.

"And the Lord," Barbara said, moving into the room from standing in the doorway. "You live to please the Lord and everything will be all right."

Barbara fidgeted with her robe and sighed. "Now, sometimes, we all do things we're ashamed of and that don't please the Lord or anybody," she said. Barbara paused and searched Seta's face with her eyes. "And I did that tonight. I'm sorry for slapping you."

Seta looked at her grandmother. She bounded from her grandfather's lap and hugged her.

Barbara kissed Seta's forehead. "Now, it's awfully late, so get your bath real quick like and get in bed," Barbara said. "Morning will be here before you know it. You need your rest."

The two grandparents cleared out of Seta's bedroom. Seta gathered her nightclothes and stopped to look in the mirror. Her grandfather's words were nice, but she didn't believe them. She wasn't the prettiest thing around. And the person she wanted most to please didn't care two cents about her.

She trudged to the bathroom with a heart heavy and hurting.

"That really didn't go over so well," Lola said, tentatively, touching Robert lightly on the arm.

Robert said nothing. He sat at the kitchen table, drinking a cup of coffee.

"The look on her face when she found out—"

"Lola, just drop it," Robert said, pushing away from the table.

"Robert, I just think there was a better way to handle it, that's all," Lola said.

"Well, if you thought it could have been handled in such a different way, you could have told her yourself," he said. "You've seen her around."

Lola shook her head. "But, Robert, you just don't get it," she said.

"What I don't get is why you are talking to me about what is clearly not your business," Robert snapped, and Lola recoiled.

"Robert, please don't talk to me that way," Lola said softly. "When we talked of this before, you said you would tell her one day. Well, I really think it was unfair for her to find out when she was clearly already in distress. When she showed up at the door, I didn't know what to say. I was shocked myself. It all happened so fast."

She paused. "And really, this is my business, too," she said. "You are my husband and that is your daughter."

"She's not my daughter!"

Lola bit her lip. These talks were always so difficult. Robert never liked talking about the child. Lola had wanted to involve Seta in the small marriage ceremony, but Robert had forbidden it. She had tried to get Robert to invite Seta for dinner once, but he had stalked out of the house in a huff, not even entertaining the conversation. She usually tried to tiptoe around Robert's emotions, but the shock on that girl's face was too much. That child had suffered enough.

"Robert, you can't keep acting like this," Lola rubbed his back. "I love you. I just want what is best for you. I'm your wife—"

"My wife is dead!" the words flew from his mouth before he could bite them back.

They thudded into the air, leaving silence in their wake.

Lola backed away from Robert, her chin quivering. "You're not right, Robert. You're not right."

She walked quickly from the kitchen.

Robert let her go. He let out a sigh. His emotions were in such flux. That girl. His dead wife. His new wife. It was all too much.

Seta was getting ready for church Sunday when she noticed a brownish red stain on her slip. Her eyes widened. She was bleeding. Oh no, she was going to die. She quickly closed the door to her bedroom and snatched off the slip and her panties. She dug in her underwear drawer to find replacements. But she couldn't put them on without wiping up the blood.

She nervously twisted her hands. She glanced at her bedroom door. What if her grandmother saw her dart across the hall? She couldn't go out. She couldn't get dressed with blood on her either.

Seta shoved the slip and panties in a corner next to her bed for the time being. She would figure out what to do with them later. She put on her robe and grabbed clean underwear. She opened the door a sliver and peeked out. No one was in the hall. She took a deep breath and tiptoed across the hall.

Inside the bathroom, she locked the door and leaned against it. Fear made her breath come in ragged bursts. She was bleeding, and it was due to one of two reasons—neither of which was comforting. Either she had a baby in her stomach, or the Lord had stricken her for all the bad she had done and was going to let her bleed to death. Her grandmother had always told her that the wages of sin is death. And she had sinned. Just ask the guy at the party.

"Seta, come on, we're going to be late to church," Barbara called. "The Lord smiles on those who do his work with a cheerful spirit and ready heart."

"Coming!" Seta called out quickly. She looked around for a towel. How should she stop the bleeding? *Oh, God, I am so sorry for every bad thing I've ever done. Please don't let me die.* Her mind went back to the other night at the party. *And please don't let me have a baby in my stomach either.*

Bam, bam, bam! The knocking startled Seta. "Seta, open this door now!" Barbara's voice had an edge to it.

Seta jumped away from the door and hurriedly pulled her robe closed. "I'm using the bathroom," she said.

"Open the door," Barbara's voice left no room for argument.

The door inched open.

"What's going on in here?" Barbara said as she looked around.

Seta tried to look innocent. "What do you mean?"

Barbara picked up Seta's soiled underclothes from the floor.

Seta's mouth fell open. "I—I—"

Barbara shook her head. "When did this happen?"

Seta didn't know what to say. Her grandmother would beat her to death if she knew about the baby, but then, Seta knew there was a good chance she would die anyway. She'd bleed to death. It was her punishment.

She lowered her head. "This morning."

Barbara's face softened. "There is nothing to be ashamed about. That's a normal thing for young girls. This means that you're a woman now—though around here, you are still a child. It's what you call menstruating. It's something that happens to all women, every month. It's nothing to be afraid of."

Seta's eyes searched her grandmother's face. *Could it be?* Seeing the truth in her grandmother's face, Seta allowed her anxiety to seep from her stiff shoulders. The beating in her head was slowing.

"But you remember what I always tell you," Barbara said. "Don't let some boy come and get in your pants, because now that you are physically a woman, you can have a baby. And besides all that, the Lord won't like it. You keep your legs closed and keep those boys away."

Seta's anxiety was back. Should she tell her grandmother about the other night?

She decided not.

At church, Rev. Johnson bellowed about something called fornication and living in sin. Seta didn't know what fornication was exactly, but she could tell by the way he talked and the way the folks said "amen" that it wasn't good. She could also tell it had something to do with a man touching a woman—most likely in her pants. Seta sat up straighter. She knew God was looking at her now. She felt like all the church people's eyes were on her. They knew she had been fornicating.

"Stop twisting!" Barbara hissed at Seta, grabbing the offending knee. Seta made her leg still.

Services were extra long today at Mount Bethel Baptist Church Number Two. This was the fourth Sunday, building fund Sunday. The pastor took up a special offering after the sermon, money that would go to the church's new construction. Seta wasn't quite sure what the building fund would build, because all she heard every week was about the fund and the need, but she never heard anything about the plans.

Truth be told, she wondered when they would have enough for this new church. For as long as she could remember, Rev. Johnson had been collecting money for the building fund.

Phillip had given Seta two dollars early in the week. She had grudgingly set aside her 10 percent tithe. Barbara nudged

her as the building fund offering plate came around. Seta
scowled, but dug in her purse. Her hand touched on a dime.
Quickly, she moved it and found a nickel. *If God owns the*
cattle on a thousand hills like the pastor keeps saying, then God
sure doesn't need a whole ten cents from me.

Her fingers lingered over the offering plate before dropping her coin into it. She didn't care about a building fund.
Besides, old Rev. Johnson already had enough money in the
building fund. Or, he should. Seta was certain that he had
much more money than she did. She grumbled under her
breath. Barbara pinched her on the thigh, causing Seta to
swallow her words.

For the next couple of weeks, Seta refused to allow herself to think about her father's new family. Instead, she busied herself with school and with basketball. She was relieved
to know she didn't have a baby in her stomach. When she
had mentioned her bleeding to Jessica, the girl had told her
that bleeding meant you could have a baby, but if you were
bleeding, that meant you weren't having a baby. Seta sent
up prayers of thanksgiving.

But in the still hours of the night, hard as she tried to
fight them, other feelings surfaced. Seta's mind went back
over all the times she had begged her father to accept her
and to let her be his daughter. She had pleaded with him to
just please let her lay her head down in the place he called
home. She had longed for him to show a little pride in her
accomplishments, to show up at one of her games, to stand
up proudly at an honors program, and just to be her daddy.

Her grandmother had always told her that prayer solves
everything. So she had prayed as hard as she knew how—
had cried out loud, had fumed silently, had written prayers
on scraps of paper. Nothing seemed to have worked.

God must be too busy for me.

Nothing she prayed seemed to have come true. Her father had refused any affection. Instead, he had gotten another family, a prettier daughter, a more fun son. She had tried as hard as she could to be perfect.

But perfect wasn't good enough.

Chapter 11

"Seta, we can't keep going through this," a worry-weary Barbara said as she opened the door and stepped into the carport. "The next time, Mr. Abraham is just going to suspend you."

Seta shrugged her shoulders, kicking past the flowers at the front of the house and trudging into the living room. She rolled her eyes. Here Barbara went again, blabbing about little of nothing.

"Seta, do you hear me talking to you?" Barbara asked, grabbing the girl's arm.

Seta shook her grandmother's hand loose and let her backpack fall to the floor. Barbara's mouth drew into a thin line. This was the third time this school year that she had been down to the schoolhouse to hear a report about Seta's misbehavior. Each time the principal had made her stay for detention, but the next time, he would put her out of school on suspension for three days.

Barbara didn't understand her granddaughter these days. For the last several months, Seta had been withdrawn and contrary. The sweet girl who did her best always seemed not to exist anymore. The only time Seta seemed to try these days was on the basketball court.

Barbara could see the fourteen-year-old was full of attitude. If this had happened a few years ago, Barbara would have put the girl in her place. Now, in the middle of 1989, with old age settled into her bones, Barbara could only half-heartedly admonish. She managed to get the words out in slow and labored breaths. Barbara put her hand to her chest for a moment. She was only in her sixty-third year, but felt like she was twenty years older sometimes. She walked to the bathroom and opened the medicine cabinet.

She needed a nerve pill.

Seta closed herself in her bedroom. The fight hadn't been her fault. Stacy Green had jumped in her face talking about some boy. Seta had told her to shut up, but Stacy just kept on talking. Stacy wanted to know why Seta had been talking to Joe the other day.

"Why were you all up in my boyfriend's face?" Stacy had said, her eyes daring Seta to respond. Seta could see the girl's face in her mind's eye. Stacy had tiny eyes spaced too closely together, and her nose looked more like a bird's beak. Seta had flipped her long, wavy hair and folded her arms across her chest.

"I wasn't in your boyfriend's face," she said, with all the confidence of someone who had recently discovered she was pretty.

Where Stacy had the usual teenaged pimples and spotty skin, Seta's was smooth. It was medium brown, halfway between milk-stirred coffee and the brown of those chocolate kisses. Her hazel eyes were striking in a way that instantly drew attention. And her hair was thick and hung in wavy layers down her back. She had outgrown that tomboyish awkwardness that had marked the last few years. Her words were laden with condescension.

"Maybe he was in my face. Maybe he liked what he saw," Seta said. A few snickers broke out. Stacy was embarrassed. She stepped closer to Seta and drew in a deep breath, the air hot on Seta's face. "So, what are you trying to say?"

Seta cocked her head to the side. She paused just long enough to command more attention. "I'm not *trying* to say anything." She raised one eyebrow and stared into Stacy's eyes.

Seta took a step backward, bored with the confrontation. She didn't want to fight. If she did, she knew she would get into trouble, with her coach, with her principal, and with her grandparents. She didn't want to hear Barbara's mouth. Nor did she want to ride the bench. Besides, the basis for the argument was silly. Actually, Joe was someone she used to play basketball with on the court at the park. They had just been speaking.

She dismissed Stacy with an air that told the other girl she was of no consequence. When Seta turned to walk away, the slap caught her just at the jaw line. The hit didn't hurt, but that didn't matter. Nobody was going to punk her and get away with it . . . nobody.

Seta whipped around to face Stacy, raising her hand to punch the girl. A strong arm caught hers in midair. She grimaced. It was Mr. Abraham, the principal.

"She started it," Seta said. Mr. Abraham sighed. He saw girls like Seta everyday. He had been a teacher at her junior high school and had seen her at her best. Seta had ended her eighth grade year as one of the top students in her class. Now, in ninth grade, her grades had slipped and it seemed that trouble followed her.

Mr. Abraham pointed down the hall. "That doesn't matter. Into my office."

Seta stifled a groan. She hoped he wouldn't tell coach. She shot a resentful glare at Stacy, who rolled her eyes.

A knock on her bedroom door snapped Seta from her thoughts. "What?" she replied.

A moment later, the door slowly inched open. It was Poppy. He poked his white-haired head into the bedroom. Seta sat up straighter. She should have known her grandmother would tell her grandfather.

"Mind if I come in?" Phillip asked.

Seta knew she couldn't say no. She stood. "Sure."

Phillip spoke in a slow, soft pitch. "Seta, you can't keep getting into trouble like this, baby," he said. His hands shook slightly as he took a toothpick from the top pocket of his overalls. He put it into his mouth before turning his eyes back to her. They were watery with age, a thin film around the edges.

Phillip was short and round. As she sat there looking at her grandfather, Seta wondered how he had managed to produce a daughter as tall as her mother had been. They looked nothing alike. The old people said physical features sometimes skipped a generation. They must have. Seta decided that her mother must have taken after her own grandparents, because Rose hadn't much resembled her mother and looked nothing like her father.

Nevertheless, Seta couldn't think about that now. She felt instantly remorseful. Her grandparents were doing all they could to give her what she needed. Taking on a job at a local supermarket, Phillip had gone back to work part-time several months back. They bought her name-brand clothes and gave her money for movies and outings with friends. She knew the money they gave her meant less money for other things.

She knew her grandparents had gotten old. She wasn't sure when exactly it had happened, but it had. Both walked with slower steps. Barbara let way too many infractions slide these days, and Phillip often sank into his now-ratty recliner and fell asleep after working, without even changing his clothes.

Seta stared at her feet.

"No, look up at me," Phillip said. "What has gotten into you?"

Seta shifted from one foot to the other. She finally looked up at her grandfather. "I don't know," she said with a half shrug. "Sorry, Poppy. I'll do better."

Phillip studied her face for a moment. He tried never to say cross words to her or be hard on her because he felt she had a hard enough time already. Sometimes, Barbara said he was too easy on the girl, but he knew Seta needed somebody in her corner. It couldn't be easy growing up not even five minutes away from your father, yet barred from his life.

Satisfied with her promise, Phillip kissed Seta on the forehead and left the room.

Two hours later, Seta sat in a sulking teenage silence at dinner.

"Seta, do you want to go on the church youth trip next week?" Barbara asked. It would mean paying for overnight lodging, but if the child wanted to go, they'd manage.

"No."

Barbara cleared her throat and tried again. "Well, I've been thinking it's time to redecorate your bedroom. How would you like a new bedspread, maybe some new curtains? We could go shopping this weekend."

Seta's bedroom window wore the same yellow curtains that dressed it when Robert had refused to let her return to his home all those years ago. Except for the wear from many washings, the curtains looked the same. And her bed was covered with a patchwork quilt Barbara had made many years ago.

Seta said nothing. She pushed her food around on her plate. Phillip shifted in his chair. "I think there is a basketball game on TV tonight," he said around the toothpick in his mouth. "You want to watch it with me?"

Why were they bothering her? Seta's sigh was full of attitude. "No."

Phillip and Barbara exchanged a look, then began talking about church and the new neighbor at the end of the street. Seta finished her food and stood.

"I have to study," she said.

Barbara smiled hopefully. "Oh, good," she said. Maybe Seta was going to get back to making high marks. "Well, I'll do the dishes. You go on to your room."

Seta stomped down the hall and closed her door behind her.

She peered into the mirror. People said she was pretty, but she knew they were just being nice. Sometimes, though, she could almost make herself think she actually was pretty, maybe even beautiful. That's how she was able to go off on that Stacy girl.

Looking at her face now, Seta knew nobody believed her lie. She frowned and stuck her tongue out at her reflection. Days on outdoor basketball courts had resulted in a few sun-streaked highlights in her otherwise dark, wavy hair that hung past her shoulders. Her skin had settled to a deep caramel. Her lips had a slight pout to them and her chin showed the rebellion that often surfaced these days. No, she wasn't beautiful. She couldn't be. Fathers didn't give away beautiful children. Nobody rejected them. Everyone wanted to be around them. She only wished she could be beautiful.

Seta's eyes roamed her bedroom and landed on the clock. It was time. She stood perfectly still and held her breath. She didn't hear any movement. She tiptoed to her closet and quickly changed into a jean skirt and walked to the window. She waited another moment to see if her grandparents moved, but hearing only silence, she slowly lifted the window, careful to inch it up so it would not make a sound.. A slow, warm breeze tickled her nose. With one last glance toward her closed door, she climbed out the window. She looked to the right and then to the left. No one was around.

Seta walked quickly down the street to the waiting car. She pulled the passenger door open and slid inside.

"Hi," she said.

Robert took his glasses off and rubbed his nose. The writing on the page was getting smaller. Or maybe his eyes were just getting worse. He needed to take a break anyway. He looked up from the paperwork. His eyes fell on the picture of Lola.

He sighed. He picked it up and searched the eyes. He placed the frame back on the desk. He had hoped the love would come, that maybe it would even consume the feelings he still held for his first wife. But it had not. Lola was a nice woman, to be sure. She was pleasant enough to look at, with wide, kind eyes and hair that still had its color. She had a ready smile and a kind word always.

Still, she was no Rose.

Even after all this time, nearly fifteen years, Robert could still see Rose's face clearly. He could still recall the exact timbre of her voice when she was excited. He could see the fire in her eyes when she was angry and hear the clipped tones she used when she was annoyed. If only she hadn't died. If only . . .

"Dinner is ready," the words came from the doorway. Robert looked up. He cleared his throat and smiled quickly.

"I'm working," he said. "You all go ahead and eat." His eyes didn't quite connect with Lola's.

"All right," she said. She smiled too, but it dimmed slightly when she left the room. She could tell he had been thinking about *her* . . . again.

Chapter 12

Seta giggled as she stood. Someone reached out a hand to steady her. "I'm all right, I'm all right," she said, swatting the hand away. The other hand held onto a beer bottle. Bobby Brown's song, "Don't Be Cruel," played in the background. She swiped her bangs from her eyes.

Jessica and Amy exchanged a look. Jessica disentangled from the arms of the boy in whose lap she had been sitting.

"Seta, you sure you are all right?" she asked. Jessica frowned.

Seta rolled her eyes. Jessica took the bottle from her hand. "Yeah, but I do need to get on home. I need to get back in that window before the folks discover I'm not there."

"Well, Big C isn't here right now, and he's the only one with a car," Jessica reminded Seta.

Seta shook her head. "I'll walk."

"It's too far," Amy chimed in.

They were in the basement of Jessica's house, drinking cheap beer and telling jokes. None of the girls really liked the taste of beer, but they drank it anyway because that's what Big C bought. Big C had picked Seta up just outside her own home. He had left Jessica's a while ago, saying he would be back.

Jessica didn't like this. She didn't think Seta should walk home alone, especially since it was after dark. Besides, she certainly didn't need to go as drunk as she was.

Jessica's father was away on business and her mother was sleeping. Her mother never came to the basement, certainly not to this part, which was on the opposite end of the house from her upstairs bedroom.

"I'll take you home," Jessica said to Seta.

Seta tried to wave her off. "That's okay," she said. "Besides, you're not old enough to drive."

Jessica puffed out her chest. "Well, my daddy has been teaching me how to drive a car and I think I'm getting pretty good. So come on, if you are ready. But shhh, be quiet. You might wake my mom."

Jessica eased open the basement door. A moment later, she was back with keys in hand. She turned to Amy and the others. "You guys better keep it quiet," Jessica said. "I don't want my mom to come down here and see all this."

Jessica drove slowly through the neighborhood. She bumped the car off a curb and rolled through a stop sign, but they made it to Seta's in one piece, laughing all the way. "This is so much fun!" Seta giggled, as a blue sedan served to avoid their car as Jessica passed too closely.

"I know!" Jessica said. "People act like it's such a big deal, to drive, but it's a piece of cake," she said, stopping some distance from Seta's home. "Okay, I'll wait here until you get in."

Seta climbed out of the car and ran to her window. Seta eased back through the window, bumping her knee on the windowsill.

She quickly pulled off her skirt, shoes, and shirt and climbed into bed.

* * *

"Seta, you're going to be late for school," Barbara called to her from the doorway. The room was still cast in shadow. Seta rolled over and mumbled. Barbara tried again. "Seta, wake up."

Barbara stood a moment longer in the doorway and then walked over to her granddaughter. She pulled the covers from Seta's head. Barbara smiled indulgently. The girl must have fallen asleep studying. She hadn't taken a bath and hadn't put on her bedclothes.

She shook Seta. "Nooo," came a sleepy response. Barbara turned her head. Seta's breath stung her nostrils.

"Baby, baby," Barbara gently shook her, "come on, you have to go to school."

Seta's eyes slowly opened. She blinked her grandmother into focus. "Oh," she said, grasping her head. Her head felt like someone was running back and forth, kicking at her brain. She cursed herself for drinking so much the night before.

But she had been having fun. And at least she had forgotten—for a moment—the pain in her heart.

"All right, all right, Grammy," Seta said. "Just give me a sec."

Barbara paused after she kissed Seta's forehead. A musty smell—one that almost reminded her of stale beer—assaulted her nostrils. She looked at Seta for a moment, and then shook her head at the possibility. She left the room, dismissing the thought.

Barbara went to the kitchen and rummaged through the cabinets for something to fix her grandchild for breakfast. Barbara put a couple of slices of bread with butter in the oven and poured a glass of milk. She smelled the milk to make sure it was not spoiled. It was past the expiration date, but it seemed all right. She warmed a couple of pieces of ham on the stove.

Seta entered the kitchen, her backpack over her shoulder. Her eyes were red and she had pulled her hair back into a clumsy ponytail.

"Here, have some breakfast." Barbara pushed the plate toward Seta.

Seta shook her head. "No, I'm not hungry," she said. Even the slight movement hurt. Her eyes felt like she had been crying and her stomach wanted to throw up. The smell of the cooked meat made her gag.

"Seta, baby, you sure?" Barbara knew the breakfast wasn't much. However, Seta was never one to turn down a good, thick slice of ham.

Seta drew in a steady breath. "Yes, Grammy, I am," she said. "I'm going to be late for school. I'll see you later."

"Well, take it to eat on your way," Barbara insisted.

"I don't want some stale bread and hunk of meat!" Seta scorned. "I'm so tired of all this. Why am I the only kid whose family is poor?"

Barbara recoiled. "Well, some children would be happy to have anything," she snapped back.

"Well, go feed it to them then!" Seta said. Her head was feeling worse. She knew she should be quiet, but her tongue was loose.

Barbara eyed her for a moment and then grabbed her arm.

"What's that smell?"

"What?" Seta's eyes were wide. She had brushed her teeth to get rid of evidence of last night.

Barbara leaned in closer and sniffed. Seta half turned. "Open your mouth!" Barbara insisted.

"For what?" Seta tried to step away, but Barbara's grip was tight.

"You been drinking?"

"No, Grammy!" Seta denied.

Barbara's eyes narrowed. "You better not be lying!" she

said. "Seta, we can't keep going through all this trouble with you. I promise, I will beat you down if I find out you've been getting into devilment. I won't be raising a fast-tail girl!"

"I said I wasn't drinking!" Seta yelled and jerked away. Her grandmother slipped but regained her balance, but Seta didn't care.

"I might not see everything you do, but God sees!" Barbara reminded.

"Forget God!" Seta snapped, pulled her backpack tighter and stormed out the door.

Barbara let her go.

She sat down at the plate she had prepared for Seta. She prayed over it and took a bite of the bread. She stared unseeing into space. *Lord, I just don't have the strength to do this.* Seta was becoming a handful. The trouble in school, and now, what if she was drinking?

Barbara sighed. Something was going on with her granddaughter. She just wasn't sure what. She couldn't put her finger on exactly when the change had come. But now, Seta was surly and short.

Barbara felt inadequate. She knew whatever was going on with her grandbaby must have something to do with growing up without a mother and a father. Barbara and Phillip tried to give Seta what she needed and had tried to fill in the gaps, but Barbara knew there were some things only a parent could do.

Barbara had tried to do right by the girl. Augusta wanted to have Seta come live with her when all this trouble started. Of course, Barbara staunchly refused. The last thing she wanted was to shuffle the child to someone else. She didn't want Seta feeling as if she had been given away again. So Augusta filled in the gaps where she could. Her own boys were grown now, so she sometimes sent money for Seta. But Augusta felt the girl needed something more.

Augusta said Barbara should put something on Seta's

rear to curb what she called "fast tail attitudes" and felt her mother was getting soft in her old age.

Barbara's mind went to Phillip. She stared down at her gnarled fingers, knuckles big with arthritis. On some days, her wedding band refused to fit. But on this day, it was there. She and Phillip had been married for fifty years. Fifty years.

Those first few years had been rocky. She hadn't wanted to get married, but her parents had made her. They said he was a good man and would be able to provide a good life for her. She had been reading books about women who did wonderful, amazing things and wanted the same for herself. She wanted to finish school and maybe even go to college.

At thirteen, Barbara dreamed of being a younger Florence Nightingale or a Marie Curie, both females and pioneers in their fields. Those were the thoughts that helped her make it through the long hours of bending to pick row after row of cotton. Her fingers would turn raw and the skin at the tips would become jagged with the constant tugging at the white pieces of cotton. She struggled not to get any stems or leaves in her bag, knowing whoever inspected her take would scowl at her in anger and disgust.

The sack would grow heavier as the sun climbed into the middle of the sky and then began its slow, slow descent toward the earth. She would sometimes struggle as the day's work trailed behind her, the straps digging into her bony shoulders. She and her siblings each had to turn in full bags so the family could collect a few dollars for a day's work. The thing that got her through was the knowledge that one day she wouldn't be a cotton picker. No, she'd be a famous scientist or singer or, well, anything. She wouldn't be stuck here.

Sometimes she would hide under her covers with books, taking in the lives of Nightingale and Curie and other famous women. She imagined she was the one to discover something new that benefited the world greatly. Other times, she visualized herself as a hot jazz singer, stunning audiences with her powerful vocals. Science or music, it didn't matter, just as long as she was doing something grand and important, with the world watching.

Her mother had told her those were foolish notions. A young girl's purpose was to marry a nice man and have babies. And the Wright boy was a nice man. So, it was settled. She would marry Phillip Wright and put all those crazy thoughts to rest.

They had married at Mount Bethel Baptist Church Number Two, just as her parents had before her. She cried the entire night before. Her mother asked her what was the matter. Barbara sniffled and said nothing, blowing her nose on the handkerchief her mother shoved into her hands. Her mother pursed her lips. "Do you not want to get married? You can stay in the house with all the rest of us and pick cotton. We'll continue as we always have. It's nothing big and fancy, and we don't always have the things we need, but we'll make do. The Lord has always provided. Just tell me now what you want to do. Do you want to stay here with us?"

Viola stared squarely at her middle child. Barbara was the fourth of seven children. An older sister had been married off the year before and already had a baby. Her oldest brother had gone up north to find work, sending home a few dollars each month. Bill, the brother a year older than she, wasn't spoken of. He had gone and gotten himself killed one night after he crawled across a white man's lawn looking for his vegetable patch. Bill had sought to grab a few tomatoes and ears of corn after a particularly lean week. Unfortunately, Mr. Luke had come out shooting first and looking later.

Barbara looked down at her feet. She knew her mother

didn't want to hear anything but one word. "No. No, ma'am," she said softly.

Viola smiled and patted her daughter's cheek. "That's what I thought. Now, dry those tears up and get to bed. You're getting married in the morning."

Barbara had resented Phillip. She felt it was his fault she had to give up her dreams. Everything she did in those first few years of marriage was done in a spirit of anger and hostility. She had refused to even sleep in the same bed with her teenage husband for the first six months of marriage. If it wasn't for him. . . .

But Barbara didn't want to think about all that anymore. She shoved away from the table to clear her head. Those were terrible times, and it wouldn't do good to dwell on them. She had made some shameful mistakes. Mistakes it had taken a lifetime to overcome.

Robert stopped abruptly. Something was different. His eyes searched the living room, and then returned to their original spot. He went in search of Lola and found her humming in the kitchen.

"You cleaned the living room?" Robert said. It was more of an accusation than a question.

Lola finished scrubbing the cucumber before answering. She looked up at her husband and replied. "Yes, I did. I clean every day. You know that."

"So, did you move anything?"

Lola resumed scrubbing. "Anything like what?"

Robert was tired of the word game. "Where is the picture that used to be on the wall?"

"You mean the picture of your first wife?"

Robert clenched his teeth. A muscle flexed in his jaw line. "Yes, that picture."

Lola sighed and put down the cucumber. "I took it down. I put it away."

"Why? You had no right to come in here moving things!"

Lola's voice was soft. "Robert, we've been married a year. I let it stay up as long as I could. But, Robert, this is my home now, my home. And I can't have your dead first wife staring at every move I make."

"Where is it?" He couldn't believe Lola had done such a thing, the nerve to go and take down Rose's picture. This was Rose's house before it was hers.

"I put it in the attic." She picked up another cucumber.

"In the attic with all the boxes and junk?" This was bad. How could she have been so inconsiderate and careless? Rose hated clutter.

Lola swallowed at the anger in his voice but held her ground. "Robert, I married you knowing you still grieved your wife. I told you I would give you time. And I think I have. But I can't live in her shadow. I can't. I have to feel like this is my home too."

"Well, it's not!" He wanted to snatch the words back, but they were already in the air. Lola's breath caught in her throat in a surprised, and then hurtful, gasp. The cucumber broke in her hands.

Robert knew he should apologize. However, he had never been good at taking back words. He did the only thing he knew to do. He turned and walked away.

The girls' basketball team had just won another game. The crowd was dispersing and the players had showered and were leaving with their families. Jessica stood with her father's arm around her shoulders. The man kissed the top of her head. "You did an outstanding job out there," he said, pride evident in his eyes.

Jessica beamed. "Thanks, Daddy."

Seta stood awkwardly watching the scene. She felt like she was intruding on a private moment. But she couldn't make herself turn away. Instead, she ravenously devoured the scene, secretly imaging that it was her father standing there hugging her and praising her work.

Jessica's father made a joke and the two laughed.

"So, your mom and I were thinking we would take you out to dinner tonight to celebrate," Jessica's father said after the laughter passed.

Jessica's eyes widened. Her father was hardly ever home, because he traveled on business a lot. "Really? That would be great, Daddy. Where are we going?"

Her father made an expansive gesture. "Wherever my little girl wants to go."

Jessica's mother strode up. She had been to the restroom to repair her makeup. "So, are we all set to go?" she asked, the familiar department store medley of fragrances in her wake.

Jessica nodded. "Yeah, I'm ready!"

Jessica's mother looked over at Seta, who was standing three feet away, alone. "Would you like to join us, Seta?" The woman smiled with benevolence.

Seta felt self-conscious. She was embarrassed to have been caught gawking at the family. "No, I see my grandparents across the way," she lied. She pretended to wave to someone. "I have to go."

She began walking off, and then half turned back to Jessica. "I'll see you later, Jess."

Jessica wasn't paying attention. She was basking in the attention of a mother and father.

Seta listened intently to Coach Malone. He was a short, stubby man, and looked nothing like a basketball coach, but looks were deceiving, in this case. He spoke gruffly but he was never mean. Her junior high coach had been a woman, Coach Bailey, and she had liked playing for her. Seta had done well because she liked to excel. But this was different. She worked hard because she needed her coach to be proud of her.

Seta ran bleachers with the rest of her teammates. Where they groaned and complained, she held her tongue. This was all part of working hard and getting better. When practice was over and everyone else raced to the locker room, Seta hung back. She practiced more lay-ups and free throws. She would be the best.

Coach Malone blew the whistle. "Okay, good practice," he said. "Hit the showers."

Seta threw the ball into the basket.

"Go on, Armstrong," her coach nodded to Seta.

"Come on, Coach, just a few more," she pleaded.

"All right, just a few more, then hit the showers and get out of here," he said. He turned to look at her. "And if I hear of another fight, you're coming to my office."

Seta's eyes widened. So he had heard. She felt instantly remorseful. Coach wouldn't like her if he knew she got into fights. "Sorry, Coach. It won't happen again."

Seta stared after him as he walked off the court.

Jessica and Seta sat on the steps of the school waiting for Jessica's mom to pick them up. Amy had been absent and Diana had decided to walk. "So, I hear that Corey likes you," Jessica said with a sly smile.

Seta sucked her teeth and shook her head. "I don't even know anything about him."

Jessica elbowed her friend. "Well, there is only one way to find out." She lowered her voice. "Shhh, here he comes."

Corey was tall and walked with a self-assured swagger. He also was a junior. Seta looked up. Juniors didn't talk to freshmen every day.

"So, how are you two fine ladies doing?" Corey asked, looking directly at Seta. He licked his lips and smiled as if he knew he was cute.

Jessica elbowed Seta and looked at her. "Oh, we're fine," Jessica said since Seta didn't say anything. She elbowed Seta again.

Corey looked quizzically at Seta. "What, you aren't talking today?"

Seta couldn't think of anything to say. Nothing she thought seemed cool enough. She didn't want him to think she was dumb or stupid. Suddenly, she wished she had taken a shower after practice. She self-consciously brushed her hair.

Jessica jumped in. "Oh, she's just tired from practice. She was really lighting up the court."

Corey let out a slow whistle. "Yeah, I've been checking her out on the court."

His eyes never left Seta. Now he turned his conversation back to her. "So, what are you waiting on?"

Seta finally found her voice. "Oh, we're waiting on her mom. She's going to give us a ride home."

Just then, Jessica's mother drove up. Both girls rose from the steps.

Jessica tried to catch Seta's eye. "Well, I'll see you later," Jessica said, hinting.

"So, can I give you a ride home?" Corey asked Seta.

"No, I'm riding with—"

Jessica jumped in. "Sure. My mom has to run an errand anyway." She gave a thumbs-up sign to Seta behind Corey's back. "See you later!"

With that, Jessica was gone. Jessica's mother waved to Seta as they drove off.

"So, I guess that settles it," Corey said, smiling. He picked up her backpack. "Come on, my ride is this way."

He led her to a red coupe. The wheels were shiny and the leather seats were spotless. Tint darkened the windows and a fuzzy covering adorned the steering wheel.

Once settled in the car, Corey turned the radio down. "So, you want to stop and get something to eat?"

Seta shook her head. "No, I should probably be getting home," she said. He was so fine. He wasn't like all the guys in her class who tried to act like thugs. This was a real man. He was clean-cut and actually drove a car.

"Okay," he said. "But next time, I'm taking you somewhere."

Seta giggled. "All right." She gave Corey her phone number when she got out the car and told him, "Don't call after nine."

The next day, Corey was waiting for Seta after practice. This time, she had showered. "So, you want a ride?"

Jessica and Amy waved her off. "We'll talk to you later!" they sang as they walked away.

Seta smiled. "Sure."

He picked up her backpack and carried it to the car same as he had done the day before. He opened the door for her and waited until she was settled before closing it. He walked around to his side.

"So, you want to get something to eat?"

Seta knew she should be getting home. It would be dark in a little while.

"No, I really can't," she said. She wanted to say yes, though, because she didn't want him to think of her as a baby.

"No problem," he said. Then he hit his palm to his head. "Oh, I just remembered that I need to stop by my house for a quick second. I need to pick up something."

He waited for her to say it was all right. Seta hesitated. She didn't want to stop, but he did say it would only be for a moment. "Okay."

Corey stopped the car in front of a house. "This is it right here. You want to come inside?"

Seta's heart beat fast. She knew she shouldn't go in there alone. Her grandmother had drilled caution into her head enough. He waited expectantly. She didn't know what to do.

"You coming?" he looked at her with waiting eyes.

She didn't know what to do. It would only be a moment. And she did like him. What was more, he seemed to like her. "All right," she said. She could hear her grandmother's words in her mind, but shrugged them off. *I'm not doing anything bad.*

Once inside the house, Corey was in no hurry. He flicked on the stereo and checked the answering machine. He opened the refrigerator. "Hey, you want something to drink?"

Seta stood in the middle of the living room. "No, no thank you," she called.

"Well, if you do, just let me know," he said. He walked down the hall. Seta wished he would hurry. She had never been to a boy's house alone before.

"Hey, why don't you come back here?" Corey called from whatever room he had disappeared into.

"Uhm, I'm fine, I'll wait right here," she said.

Corey called back, playfully. "What, are you afraid I might bite you?"

"No." Seta didn't want him to think she was afraid. She took one step and then two. A moment later, she was in his bedroom. She looked around. He had posters of football players on the wall and stacks of tapes piled on the table and floor.

He was sitting on the bed. "Why don't you come take your shoes off?"

Seta knew she shouldn't sit on his bed. She could hear her grandmother's voice, again telling her to watch herself, that God wouldn't like this. *But God doesn't like too much that's fun, so I don't care.* Besides, what harm could it do? She slowly sat on the bed, the mattress sinking under her weight.

Corey waited a moment and then lightly touched her hair. "You are so pretty," he said.

Seta smiled shyly. Lately boys had been taking notice of her. Her grandmother said it was her inner beauty. Seta had spent her early years resenting her long hair and hazel eyes because they separated her from the other girls. However, she knew both now were providing a gateway to the boys' affection. And she was happy to have admiration. She welcomed the looks of approval instead of resentment or disgust.

He leaned in closer. "You going to let me kiss you?"

Seta couldn't speak around the lump in her throat. She had never been kissed by a boy before, well, except for that one gross time at that party. Her grandmother told her only bad girls let boys kiss them. But Corey looked so kind and he was so sweet to give her a ride. Besides, she really did want him to like her.

She nodded. He pushed his lips to hers. Then, somehow, his mouth was open and his tongue begged entry to hers. Her first reaction was to pull away, but he held her tightly.

She turned her head away. "I need to go home," she said, looking at him.

He looked into her eyes. "Okay," he said, "but first let me kiss you again."

The next day Corey came by just as school let out and without asking, picked up her backpack. "Come on, I'll give you a ride."

Seta was scared and excited at the same time. She didn't want to do the kissing thing again, but she couldn't believe that so nice of a guy actually liked her. He had hugged her when they left his house yesterday. He had actually hugged her.

When they were in the car, he touched her hand. "So, you mind if I stop by my house?"

Seta bit her lip. She didn't want to. Then she thought that if she didn't, he might not like her anymore. And she knew what it felt like not to be liked by someone you wanted to like you. She smiled an unsteady smile. "Sure."

Chapter 13

Robert had made a halfhearted apology to Lola. She nodded her acceptance. Still, her hurt eyes gave lie to her action. Robert knew she was right, that he should not have Rose's picture up on their wall. Knowing she was right didn't change his heart though. He pulled the picture from the attic and put it in his office.

Lola saw the picture but said nothing. She had married him knowing he didn't love her, and so she bore her pain in silence. She had lain awake at nights wondering if she would ever marry again after the divorce. So anxious was she to have a husband again and to have a father for her children that she had ignored her need for love. Maybe in time things would change.

As Robert put the picture in his office, though, his mind went to Seta. They hadn't spoken since that day a year ago when he had told her he was married. He knew he should attempt to talk to her, but he didn't know how. He wasn't used to making overtures, certainly not to her. He had built a whole lifestyle on his resentment of her.

I don't know where to even begin with her. The hard edges of resentment had dissolved, but he still didn't know how to relate to the girl. He didn't know if he even wanted to. To invite her into his life would be an acknowledgement that he had been wrong to shut her out in the first place.

And Robert wasn't ready to admit that.

"Daddy, I need help with my homework." Berrie barged into his office. He smiled as she placed her hands on her hips and pointed a finger at him. Thoughts of Seta vanished from his mind. Berrie was cute in her seriousness.

"I need help now," she said.

Robert picked her up and nuzzled her, his short facial hair scratching her cheek. Berrie giggled. "Oh, Daddy!"

He enjoyed these children. They helped to relieve the tension between Lola and him. They gave him a reason to smile.

He put Berrie down and she grabbed his hand, leading him to the kitchen table where her notebook lay open.

Yes, he was glad to be a daddy.

Seta didn't go to Corey's house the next day because she had a game after school. She was actually relieved to have an excuse not to go over there and have him kiss her. She was so confused. She liked it when he hugged her and talked to her nicely, but she didn't like what came afterward. She didn't like the kissing, and she knew it was wrong to let him touch her bra. On the other hand, it felt nice to be liked.

The next Monday, Jessica pulled her aside. "So, what's up with you and Corey?" she asked.

"What do you mean?" Seta asked, nonchalance in her voice.

"Well, you have been hanging out with him a lot lately," Jessica whispered. "You're not going over to his house or anything, are you? You're not letting him touch you, are you?"

Jessica was worried about Seta. If Diana had been in Seta's position, Jessica wouldn't have minded. Diana could take care of herself. Seta, though, she wasn't sure. Seta was naive.

"I thought that's what we were supposed to do. Don't you let guys touch you?" Seta asked.

Jessica sighed. "That's different," she said. She had let a few guys touch her and kiss her, but that was it. Amy had done the same. She knew Diana had gone all the way. But she didn't want Seta to do that . . . not Seta.

Seta was confused. They always talked about boys, which ones they would let touch them and which ones they wouldn't. "So, what if I did?"

Jessica frowned. "Seta, I don't think you should go to his house."

Seta grew defensive. How was Jessica going to come and try to tell her what to do, especially when Seta knew Jessica had been to boys' houses before? "Well, it's not your business."

Jessica opened her mouth to say something, but closed it when Corey approached. He smiled. "So, you ready?"

Jessica narrowed her eyes at him. She knew his game. She could see it in his eyes. He reached to pick up Seta's backpack, but Jessica grabbed it.

"We're fine. We're waiting on our ride," she said pointedly. He glanced at Jessica, then turned back to Seta.

Seta's eyes went from one to the other. "Come on, Seta." Jessica's voice was firm.

Corey raised an eyebrow. Seta didn't know what to do. She knew her friend was right, but Corey might want to be her boyfriend. She got the impression that maybe Jessica was trying to ruin it for her. She snatched her backpack from Jessica.

"I'll see you later," she said defiantly and turned to Corey.

Jessica's chin jutted out. "Fine."

At Corey's house, he clicked on the radio in his bedroom. He walked around and stood in front of Seta. He pulled off his shirt, then tugged at the top button of hers.

"So, are you going to let me see your beautiful body?" Maybe if he hadn't called her beautiful, or maybe if he hadn't looked so sweet saying it, she would have said no. But she didn't.

She let him tug at her blouse, his fingers deftly unhooking the buttons. He eased the pink shirt from her thin shoulders and then slid her white bra with its tiny pink bow from her body. She felt her face grow hot with embarrassment when he eased off her jeans and white panties too, the radio playing in the background.

She wanted to snatch her clothes back on, but the desire to be liked was too strong. Her grandmother's voice rang in her ear: *God is going to*—she squeezed her eyes shut against the thought.

Forget God. Anger and resentment cradled the thought. God wasn't here. Corey was. And right now, Corey was giving her a lot more than God ever did. Besides, what harm could it be in just a look? Looking never hurt anybody. *All those horror stories were just old people's ways of making sure nobody had any fun.*

Seta stood before Corey, naked. She covered her breasts with her hands and tried to hide her private area by standing with her legs crossed. The hair on her arms stood and chill bumps rose.

Corey nodded appreciatively. "I knew you were going to look good," he said. He tugged her to him. She moved toward him, feeling awkward and exposed.

"You just want to look, right?" she asked worriedly.

He nodded. "Yes, baby. That's all I want to do."

He gently pushed her to the bed. "Why don't you lie down though?" Seta wanted to remain standing. Actually, she wanted to put her clothes back on—but she did as he asked.

"Close your eyes," he said, and she obliged.

He kissed her lips. Then, he kissed her breast. She drew in a sharp breath and her eyes flew open. "Wait."

Corey laughed, slowly and lowly. "Hey, it's okay. I'm just looking. You said I could look."

Well, that was true. She did say he could. She closed her eyes again and tried to relax. In a moment, he was lying next to her, naked also. Her eyes searched his face. She didn't like this. But she didn't say anything.

He lay there holding her in his arms, brushing her hair. No one said anything for the longest. Seta smiled. This was nice. She wished he would hold her in his arms forever.

"You know, I love you," Corey said, his breath a flutter against her ear.

Seta's eyes widened. Corey loved her? He really loved her? Her heart was full and she couldn't speak. The only people who had told her they loved her were her grandparents and her Aunt Augusta.

"Are you going to let me show you how much I love you?" he said.

All Seta could do was nod yes.

The phone was ringing when Seta walked into the house. Barbara called to her. "It's Jessica. She's been calling here all afternoon," she said, passing the phone to Seta. Barbara still didn't care too much for Jessica.

Seta took the receiver. "Hello?"

Jessica's voice came through. "It's about time you got home," her tone was angry. "So, what did you do?"

Seta's face grew hot at the memory of the afternoon.

Guilt and confusion washed over her. She needed time to think. So much had happened. "Don't worry about what I did," she snapped.

There was a silence on the other end. Finally, Jessica spoke. "Seta, I really hope you didn't do what I think you did."

Seta didn't have time for this. Besides, Barbara was within earshot. "Look, I have to go." She hung up.

Back in her bedroom after dinner, Seta lay on the bed and stared at the ceiling. She had taken a shower and told her grandmother she was going to bed early so they would leave her alone. Actually, she just needed time to get her thoughts together.

She felt sinful and ashamed, even as she tried to convince herself she didn't care. She knew what she had done was not right. *I'm horrible. No wonder my mother left me and my dad doesn't want to be bothered. Who would want a child like me?* She knew she was the worst type of person and would surely be struck to death by lightning. Or she would burn a thousand deaths in hell, with the weight of her sin heavy. Fighting that feeling, though, was the need for Corey to love her as he said he did. He must love her for him to do all those things to her. And afterward, he hugged her again.

Seta wondered if she could get him to love her without having to do all those things again. But still, her conscience raged. She tried to shake loose of it, though. *I don't care what God thinks!* She fumed, trying to get past the guilt that washed over her. The crucifix that hung around her neck seemed to be burning a hole into her skin. She tore it off and flung it across the room. "I don't need this!"

But she couldn't get rid of the shame that tied her stomach into knots. Maybe she could get rid of the shame but keep Corey. Maybe they wouldn't have to do all those things again. If he would just hug her, that would be enough. She didn't need the nakedness. The nakedness had been for him.

Jessica didn't say anything else about their conversation, not with words anyway. With her eyes, though, she said plenty. She was disappointed in Seta. Seta was the good girl. And now, she had done it. Jessica had never even done it, not that. She had always thought Seta was the innocent one of the bunch.

But now she wasn't.

Jessica felt guilty. It was her fault Seta had gone home with Corey that first day. Now, look what had happened.

Amy felt the strain. She nudged Seta with her elbow as the four ate lunch in the cafeteria. "What's up with you and Jessica?"

Seta feigned ignorance. "What are you talking about?"

"Well, I don't know. It's just something weird going on. Are you two mad at each other?"

"It's nothing," Jessica said, turning to Diana. "So, you getting drunk this weekend?"

The girls had taken to drinking on the weekends, usually when Jessica's parents were busy. They always had privacy at Jessica's house. It was their way to unwind, especially after a week of hard practices.

"Yeah, that sounds good to me," Diana said. "I'll get Big C to go to the store for us."

Big C was Diana's cousin. He was twenty-one and bought alcohol for them. Sometimes, he also introduced them to some of his friends, guys who were much older than they were. The guys would sometimes give the girls money if they would let them see their breasts. Jessica and Diana would acquiesce, but only after a few drinks.

"You coming?" Diana asked Amy, who nodded.

"You?" Diana asked Seta. She tolerated Seta because the others seemed to like her. She was cordial, but that was it.

"I don't know," Seta said, looking at Jessica.

Corey walked into the cafeteria. "Hey, there is your boy-friend," Amy whispered.

Seta giggled. "He's not my boyfriend," she said, even though she felt like he was. They just hadn't talked about it.

"Well, you two sure have been cozy lately," Amy kidded with her. "I saw you getting into his car the other day."

Corey would be her first boyfriend. Seta knew he would ask her soon.

Corey was walking toward the table. Seta sat up straighter and smoothed her hair.

"Do I have any food in my teeth?" she hurriedly asked Amy, who shook her head no.

But Corey walked on by and went to a table full of ju-niors and seniors. Seta smiled. "He must not have seen me."

She turned back to her food, and then looked up again when Amy kicked her under the table. "Look!"

Seta looked up to see Corey kissing a cheerleader named Holly. Seta blinked, as if she was seeing things, but the sight remained unchanged. Corey whispered something in the girl's ear and sat next to her. The girl giggled bashfully.

Her friends' eyes were on her. Seta willed herself not to react. She smiled gamely. "Oh, that's nothing," she said. However, the words sounded uncertain, even to her ears.

Inside, Seta was struggling. What was Corey doing kiss-ing another girl, especially after he said he loved her and after all the things she let him do to her? Seta didn't under-stand.

Robert stepped into the house after work. He breathed in the scent of baking bread and chicken. Bennie raced to him, talking excitedly.

"They're having father-son day at school, can you come?" Bennie asked.

Lola and her husband had gotten a divorce when the boy was two years old. Bennie hadn't grown up with his father, who showed up irregularly at first, and then not at all. Bennie seemed to welcome Robert into his life. Both of Lola's children immediately embraced Robert, so starved were they for a father's attention.

Robert smiled at the boy and playfully pulled his ear. "Sure," he said.

Lola called from the kitchen. "Dinner will be ready in five minutes," she said. It did her heart good to see how her children eagerly accepted Robert into their lives. That made everything worth it.

Robert and Bennie went to wash their hands. "Where is your sister?" Robert asked.

"I think she is in the kitchen with my mama," Bennie replied.

And that's where she was.

"Hi, Daddy, look what I made," Berrie proudly showed off a bowl of rice to Robert as he entered the kitchen with Bennie at his side. Beryl, or Berrie as she was called, was, at nine, a year older than her brother. Beryl had been a bit reserved initially, but had warmed up to Robert after seeing how eagerly her brother took to him.

Hearing the word *daddy* still sounded strange to Robert's ears, but the children had started calling him that on their own. And Lola hadn't disapproved.

Robert sat down at the table. The food looked and smelled delicious. This was what home was all about. Though, as he sat around the table surrounded by his new family, a nagging sense of guilt reminded him that one of his children was absent.

Corey hadn't come by to drive her home after school, and he didn't answer the phone when she called him that night. Finally, after the eighth ring of the third call, some-one answered the phone.

"Hello?" a female answered the phone. Seta hadn't met her, but it must be his sister, Michelle.

"Hi, I was calling for Corey," she said.

There was a pause. "He has company right now. Can he call you back?"

"Could you tell him Seta called?" Her voice was small.

Seta looked for Corey at school the next day. He was in the eleventh grade, so they had no classes together. She didn't see him in the hallway, so she decided to wait around for him after school in the spot she always waited in, but Corey didn't show.

The weight of the backpack seemed like a thousand-pound man to Seta. She wanted to drop it, but knew she needed her books. She trudged home slowly, each step feel-ing like it would be impossible to follow it with another. She didn't understand why Corey was doing this to her. What had she done to him? A thought occurred to her. Maybe he had come looking for her, but she wasn't there. She decided to stop by his house.

His car was there. She smiled. The weight had been lifted. She bounded up the steps and knocked.

No one answered the door. She knocked again. Finally, a shirtless Corey answered the door.

"What are you doing here?" he asked, clearly perturbed.

"I waited for you," she said, simply.

He shifted from one foot to the other. "Okay, well, now is not a good time."

"I called you yesterday," Seta said.

"Look, girl, you need to leave me alone." Corey's teeth flashed.

Seta blinked. *Why is he being so mean to me?*

"Baby, who is at the door?" a distinct female voice came from somewhere inside the house.

Corey shrugged. "Look, my girlfriend is here. You need to get out of here."

"Your girlfriend?" The word stuck in her throat. "But—"

A moment later, the girl Seta had seen Corey kiss at lunch the other day appeared behind him. Her eyes narrowed when she saw Seta.

"What's going on here?" the girl asked, her hands on her hips.

Seta looked at Corey. He tried to look nonchalant. "This girl just stopped by. She was looking for directions. That's all."

The girl looked suspicious.

Seta started to let the lie go unchallenged because she just wanted to get out of there. Then something clicked. He wasn't going to get away with this. "I think I left something in your bedroom the other day."

The girl's expression changed. Seta smiled sweetly. "You must be his sister?"

The girl shoved Corey. "His sister?" She stood inches from his nose. "Baby, am I your sister?"

Corey squirmed. He didn't know how he would get out of this. "Baby, I know you are not going to believe this crazy girl. You know how girls always be lying on me, everybody claiming some crazy stuff. That's because they don't want us to be happy."

The girl seemed to consider this. Then, she turned to Seta. "So what does his room look like?"

Seta pursed her lips and went to describing the stack of tapes, even the posters that covered his walls.

"Girl, you are lying!" Corey looked like he wanted to hit her.

The girl's eyes narrowed and she turned an angry stare at Corey. "Oh, so now you're fooling around on me?"

She jabbed a finger in Corey's face. He dodged and held up his hands. "Hold up, baby. This is all a misunderstanding. She's lying. You know how—"

The girl shoved past Corey. "I'm getting my stuff, and I'm leaving."

Corey cast a disgusted glance at Seta, who stood on the doorstep. Seta wanted to say more, except the words wouldn't come.

She stomped down the steps.

The door slammed behind her, but she could still hear the raised voices as she walked away.

Seta tried to watch television with her grandfather, but her mind wandered. She felt dirty and used. Corey had lied to her. But why? Why had he said he loved her when he didn't? The reality sank in that she was back to being unloved. Unloved and unwanted.

"Seta, baby, what's on your mind?" Phillip passed her the bag of potato chips. She pushed it back his way.

"Nothing," she said. "I'm just watching the game."

Even though the Chicago Bulls were leading by double digits, she couldn't concentrate on the moves. Her mind kept playing over and over the scene on Corey's doorstep.

"Come sit on Poppy's knee," he said, patting his leg. His knee had been one of Seta's favorite spots to sit when she was little.

Today, she only shook her head. "Poppy, I'm too big to sit on your lap," she said, with irritation lacing her voice. They still treated her like she was ten instead of fourteen.

Phillip nodded. He could see that she wanted a bit of independence. "You might be too old to sit on Granddaddy's knee, but you're never too old to come and talk to me," he reminded her.

"Are you having problems at school?" was the only thing he could think to ask. What else could be wrong with a fourteen-year-old? She had enough food. They bought her clothes that were nicer than anything they were wearing. She was the star of her team.

"No, Poppy, I'm fine," Seta said, standing. She knew she would get no peace tonight. She would expect a barrage of questions from her grandmother, but not from her grandfather. He was usually a man of few words. Her grandmother must be rubbing off on him.

Seta walked down the hall and slammed the door to her bedroom.

Barbara stood in the doorway to the living room. "What was that all about?"

Phillip shook his head. "I don't know," he said. "She wouldn't talk to me. Give her some time. She'll come around. She always does."

Barbara looked down the hall. "I don't know, Phillip. Something is just not right."

Phillip looked at the woman whose life he had shared for half a century. If he closed his eyes, he could still see the young girl he married. He hadn't known anything about pleasing a woman or maintaining a household, but he had wanted her for his wife all the same. He worked hard to prove it too.

Those first years had been fierce. Barbara hadn't wanted to get married—she had been a child, really—but had married him at her parents' insistence. They were just happy to have one less mouth to feed and were glad to send her to adulthood.

The country was just coming out of the Great Depression when they wed. Still, times were hard, especially for a Negro boy who hadn't finished school. Barbara hadn't liked living with his family for those first few months until they were able to scrape up enough money to find a small place of their own.

Phillip spent much of the early years away, first during

the war, then at a rail yard in another city before moving to one closer to home. When he had finally returned home to be a husband—and yes, a father,—he had found a distant and unhappy Barbara.

He didn't want to think about that now though. He had spent years trying to get over that and regain trust in their union. He smiled at his wife. "It'll be all right."

Chapter 14

Seta noticed the stares before she heard the whispers. She walked down the hall toward her first class and found Virginia Peterson gawking at her. This gawk was beyond the usual glances of contempt she sometimes still received from girls. This look was withering. Seta at first didn't know what to make of it, that was, until she heard words that would earn her punishment for a week if she were to dare utter them.

Who could they be talking about? Whoever it is must have done something pretty bad. Seta's eyes widened when she heard her name in a sentence and looked over to find three girls bunched together, staring her up and down. The crowd parted to produce the girl Seta had seen at Corey's house the other day, the cheerleader.

The girl's mouth curled into a sneer at the sight of Seta. "There she is," the girl said. "That's the skank who was sleeping with my man."

Seta's mouth fell open in disbelief. Why was this girl attacking her? She felt just as betrayed by Corey. It wasn't like she knew he had a girlfriend. Heck, she thought she was his girlfriend. Seta could hear her grandmother's voice in her head saying, "Just ignore them and hold your head up."

Seta drew in a steadying breath and held her backpack tighter. She looked the other way and tried to walk past.

"Hey, you!" said Marie, one of the other girls. "You like to sleep around, huh? Always want to mess with somebody else's man?"

Seta had no choice but to acknowledge the girl. Curious eyes glared at her from every corner. In the distance, someone laughed. She bit her lip and swallowed. "Look, I don't know what you're talking about," Seta said.

The girl baited her. "Yeah, right! Look at you, trying to break up a happy couple," Marie said. "But it's not going to work. My girl, Holly, is still going to be with her man! You can't steal him."

All Seta wanted to do was get to class. She didn't want to fight, and she didn't want to be called names. "I wasn't trying to take anyone from anybody," she said softly. "I thought he was my boyfriend."

The girl named Marie laughed derisively. "What?! Why would he be your boyfriend? You're just a stupid freshman. Plus, you're not even cute," the girl spat. She took two steps closer to Seta, invading her personal space. The girl named Holly smiled with a self-satisfied gleam in her eye.

Seta shook her head. "Look, I just want to get to class." She was not going to let this girl get to her. She wouldn't let them see her react. Nonetheless, the words burned at her. Why was it that no matter what she did, she could never have people like her?

Seta moved to step around the girl and was bumped from behind. She stumbled and looked back to see a vaguely familiar face staring at her, daring her to strike. Her mind tried to put a name to the face, and then it clicked. It was that bird-faced girl, Stacy Green, the girl from the fight the other week.

This time, though, Stacy seemed empowered. She was feeding on the hostile feelings directed toward Seta. Stacy hadn't forgiven Seta for embarrassing her the other week. She had been waiting for her chance to get back at her, Seta knew.

"Hey, watch it," Seta said to Stacy.

"And if I don't?" Stacy asked, full of attitude. Her eyebrows drew together.

Before Seta could respond, someone shoved her from the other side. The push sent her crashing into a wall of lockers. She put her hand out to break her fall.

The crowd came alive. Someone screamed. Someone else hit her. Seta struggled to get up but was shoved back down. "Let me at her!" someone said. "I'll teach her a lesson. I'm going to cut that precious hair of hers. Then we'll see how cute she thinks she is. We'll see if she can take anybody's man then."

Seta looked up to see scissors coming at her. She rolled to the side and the scissors struck the locker. Anger suddenly flashed in Seta's eyes. *These girls are crazy,* she thought as she jumped to her feet. She grabbed the hand attached to the scissors and jerked. Seta heard a wounded yelp and looked at the face. It was Marie.

Seta hit the girl in her face and snatched the scissors from her. "Now, who else wants a piece of me?" She looked around, her eyes wild with defiance. If they wanted to come at her, she would beat them all up too.

Someone grabbed her around the waist before she could raise her hand again. She flailed wildly. "Let go of me!"

"Seta, stop it," the guy's voice said. With an eerie feeling of déjà vu, she knew who it was without seeing the face. It was Mike, coming once again to rescue her.

"Leave me alone!" Seta tried to jerk away from him, as much out of defiance as embarrassment. His grasp on her tightened.

"Seta, you're going to get in trouble," he said. "Just let it go."

He turned to the other girls. "You need to leave her alone," he said in a voice that was deeper than she remembered it.

Mike loosened his grasp on her and Seta took the opportunity to lash out again at the girl. She would show her. Nobody was going to get the best of her. She hadn't gone looking for the fight, but she wasn't going to back down. She had had enough of being run over as a young child. These days, she was in charge.

"Break it up! Break it up!" The booming voice caused a sinking feeling in Seta's stomach. It was Mr. Abraham.

He shook his head when he saw Seta. "What are you doing with those scissors?" he asked.

She dropped them like they were hot. "I—I—"

"Into my office, Armstrong," he barked, and then turned to the girl on the floor. "You too. The rest of you, back to class."

Mike, who had tried to help her, now looked at her hopelessly. He shook his head.

Marie slowly stood. Her pride seemed to be the thing most hurt, but she limped as if her leg was broken. Mr. Abraham ignored the obvious act and she soon lost the limp. She sulked behind him.

Mr. Abraham listened to Marie's statement, and then beckoned in a short gesture for Seta to step into his office. She hesitated and then crossed the threshold. He sat behind the large, mahogany desk, his elbows braced firmly on the surface. He clasped his large hands in front of his face. His eyes drilled into Seta.

After a moment of screaming silence, he slid the phone across the desk to her. He nodded, his expression grim and expectant. Seta groaned. Telephoning her grandmother was the last thing she needed. Grammy would kill her.

But that wasn't the worst of the news. "You're suspended," the principal told Seta. "Three days."

She stood, her startled eyes glaring back at his. His eyes moved from her to her seat. She sat back down. "But, Mr. Abraham, it wasn't my fault," Seta pleaded.

"It never is," he said, turning to scribble something on his notepad.

Seta tried again. "Come on, Mr. Abraham. Please don't suspend me."

He looked at his watch. "You'd better be glad I'm not expelling you for having the scissors."

"They weren't mine!" Seta's voice raised a notch. "I took them from her before she could get me."

The door opened. She looked up to see her coach standing in the doorway. Seta closed her eyes.

"Seta, what's this I hear about a fight?" Coach said.

Seta looked nervously from the coach to the principal. Since Mr. Abraham wouldn't listen to her, maybe her coach would. "Coach, it really wasn't my fault," she said. "I was just trying to get to class and they started calling me names and pushing me."

Her coach shook his head. "I'm disappointed in you, Seta."

His words hurt worse than the suspension. His eyes looked sad and Seta felt her heart break again. She didn't like seeing that look in his eyes. She just wanted him to like her.

She tried again, "Coach, please. I—"

But he had heard enough. He turned, his words directed at the principal. "She won't be able to play on the team for the next two weeks. One more infraction and she is off the team."

Seta looked from one to the other. She jumped from her

seat and stood in front of her coach. "Coach, you can't do this to me. You can't!"

"Seta, sit down." His voice was firm.

The secretary buzzed the office. "Mrs. Wright is here." Seta's eyes widened. Who had called?

"Send her in," Mr. Abraham said.

A moment later, Barbara stepped into the office. Her lips were drawn into a straight line and her purse hung from the crook of her elbow. Her black wig, hastily donned, was slightly askew. Seta dropped her head to keep from looking into the piercing eyes.

Barbara jerked Seta's head up. "Look at me," she said, her grip firm on Seta's chin. Anger seemed to jump from Barbara's eyes.

Seta took an involuntary step backward. She hoped Barbara wouldn't embarrass her here, but instead, would wait until they got home. She didn't want her coach and her principal to witness her humiliation. Barbara's nose flared and she turned to the principal.

"Mr. Abraham, I am so sorry to be so much trouble," she said. "I just don't know what has gotten into her."

Barbara sucked her teeth and peered at Seta. "What I do know is that we're going to handle this problem. She will come back to your school a whole new person. I guarantee it."

Seta shook her head. Man, they just didn't understand. Her grandmother hadn't even asked her what happened. Hadn't bothered to see whose fault it was. Even worse, her coach and principal weren't interested in her story either.

Ten minutes later, Seta was in the Cutlass with her grandmother. It took a few tries before the engine turned over, but it finally revved. Neither said anything. Seta sat straight up in the passenger seat, slipping quick glances at her grandmother out of the corner of her eye. Barbara's jaw was set. She drove with both hands on the steering wheel.

The car was barely at a complete stop in the driveway before Seta climbed out and walked into the tiny, brick house. She glanced back over her shoulder at her grandmother. It made her nervous that Barbara hadn't said anything. Barbara turned away. Seta slinked off to her bedroom.

A few hours later, Phillip arrived home from work at the store. He knocked on Seta's door. "Come in," she said.

He stepped into the room. "Hey," he said, standing in the doorway.

Seta shrugged. "Hi."

Phillip picked his nose and rubbed his chin. He looked skyward, and then sat at the foot of the bed. "Seta."

He waited for her to acknowledge his words. She didn't. He plunged into his talk anyway. "Seta, you can't keep doing this," he said slowly. "Your grandmother wanted me to talk to you. She says she is too angry to speak to you right now. Seta, if you keep getting into trouble like this, you're not going to be able to live here." The words pained him. He hadn't wanted to put it to her like that, but Barbara insisted. Phillip touched her arm to soften the sting of his words. Seta jerked away.

"You're going to put me out?" the question squeaked out. She blinked hard so the tears wouldn't come. She would not give them the satisfaction. They just wanted an excuse to get rid of her . . . just like her dad.

Phillip wanted to take the words back but couldn't. "Well, we all have to live by rules," he said, speaking slowly, searching for the right words. "We've tried everything we can. We've tried to provide you with all of the things you need and some of what you want. We've tried to raise you in a decent and loving Christian home. But we can't have you running around getting into fights every week and threatening people with scissors."

"It wasn't my fault!" Seta yelled the words. Why was nobody listening to her?

Phillip let the raised tone go unchallenged. This person who sat before him wasn't his Seta. He didn't know what had gotten into his little girl, but the child he raised wouldn't act like this. Something was definitely the matter.

"You didn't even ask me what happened," she said, hurt and anger making her voice crack. She cursed herself for having a wavering voice. "You just want to put me out. But that's all right. I don't have to stay here."

Phillip knew Barbara wanted him to mete out discipline. However, he couldn't do that right now. He had to comfort his child. He reached for Seta, but she didn't respond. He inched closer and put his hand on her shoulder. "Seta, listen," he said. "You will always have a home here. We will get through whatever this thing is that you are going through. It will be all right."

Seta's chin quivered. If he had spoken to her with anger, she could have lashed out at him in like manner. However, his soft tone touched her and the hurt of the past few days flooded forward. She sniffed hard to keep from crying.

She looked at the white-haired man next to her. In all her years, she couldn't remember him ever speaking to her harshly or whipping her. He had always been her shelter. Even now, he seemed to be ready to wipe away a tear.

Her grandfather had been the one male constant in her life. She turned to him now. "Poppy, I'm just so confused . . . about everything."

"Tell me about it," he said. She smiled a little. He would always use those words when she was little.

So she did. She told him about Corey and about the fight. She edited the story slightly, though, leaving out the fact that she had gone to Corey's house and all that ensued there. "We talked a lot and he gave me a ride home," she said. "Then this girl thought I was trying to take her boyfriend. That's when they all tried to fight me."

A light of understanding clicked for Phillip. Of course, boy problems, that's what had been bothering his child. "Well, it seems to me that those girls are just jealous," he said. "They just wish they were as smart and pretty as you. That's all. And as for that little knuckleheaded boy, don't even pay any attention to him. He's not worth your time."

Phillip rubbed his chin. "I know it wasn't your fault," he said. He lowered his voice. "Between you and me, I'm glad you knocked that girl out. The next time somebody comes in your face and pushes you, you make sure you lay them out. That'll teach 'em."

Seta leaned on her grandfather's shoulder. Then, she looked up at him. "What about Grammy?"

"I'll talk to her," he said, standing. "You're still going to have to be on punishment. But it won't be too bad. I'll tell her it wasn't your fault. You were only defending yourself."

Seta spent her suspension in her bedroom. Barbara listened to Phillip's explanation of what happened and softened somewhat, but she still told Seta there would be no telephone privileges, no television and no radio for the duration of the suspension. Seta wasn't allowed to go anywhere, aside from a trip to church Sunday morning.

Her grandparents had started allowing her to sit with some of the other children her age. On this Sunday, however, Barbara made Seta sit with her. Seta didn't much mind that because the other children weren't really her friends.

Seta sat through the sermon of the new pastor, Rev. Franklin. She didn't much care for him. Rev. Johnson had died and this new minister had a decidedly different air. Where Rev. Johnson had been mellow and nurturing, this new man was flashy and flamboyant. His sermons were extra long too, Seta noted with resignation. Seemed like he thought the Lord couldn't ever hear him, so he seemed to repeat everything.

"Lord, we need a blessing today," the pastor shouted to the roof. "Lord, I said we need a blessing."

Seta wanted to roll her eyes, though she didn't dare for fear her grandmother might see. And she was already on her bad side. "Lord, your children need a word from you," he said. "Lord, a word from you, that's what your children need."

"I think we're getting plenty from you," Seta said under her breath before she realized it.

Barbara glanced at her quickly and put her finger to her lips. "Shhh," she told Seta, frowning.

Seta tuned out Rev. Franklin. He didn't wear a robe like the one Rev. Johnson had. His suit was crisp and dark. His shirt was monogrammed and adorned with cuff links. *He is too young,* Seta thought, having gotten used to the grand-fatherly Rev. Johnson. This new guy didn't look old enough to know how to explain the stories of Moses and Jesus, Jeremiah and all the others.

She could sometimes see the shine of his clear coat manicure flash in the pulpit light.

Nope, she decided, he wasn't a real pastor. Besides, she didn't need somebody else telling her how hard it was to reach God. She already knew.

At the exact moment she thought she would run screaming from the room if he repeated himself once more, he sat down. A secretary reminded the congregation to place some money in the offering plate for the building fund on their way out. Seta didn't know about the rest of them, but she wasn't putting another dime in that building fund until she saw some proof that there would be a new church.

She stood on the church steps waiting for Barbara to finish greeting Sister Mary and praying with Sister Benson. *You'd think she would have said all the prayers she needed to inside the church,* Seta grumbled.

"Hi, Seta," she heard a shy voice call to her.

She looked around, searching out the face that belonged to the voice.

"Hi," she said. It was the pastor's daughter, Hannah. The new first family had been coming to the church for about two months, but Seta hadn't exchanged any words with the pastor's children, though the congregation had welcomed them with a dinner in the fellowship hall.

The girl wore a puffy, ruffled dress with ankle socks. Her hair was pulled back in braids. *She is tall enough to be my age, but those clothes make her look like a baby*, Seta thought. She looked like her mom still dressed her. *What could she want with me?* Seta wondered.

"I saw your fight last week," the girl said. Seta bristled.

"Oh yeah?" Seta asked. She glanced nervously at her grandmother.

"Yeah, I didn't think it was your fault," the girl said.

"Yeah, well, it wasn't," she said, cutting the girl off when she saw Barbara approaching. She didn't know where this girl was going with her comments, but Seta didn't want to hear. She had had enough of girls and their jealous ways.

"Come on, Seta," Barbara said with an edge to her voice, before smiling a greeting at Hannah.

Seta returned to school Monday. Amy was the first to see her. She rushed over, her eyes big with curiosity. "So, did your grandmother beat you?"

Seta frowned. "No, Amy," she said. Amy looked disappointed for a second, then, "So, did Coach kick you off the team?"

Amy was always looking for gossip. Her shyness had worn off and in its place was a gregarious soul whose purpose in life seemed to be to spread information.

"No, Coach didn't kick me off the team," Seta slammed her books into her locker. She didn't feel like a verbal assault.

Amy persisted. "Oh, well, I heard he did," she said, waiting to see what Seta would say.

"Well, he didn't." Seta closed the locker.

Jessica strode up with Diana. "Good to see you again," Jessica said coolly. She still was annoyed at Seta.

"Yeah, you too," Seta mumbled, heading to class.

"Hey, wait up," Amy said. "Why are you trying to leave us?"

Seta stopped and turned around. "Look, I just want to get to class. I don't want any problems. If you want to walk with me, fine. If you don't, that's fine too."

The three looked at each other. The old Seta would have never said anything like that. Jessica beckoned to Diana and Amy. "Come on," she said.

They walked in silence.

Holly purposely walked near Seta's table at lunch. Holly hissed down to her, "You'd better watch your back."

Seta looked up to see if anyone had heard. No one had. She tried to refocus on the conversation with the other girls on the basketball team, but her ears perked when she heard her name at the neighboring table.

"Yeah, I heard she slept with Corey," one voice said.

"Yeah, and I heard she was chasing him down too," someone else chimed in.

"Well, a reliable source told me she slept with that girl Stacy's boyfriend," another voice said to gasps.

"I always knew that Seta was no-good," said the first voice. "She was always so quiet, acting all innocent like. But I knew better."

Seta's face burned with embarrassment. She felt small and exposed. How could these people say such things about her? They didn't even know her. She wanted to turn around and confront them. However, she knew she could ill afford a fight at school.

She hoped none of her friends had heard. She glanced up and caught Diana's eye. Seta's heart sank as she realized Diana had heard the same words as she. Diana stared at her for a moment, and then turned back to her own conversation.

"So, what do you think, Seta?" Jessica asked.

"Huh?" Seta tried to refocus.

"So, what do you think about us all getting together at my house for your birthday? We haven't been drinking in a while," she said.

Seta wasn't in the mood to party, but she nodded. "Yeah, sounds good."

"All right," Amy said, rubbing her hands together. "I hope Big C brings some of his friends," she said, elbowing Diana.

The words from the other table replayed over and over in Seta's mind that afternoon. It seemed that everywhere she went now people were calling her horrible names and saying unmentionable things about her. A guy had even groped her on her way out the cafeteria, saying lewdly, "I hear that's what you like."

She had swatted his hand away and raced to her next class.

Her next class was no better, though, because Stacy and another girl sat directly behind her and hissed foul words at her whenever the teacher's back was turned. Seta tried to ignore their calls, but she couldn't. She doodled on her notepad and chewed her lip until it bled.

She wished she had never met Corey. Her heart hurt over her lost innocence, and the words people now used to describe her made her feel filthy. Those words painted nasty women, and they were being applied to her. She knew she was now like those women—"Jezebels" her grandmother called them—who did terrible things with men. She had done those terrible things. Seta knew she would go straight to hell.

She vowed never to do those things with another boy.

The pain just wasn't worth it.

Coach Malone made her sit on the bleachers during the entire practice. Seta burned to be on the court. After practice, she approached Coach Malone in his office. He looked up from papers, his eyes peering above the glasses on his nose. His sandy hair was thinning at the top of his head and his office smelled like old sneakers. Posters with scribbled autographs of former players lined the wall behind him.

"Hi, Seta," he said. "I was expecting you."

She launched into her spiel. "Coach, please don't make me sit out the next two games. Coach, the team needs me."

"The team needs you to behave even more," he said.

"Come on, Coach," she said. His stare was unwavering. She tried another angle. "Well, can I at least practice with the team?"

"Seta, you are one of the most talented girls I've seen in a long time," he said. He closed the book in front of him and clasped his hands, the fingers interlaced. "Next year, you'll be up for the varsity team, and I'm sure you will make it. You could get a scholarship and play at college. But you are not going to go far if you let your emotions get the best of you."

Seta opened her mouth to argue, then thought better of it. It didn't matter. Nobody—well, nobody except her Poppy—even wanted to hear her side of the story. "Okay, Coach."

Coach Malone nodded appreciatively. Maybe she was learning. He stood. "All right, I'll tell you what. You'll still miss this week. However, I'll let you back on the court next week. If you're not rusty, I'll let you play."

Seta broke into a large smile. "Oh, Coach, thank you!" She rushed to the other side of the desk and hugged him. A startled Coach Malone awkwardly hugged her back.

Seta lay in bed that night listening to the silence. For the first time in a long time, she fingered the picture of the woman. She wondered what she was like for everybody to love her. Seta wished she could be like that—whatever that was. She imagined that life for her mother must have been easy. It had to have been. Everybody loved her. She was beautiful. At just the mention of her name, people would get sad with missing her.

Nobody would ever miss her, Seta knew. They didn't even want her around. Her grandmother wanted to put her out and her father never even called for her. Seta slammed down the picture. Seta tried to squeeze thoughts of her father from her mind. But sometimes, her mind defied her. And when her mind focused on him, anger now replaced the longing she once had felt. Now, she couldn't stand even the thought of Robert Armstrong.

He didn't want her. Well, she sure didn't need him.

Lola entered Robert's office to find him leaning back with his eyes closed. She paused in the doorway for a second before calling to him softly. His eyes fluttered open.

"Yes, dear?" he said. Lola bristled slightly. Whenever he called her dear, it meant he had been thinking about that other woman. He always tried to use that term to cover up his distant thoughts. She ignored the bottle next to his hand.

"It's late. Don't you want to get ready to go to bed?" Lola let her bathrobe fall open, as if by accident. She had put on a bra under her gown so her breasts wouldn't hang. She sucked in her stomach and put one hand on her hip. At forty, Lola was a handsome woman. She was round, with strong features. Her nose was broad and her forehead still unlined. She wouldn't win any beauty contests, but she was pleasant to look at, she felt.

She had come prepared to seduce. Her mouth was burgundy with lipstick and her hair was pulled back. She had showered and put on sweet-smelling lotion. Their sex life was pretty nonexistent, though Robert sometimes obliged. She felt as if she had to pursue him, and the thought made her sick. She was getting tired of the sham of a marriage.

Still, she knew she wasn't going anywhere. Robert earned a good salary, and her children had a man to call daddy once again. No, she wasn't leaving. Therefore, she would try to make do and try her hardest to let this man know it was not a crime to fall in love again.

"I'll be up in a little while," Robert said, shifting in his seat. A single sheet of white paper was in his right hand. A chill went through Lola. She knew without examination that it was that letter. Robert didn't know she knew about it. She knew Rose's words by heart, though, and she was sure Robert did too.

Lola stepped into the room. "Robert, don't do this, please," she said. Her chocolate eyes were a sea of begging. "You keep reliving it. It's not healthy. You have a new wife now, a new family."

When Robert didn't say anything, she tried again. "Come to bed. Let me help you forget."

Robert's eyes sought the floor. He looked back up. "Give me a moment. I'll be up to bed in a sec."

Lola stared at him for a moment and then turned on her heel.

Robert sucked in a deep breath and held it. He let it out slowly. So many emotions raced. Tomorrow would mark fifteen years since Rose had died . . . and fourteen years since he had given away their child.

* * *

Barbara fixed Seta a birthday dinner of her favorites and allowed her to invite friends over to celebrate. Seta hadn't really wanted Jessica, Amy, and Diana to come over—especially Jessica, who lived in such a nice house—but her grandmother insisted.

Seta hid the chipped dishes and pulled out the Sunday plates. She put a pillow over the tear in the fabric on the couch and hid her grandfather's worn slippers in his bedroom. She wished she could hide the garden in the backyard, but maybe her friends wouldn't look out the window. None of them had to grow any of their own food. She didn't want them to know her family produced some of its own.

Her friends had been in her house only a handful of times before, usually for never more than a few minutes while they waited on her to get dressed, but they had never spent any prolonged time there. This time, they would have time to pick apart her home—to see the ragged and worn furniture, to observe how slow her grandparents now were, to see the threadbare rugs.

Amy walked in, taking in the walls, floors, everything. Seta could see her making mental notes.

Diana was her usual aloof self. Seta hadn't been sure Diana would come, but she had. Diana handed her a small gift wrapped in silver paper. Seta's smile revealed her surprise. "Thank you, Diana."

"Yeah," Diana said, brushing past her and stepping into the living room.

Jessica was last to arrive. "Happy birthday!" she sang. She had decided to let Seta's indiscretion go.

The girls laughed over dinner and finished it with cake. Amy took only a bite because she didn't want to eat too many calories. Diana had two slices, though, and Jessica and Seta each had one.

"Your grandmother sure can cook," Jessica said, nodding. She licked icing off her finger.

"Thanks," Seta said. Jessica was right.

Jessica turned to Barbara. "So, Mrs. Wright, is it all right if we take Seta out, maybe to the movies?"

Barbara still didn't care too much for Jessica, who dressed like a grown woman. However, she was grateful the girls were her granddaughter's friends. She smiled. "Sure," she said. "But she can't stay out too late."

"How are you going to get there?" Phillip chimed in.

Each girl had been dropped off at Seta's. They looked at each other. "We're going to walk to Amy's house and her dad is going to drop us off at the movies," came Jessica's quick response.

Satisfied, Phillip nodded.

Thirty minutes later, the girls were settled into Jessica's basement with a bottle from her parents' wine collection. Seta still did not like alcohol's taste, but she used it to assert her independence. She found herself most likely to drink if she thought of her father. She imagined—though she didn't know for sure—that drinking was something of which he would disapprove. So, that made her want to do it even more. She would do anything to prove that she didn't care what he thought and to show that she didn't need his approval.

She drank for the same reason that she now had harsh words for her grandmother and found herself getting into trouble. She told herself she didn't care. She didn't care what happened to her. And if she got into trouble, so what? Nobody else cared what happened to her. So why should she?

Seta finished her ninth-grade year without incident. She tried out for the varsity basketball team and made it. Diana also made the team. Amy tried out, but didn't find a spot on the team. Jessica decided she'd rather be a cheerleader.

Seta wondered what would happen to this network of friends now that they were all doing different things.

She felt scared that without the common thread of basketball, they would no longer like her and they would all become distant. She hoped that didn't happen, though, because the memory of being without friends was still fresh enough on her mind for the thought to be painful.

She was at last comfortable enough with her friends to speak freely with them. She broached the subject with Jessica, who sometimes treated her like a kid sister even though they were the same age.

"Oh, girl, we'll be friends for life," Jessica assured Seta. "There is nothing that can tear us apart."

Chapter 15

"Take the shot! Take the shot!" Seta heard the voices coming at her. She glanced to her right and saw Diana being guarded. She looked to her left. The game clock was running out.

"Take the shot!"

Seta set her feet and aimed. The ball went cleanly into the hoop as the buzzer sounded. The crowd erupted into a frenzied mass as the game ended with a win for her team.

Someone hoisted her in the air. There were screams all around. Folks flooded onto the court. Seta smiled widely.

"Girl, that was a good game you played," Jessica said, her cheerleading uniform tight across her chest. The skirt flirted around her legs.

"You could have passed the ball a little bit more," Amy chimed in. Seta ignored her.

Her grandparents smiled from the bleachers.

Seta waved to them and ran into the locker room with the rest of the team.

* * *

Robert cut the picture from the newspaper. A smiling girl was perched atop her teammates' shoulders. Robert stared at the photo. Her eyes looked just like her mother's. Her hair was pulled back in a ponytail, but it was wavy, just like her mother's. Her skin and hair were darker, though. Still, there was no mistaking the resemblance.

Robert gritted his teeth. He placed the clipping into the photo album with the rest of the newspaper articles and miscellaneous memorabilia he had begun to collect. He wasn't ready to embrace her, but he wasn't angry with the girl anymore.

He didn't really know what he wanted from her, or with her. Guilt replaced the anger these days whenever he thought of her. He was ashamed of the way he had treated her. He knew he had hurt her and that his acts weren't to be forgiven.

He wanted to approach her, maybe to ask if she could ever let him be a part of her life. Somehow, his pride wouldn't allow it. So, he just watched her from a distance.

He watched and he said nothing.

"Daddy, look!" Berrie raced into the den, interrupting Robert's thoughts. He pushed the photo album to the side.

"My teacher said I should try out for choir next year." Berrie showed him the letter from school.

Robert smiled. "That's great," he said. He brushed her hair down. She was so excitable. "You do have a beautiful voice."

Robert marveled at the innocence. Bennie and Berrie were good students and well behaved children. He spent time with them in the evenings, going over homework and playing word games with them. They all spent time reading before bed. It was a family ritual.

Robert stared unseeingly long after Berrie was gone. He loved these children.

*   *   *

The ringing of the phone broke into Seta's consciousness. A pencil was in her mouth, gripped between her teeth. Her hand was to her forehead. These geometry problems were something else, but she was figuring them out. Math and science were her favorite subjects.

She ignored the phone, thinking her grandmother may answer it. Finally, she grumbled and snatched up the receiver. "Hello?"

"May I speak to Mr. Wright?"

"Who's calling?" Seta asked.

"This is his job. I was calling to see if he was planning on coming in to work today," the person on the other end said. "He's two hours late."

Seta frowned. That was weird. Her grandfather was a stickler for time. He was never late for anything and never missed work. "Are you sure?" she asked.

"Yeah, he's on the schedule," the other person said. "Is he there?"

"Hold on," she said and put the phone down and headed toward her grandfather's room.

She knocked on her grandfather's door. "Poppy, there is somebody from your job on the phone. They say you're supposed to be at work." Seta frowned.

Phillip looked at her absently for a moment. "Work?"

"Yes, Poppy, you know, at the grocery store?" He could sometimes be so distant, especially lately.

Phillip rubbed his chin. "Oh, yes, that's right," he said quickly, but without much conviction. "I must have just forgotten. I remember now."

He scurried to find his shoes and headed off to work.

Nettie reclined in Phillip's overstuffed chair after having dropped in unexpectedly to see Barbara. Seta was in her bedroom. Phillip was at Augusta's house helping her husband repair a window. Nettie had brought a bag of clothes for Seta—she often brought some gift for her friend's family. The clothes came from one of her granddaughters.

"It's a shame I have to chase you down these days," Nettie chided her friend gently. She had seen Barbara in passing a few times at church but hadn't talked to her for any length of time in months.

Barbara shrugged her off. "Oh, nonsense," she said.

Nettie wasn't put off that easily. "So, what's been going on with you?"

Barbara hunched her shoulders. "Oh, nothing," she said. "Just this and that."

Nettie narrowed her eyes. "Uh huh. Like what?" she peered at Barbara closely. "I didn't see you at choir rehearsal the other day. And you're looking a little puny, if you asked me."

"Well, I didn't ask you," Barbara said. She was on the defensive. They were all getting older. What about it?

Nettie took a sip of her tea and looked around the living room. "Well, don't let it be said I didn't ask," she said, "if you want to talk, you know where I am."

Nettie knew it would do no good to pry. She looked at her friend thoughtfully. Barbara seemed to be moving a bit slowly these days and her living room wasn't spotless. Not that it was dirty—far from it—but it didn't have the usual flawless look Nettie had come to expect. Barbara hadn't even called her to complain about Robert—a sure sign that something was wrong.

Barbara changed the subject. She didn't want to talk about what was going on with her. Nobody wanted to hear about bills and ill health. "So, how is Charles?"

Nettie rolled her eyes. "Sister, those children of mine want us to have a wedding or some such," Nettie said. "Our fortieth wedding anniversary is coming up in a few months, and the children want us to renew our vows. I told

Charles after all time, I've forgotten the vows," she said, laughing at her own joke.

Barbara smiled. "Well, it would be nice to have a little ceremony. Forty years is a long time."

Nettie stretched. "I know that's real. Forty years. Girl, I never thought we'd make it through forty years of snoring and belching and bad moods," she said. "But I guess Charles is a patient man."

"He just doesn't know any better," Barbara joked. Charles adored his wife.

"Yes, well, I told him don't think everything is going to be just like it was when we first got married. Specifically, some things that used to be up are going to be down now," she said, raising an eyebrow, "if you know what I mean."

Barbara chuckled. Life had taken its toll on them all.

"I told Charles too that I can't be kissing like some youngster. I paid too much for these dentures to have our teeth clicking and clacking against each other," Nettie said, waving her hand in the air.

"Child, be quiet," Barbara couldn't stop the laughter. Nettie would say anything.

Nettie stared in mock seriousness. "I don't see why you're laughing. I am dead serious. Don't you know how much these here teeth cost?

"Charles told me, don't worry about the teeth. He said if I wanted to, I could take them out—he had no use for them," Nettie said. "I told him, 'you better watch yourself.' "

Barbara scooted out of her chair. "Girl, I am not paying any attention to you. Lord knows I'm not. You are outrageous. Let me go and check on this food on this stove."

Nettie nodded and called after her friend when she downed the last of her tea, "Yeah, you do that. Why don't you fix me a plate to take home to Charles?"

* * *

Seta wiped her lips with a napkin. "Grammy, this is really good. Is there any more?" Seta said, putting the last bit of meat into her mouth. She glanced toward the stove.

Barbara paused, her fork halfway to her mouth. She put the fork down and shook her head. "No, but why don't you have the rest of mine?"

Seta frowned. "No, Grammy, I can't take your food."

Barbara was already pushing her plate toward Seta. "No, it's fine, baby. Here." She slid the meat to the edge of her plate. "I'm not hungry."

Seta glanced from her grandmother to her grandfather. They looked at her expectantly. Her grandmother nodded. "Take it, baby. You need your strength."

After a moment, Seta scraped the beef patty and gravy onto her own plate. "Thanks, Grammy."

Barbara remembered Nettie's visit. "Sister Bradshaw brought you some clothes by here today," she said. "Some really nice things."

Seta frowned. She was not going to wear hand-me-downs. But she quickly erased the look from her face. Maybe she would glance at the bag. Who knows, she might find something that still had the tags on it. She thanked her grandmother.

The three chatted about Seta's latest basketball game. Then, the conversation turned to church. Sister Mary's brother was in the hospital and the choir would be traveling to Shady Grove Church next Sunday. Grammy had missed a few rehearsals lately on account of being tired.

"I think I'm going to skip the Shady Grove trip," Barbara said.

Seta glanced quickly at her grandmother. Barbara rarely missed a singing event. "Grammy, you're missing a choir trip?"

Barbara absently rubbed her chest. "Yes, I've been a little

tired lately and I just don't feel like it," she said. Seta and Poppy exchanged a look. Something wasn't right here.

Seta opened her mouth to say something, but the telephone rang. She sprang to answer it. She picked it up and smiled. It was her friend Jessica.

Seta grabbed her lunch from her locker and headed to the courtyard to find her friends. "Seta," someone called her name. She looked around. Her eyes widened when she saw that it was David, one of the football players. He was tall and always had girls around him.

"Yeah?" she asked.

He gestured with his head, telling her to come to him. She hesitated, but went anyway. "I was wondering if you wanted to go out this weekend?" he asked.

She recalled what happened the last time a cute guy had approached her. She shook her head. "No, but thanks."

He wasn't easily deterred. "Come on. I've been checking you out and think you're fine. We can go to the movies or something."

His eyes took in her hair, her pink top and her jeans. Seta was leery, but her heart leapt at the way he looked at her, as if he may actually like her. She nodded. "Okay, give me a call." She scribbled her number on a sheet of notebook paper, tore it out, and gave it to him.

He winked at her and disappeared.

Seta was back to studying and doing well in school. She was glad junior high grades didn't count in her high school grade-point average, or she might have some trouble. As it was now, she would have to work hard to regain her high academic position at the top of her class. She was one of the highest-ranking students in her sophomore class. Still, being one of the highest wasn't good enough for her. She wanted—needed—to be the best. She reminded herself the reason she worked so hard was to gain a good scholarship and ultimately become a family lawyer and prosecute fathers who neglected their children.

But she knew the real reason—though she swallowed the thoughts each time they arose—she craved the top of her class was to prove that she was good enough for her father's love. But she shook those thoughts away. Seta convinced herself that she was pushing herself to get the type of scholarship she wanted, that was all. She still had two more years to work hard, but she knew that if she kept at it, she could have both academic and athletic scholarships.

She knew scholarships were her only ticket to college. Her grandparents tried to hide their strained finances from her, but she wasn't blind. Her grandmother's blood pressure medicine and whatever other pills she took were expensive—Seta had seen the paperwork. She wanted to get an after-school job, but Barbara would hear nothing of it. She said Seta's job was school. Case closed.

"Hey, hotshot." The voice behind her was familiar. Seta turned around when she heard it. She smiled. It was Mike. He was driving a Honda Accord.

He climbed out of the car and gave Seta a hug. He was now well over six feet tall, with long arms and a smattering of hair on his chin. The beat-up sneakers he used to wear were replaced with Jordans.

"Hey, yourself," she said. Her heart did a strange flip-flop. "So, I hear you're going to A and M next year."

He smiled proudly. "Yeah, I am, on scholarship. All those days on the court paid off," he said.

"I see," Seta said. An awkward silence settled between them.

Seta twirled a strand of hair around her finger and looked away. "I see you have a ride now," she said, stating the obvious.

"Yeah, I've been flipping a lot of burgers," he said. "But

that's okay. I won't be doing that when I go to college next year. You want a ride home?"

Seta was suddenly shy. She hadn't spent a lot of time with Mike in the last couple of years, but he always seemed to pop up every now and then. This would be his last year around before going off to college.

She had never told him how grateful she was that he took her under his wing all those years ago. She wanted to say something now, but a girl bounded up to them before she had a chance to do so.

"Hey, baby." The girl kissed Mike squarely on the lips. He glanced at Seta and cleared his throat. "Seta, this is Michelle, my girlfriend. Michelle, this is Seta."

Michelle smiled. "Oh, you're the little girl he used to walk home from the basketball court," she said.

Seta felt an unfamiliar emotion she couldn't describe. She managed a smile. "Yes, that would be me." She playfully punched Mike on the arm. "That's our Mike, always coming to save me."

Michelle entwined her arm in Mike's. "Yes, he's like that." She turned back to Mike. "Oh, I finished up early, so I ran out here to catch you. I saw your car pulling off. I was glad when you stopped."

Mike gestured to Seta. "Yeah, I just offered Seta a ride home. Come on, we can drop her off, then I'll take you home."

Seta shook her head. "No, that's all right. I don't want to get in the way. You two go on."

Michelle wouldn't hear of it. "You're not in the way. Come on. Let's go."

Seta looked from one to the other and then climbed in the backseat and let Mike drive her home.

Seta looked up from her research paper to notice two girls staring at her across the library. She groaned inwardly, and then looked back down at her work. Even after all this time, girls still acted as if they didn't like her.

One of them strode to her table and sneered. "So, I hear you're going out with David Buchanan."

"What about it?" Seta raised one eyebrow.

The girl leaned in closer. "You know a lot of girls like him," she said, her breath on Seta's face. "I'd keep my eyes open if I were you. A lot of folks wouldn't want to see you end up with him."

"So what's it to you?"

The girl laughed a one-syllable grunt. "Look, I'm just trying to look out for you. I just wouldn't want to see you get your hopes up. He could go with anyone he wants. Why would he pick you?"

Seta looked pointedly at her papers spread over the table. "You let me worry about that," she said. "Now, as you can see, I'm busy here."

The girl pursed her lips. "Uppity broad."

Seta's eyes narrowed and her mouth opened, but she saw the librarian eyeing them suspiciously. She cleared her throat and shifted in her seat. The girls glanced at the librarian and left.

Seta doodled on her paper, absently filling in all the circles on the page with the black ink of her pen. She didn't know why girls had it in for her. She didn't even like David all that much. He was just some cute guy who had asked her out.

As if on cue, David stepped into the library. He glanced around the room and his eyes settled on Seta. He smiled and strode over, confidence oozing from every pore. "Hey, beautiful," he said.

The word sounded so odd when applied to her. Seta blushed. "Hi."

"I was looking for one of my boys in here, but I'm glad I

spotted you," David said, pulling up a chair. He put his backpack on the table.

"What are you working on?" he asked.

Seta blinked at his question. Nobody was much interested in what she was doing, not unless she was on the basketball court, anyway. "Oh, just a research paper."

David groaned. "Oh, I know how those things are. I have one due tomorrow," he said. He seemed to think for a moment, then looked at her. "Hey, can you help me with my paper?" He paused, dramatically. "Well, I don't know. You are a sophomore, and this is for a senior class. It may be too much for you."

Seta leapt at the chance. "Oh, no, I can help you. What do you need?"

David quickly looked around and then pulled out his notebook. He lowered his voice, as if to conspire. "Well, I have this huge paper that's due and I have got to go to football practice. I don't know if I'll be able to get everything done."

Seta understood his quandary. It could be a hard time, trying to balance class work and practice. Seta pushed aside her own work and looked at his assignment. "I can help you with it. That's not a problem."

Her eyes searched for approval in his face. After a moment, he nodded, as if considering. "You've convinced me. I'll let you help me, but only if you think you can do a good job."

Seta stood. "I'll go and pull some books. We can figure out what to include in the paper and I can type it after we go through some of these books."

David looked at his watch, and then hit his forehead. "Oh, man, look at the time. I have to go to practice. Hey, I trust your judgment. Why don't you just research it and type it like you want it? I'm sure it'll be fine."

Seta hesitated but didn't want his smile to disappear. It was a smile directed at her. She nodded. "Sure."

She flipped through encyclopedias and reference books researching David's topic. She was typing the paper when the librarian announced the library would be closing in twenty minutes. Seta looked up, her mouth open in surprise. "Twenty minutes?"

The librarian nodded. Seta could finish typing the rest of David's paper by then; however, she wouldn't have time to finish her own assignment, which was due the next day. She walked to the librarian. "Mrs. Cain, is there any way I can stay a little late? I have to finish this paper."

Mrs. Cain shook her head. "That's the problem with you athletes. You always think you're supposed to get special treatment. No. The library closes in twenty minutes. Period."

"No, I wasn't looking for special treatment because I'm a basketball player. I was just thinking maybe I could stay while you do your last-minute work straightening up or something, that's all."

Mrs. Cain picked up a stack of books. "I'm doing that now. I am closing this library in exactly—" she looked at her watch, "eighteen minutes."

"Fine." Seta turned and went back to her seat. She didn't have a computer at home and didn't have a way to type up her own paper. She banged out the rest of the pages for David's work just as Mrs. Cain turned off the lights. "Time's up," the woman said curtly.

Seta scowled but slammed the book shut and printed David's report. She grabbed all her materials and strode out the library. She dreaded the idea of walking home with all those books, but had no choice. She had to find some kind of way to get her own paper done.

She was pondering as she began the trek home with the

glare of the late afternoon sun in her eyes. She thought she heard her name and looked around. It was the two girls she saw in the library. One of them strode up to Seta with purpose.

"So, you looked like you wanted to say something while we were in the library," she said, rolling her neck. "What do you have to say now, ugly?" the girl said.

Blood rushed to Seta's head. She would show them who was ugly here. She threw her backpack to the ground and planted her feet firmly apart. "Who you calling ugly?" Seta shot back.

The first girl took a step back and said with a little less force. "You."

Her friend egged her on. "Yeah, she was talking to you. Did she stutter?"

Seta wasn't going to let anybody talk to her like she was nothing. In the back of her mind, a little voice reminded her that she needed to be on her best behavior, that she had already had enough fights to last a lifetime. She tried to draw a calming breath and was poised to walk away when the first girl shoved her.

That was too much.

Seta shoved back and lunged at the girl, knocking her to the ground. Seta punched her in the mouth. "Next time you want to call somebody a name, you might want to think twice," she said, slamming the girl's head to the pavement.

The girl's friend jumped on Seta's back, knocking her to the ground. They double- teamed her, one punching her in the face, the other in her stomach.

Seta struggled to climb from under the pile when a third person appeared. Only this person wasn't hitting Seta, she was hitting the other girls.

The first girl yelled in angry surprise at the outsider, who punched her hard in the stomach. The first girl doubled over, crying. Seta punched the other girl and stepped away. Seta breathed hard, her hair all over her head and her shirt askew.

She looked at her savior. It was Diana.

The house was quiet when Seta opened the door. An eerie feeling sent a chill through her, but she shook it off. Poppy must have had to work late. "Grammy, I'm home," Seta called, opening the refrigerator. She looked around quickly and took a swig out of the milk carton. She wiped her mouth with the back of her hand and put the carton back in the refrigerator.

That's strange, she thought as she looked at the stove. Nothing was cooking and the stove looked like it hadn't been used all day. "Grammy?"

Seta's eyes took in the empty kitchen. Something wasn't right. Grammy was never gone when she got home from school. Maybe she was in the bathroom.

"Grammy?" Seta walked slowly down the hallway. She quickly smoothed her hair back in place and made sure her shirt was intact. The bathroom door was open, so she knew she wasn't in there. She peeked into her grandparents' room. Relief coursed through her when she saw her grandmother lying across the bed. That was before she remembered her grandmother hardly ever took naps.

"Grammy, are you sick?" Seta tiptoed to her grandmother and shook her. Nothing happened. She shook Barbara a little harder. "Grammy!"

Barbara was cool to the touch. Seta leaned in to feel or hear her breathing but could sense nothing. Seta began shaking her fiercely. "Grammy, Grammy, wake up!" She looked around frantically. Something was wrong with her grandmother.

Seta ran to the kitchen and grabbed the telephone. She punched in 9-1-1.

"Nine-one-one, what is your emergency?"

"My grandmother isn't breathing! Please, get somebody over here, quick!" Seta screamed the words.

"Ma'am, please tell me what exactly is going on with your grandmother," the operator's voice was firm.

Seta spoke in a hurried burst, her words tripping over each other as they spilled from her mouth. She rattled off the address and hung up. She ran back to Barbara. She was in the same position as before.

Seta cradled her grandmother in her arms and rocked her back and forth. Silent tears fell from her eyes. "Grammy, please don't leave me," she said softly. "Please."

The paramedics found her sitting on the edge of the bed, the grandmother in the teenager's arms. They pried Barbara away from Seta. One of them looked at Seta with a sad expression, but that was it. Seta knew taking her to the hospital was no use. Still, she let them take her away. Seta didn't go with them. She just sat on the bed, rocking.

That was how her grandfather found her an hour later.

"Seta, baby, what's the matter?" Phillip wiped his hands on his pants. Dirt from the produce he had stacked in bins at the grocery store stained the front of his clothes. He looked around. "Where is your grandma?"

Seta kept rocking.

"Seta?" Phillip touched her gently on her shoulder. She continued to rock and stare straight ahead.

Phillip looked around and repeated his question. "Seta, tell me where your grandma is."

Still rocking, she uttered the one word. She didn't take her eyes off whatever distant thing at which she was staring. "Gone."

Phillip grew uneasy. "What do you mean?"

Seta's voice was a dull monotone. "She's dead, Poppy."

Phillip stood still. It felt like his heart stopped beating in his chest. It couldn't be. "When?" He lowered himself on the bed and put his elbows to his knees.

"I don't know. I just got here from school and found her. She was lying on the bed. The paramedics took her, but I know she's dead. I just know it."

Chapter 16

Seta was right. Barbara died of a heart attack. Her heart had been working too hard, at least according to what Seta could gather from eavesdropping on her aunt's whispered telephone conversation. Barbara had stopped taking some of her medications. When Seta found out, she was sure it was because of the expense. One medication was to thin Barbara's blood, another to address heart disease—which Seta hadn't known about—and another was to regulate her blood pressure. The doctor said if he had known, he could have prescribed something less expensive or could have told her which medications she couldn't stop taking. Seta's eyes flashed with anger. How could he have not known her grandmother was struggling? *He probably prescribed the most expensive medicine he could find,* she thought.

Seta tried her best to comfort her grandfather. He sat around in silence that first night without Barbara. Seta had fixed him a sandwich, but he had waved it off. She urged him to make the funeral arrangements, but Phillip couldn't make a decision on a casket, on a date, on a time. Therefore, Augusta took over.

She set the date, reserved the church and wrote out what should be included on the obituary. Augusta stayed at the house, cleaning and cooking. She had never seen her father in such a still, quiet state. He had never been a rowdy person, still his absolute silence made her uneasy. She turned to her mother's remedy for any illness.

"Daddy, do you want me to bake you a cake?"

Phillip was notorious for his sweet tooth. He shook his head. "No, nobody can bake a cake like your mama."

"I can use her recipe," Augusta said. "It's in her big recipe book."

Phillip wasn't interested. Nobody could cook like his Barbara. A half century had come to this. She was gone and had taken with her his identity, his frame of reference, his world. Aside from his time away at war and rail yard work in the early days of their marriage, Phillip had never spent more than a day away from Barbara. He couldn't sleep that first night. He missed the way she always coughed first thing in the morning and the way she looked at him when she was joking.

Phillip was lost.

People crowded into Mount Bethel. Many knew Sister Barbara and they came from all around to pay their respects. Her work on the usher board and the deaconess board was lauded. Her leadership in the choir and the way she had planned the last choir anniversary all were applauded. Beulah Montgomery, with her wide, gold-trimmed hat, started shouting. Rev. Franklin's voice rose and fell as he extolled Barbara's virtues. The choir moaned a stirring rendition of "Swing Low, Sweet Chariot" in soulful tones. By the time they finished, tears streamed down the faces of half those there.

The pastor led a call and response that reminded Seta of a farmer calling to mooing cows. The rise and fall of the congregants' voices sounded almost like they were in pain as they half sang, half moaned, "I love the Lord, he heard my cry, I-I-I—"

Augusta dabbed at her eyes with one of her mother's embroidered handkerchiefs and fanned Seta with a fan that had a giant picture of Martin Luther King, Jr., on one side and the name of a funeral home on the other.

Except for when she passed to view the body, Seta's eyes remained cast down. She fidgeted with her already short fingernails and chewed her lip. She wouldn't cry because she knew her grandmother wouldn't like it. She swallowed hard to move the golf ball out of her throat, but it wouldn't budge.

When Seta turned to walk out the church, she saw her friends in a row in the center of the church. Jessica gave her a tiny smile and waved. Amy dabbed at her eyes. Diana was looking down at her lap. Mike sat in a row behind them. Mrs. Bradshaw gave her a tight smile of encouragement.

Seta's eyes locked with Robert's. Her breath caught in her throat. She forced herself not to react. A small part of her was happy to see him, but that happiness was immediately replaced by a dark anger and resentment. How dare he come to her church, to her grandmother's funeral after what he had done? He wasn't a part of this family. Her eyes moved to the person next to him and Seta almost lost it. It was that woman, his new wife, sitting there smugly, with her hand resting on his thigh. Seta's eyes narrowed and returned to her father's face.

He looked away.

She refused to look at him as she walked past, her back as straight as she could make it.

Robert saw Seta before she saw him. She was tall and her hair was pulled back off her face with a clip. She wore a crisply ironed black suit that only highlighted her slender build. A tiny cross that dangled on a necklace around her neck was her only jewelry. He wasn't sure about attending the funeral but knew he had to. For as much as he disliked Barbara, she was his wife's mother. He knew Rose would want him to be there. Besides, it would give him a chance to see his child from afar.

Besides, something wouldn't let him stay away. For as hateful as Barbara had been to him, he knew she loved Rose, just as he did. And all the hard feelings of the past seemed to dull for Robert. He had been experiencing so many new emotions lately. Maybe those sermons he had pretended not to hear had sunk in. His anger toward God was even lessening, though he wasn't ready to go there.

He could only deal with so much at a time. And now, now was about Seta.

Seta's eyes locked with his for a second. Hope leapt to his chest. Maybe she would let him make it up to her. Robert wasn't sure if he was ready to be a real father to her. Still, he wanted her to be a part of his life now. Being with Berrie and Bennie made him realize how much he missed being a part of his own daughter's life. And Barbara's death was a reality check. Another connection to his Rose had been severed.

He saw Seta visibly stiffen when her eyes raked over Lola. He groaned inwardly and shifted in his seat. He hadn't wanted Lola to come, but she insisted. She said she would be there to support him. Robert knew she came only to watch over him and to remind him that though he was at the funeral of his former wife's mother, his current wife was only an inch away. A muscle jumped in Robert's jaw as he clenched his teeth under Seta's gaze.

If he could just talk to Seta, maybe he could explain away his behavior and maybe she would allow him to be a part of her life. A nagging voice of guilt taunted him though.

Why should she let him in after he had acted in such a way? In that instance when their eyes locked, he saw a hostility so fierce he was forced to look away from the burn of her gaze.

Her back was straight as she brushed past him. He wanted to reach out to touch her, but didn't dare. She looked just like her mother, only with black hair instead of sandy, red strands. She was tall and regal and seemed to float across the room.

Finally, it was the turn for Robert's row to file out of the church. Everyone paced to the graveyard. Augusta's two boys, grown and tall now, with families of their own, stood next to her. Augusta stood next to Phillip and next to him, Seta. Robert stood at the back of the crowd.

As the pastor's words came out strong and firm, with a touch of sadness, Robert's mind went back to a funeral fifteen years before. He glanced to his right and could see Rose's grave. The flowers he had placed there last week were gone. He drew in a deep breath.

It was time he made up with her child.

Seta returned to school the following Monday. Nobody said anything about the fight. Her teacher told her not to worry about her research paper. David though, didn't have the same thoughts. "Yeah, I heard about your grandma," he said, shifting anxiously from one foot to the other. "Sorry to hear that. But, uh, what's up with my research paper?"

Seta sighed. She hadn't thought anymore about David or his paper. She put her backpack down on the floor and unzipped it. She handed him the pages. "Hey, thanks, baby." He let out a short laugh and raced off.

Seta stared behind him, and then shook her head. Guys were so insensitive. The only one who was decent at all was her grandfather . . . and maybe Mike. Mike? Where had that thought come from? Seta frowned as she zipped her backpack and walked to class.

"Seta, I was sorry to hear about your grandmother," someone said to her left. She didn't feel like talking, but turned to see who was speaking to her. It was Hannah, the pastor's daughter.

"Yeah, thanks," Seta said and turned away, continuing to walk.

"She was a really nice lady." The girl ran to keep up with her.

Seta paused. "Yeah, okay, thanks," she said.

The girl was walking beside her now. "If you ever want to talk or pray or anything, just let me know," Hannah said. Her eyes searched Seta's hopefully.

What a weirdo, Seta thought. "Yeah, I'll do that."

The girl seemed to wait awkwardly for a moment. Seta glanced at her watch. "Yeah, well, I've got to get out of here or I'm going to be late for class."

The girl opened her mouth, then closed it again. "Sure. I'll see you at church."

Seta was sitting with Jessica and Amy at lunch when Hannah walked by. "Hey, I hear her mom still combs her hair and picks out her clothes," Amy whispered loudly.

"She looks like it too," Jessica said. Hannah's hair was in pigtails and her ankle-length dress was a dull blue and gray.

Hannah looked around for a table at which to sit. Her eyes caught Seta's with a question, but Seta looked away. Hannah's shoulders seemed to slump as she walked to an empty table and pulled out a chair. She opened her milk carton and took a sip.

Seta felt a moment of guilt but brushed it off. It wasn't her job to be that girl's friend.

* * *

That afternoon Seta saw Diana in between classes. She hadn't thanked her for helping her that day when the two girls attacked her. "Hey, Diana, hold up," Seta called out

Diana halted. Seta caught up to her and the two began walking together. Silence dominated the space between them. Seta spoke first. "Uh, I just wanted to say thanks for your help last week. With the fight," she said. Diana was the last person she would have thought to help her. Even now, it was as if Diana didn't like her all that much.

Diana smiled slightly. "Well, I couldn't just stand there and let you get beat up," she said. "You are my friend, after all."

Seta looked at Diana in wonderment. After all the hard times Diana had given her, she just knew Diana couldn't stand her. Diana must have read her face. She shrugged. "Well, I didn't always feel that way. But that was before I knew you. I used to think you were stuck-up. Now I know you're not. You're all right."

A lump settled in Seta's throat. Acceptance felt good.

"I'm going to take the children to the park," Robert told Lola Saturday afternoon. Lola smiled. She was happy he loved her children, but a tiny sliver of jealousy slithered through her being. Why couldn't he love her as he loved her children? Why couldn't he replace his dead wife with her, just as he had replaced that child of his with Bennie and Beryl?

"That's great," she said. "I hope you have a wonderful time. Don't feed them any junk because I'll have dinner ready when you return."

Robert kissed her on the cheek. "I won't," he said.

"Come on, children, let's head out!" he called up the stairs. A moment later, Bennie and Beryl raced down the stairs.

"I get to sit in the front!" Beryl called.

Bennie screwed up his face. "No, I want to sit next to Daddy! You sat next to him last time!"

Robert laughed. "Hey, there is plenty of me to go around," he said, tickling Bennie, who giggled uncontrollably. Beryl didn't want to be left out of the fun, so she nudged into the fray. Robert gathered them both in a hug. They walked out the house, laughing and chatting, engrossed in each other and forgetting to say good-bye to Lola.

Robert stood between the swings that held Bennie and Beryl. He alternately pushed each of them, each calling to go higher and higher. He pushed them but was careful not to make them go too high. He didn't want the children to fall or hurt themselves.

As he responded to their giggles and chatter, that feeling he had earlier washed over him again. He knew it wasn't right that he had cast off another child long ago. He knew he had to find a way to make it up to her.

He was finally ready.

Augusta sat at the table with Phillip and Seta. Seta's arms were crossed in front of her and her jaw jutted out stubbornly. Augusta tried again. "Seta, I really think it would be good for you to come and live with me for a while, just until Daddy gets things together here."

Seta shook her head. "No, I'm not leaving Poppy."

Augusta sighed. "Seta, Daddy needs some time to adjust to living on his own right now. He doesn't need to have to worry about a teenager, and I'm happy to have you come live with me."

Seta looked to her grandfather for some guidance, but he said nothing. He stared at his hands. She tried another approach. "Auntie, I am fifteen, almost sixteen years old. I can take care of myself. I won't be any trouble here. If anything, I'll take care of him. Poppy needs me."

Augusta shook her head. Her sister's daughter could be so difficult. "Seta, listen to me. You're a growing girl. I'm sure there will be things going on in your life where you will need to talk to a woman. I want to be there for you. You can come and visit your grandfather anytime."

Augusta knew how Phillip doted on the girl. Augusta didn't think her father would be a strong disciplinarian, nor would he have insight into teenage problems or concerns. Besides, he was in shock and needed to have time to recover, without having to look after Seta. Augusta knew Seta could be a handful—Mama used to tell her about all the fights and the attitudes. That fast tail girl needed structure.

"I don't want to live with you," Seta's voice was firm. Her aunt was nice, but she could also be tough. Besides, she always had all those grandchildren running around. Who wanted to deal with that all day?

Augusta raised an eyebrow and cast a glance at her father, who was still silent. "It's not always about what you want," she said with steel in her voice.

"Well, it's not always about what you want either." Seta wasn't backing down.

Augusta had a trump card. "Well, then, you can go live with your father. I spoke with him yesterday. He said he'd love to have you."

The silence was thick. Seta sat up straighter in her chair. "I would rather freeze on the street than go live with him," she said, her voice just as steely as her aunt's.

Augusta smiled in victory. "Well, I guess it's settled then. If you don't want to live there, you'll live with me."

Phillip spoke for the first time. "Leave the child be, Gussie," using the nickname he had given Augusta as a child.

Augusta cast a dark look at Seta, who gloated, then turned

to her father. Her voice softened. "Daddy, I'm just trying to help you out."

"We'll be fine here," he said, pushing his chair back from the table.

Augusta jumped up, following closely at her father's heels. "But, Daddy—"

Phillip shooed her away. "Gussie, the child will be fine. She's 'bout grown anyhow."

Augusta tried to reason with her father. "But, Daddy, that's just it. She's not grown."

Phillip wasn't listening. He closed the bathroom door behind him.

Seta tried to contain her smile of victory. Still, it tugged up the corners of her mouth. Augusta hastily gathered her purse and keys and left in a huff.

Chapter 17

"Come on, Poppy, you have to eat something," Seta pleaded. Phillip sat in his favorite recliner, staring listlessly in space. He still had on his dirty work clothes.

He waved the girl off. "I'm not hungry, baby," he said. Seta pouted. She had tried fixing something she knew he liked, pepper steak, but the chunks of meat were black and tough, and the rice stuck to the pot. She hadn't spent much time in the kitchen growing up. Her grandmother said her job wasn't to be a cook, so she didn't have to learn. Her grandmother told her to focus on her dreams instead—her basketball and her studies so she could go to a good college and become an attorney.

At the time, Seta had been glad Barbara hadn't made her learn to cook. Now, though, without her grandmother, Seta wished she had at least learned the basics. She did know how to boil macaroni, and rice too—though you couldn't tell by today's offering—but most other things were beyond her.

Seta plunked her grandfather's plate down. She tried to

saw into the meat, but dropped the knife after a moment. Maybe it was good he wasn't hungry.

As Seta dumped the plate in the trash, she felt a pang of guilt. Her grandmother hated to waste food. At the thought of Barbara, a huge sadness washed over Seta. She knew she had been difficult at times, but she hoped her grandmother knew she loved her.

Seta wondered why God took everybody away from her. What had she done to deserve such treatment? She tried to erase the thought. She could hear her grandmother's voice in her ear talking about "blasphemous thoughts," or some such. People shouldn't question God, her grandmother always said.

Seta sat on the bar stool at the counter. She knew her grandmother would want her to take care of her grandfather. And to think Augusta tried to tear them apart. Seta grunted. There was no way she was leaving her Poppy.

Her mouth hardened into a straight line in regards to what else Augusta had said. Robert wanted her to live with him. Seta didn't believe that. Even if he did want her to live with him—after all this time—she didn't want to. She admitted there was a time when she would have gladly given anything to be able to live with him. Not anymore, though. Not after the way he had treated her.

Seta stopped by the grocery store her grandfather worked at for some boxed dinners. Those would be rather easy. According to the package, all she had to do was put them in the microwave. Maybe her grandfather would eat then.

She was closing the freezer when she looked up and stopped. "Oh, Daddy, you are so silly!" the girl said and swatted at the man. The man looked up. His eyes locked with Seta's.

He froze but quickly regained his composure. "Hello," he spoke.

Robert was amazed that his voice sounded so steady when he felt quivery inside. He had been caught off guard when he rounded the corner to come face to face with the daughter he had locked out of his life. His new daughter leaned into him. Her skinny arms hugged him around the waist.

Seta's eyes went from one to the other. Her breath caught in her throat and it was like she couldn't take in any more air. Her blood rushed in her ears and her palms were sweaty. She could hear her grandmother's voice in her mind telling her to stand straight and tall. So she did. With everything in her, she managed to pull her spinal cord straight. She began pushing her buggy past the man and the girl.

"Daddy, who is that?" the girl asked. She looked to be about ten or eleven, with a neat ponytail pulled to the side and bangs. She spoke to the man with obvious affection. Her clothes were nicer than any Seta had had at that age, Seta noticed in that long moment. Her shoes were even name brand.

Robert touched the child on her arm without looking away from Seta. "Shhh."

"But, Daddy!" the girl's whine rose an octave. "Who is that? And can we hurry? The ice cream is going to melt."

Robert reached out to touch Seta's arm as she walked past. He needed to touch her, to say something to her. He placed his hand on her forearm. Seta stared at him with a gaze so cold he recoiled.

"Daddy . . ." the girl's whine was insistent.

The word ran around and around Seta's consciousness. All she heard was the girl's word, over and over. *Daddy. Daddy. Daddy.*

Robert tried again. He reached out his hand, but Seta

jerked away. "Don't you dare touch me," she said in a low whisper through her teeth.

Robert was dumbfounded. He knew she would be angry, but he hadn't thought she would talk to him with such hostility. He remembered a time not too long ago when she had pleaded for him to take her home with him.

Seta wheeled her buggy forward. With as much dignity as she could muster to legs that felt like stiff and wooden planks, she walked away.

Seta was seething by the time she left the grocery store. How dare he bring his new daughter into her grand-daddy's grocery store! How dare he think he could touch her and flaunt his new family in her face! He looked like he wanted to say something, but there were no words in the English language that would come from him that she would want to hear. None. She had tried to get him to love her and now all she could do was hate him.

Seta climbed into the car. A dent on the front fender spoke of her inexperience. Other than that, she had kept the car in decent shape, though the seats were worn and the upholstery tattered in places. She didn't think her grand-father would even know she had taken it. She tried to crank it, but nothing happened. She tried once more, still nothing. She fumed silently, hopped out, and lifted the hood.

She had learned a few things about cars from hanging out with her basketball buddies. She looked around for someone who might be able to give her a jump with some jumper cables.

"Hi, you need some help?" a voice asked her. She turned.

Standing before her was a guy a tad taller than six feet, with skin the color of dark chocolate and piercing black eyes. She could tell by the way that his shirt hung on his chest he worked out. His starched pants didn't do much to hide a trim waist and muscular thighs.

"As a matter of fact, I do," Seta said. She felt shy suddenly, but pushed those thoughts away. He was just here to help her get her vehicle started.

The guy rubbed his hands together. "Let's see," he said.

"I think it's my battery," Seta said softly.

The guy nodded. "You're probably right. Wait right here. I have some cables in my car," he said. When he turned his back to go to his car, Seta hurriedly brushed her hair down and smoothed the front of her yellow shirt. A moment later, he was back.

"I hate to see you get dirty," Seta said, looking at his linen shirt.

He waved her off. "Not a big deal. That's why God made dry cleaners." He smiled to reveal beautiful, white teeth that had a tiny gap between the two front ones.

"My name is Gabe," he said.

"Oh, I'm so rude," she said, rolling her eyes. "My name is Seta."

"Interesting name. Where does it come from?" he asked as he hooked the cable to her battery and pulled it to his own.

Seta's smile dimmed, but she regained it. "Oh, I don't know," she lied. She couldn't very well tell him the truth.

He worked with the cable and got inside his car. A moment later, he called to her. "Okay, try to start it."

The car started immediately. The guy strolled over to her window. Seta smiled. "Oh, thank you. I don't have any money to pay you," she said.

Gabe smiled. "No, that's all right. But I can think of another way you can repay me. How about dinner?"

Seta's eyes widened. He had to be at least twenty years of age. "Oh, uh . . ."

Gabe cocked his head to one side. "You're not going to deprive me of the company of a beautiful lady, are you? Not after I came to your rescue?"

Seta fidgeted and stared at her shoes. She hated it when people called her beautiful because she knew she wasn't. "I can't—"

She stopped in mid-sentence. This guy didn't know her house rules, no boyfriends or dates till she was seventeen. Besides, she'd be seventeen soon enough. She was her own woman. "Sure. Here is my phone number."

She scribbled her number on a sheet of paper he produced.

Gabe tucked it into his shirt pocket. "I'll call you. Be careful out here, Seta."

As Seta drove home, she felt a strange sense of elation. A man had called her beautiful. And he acted as if he liked her. She giggled. Maybe he did.

Seta heated two frozen dinners in the microwave. She plunked them down on the table, then thought better. Maybe she would make things look a little homier. She was no culinary wizard, but even she could dump food onto a plate. She went into the cabinet to get some of the everyday dishes. She scraped food onto a plate for her grandfather and another onto a plate for herself.

"Poppy, why don't you come and eat?" she called to Phillip, who sat slumped in his recliner. The news was on, but he wasn't paying attention. Phillip didn't say anything. Seta gently shook his shoulder. "Poppy, I made you some peas, corn, mashed potatoes, and steak."

"Okay." Phillip nodded absently but didn't move.

Seta groaned. "Poppy, you've got to eat. I'm trying really hard to take care of you, but you've got to help me."

Phillip had been to work that day in the same clothes he had worn the past two days. Dirt from the produce had taken up residence underneath his fingernails and his shirt sported stains that Seta couldn't even begin to identify.

"Poppy, you're going to have to get a bath tonight. And

I'm going to wash your clothes," Seta said. Barbara had shown her how to do laundry and some other chores, though nothing in the kitchen.

"Okay." Phillip nodded, but again, he didn't budge.

Seta stomped back into the kitchen. She couldn't make him eat. She picked up her own plate and stuck the fork in her mouth. She didn't much feel like eating either.

The knocking at the door startled Seta. She glanced at the clock on the wall. It was nine o'clock at night. Who would be at their door? She swallowed a groan as she hoped it wasn't her aunt. She was in no mood to see Augusta. She didn't think Augusta was in the mood to see her either, but who else could it be?

Seta peeked out the lace curtain over the window in the door. Her eyes widened. It was Diana. She opened the door. "Hi," Seta said, surprise in her voice.

Diana shifted from one foot to the other. Her hands were shoved into her pockets. "Hi," she said. "I was just in the neighborhood and thought I'd stop by to see how you're doing. Since, well, since . . ." She didn't want to say, since Seta's grandmother had died, but how else could she phrase it? Seta instinctively knew.

She stepped aside to let Diana in. "I'm fine," Seta said. Jessica had called her a couple of times, still she was happy to see Diana. She hadn't heard from Amy though.

Diana stayed for a few minutes, chatting about basketball and school. Diana was still trying on this newfound acceptance of Seta. When Diana stood, signaling she was ready to go, Seta thanked her for stopping by. Diana gave Seta an awkward hug and left.

Seta felt so alone. At night, when she was away from her friends and off the basketball court, she lay in bed and fingered that picture she had turned to so long ago. It had been years since she had pulled out her mother's likeness, but these days, she needed it. Barbara had been the closest thing she had had to a mother, and now even she was gone.

Seta felt hollow inside, like something was missing. She couldn't comfort her grandfather because he wouldn't talk to her. Even if he would talk to her, she didn't know what she would say. Her heart ached. Why had God taken her Grammy? Why had God taken her mother? Why had God taken her father's love?

She quickly corrected her thoughts. She didn't need her father anyway. He was as good as dead to her. After all, that's the way he wanted it.

Seta's sixteenth birthday passed without much fanfare. She didn't mind though. With her grandmother gone, it didn't seem like a day worth celebrating. Barbara had always made a big to-do out of such things, no matter how tight times were. Seta smiled a little when she thought of her last birthday, with a party at the house and a beautiful homemade cake.

She thought her grandfather might remember, but he didn't say anything. So, neither did she. She didn't want to seem like she was searching for a gift. It stung a little that he would forget, but she knew he was wrapped in his own grief. Her aunt hadn't said much to her since that day in the kitchen, so Seta knew she would get nothing from her.

She checked the mail when she arrived home from school. She found two envelopes addressed to her. She turned them over. One was from her aunt. The other had no return address on it.

She smiled, so her aunt was speaking to her again—or at least, writing. Seta tore open the envelope. It contained a card and a twenty-dollar bill. Just what she needed. She shoved the money into her pocket. Curious, she gingerly pulled open the other envelope.

In it was a delicate card embossed with fancy calligraphy on a flowery paper. "To a beautiful daughter, on her Sweet Sixteen. Love, your dad."

Seta dropped the card in disgust and traipsed to the kitchen. "Love, your dad? Whatever!"

She snatched open the refrigerator door and scoured the shelves for something to eat. Her grandfather wouldn't be home for another two hours. She wondered what she should fix for dinner—not that he would eat it.

I need a drink, Seta thought as she pulled out meat and bread to make sandwiches. She would get something from her beer stash in her room. She could see her grandmother's disapproving glance in her mind's eye but ignored it. Grammy just didn't understand all the pressures. Trying to stay on top of her basketball game so she could get a good scholarship, doing her best to ignore the hateful words of girls at school, and fighting against her father's rejection was all a bit much to handle sober.

She sat on the floor next to her bed and gulped down half a can of the beer that she hid under her bed. It didn't taste all that great. Still, it took the edge off the knife pricks that seemed to jab at her insides. "Happy birthday to me," she halfheartedly sang. She leaned her head against the wall. The gray, January sky reflected her mood.

She sat there for about thirty minutes, then wiped her mouth with the back of her hand. She needed to get to her homework. Besides, it wouldn't do to drink too much of this stuff. She hadn't gotten where she was by getting drunk.

She was doing homework when the doorbell rang. A moment later, before she could get to the door, keys jingled in the doorknob. Augusta stepped into the house. "Happy birthday," she said.

Seta didn't know what to make of her aunt's appearance. Augusta's expression was sour. *I guess she's still mad about the other day*, Seta thought.

"Thanks for the card," Seta said, jerking her head toward the table where it lay.

Augusta smiled tightly. "You're welcome," she said. "You didn't think I'd forget your birthday, did you?"

Seta swallowed her retort. "No, Auntie."

She didn't feel like being bothered with Augusta today, especially if she was going to act all sour. Seta bowed her head to her homework, making it clear she was busy.

Augusta ignored Seta's obvious attempt at business. "So, how has your day been?" Augusta eyed the half-eaten sandwich.

"Fine. I'm just doing homework," Seta said, praying Augusta would leave. She didn't feel like being fussed at or interrogated.

Augusta sat down at the table. She paused for a second and then peered at Seta. "I smell something," she said. Seta sat absolutely still. "If I didn't know any better, I'd swear I smelled alcohol. But I know Daddy doesn't drink."

Seta hunched her shoulders. "I don't smell anything."

Augusta refocused on the reason for her visit. "I'm sure it's nothing. Anyway, why don't you finish that, and I'll take you to dinner for your birthday."

Seta looked up, surprised. Augusta rolled her eyes and smiled. "Don't look so surprised. I'm not the Wicked Witch of the West, you know. So, where do you want to go?"

"Well, I really can't. Poppy will be home in a little while."

Augusta waved that off. "Oh, I called Daddy at work and told him I was going to come by and get you for a while. He said that's fine. So, where do you want to go?"

A bit of excitement inched into Seta's heart. Maybe her birthday would turn out all right, after all. She had tried to tell herself it wasn't important, but really, she was glad someone wanted to do something special with her today. She missed her grandmother and hoped the outing with her aunt would take her mind off the loneliness.

"What about Little Italy?" she asked.

Augusta nodded. "If that's where you want to go. Go get changed and we can go."

Seta was wearing warm-ups. She wanted to argue that she didn't need to change, but one look at her prissy aunt, and she knew she would lose that argument. Her mother's younger sister was somewhere in her mid-forties, Seta knew. Augusta had always been slender, though she had put on a little weight in the last couple of years. Even that weight didn't make her fat though. She had the body of a "real woman" as Barbara would say.

Augusta hadn't turned out to be the doctor Barbara would have liked, but she was a principal at a private elementary school across town. She was fond of wearing skirts and blouses. Today was no exception. Tiny pearls adorned her ears. Her wedding ring was on one hand and on the other was a birthstone ring.

Barbara had instilled in her the virtues of being a lady. You wouldn't ever find Augusta out in public dressed in anything less than a perfect ensemble. She didn't use improper English and frowned upon people who did.

Seta went to her bedroom to find an outfit that would pass muster. She came back with black pants and a pink shirt. Augusta nodded with approval.

The two drove to the restaurant in relative silence. Seta didn't know what to talk to her aunt about. She rarely saw Augusta smile and knew they didn't have anything in common.

Once they placed their order, Augusta dug into her purse and pulled out a plain, white envelope. She handed it to Seta.

Seta curiously tore open the top. Another birthday card? She liked cards, but jeez.

However, there was no card inside. She pulled out the

lined paper. She unfolded the letter and saw the opening. "Dear Joy,"

Seta frowned and looked at her aunt. "This isn't for me. It's for somebody named Joy."

Augusta smiled. "It is for you. Just read it."

Seta began reading with a quizzical expression. She had never seen handwriting so pretty.

"Dear Joy," she started. "*Today is your sixteenth birthday. I know you're a beautiful young woman, inside and out. I just know it. It breaks my heart that I'm not there with you, but I hope that I'm somewhere in your heart.*"

Seta didn't get it. What was this all about? She looked up at her aunt with a confused expression. Augusta gestured for her to finish reading.

Seta looked back down at the paper and continued reading to herself. "*It's so hard for me to write this, knowing that it must be even harder for you to read it. I tried to think when would be the best time for you to get this letter, and I decided it had to be your Sweet sixteen. Every girl's sixteenth birthday should be special. And every mother wants to be a part of it.*"

Seta's mouth fell open as realization washed over her consciousness. She looked up at her aunt. "This is from my mother?"

Augusta swallowed hard and blinked away tears. She dabbed at the corner of her eye with one of her mother's handkerchiefs. "Yes."

Seta hungrily read the rest. "*I just want to let you know I am so proud to be your mother. If only for the briefest of moments that I got to hold you when you were born. I am so happy. I hope you know how special you are and how loved. You were the missing key to my happiness. My life was not complete until I had you.*

"*I'm only sorry that I am not there to share that with you and to shower love on you every single day of your life.*"

Tears streamed freely down Seta's face. She could hear her grandmother's voice telling her to stop all that nonsense, but she didn't care. She didn't even bother to wipe away the tears. She held onto the letter, her heart pounding in her chest.

"I prayed that God would give you to me for so long and now, he's finally answered my prayers. But I think he got the last laugh. He gave me you, but he won't give you me. I don't think I'm going to make it out of this hospital, Joy, baby. I don't think I'm going to be around to share in your scrapes and bruises, your first loves and the great things you do.

"But I want you to know that no matter where you go or what you do, your mother loves you. She loves you very much and she wants you to know that always. I was so happy when I found out I would have you.

"I want you to always do your best and to always believe in yourself. You are smart, gifted and beautiful. You are precious."

The waiter came with their meals. Seta snatched the letter off the table. She didn't want any food to get on it. Angelo, the waiter, looked at her curiously but didn't say anything. He plunked down her plate and Augusta's.

"Do you need anything else? Maybe a tissue?" he asked pointedly.

Augusta spoke up. "We're fine. Thank you, young man." She had on her principal's voice.

The waiter shrugged and disappeared.

Seta didn't have an appetite. She wanted to get back to her mother's words. Augusta slid the plate out the way. Seta held the letter in *both hands again.*

"Well, baby, if I know your father, he had a hard time getting used to the idea of me being gone. But I know he's taking good care of you. Please take care of him too. He's a great man. Take care of your daddy for me. Even when he makes you mad—and he will make you mad, trust me—love him and let him know you'll be there. He needs you and you need him.

"Well, Joy, I guess I'll close this letter now. Happy birthday, baby. And always remember that I love you. You are truly my shiny Joy."

The letter was signed *Mama* with a flourish.

Seta sat speechless. She finally looked up at her aunt. "But, Auntie, how?"

Augusta took a sip of water. Her voice was husky with emotion. "Your mama knew she wasn't going to leave that hospital. She called me into her room and gave me two letters. One for your daddy, and this one for you. She told me to give it to you on your sixteenth birthday. So, I've kept it all these years. That was my big sister, always full of surprises. She thought of everything."

Seta sniffed. Her grandmother would surely roll over in her grave if she let another tear fall. She wiped her eyes with her sleeve. Her mama had left her a letter. A love letter. And to think, she thought nobody would remember her birthday.

Chapter 18

That night, Seta traced in wonderment the outline of the woman's face in the Polaroid picture she had held onto for years. On that night, she couldn't get enough of the woman's face. Nor could she get enough of her words. Seta sat on her bed, alternately staring at the face and reading the words over and over.

Her mama loved her. Her mama wanted her.

For the first time in her sixteen years, Seta felt that maybe she was special. Her mama had told her so and had even taken care to leave her a birthday present. Her mama loved her.

The words echoed in Seta's consciousness. If she never got another birthday present as long as she lived, that was all right with her. Nothing could top the words her mother had penned for eternity.

Her mother said she was smart and beautiful. Her mother wanted her to do her best.

Seta resolved that she would.

* * *

"Poppy, what are you doing?"

Phillip was walking through the house, sticking his head into each room. He looked around, a thoughtful expression on his face. His shoulders slumped forward and he walked with a seemingly perpetual bend in his back. He shuffled through the house, his slippers snagging the carpet.

"Poppy?" Seta cocked her head to the side and waited on a response.

Phillip stuck his head in the bathroom. "I'm looking for your grandmother. She didn't tell me she was going out. She knows I don't like it when she just goes out and doesn't tell me."

"What are you talking about?" Seta was confused.

Phillip looked at his granddaughter as if she were ten years old again. "Your grandmother. Don't you know who your grandmother is?"

"Yes, but . . ." Seta knew something was definitely not right here. Didn't he know that Grammy wasn't here anymore?

Phillip stuck his head in Seta's bedroom. "Well, she's not there either." He glanced at his watch. The belt on his bathrobe hung loosely around his waist. His T-shirt peeked through the open top. "I guess I'll just sit in my easy chair and wait for her."

Seta didn't know what to say, so she did the only thing she could think to do. "Okay, Poppy, You wait right there," she said softly and patted his hand. Her eyes misted as she choked back the tears.

"Hello?" Seta caught the phone on the fifth ring. Her grandfather was sleeping.

"Is this Seta?" the voice on the other end asked.

"Uh, who is *this?*" she challenged.

A sexy laugh came over the phone line. "Feisty. I like that," the male's voice was soft and silky. "This is Gabe."

Seta frowned for a second, then the name registered. The guy with the linen shirt. She smoothed her hair self-consciously, even though he couldn't see her.

"Oh, hi, Gabe. How are you?"

"I'm doing great, babe. You were just on my mind, so I thought I'd call and see what you were up to," he said.

Seta lowered her voice. "Nothing . . . just getting ready to go to bed."

Gabe laughed suggestively. "Hmm. I can dig that. You want some company?"

Seta giggled. "No, I don't think so."

Gabe feigned disappointment. "Oh, darn. Well, I had to try. So, how about that dinner you promised me?"

"Oh, I promised you, did I?" Seta said.

"Well, not exactly, but I was hoping I could make you think you did," he said.

Seta liked him already. She twirled a strand of hair around her forefinger.

"So, you going to let me take you out?" he asked.

Seta thought. Her mother's letter came to mind. Though she didn't really know her mother, she had a feeling Rose wouldn't want her going out with a guy so much older than she. "I don't know. . . ." Seta said hesitantly.

"What do you mean?" Gabe asked.

"Well, I'm only sixteen," she said. "I'm not allowed to date."

Gabe laughed. "Oh, that's easy. I thought you were going to tell me something hard. It doesn't have to be a date. I just want to see you again."

Seta paused. "So it won't be a date?"

Gabe's voice lowered suggestively. "Baby, it can be whatever you want it to be."

Seta was uncertain. She was trying to be good, for her

mother. Maybe she shouldn't go out with this guy. He did seem nice though. "Well, all right, but only as friends."

She could tell Gabe was smiling when he spoke. "That's fine, baby."

"We always find it easier to blame others for our own situations!" the pastor said, eliciting a heavy "amen" from the congregation.

"But most of the times, if we just look at ourselves, we will realize we are the cause of our own problems!"

"You got that right, preacher!" a deacon called, and a chorus of "amens" erupted.

Robert gulped. He tried to turn his mind to other things, but he couldn't distract himself from the sermon. The pastor's words struck Robert hard. The pastor bellowed about faith and forgiveness, and about not holding grudges. The harder he tried to tune out the words, the more they seemed to sting him. He even found himself finding the scriptural references in the Bible.

I don't know what it was about today, he mused after service ended. He had heard hundreds of sermons, but something about today's seemed to be expressly for him.

As the family drove back home following church, Robert was silent. Maybe God hadn't been the cause of all Robert's problems. *Maybe I should look at myself a bit more*, Robert thought.

He had gone to church all those years before to find his dead wife; and here he was, finally, finding a way to God. *I could have made some different choices in life and could have avoided some of the heartache I've had.*

"Are you okay?" Lola asked.

"Huhn?" Robert asked, glancing at her before returning his eyes to the road as he drove.

"You've been very quiet all the way home," Lola said.

He reached out his hand and touched hers. "I've just had

a lot on my mind," he said. "That sermon . . . it made me think."

He squeezed his wife's hand. "I'm sorry for the way I've treated you."

Tears welled in Lola's eyes and she smiled. "It's all right," she said.

Robert pulled the car into the driveway. He stayed Lola with his hand. "Really, I am truly sorry. I hope you can forgive me."

"I already have," Lola said.

The family climbed out of the car. Robert walked into the house and turned to his wife. "I'll be in my study. I need to make a phone call that's been long overdue."

Lola nodded. She hugged him. "You go do that."

Robert picked up the telephone. It had been years since he had dialed the number, but he still knew it. A familiar voice answered on the third ring. "Hello?"

He drew a deep breath. He imagined all the horrible things that could go wrong—and he knew he would deserve whatever words she had for him. "Hello, Augusta."

The long silence almost made Robert wonder if the phone had gone dead. "Hello, Robert. How can I help you?"

He knew if he didn't say the words now, he'd never say them. "I want to be in my daughter's life."

"Oh, so now you have a daughter? Funny, but I don't recall you acting that way in any of the past fifteen years." The sarcasm was thick.

Robert grimaced but ignored it. "Augusta, please help me get my daughter back."

He knew Augusta was his only hope. She was his link.

"I don't know, Robert." Augusta's voice was unsure. Her mother had told her how Seta had longed for her father to come and rescue her, but those feelings had long given way to a hard emotion Augusta feared may be hate. Hate in the heart of a child could be a torturous thing.

"Augusta, please." Robert hated to come crawling to her, but he swallowed his pride. He was finally ready to do what it took to have a relationship with Seta, even if that meant groveling at her aunt's feet.

"So, why should I help you after the way you've treated that child—your own flesh and blood?" Augusta had picked up on her mother's dislike of Robert.

"Because you know she needs a father."

Augusta let out a derisive laugh. "You call yourself a *father?*"

Robert knew he deserved that. "You're right. I've not acted much like a father. Still, I want to try."

Something in his tone began to thaw the ice around Augusta's heart. She hated to admit it, but she did feel sorry for Robert. She didn't know what it was like to lose a spouse. She could only imagine how she'd feel if she lost her husband.

She made up her mind. "Okay, Robert. I'll see what I can do."

Augusta twirled spaghetti around her fork. Phillip had gone to bed early. Seta sat across the table from her.

"So, how is Daddy doing?" Augusta asked.

Seta quickly searched her aunt's face for any telltale signs that Augusta may know something. "He's fine," Seta said.

Augusta took a sip of tea and dabbed at the corner of her mouth. "Well, he just seems to be sleeping a lot lately," she said. "Maybe I should take him to the doctor."

Seta immediately sat up straight in her chair. "Oh, no!" She softened her tone at Augusta's curious look. "I mean, no, he's all right. He just likes to go to bed early, that's all."

Augusta was quiet for a moment. "I know I don't get by here as often as I should. Work has been so busy for me."

A twinge of guilt nipped at Augusta's consciousness. Truth be told, she was doing a terrible job of making sure

her father and niece were taken care of properly. She ratio-
nalized her absences by reminding herself that Seta was a
very mature girl. And her father was a grown man, after all.
A visit once or twice a week was a good effort, she told herself.

"Oh, that's okay, Auntie," Seta said, smiling reassuringly.
"Poppy takes really good care of me. He makes me go to
bed on time and everything."

For good measure, she added, "He even put me on punishment last week because I got in late from basketball
practice."

Augusta pursed her lips. "You're not being too difficult
for him, are you?"

Seta shook her head. "Oh, no, I didn't even give him a
hard time about the punishment." The lie stumbled out of
her mouth. Seta coughed to cover her uneasiness.

Augusta's cell phone rang. She held up a finger to Seta.
"Hello?" She paused. "Speaking."

Augusta talked about something school related, and then
hung up. She turned her attention back to Seta. "Now,
where were we?"

"We were just talking about—"

"Didn't your grandmother teach you not to talk with
food in your mouth? Swallow, then speak," Augusta said.
Her disapproval wasn't sharp.

The two ate in silence for a moment. Augusta spoke first.
"Seta, I'm sorry I've been busy lately. I will do better, I
promise. I've let a lot of things slide. I do need to be more
involved with what's going on over here, especially now
that Mama is gone."

That's the last thing I need, Seta thought. She didn't need
an overly attentive aunt getting into her business or her
grandfather's business. "Oh, Auntie, we're fine, really."

Augusta ignored the nagging doubt in her mind. She
searched Seta's eyes for a moment, and then nodded. "All

right, but you have to let me know if any problems come up. And I'll talk to Poppy later and let him know he can count on me. If you two need anything. . . ."

Seta's mind worked fast. "Oh, I'll tell him in the morning." She didn't want her aunt going out of her way to talk to her grandfather.

Augusta pushed her plate away and clasped her hands in front of her. She sighed and reached out for Seta's hand. Seta placed hers in her aunt's. "What's wrong, Auntie?"

Augusta licked her lips and paused. "Seta, your father really wants a relationship with you."

Seta snatched her hand back. "I don't want to talk about him."

Augusta rolled her eyes skyward and gritted her teeth. "You're being difficult, Seta. He's trying. He really is. He just wants you to talk to him."

Seta stood. "I'm not hungry."

She snatched up her plate, dumped her spaghetti in the trash and dropped the plate in the sink. She turned on the hot water, a pointed attempt to end the conversation.

Her father was one man she didn't want to discuss—or see—again.

Seta couldn't get her mother's letter off her mind. She hadn't realized how much she needed those words until they came. They produced an immediate change.

Seta stopped drinking. She took to doing her schoolwork with a diligence that surprised even her teachers. She had always been a good student—when she wanted to be—but the new fervor with which she worked was startling.

She turned up her intensity on the basketball court as well. Her junior year, the coach moved her to the point guard position. Seta studied her new position. She stayed after every practice and did any drills she could do on her own.

She went ahead to dinner with Gabe. However, the nagging thought that her mother wouldn't like the fact that she was out with an older man made her tell him she couldn't see him again. He acted like he understood and asked if it would be all right to call and check on her from time to time or maybe even stop by. He said he had an uncle who lived somewhere in her neighborhood. She said yes.

Seta's relationship with her aunt even took on a different tone. Suddenly, she didn't see Augusta as the enemy. She asked Augusta to teach her to cook. Her aunt agreed. Augusta still wanted Seta to move in with her, but Seta steadfastly refused. She wasn't going to leave her grandfather. Augusta said she would allow the situation to remain as it was, as long as Seta was doing well in school and causing her grandfather no trouble.

Phillip was still going to work at the grocery, but his hours were getting shorter and shorter. He seemed to spend more and more time in his recliner. Sometimes, he was talkative and attentive, even fun to be around, like old times. But more often, he was becoming disoriented and sometimes downright hostile. When he got in one of his moods, Seta tried to stay out of his way.

She felt it was her responsibility to look after him. She learned how to make chicken the way her grandmother did, but most other culinary secrets remained just that, secrets.

"Auntie, I just don't get it!" Seta said in disgust, throwing down the pot holder. She had tried to make a cake, but it had fallen, resulting in a lopsided mess. "I follow all the directions on these stupid recipes, and they still turn out ugly!"

Augusta stifled a smile. Her sister's child couldn't master cooking to save her life. It was funny, really. Seta was a whiz at everything else—her grades were stellar, her basketball game couldn't be stopped. She would surely have her choice of scholarships. But in the kitchen . . . that was a whole different story.

Augusta was amazed at the change in her sister's daughter over the course of a year. The surly, uncertain girl was gone and in her place was a more confident, conscientious high school senior.

There was one thing missing though. Augusta took a deep breath. She hesitated to bring up the subject because every time she did, Seta would shut down and either storm off in a huff or flat out refuse to discuss it. Still, Augusta thought she would give it another try.

"So, I talked to your father today." Augusta tried to sound casual.

Seta's back was to Augusta. Her aunt could see the immediate tensing of Seta's body. "Seta, I think you should at least talk to him."

She knew Augusta was right. Seta had tried to live up to everything in her mother's letter—well, everything except for that part. She just hadn't been ready. Her mother's words came back to her mind. Her mother had asked her to love and take care of Robert. Or at least be nice to him. Seta took in a deep breath. She would try, only for her mother.

"Okay," Seta mumbled.

Augusta's eyes widened. She hadn't been ready for that response. She quickly collected her wits. "Really? Well, what if I fix dinner and invite him over to my house? I could leave you two to your own conversation."

"No!" Seta's head was spinning. "I can't just sit down and have a meal with him. It would be too much."

She searched her aunt's face for understanding. Seta was finally ready to try to forgive her father for hurting her, but she didn't know if she was ready to do it in person just yet. Certainly not in so intimate a setting.

Augusta touched the girl's shoulder. "All right, we'll figure it out together."

Chapter 19

Coach Allgood blew the whistle. "Hit the showers," he said. "Armstrong, wait up a minute."

Seta looked at Diana, who shrugged her shoulders. Seta hoped she hadn't done anything wrong. "Okay, Coach," Seta said.

As the girls cleared the court, the coach beckoned Seta to follow him to his office. He gestured for her to have a seat. Nervous, Seta sat. "Yes, Coach?"

Her former coach, Coach Malone, had been nice, but not in the way that Coach Allgood was. Coach Allgood felt almost like a father. His walls were dotted with pictures of him with his players as well as trophies and banners. He had been voted coach of the year two of the past three years. Photos of his family dotted his desk. He leaned forward, his hands clasped in front of him.

"I just wanted to bring you in for a second," he said. "How are you doing?"

Seta nodded slowly. "I'm fine," she said. *Where was this going?*

Coach Allgood paused, looking at her. She shifted uncomfortably. "Good. I just wanted to make sure you're all right. I know you're doing fine on the court. You're playing harder than I've seen you play in a long time. How are you doing since your grandmother passed?"

Seta hated questions like this. They always made her sad. Even after all this time, people still asked her how she was faring. She smiled brightly. "Oh, great. I'm doing well in school. You said yourself that I'm doing fine on the court. I miss her, but I'm all right."

"And your grandfather?"

Seta's eyes shifted. "Oh, he's fine too." She crossed her fingers over the lie.

Coach Allgood stood in front of her. "Well, I just want you to know your basketball family is here for you. Your teammates love you. I love you. My family loves you," he said. "If ever you need anything, you can come to us. You hear?"

Seta waved off the attention. She felt unworthy. "Sure, Coach," she said with an uneasy laugh. Coach Allgood was like a father to some of the girls, but she wouldn't allow him to be so to her. She knew about fathers.

The coach searched her face, and then stood. "You can go hit the showers now. Just remember, you can call me any-time."

Seta sat across the table from this man she had once begged to be in the same room with her. She sat there, and she studied him. His face had a look of sadness to it, yet his eyes were full of life. He didn't have any hair on the top of his head. He was tall, taller than many of the basketball players at school. Yes, he was a stranger, she decided, a stranger whose blood ran through her veins.

She waited for him to speak. She didn't mind talking to him. However, this was his idea to get together. She wasn't going to make it easy for him.

She drummed her fingers on the table.

Robert glanced from under lowered eyelids at the girl who sat across from him. She was dressed plainly—in a T-shirt and jeans—but that did nothing to hide what a stunning beauty she had become. *She has her mother's eyes,* he thought with thick emotion forming in his throat. Seta's hazel eyes had more gray, though.

Her cheekbones were high too, just like Rose's. Her hair was like his. It was almost as dark as his was. *Well, almost as dark as mine had been at one time,* he thought wryly. Now, much of the color had left and with it, much of the hair itself. Seta's hair was wavy and black with lighter highlights.

She was slender, but athletic and strongly built. He suspected she would be able to take care of herself in any situation, just like her mama.

The silence was getting uncomfortable.

"So," Robert began, "you decide where you want to go to college?"

Seta was at the beginning of her senior year. By now she had traveled with her aunt to visit several colleges.

She shrugged. "I don't know." She could have said more, but she wanted to punish him in some small way. No, she wouldn't make this easy.

Robert looked around uneasily. "So, do you want to order?" They were at the ice cream parlor down the street from her high school.

"No, not really. I can't stay long. I have to meet some of my friends and go over what coach said in practice ... since I left practice early and all to come meet you."

She wanted him to know he was inconveniencing her. The barb registered with Robert. "Oh, I'm sorry for interrupting your practice. I just thought this would be a good time for us to get together."

In truth, he had tried to find a time when he could meet when Lola would think he was still at school. He knew if she had known about his meeting with Seta ahead of time, she would have insisted on coming.

Seta made an obvious attempt to look at her watch. "Yeah, well, like I said, I can't stay long." Sitting there looking at him squirm gave her some dark pleasure. It was only what he deserved.

She had considered being ridiculously late, but her grandparents had drilled into her the importance of keeping your word. And if you said you were going to be there at a certain time, then that's what you needed to do, her grandmother would say.

Robert signaled the waiter over anyway. "We'd like two chocolate shakes." He took a guess at what his daughter would like.

Seta raised her eyebrow. Surely he didn't presume to know her—though chocolate was her favorite shake flavor.

Robert shifted in his seat. He looked around the room. "So, tell me what's been going on with you."

"Oh, do you mean over the past sixteen years?" Seta asked, pointedly.

Robert held up his hands. "You know, this isn't going too well. Let's start over." He stood and drew a deep breath. He pretended to make an introduction. "Hello, miss. My name is Robert, and I've been a butthole. Might I join you for a moment?" He gestured grandly to the seat he had just vacated.

His levity caught her off guard. Her stern look dissolved into a tiny smile. Maybe she was being a little too hard on him. She nodded. "Sure. Please have a seat, sir."

Robert settled into his chair. "Seriously, I do want to apologize. I'm so sor—"

Seta wasn't ready to hear all that. She held up her hand. "Let's skip all that right now. Maybe later, okay?"

At this moment, she could deal with something light and fun, but she didn't want to have a heavy conversation. She had to get used to talking to him first before she could really listen to him.

Robert nodded.

"Harder, Armstrong, harder!" Coach Allgood yelled at her from downcourt. "You have to push it! You can't let up."

Seta gritted her teeth against the assault. She was playing as hard as she could, but Coach pushed her even more. "Coach, I'm trying!" she said, sounding out of breath.

"I know you're not getting soft," he called back. "When you finish practice, you will be running the bleachers."

Sweat ran into Seta's eyes. She let out an exasperated sigh as she made her lay-up. Coach was picking on her. "Don't worry about it," Diana said under her breath as Seta came back to the edge of the court.

After practice, Coach Allgood pulled Seta aside. "Look, Armstrong, you did good out there, but I know you can do better," he said to Seta, who stood with her arms folded across her chest and her eyes staring at the wall above his head. "You have to push hard," he said.

Seta refused to look at him. It was so unfair. Kayla Brown had missed way more shots, and he hadn't said anything to her. Coach touched her arm. Seta jerked away. "Come on, Seta, you know I'm right." Coach said.

"You're not!" she said. "You're being so mean to me. I bust my butt every day in practice and you yell at me. I made way more of my shots than Kayla, but you didn't say two words to her. It's not fair!"

Coach Allgood looked off to the side. "Hey, baby, come on over. I'll be ready in a second." He gestured to his daughter, who was walking into the gym. He turned back to Seta. "Seta, you are an A-one player. You should know by now that I am going to push you every single time you step on my court. Now colleges are looking at you and they need to see you at your best. You have the potential to do some great things and to have your pick of colleges. You can't slack off."

"Coach, I'm not slacking!" Seta rebutted.

"And that's why I'm going to stay on you," he said. He smiled and put his arm around her shoulders. "Now go ahead and hit the showers."

"Poppy, where are your shoes?" Seta asked Phillip. Jessica had just dropped her off at the house. Phillip was outside, watering the lawn in his socks.

"What did you say?" Phillip asked, smiling.

Seta gently took the hose from Phillip. "Poppy, you can't keep doing this. Now, let's go inside."

Phillip had taken to forgetting simple things, like putting his shoes on when he went outside. He didn't go to work anymore. After forgetting to show up several days in a row, only to arrive there at an unscheduled shift on another day, the manager had called the house and told him not to worry about coming back.

Phillip smiled absently as he trailed behind Seta, with her holding his hand. "Do you want something to eat?" she asked her grandfather.

He shook his head no, but she fixed him something anyway.

"Hey, where are you off to in such a rush?" Diana asked. Seta was rushing to class. Diana sped up to catch up to her.

Seta didn't have time to talk. "I'm late for class. Man, if I get another tardy, I'm going to get into trouble," Seta huffed

"Why are you late?" Diana asked.

Seta waved her off. "My granddad. Look, I can't talk. I just told you I'm late. I have to go." She picked up the pace. Diana raced to catch up with her. "Hey, hold up."

Seta was getting annoyed. Diana hadn't been all that interested in her comings and goings before. And she wasn't in the mood to hear Diana give her a hard time. "Look, really, I can't talk, Di!"

Diana grabbed her by her shoulder. "Look, I'm working in the library this period. I can give you a pass. We can say you were in the library. That'll keep you from getting a tardy."

The worry evaporated from Seta's face. Her eyes narrowed suspiciously. "Why are you being so nice to me?"

Diana shrugged. "I don't know." She put a hand on a hip. "So, do you want the pass or not?"

Seta quickly looked around. Maybe Diana was being for real. "Sure."

Diana lowered her voice. "Come on. The librarian isn't in there right now. I can just get the pass and use her signature stamp. Hurry up!"

Seta found an unexpected ally in Diana, the girl who had spent years giving her a hard time. After that, Seta and Diana became closer. Seta had missed the bond she had begun to form with Jessica, but after the incident with Corey, things just weren't the same between them, though they were cordial. Seta wasn't comfortable enough to share the stress of trying to take care of her grandfather or any of that, but it was nice to have Diana to talk to about life and scholarships and basketball. Diana was the eldest of six children, so she knew the hunger to earn a college scholarship.

"Maybe your dad can help you pay for college if you don't get a scholarship," Diana told her one day.

Seta didn't stop painting her nails. "I'd rather die first."

Seta wasn't at the point of forgetting how Robert had made her feel all those years, but she was trying to forgive. She was trying to live out her mother's words. If she could just find it in her heart to let that hard lump of anger dissipate, she knew she would be able to fulfill every one of her mother's requests. However, she couldn't.

She recalled a visit from the woman who had been her grandmother's best friend when she was living, Nettie, just the week before. Ms. Nettie had brought some crispy fried chicken by the house just before nightfall.

"Thank you so much!" Seta had gushed, as it was a day when she did not have time to prepare dinner for her grandfather because practice had run long.

"I'm happy to help out," Ms. Nettie said, plopping a chicken leg onto a plate and a thigh onto another. She spooned some rice from a foil-covered container.

"Here, eat this," Nettie said, passing one of the plates to Seta and putting the other on the counter.

"Let me get my grandfather from his room," Seta said, but Ms. Nettie stayed her with a touch on the forearm.

"You just let him rest a while," Ms. Nettie said. "I wanted to share a few words with you, if that's all right."

Seta nodded. Ms. Nettie had always been nice to her. "Sure."

"Well, I know I'm not a prayer warrior like your lovely grandmother was," she said, "but I've had you heavily on my heart lately. I've been praying that the Lord will give you strength—"

"Oh, Ms. Nettie, I can save you the trouble," Seta said. "God doesn't answer prayers with my name in them."

"Seta!" Ms. Nettie said. "That couldn't be further from the truth."

"No, I'm serious," Seta said. "But it's okay. I used to be really angry with God about jerking me around, but now I know I'm just not a good enough Christian for Him. I know when I become good enough, things will change."

Ms. Nettie shook her head. "Oh, baby, that isn't how it is," she said. "God answers prayers all the time. And He gives us all so many blessings. We can't earn them—we could never do enough to earn His favor—but He gives them to us freely."

Seta looked askance. That hadn't been what she had grown up hearing. "I don't think that's exactly right," she said, then quickly added, "no disrespect."

Nettie nodded. "It's all right," she said. "I know you're not being disrespectful. It just always boggles my mind, though, how confused we can get sometimes over what God wants for us and even over something as simple as what it takes to reach Him."

"What do you mean?" Seta asked, taking a bite out of the chicken. It was juicy and perfectly seasoned. It may have took some years of learning, but Nettie had finally gotten the art of frying chicken right.

"Well, for all our studying, we will be forever learning about God," Nettie said. "We make it so complicated. We have all these different denominations and rules and traditions that don't have anything to do truly with who God is. All of that is some made-up stuff we have created for our comfort. Sometimes the rules are aimed at scaring people into doing right. Other times we use rules to control people. And still other times, we just have rules to make ourselves look and feel good. But God isn't about scaring us, and He isn't about punishing us or causing us to live in fear. He is love. He asks just that we love Him and try our best to honor Him by doing good. But He isn't like us; He doesn't only hand out His blessings and favor if we are quote 'good enough.' We are good enough because we were born. We are His children and He loves us and wants to bless us. Period."

Seta mulled this over. Is it possible that she didn't have to work vainly to earn God's love? Is it possible that He loved her, as Ms. Nettie said, just because she was born?

"I don't know. . . ." she said slowly.

Nettie stood from the table. "Well, I need to run along home. But just think and pray on what I said. You don't have to earn God's love or work to be perfect. Just love Him and do your best, and that's good enough. And try to give others the same benefit of the doubt that God gives you. We all make mistakes." She paused. "And please, don't give up on God. Even if at first it appears He hasn't answered your prayer, just keep your heart open. Sometimes, He speaks to us but we're so busy talking that we can't hear what He is saying."

Seta sat at the table for several moments after Nettie left, going over the conversation in her head. This was so different from what she had learned, but it would be such a relief if she didn't have to be perfect before she could talk with God.

Maybe she didn't have to sacrifice who she was to spend time with God.

But if He could forgive her imperfections, could she forgive others'?

The phone was ringing as Seta stepped into the house. She dropped her backpack on the floor and hastily walked to the kitchen. "Hello?"

"Hi." It was Robert. He waited.

Seta took in a deep breath and sat in her grandfather's easy chair. "Hello, how are you?" she asked. *I'm trying.*

"Fine. I was wondering if you'd like to come over for dinner." Robert chewed the side of his lip as he waited for her response. He was trying to make things right with her.

Seta shook her head, but realized he couldn't see her. "No, I don't think so," she said.

"So how was your day?" Robert said.

"Fine."

He cleared his throat, casting about for any other conversational opening. "You like the weather?"

"It's all right."

"How is your grandfather?"

"Okay," Seta said.

It was all she could do to have even these words with Robert. That's all she could manage. She wasn't there yet. She couldn't see other children calling him daddy, or watch him pour out the affection on them he had so stingily withheld from her all those years.

"Well, I'm sorry for interrupting your evening," Robert finally said, giving up after Seta's apparent disinterest.

"Okay, bye," Seta said.

Seta shrugged as she placed the phone back on its base. She was trying, really. Tiny darts of anger still pricked her when she thought of his sudden interest. He wanted to invite her into his life, but she couldn't forget that she had spent years—years—craving entry to his.

The phone rang again. She snatched it up. "Hello?"

"Hi, it's me again." It was Robert.

"Yeah?" She frowned. *Why is he calling again?*

"I was wondering if you'd like for me to come to your next game," Robert said.

Seta wrinkled her nose. "It's a free country."

"But do you want me to come?" he pressed.

She rolled her eyes. "Doesn't matter to me."

After that conversation, he came to her next game and attended every game after that regularly. He replaced her grandfather in the stands.

Phillip didn't leave the house much these days anymore, not even to go to church. He would sit for hours on end in his easy chair, sometimes smiling to himself, sometimes sleeping. Sometimes Seta would arrive home to find him walking down the street, maybe with shoes on and maybe without. It was those times that her heart beat fast as she imagined all the bad things that could have happened to him. But he never seemed to get flustered, even as she ushered him back into the house. He'd just smile and pat her arm, as if comforting a small child.

Seta tried to convince herself that he was all right. Still, something in the back of her mind told her that his actions weren't normal. She shook those thoughts away though. "He's fine," she told herself as she looked in the refrigerator to pull out a casserole Augusta had brought over a few days earlier. She didn't want anything to be wrong with her Poppy.

Phillip's job loss created another concern for Seta. How would they pay the bills? Augusta told her not to worry about it, that she would handle everything. However, Seta felt that was a family matter, something between her grandfather and her. Augusta said she would get all the bills mailed to her house, but Seta stopped her.

"Hey, Auntie, I'm growing up, trying to be responsible," Seta reasoned. "Why don't you just let me see if I can handle things for a while? And if I can't, I'll let you know."

Augusta looked doubtful. "I don't know. . . ."

Seta was convincing. "Come on, you said yourself that I've gained a lot of maturity. Poppy is here. He can take care of everything, and I'll just double-check things after he does them to make sure everything is all right. It's just a matter of writing a few checks. He can do that. We'll be fine on his retirement money."

Augusta thought about it. That would make things a lot easier. As it was, she was so busy that she really couldn't fit any more responsibilities into her schedule. And while her mother hadn't left any life insurance, it was good to hear Seta say Augusta's father's small retirement income was sufficient. She knew Phillip would make sure everything was fine. Augusta gave in. "We'll try it. If things start to get hectic, or if it looks like Daddy doesn't have enough money and is having a hard time, I want you to give me a call, you hear?"

Seta nodded obediently. "Okay."

Seta mulled the bills and the money situation one afternoon as she pulled a stack of envelopes from the mailbox. "Hey there, little lady," Mr. Spivey called. Seta looked up and waved.

"Hi, Mr. Spivey," she said. He wore black socks and shorts.

"Why don't you come in here and get some of this here candy," he said.

Seta shook her head. She was a senior in high school, certainly too old to be lured by candy. "I can't," she said. "I've got to get inside and check on my grandfather."

Mr. Spivey sucked his teeth and chewed on a broom straw. "How is he doing anyway, what with your grandmother gone and all?"

Mr. Spivey had come to the funeral.

"He's fine," Seta said quickly. She wasn't going to let any strangers know her grandfather's true state.

"Oh, that's good to know," Mr. Spivey said. He scratched his armpit and waved to someone down the street.

"Hey, you should hang around and meet my nephew," he said. "He hadn't been too long moved to town from out east. He's been here not even a year, so I know he's still trying to meet new people. Pretty little thing like you, he'd love to get to know."

Seta shook her head. She wasn't in the mood. "Nah," she said, but her tone softened. The old man was only trying to be helpful. "Maybe some other time."

The car, which looked vaguely familiar, came to a stop in front of Mr. Spivey's house. A tall guy climbed out. Seta's eyes widened. It was Gabe.

He smiled a wide, toothy grin.

"Hey, Miss America," he said.

Seta giggled. She hadn't talked to him in months. She recalled him saying he had an uncle who lived near her. Who would have known it was Old Man Spivey? "How are you doing?" she asked. She tried to hide the bills that were in her hand.

Gabe closed the car door and gave Mr. Spivey a one-armed hug. "Hi, Uncle, I bought you some magazines," he said and handed over a brown paper bag.

Mr. Spivey grinned conspiratorially. "Oh, did you now?"

"Yeah, I think you'll like them," Gabe said and winked. "Some of my pictures are in this issue. Check them out and tell me what you think."

He turned to Seta. "So, how have things been going?"

Seta glanced quickly toward her own house. Maybe it would be all right to stand outside and talk for a while. "Oh, fine. What about you?"

Gabe inched closer. She could smell his cologne. It smelled *sooo* good. "I would still like to take you out sometime."

Mr. Spivey clutched his bag to his chest. "I'm going to leave you young people to your own conversation and head on inside. Thanks, Gabe. See you later, young lady."

"Good night, Mr. Spivey," Seta said, her eyes still on Gabe. She had never seen such a beautiful man.

Gabe turned back to her. He put his arm around her shoulders. "So, how about if I take you out to eat? We all have to eat. How much harm could that be?"

He looked at her with eyes that bore into her soul. Without hesitation, she said yes.

She asked him to wait a few minutes while she raced inside and freshened up. She checked on her grandfather. He was sleeping. She knew he would be that way for the rest of the night. She ran a brush through her hair and put on some lip gloss.

A moment later, she was back outside with Gabe.

Gabe took her to a nice restaurant across town. He held the chair out for her as she sat down. She struggled to hold in a smile. No guy—aside from her grandfather—had ever done that for her before. It made her feel special.

She laughed throughout dinner. Gabe teased her and told jokes. He flirted with her and complimented everything about her. When he dropped her off at home, he asked if he could call her again. She said yes.

The phone was ringing when Seta stepped into the house. She quickly snatched it up. "Hello?"

"Where have you been?" The voice on the other end was stern.

"Huh?"

"It's after eleven o'clock on a school night. Where have you been?"

The question took her aback. The voice sounded like Robert's, but surely, he wasn't grilling her.

"Is this Robert?"

There was a pause. She knew he hated when she called him by his first name, but what could he do.

"Yes, this is your *father*," came the reply. "I've been calling since nine."

Anger welled in Seta's chest. She tried to stifle it. How dare he question her? "I was out."

Robert clenched his jaw. He was trying to build a relationship with her, yet there was a delicate balance. He tried to handle her gingerly, to be her friend because he knew he didn't have much of a right to act as a father. Still, she couldn't wander in at eleven at night and expect nothing to be said.

"Well, you need to make your way in a little bit earlier," he said.

Seta rolled her eyes. This was too much. "And who are you to tell me what to do?"

"I'm your father," he countered.

"Yeah, right," Seta spat. She was trying. Lord knows, she was. Times like this made the anger resurface though. He had no right, no right at all.

"What does that mean?" Robert's voice was strained.

"It means exactly what it sounds like," Seta said. "I didn't stutter."

Robert's nose flared and he gripped the telephone tightly. He was trying so hard to make amends. He slowly sucked in a deep breath. It wouldn't do to alienate her.

He tried again. "Look, I'm sorry. I just don't want anything to happen to you. I love—"

"Save it," Seta snapped. If he said he loved her, she would surely reach through the phone and snap his bony neck. Love didn't leave a year-old child on the doorsteps of another.

Robert could see the conversation was going nowhere, so he switched gears. "Well, anyway, I was really calling to see how things were going over there," he said. "Do you need anything? Money?"

Seta laughed. She would rather go hungry before she asked him for a dime. "Oh, now you're concerned about my well-being?"

She knew she was being harsh, difficult even, but he set her off with his attempt at suddenly being a father. Their conversations had been tentative in the few previous attempts. This was the first time he had tried to assert any type of authority.

"Seta, I want this to work," he said.

"People in hell want ice water." The retort flew out of her mouth.

Robert sighed. "Seta, I'm really trying here," he said, in a half plea, half demand.

Seta glanced at her watch. "Yeah, well, it's getting late. I need to go check on my granddaddy and get ready for bed," she said. She decided to throw him an accommodation. "I'll talk to you later."

Then, she hung up.

Chapter 20

Robert held the receiver in his hand. He recalled a conversation years ago when the situation had been reversed. He had hung up on her and left her wondering why. *They say turnabout is fair play*, he thought. Now, he was on the other end, looking for a little acceptance.

"Daddy, I can't sleep," a wide-eyed Berrie said as she walked into his office, a teddy bear in her arms. She rubbed her eyes.

Robert hoisted her onto his lap. "Did you have a bad dream?"

"Yes," she said. "I dreamed somebody came and took you away from us."

Robert smiled and held her close. "Oh, that was a bad dream. But that's all it was. I'm your daddy. I would never leave you."

A small voice reminded him that there was a child to whom he had done exactly that.

College recruiters were regulars at Seta's games. Several of them hinted that they would be glad to give her money or buy her things if that would help in her decision-making process as she narrowed down her college choices. But she knew that was against the rules. She wanted to do the right thing, so she turned them down, although money was becoming a real worry for her. Her grandfather's Social Security check didn't stretch very far at all.

She sometimes confided a few vague details to Gabe. She was allowing him to call her more often now. He complimented her and marveled at her intellect. They spent more and more time together. She wasn't going to make the mistake of letting him touch her, though, just because he told her she was beautiful. Not like she did with that guy Corey all those years ago. However, she knew Gabe was different. He didn't want sex from her. He just wanted to be her friend, and maybe, one day, her boyfriend. She could trust him.

Sometimes she talked to him about her grandfather, although never much about the bills. Somehow, he must have known.

"I might have an idea for you, if you're interested," he said. "It could be a way to make some money."

He seemed to wait for her response as they sat over dinner.

Seta was intrigued. "What is it?"

Gabe leaned in closer to her. "Well, you know I told you I'm into photography, right?"

Seta nodded. They hadn't talked too much about him or his livelihood, but she did remember that.

"Well, I think you could be one of the models. You'd make good money," he said.

Seta blinked. Her? A model? She shook her head. "Oh, no, I couldn't be a model," she said, suddenly shy. Was he making fun of her?

Gabe touched her hand. "Really, you could be. You're tall. You're beautiful. I think you'd be great."

Seta had never envisioned herself a model, someone that others longed to be like. She looked down at her hands. Maybe Gabe wasn't really her friend. Maybe he was just playing a cruel joke.

"Seta, listen to me," he said, touching her chin. She looked up into his eyes. "You are beautiful. Just come out to the studio. Trust me."

He went on, telling her how much money she could earn. Her eyes widened at the prospect. It would be enough to pay off a lot of bills and even put away some for college.

Seta toyed with her hands in her lap. She finally looked up at him, shyness suddenly making it hard for her eyes to meet his. "You really think I'm beautiful?" Her eyes searched his.

"Oh, without a doubt," he said. "So, check this out. Why don't I pick you up after practice tomorrow? We can go to the studio."

"Just like that?"

Gabe snapped his fingers. "Just like that."

The next day Seta went with Gabe to the studio. Large lights were to one side and a few guys milled around. Gabe turned to her. "Here, she will show you the clothes. Why don't you see what fits?"

Seta looked up to see a woman smiling warmly at her. She smiled back. "Go with Miriam. She'll help you change."

Seta didn't know what to say, so she just followed the tall blonde. Miriam held up several outfits, first eying the clothes, then eying the girl. She finally settled on something red. Seta cleared her throat.

"Uhm, what's this?" she asked incredulously. It was a red teddy with garters.

"Oh, you would look stunning in this," Miriam gushed.

Seta wasn't so sure. It hadn't occurred to her to ask what

type of modeling she would be doing. She looked around. "Uhm, I think I need to talk to Gabe."

Miriam waved her off. "Oh, no you don't. You'll be fine. Trust me."

Trust me was what Gabe had said to her also. *Seems that a lot of people want me to trust them,* Seta thought. She wasn't sure about any of this, especially these clothes.

"Really, I need to talk to Gabe," she said. Surely, there was some mistake.

Miriam disappeared and came back with Gabe. Gabe clapped. "Oh, that would look so good on you," he said, checking out the skimpy outfit that was hanging next to Seta.

Seta smiled nervously. "Uh, I'm not sure about this," she said, shaking her head. She hadn't been naked in front of a man since that time when she was fourteen and at Corey's house. The memory of that washed shame all over her being.

Gabe smiled. He clutched her by the shoulders and stared into her eyes. "Look, you're beautiful. Lots of women would kill to have the body you have. You need the money. It's not a bad idea."

She still wasn't too sure. He sighed. "You won't really be naked. You'll have on clothes. That thing right there will cover all the places you want covered." He paused. "Do it for me."

This isn't right. You know better. A tiny voice warned her, but she shoved it aside. Maybe Gabe was right. Maybe she was thinking too hard. After all, it's not like she was going to be nude. Besides, she wanted Gabe to like her.

Miriam gingerly placed the red item in her hands.

When she returned home from the photo shoot, Seta gingerly placed the key in the lock. "Poppy? Poppy, I'm home," she said, dropping her bag on the floor. She was tired. She closed her eyes against the memory of the afternoon, but her body wouldn't let her forget. A knot formed in her stomach and she raced to the bathroom, barely getting the toilet seat up before heaving into it.

Shame folded her stomach over on top of itself. Seta sat limply on the floor next to the toilet, her hand to her head and sweat on her brow. After some moments, she pulled herself up, flushed the toilet and washed her face. She squirted paste on the toothbrush and scrubbed the taste of shame from her mouth and, she hoped, from her memory.

She stared at the face in the mirror. Barbara frowned back at her disapprovingly. Seta closed her eyes against the reproach. Still, it would not leave. She wanted Gabe to like her, so she had done as he asked. Besides, she really did need the money.

Seta knew she couldn't do it again though. There had to be a better way.

Phillip appeared in the doorway to the bathroom. "I waited for you all day," he said in a childlike tone. "I waited and I waited. But you didn't come."

Seta turned from the mirror and managed a smile. "Oh, Poppy, you know I had to go to school," she said, kissing him on the cheek.

"When is my Barbara coming back home?" he asked, plaintively. "I'm hungry. She knows I get hungry."

Seta's brow creased and sadness crossed her face. It was getting harder and harder to watch this thing happen to her grandfather. Some days, he seemed just fine, but on other days . . .

"I'll take care of you, Poppy," Seta said, leading him to the kitchen. "Don't you worry."

Coach Allgood held out a sports drink. Seta took a long swig of it and wiped her mouth with the back of her hand. "Good practice," he said.

Seta smiled. "Thanks, Coach."

Coach Allgood spent extra time with Seta, teaching her new moves, chatting, always coaching. She sometimes still grew angry with him as he pushed her, but she knew he was only looking out for her. He had become a confidante, as he was for so many of his girls. She talked to him about grades and about her hopes, but never about her home life.

Or her secret job.

"Girl, I haven't seen you in so long," Jessica said, running to catch up with Seta after Seta's basketball practice.

Seta was late for a photo shoot. "Oh, I've been busy," she said. She had a lot going on and felt guilty for pushing her friends to the side.

"What has you so busy these days?" Jessica wanted to know. "Sometimes I see you after school, but then I look up, and you're gone. And I can never catch you on the phone."

"Oh, just different things," Seta said, busying herself with her purse.

Jessica wasn't deterred. "Like what?" Jessica had been working to regain their friendship, but Seta's schedule hadn't allowed much time to reconnect.

Seta wasn't about to share her secret. She had promised herself she would leave the photos alone, but the prospect of finally having money to pay for nice food for her grandfather, and to take care of the bills was nice. She swallowed whatever misgivings she had.

And maybe God wouldn't judge her. *After all, Ms. Nettie said God just wanted us to try our best. And right now, this is my best. I can't go back to being broke. And I can't send my grandfather away.* A few pictures won't hurt. And who would ever find out?

"Nothing, just . . . well, you know I try to spend a lot of time with my grandfather these days."

Jessica's voice immediately lowered. "Is he okay?"

Seta waved her off. "He's fine. He just misses my grand-mom, so I try to keep him company, that's all."

Seta hoped that would satisfy Jessica, and it did.

"So, do you want to go out with us this weekend?" Jessica asked. Jessica was still one of the most popular girls at school—despite the fact that she was no longer holding parties at her own house. Jessica's parents had come back home prematurely one evening and busted up one of her alcohol parties. They had put her on punishment for a month and threatened to send her to a private school. That hadn't stopped the teenager from entertaining though. Now, she held the parties at a cousin's house. She had continued to serve alcohol until police arrested Big C for drunk driving after he slammed his car into a parked truck. That scared Jessica.

Jessica flaunted her sexuality. When she wasn't wearing a too-short cheerleading outfit, she could usually be seen in something that was either short, tight or both. Where other girls would look trashy, Jessica came off looking cute—if a little seductive. The result was that she never spent a weekend alone. Today she wore a tiny shirt with DREAM GIRL written across the front and name-brand jeans with platform shoes. A fake tattoo adorned her right shoulder. She settled for the fake tattoo because her parents wouldn't allow her to get a real one.

Seta was grateful her friend included her, but Seta had her own plans. Gabe was taking her out. "I can't. I have a date," Seta said.

Jessica's eyes widened, and then narrowed. "Not with that older guy you were talking about?"

Seta's silence confirmed what her words didn't say. Jessica let out an exasperated sigh. "Seta, he is too old for you."

Jessica and Seta hadn't spent as much time together in their senior year as before, but Jessica still felt she should watch over Seta. Seta hadn't told her all of what happened

with Corey way back then. Still, Jessica knew it had hurt
Seta deeply. Jessica couldn't help but think it had something to do with Seta's immaturity. Jessica knew this Gabe
guy probably meant her no good.

"He's not too old," Seta said, though it occurred to her
that she didn't know how old Gabe was. He never liked to
talk about himself, choosing instead to deflect comments
from himself. He said he loved learning about her. Seta
soaked up his apparent interest. The result was that she
knew next to nothing about him.

"Well, how old is he?" Jessica pressed. She rubbed a carefully manicured hand through her straight hair.

Seta squirmed uncomfortably. She shrugged defiantly.
"It doesn't matter. He treats me nice."

Jessica opened her mouth to say something, but Amy
bounded up to them. She spoke in a rush. "Did you hear?
That girl named Hannah is pregnant. You know, I think she
goes to your church, Seta."

Seta had been missing services lately, but she went occasionally. Her eyes widened at the news about Hannah. *Not
little Miss Innocent. Hmmm, just goes to show. You can't trust
anybody,* Seta thought. She would have never thought Hannah to be the fast-girl type.

"How do you know?" Jessica asked with skepticism. She
knew how Amy could gossip.

"Because I heard. Jennifer Mills told Susan who told
Karen who told me."

Jessica looked doubtful. "Hannah? What's her last name,
Franklin? I can't imagine. She would be the last one I would
think to be pregnant."

"It's true," Amy insisted. "Seta, you know her. What do
you think?"

Seta glanced at her watch. She had to meet Gabe at the
studio. "Who knows? It probably is true."

* * *

Seta gathered her courage as she stepped into the studio. Her stomach flip-flopped at what she was about to do. Her first time taking pictures wearing only a red teddy had made her sick. She was home barely two minutes before running to the bathroom and throwing up.

Seta promised herself that no amount of money was worth feeling that way—or, as she listened to her grandmother's voice, going to hell over. For she knew surely she would be condemned to eternal damnation.

She promised herself she wouldn't do it again. That was before the power company sent the third notice that their lights would be turned off. Her grandfather's Social Security checks had made Seta do a double take. Who could live on that?

The check she received from Gabe for taking those first pictures paid to keep the telephone on. Seta had lied to her Aunt Augusta and told her that everything was under control and that her grandfather had taken care of all the bills. Nobody knew how bad things had become.

Seta struggled to hide Phillip's true state from everyone, including her Aunt Augusta, because she was afraid that if they found out how bad things were, they would take him away. They would put him in some stinking hospital or worse, lock him up in a nursing home. She knew her grandfather would simply shrivel up and die if that happened.

And so would she. She had to hold onto the last piece of her family as long as she could, even if that meant showing her body to pay to keep her grandfather with her.

"Hey, good to see you," Gabe said with a wide smile. He wore expensive loafers and linen pants. He took her backpack from her shoulders, and then rubbed them. Seta breathed deeply. He smelled so good and he was so nice to her. It meant a lot that Gabe cared so much for her.

"So, you ready to stun the world?" Gabe asked, gesturing to Miriam. Miriam hurried over, a purple gown in her hands. Gabe handed it to Seta.

Seta nodded.

"Look like you're having fun," Gabe said from behind the camera. "Look like you're the sexiest woman alive, because you are."

Seta wasn't having fun and struggled to see herself as sexy. But she wanted to, for Gabe. She smiled self-consciously. "Yeah, that's it. Now, wink at me."

Seta did. Gabe purred at her. "Okay, tilt your head back," he said. Seta did as she was instructed. "Now, open your legs."

Seta's eyes went from Gabe, to the guy who was adjusting the lights, and then to Miriam. Miriam nodded almost imperceptibly. The older woman seemed to be telling her to go ahead, to do it, but Seta still felt that it wasn't right.

Gabe's purr was a little firmer. "Come on, baby, we don't have all day. Open your legs. Look sexy. It won't hurt you, I promise."

Seta slowly eased her legs open and licked her lips nervously.

"Hey, that's it. Do it again. Lick those lips," Gabe said excitedly.

"Huh?"

"Your lips; lick them again," Gabe said. "That was sexy. Do it like you're making love."

Seta's only sexual experience had been with Corey, but she tried to look like she was making love. She leaned further back and licked her lips again.

Gabe got an idea. "Why don't you let your shoulder strap fall," he said.

"What do you mean?"

Miriam glanced at Gabe, and then rushed over. She slid

the strap down and Seta's breast came into view. She hastily covered herself. Gabe laughed. "No, don't do that. Just show it to the camera. Show it to Big Daddy," he said.

Seta shook her head. This was too much. "No, I can't. Gabe, this isn't right."

Gabe pressed. "Do you want to disappoint me? Is that what you're trying to do? You want to make me think you're going to help me and then you clam up and act all shy. Are you trying to hurt me, after all I've done for you?"

Seta looked down at the purple satin gown that exposed her thigh and scooped low in the front. No, she didn't want to disappoint Gabe. He had been so nice to her, to be her friend, compliment her and to offer her a job. She looked back up at him.

"No, I'm not trying to hurt you," she said. "Maybe we can just take the pictures like last time, with me just in the lingerie, but not really showing anything?"

She looked at him with pleading in her eyes. She didn't want him to be mad at her. On the other hand, she didn't want to show her body either. As it was, she already felt like she had shown too much.

Gabe threw his hands in the air. He turned to Miriam. "This isn't going to work," he said angrily. "Go on, Miriam, find her clothes. She's acting like a child. When I saw her, I thought she could be mature. I see I was wrong. Let her get dressed so she can go home."

Seta's hand flew to her mouth in surprise. This wasn't the Gabe she knew. She quickly got up from the couch and rushed to him. "Gabe, I'm sorry. I'll do what you want," she said, trying to make him look at her. He refused.

"No, that's okay," he said, busying himself with his camera. "I can't have you doing anything you don't want to do. If you're uncomfortable, then that's fine. I'll find somebody else. I was just trying to help you out. You're the one who needs the money."

"Gabe, I know you were trying to help me out, and I'm sorry." Seta was afraid he wouldn't want to be her friend anymore. "I'll do whatever you ask. Please give me another chance."

Seta didn't want him to push her away. She had been pushed away too many times.

Miriam and the guy watched the drama unfold. Seta held her breath. Finally, Gabe looked at her. "All right," he said. "I'll give you one more chance. But if you act like you don't want to do something, or that I'm forcing you, then it's off. I'll find somebody else. Understood?"

Seta nodded silently. Gabe smiled and tapped her under the chin. "That's my girl. Now, get back over there and let's do this again."

Chapter 21

Seta's senior year of high school took away her innocence. From basketball practice, she rushed to photo shoots and from there, home. She was becoming afraid to leave Phillip alone and relied on several telephone checks during the day to make sure he was all right. She made him promise not to touch the stove, and so far, he had obeyed. She shouldn't have worried though. It seemed he spent much of his time these days in his recliner or sleeping.

Augusta stopped by the house on the weekends to bring several days' worth of meals. She knew her niece would never be a good cook and felt this was her way of helping out. She told herself that she was doing her part to look after her father and her niece. She telephoned sometimes to see how Seta was doing in school and to talk to Phillip. Seta never let Phillip talk if it was late in the evening because his confusion and memory loss seemed to be more pronounced then. She didn't want him to say the wrong thing and alert Augusta.

When she did allow him to talk on the phone, Seta monitored the conversations closely and grabbed the phone if it sounded like the conversation was taking a bad turn.

One evening, she returned home to find Phillip sitting in his armchair, naked.

"Poppy!" Seta shrieked, and then tried to lower her voice so as not to alarm him. She quickly walked to his bedroom and found his bathrobe. She helped him stand, gently pushed his arms through and tied the belt around his waist. His always-portly form had become thin in the two years since Barbara had died.

"Poppy, what did I tell you?" Seta said. "You have to wear clothes. And shoes. You have to. What if Aunt Gussie had walked in? Do you want them to send you away?"

Phillip didn't look as if he were even paying attention. Seta knew it was useless to scold. "Okay, Poppy, let's go get your bath."

Phillip had taken to skipping baths. The only times he seemed to take them was when Seta insisted. She would sometimes let him go a day without getting one, but by the second day, her nose told her he could wait no longer.

Phillip let her lead him to the bathroom. She turned on the water and he recoiled. "No!" he shook his head, frightened.

Seta sighed. "Poppy, come on." She tugged on his arm. Phillip snatched back, his frail form producing a surprising amount of strength.

Seta stomped her foot. "Poppy! You have to take a bath." She tried again to tug on his arm, but he refused to budge. Seta didn't understand why he was acting like this. "Poppy, come *on*."

Phillip cowered in the corner. Seta didn't have the strength to make him budge. She finally let the water out and gave up. "Fine, Poppy," she said. "But tomorrow, you're getting a bath."

* * *

"Miss Armstrong, you need to pay attention," Seta heard from somewhere in the distance. "If you choose to party at night, that is not my concern. But you will stay awake in my class."

Seta lifted her head from her desk. Somehow, she had managed to fall asleep. She wiped her mouth and looked around the classroom. All eyes were on her. Some of her classmates laughed. "Yeah, she was probably out screwing," someone to her rear said. "You know, that's all she does these days."

Seta's shoulders slumped. Even after all this time, classmates still called her names after that episode with Corey back in junior high.

Mrs. Mack folded her arms across her chest and stared meanly at Seta. "Well, you're not going to bring your wayward self in here. Sit up!"

Seta was too shocked to say anything. How could her teacher be so judgmental? What had she ever done to Mrs. Mack? Not wanting to appear disobedient, she did as she was told.

"Now, as I was saying, where is your research paper?"

Seta regained her focus and pulled it from her backpack. She had stayed up half the night finishing her homework. Augusta had bought her a computer and printer, which saved a lot of library time.

Mrs. Mack snatched the paper from her. The teacher seemed almost disappointed to get the paper. "Oh, so you brought your homework to class, I see."

Seta frowned. What was *her* problem? "Of course," Seta said. She always brought her homework.

"What, are you sassing me?" Mrs. Mack asked with a sneer. "Don't talk back to me."

Mrs. Mack had always acted a little distant, yet had

never been downright rude to her. Seta looked around the classroom and was embarrassed to see classmates staring at her with amusement and relish at her apparent discomfort.

Her eyes fell on Hannah. Hannah smiled at her. Seta rolled her eyes. *Does she think this is funny?*

The bell rang and Seta hopped up. She couldn't wait to escape.

Seta was walking down the hall when Hannah caught up with her. "Hey, don't worry about what just happened," Hannah said hurriedly. "Mrs. Mack was just being mean."

Seta looked at the girl in disgust. Who was she that she should try to comfort her? Shouldn't Hannah worry about her own concerns—like her pregnancy? "Don't worry about me. I'm fine."

Hannah hesitated, and then spoke anyway. "Well, it just looked like you were embarrassed, that's all. I was just trying to help. I know what it's like to have people laughing at you."

Seta looked askance. "I'll bet you do, being pregnant and all," she spat the words at the girl. It bugged Seta that Hannah was always so nice to her. She didn't trust many girls, especially since so many of them had it in for her. Why this Hannah girl was so nice was beyond her. It made Seta suspicious.

Hannah recoiled as if struck. "I'm not pregnant," she said.

Seta laughed derisively. "Sure, Miss Goody Two-shoes. Always wants to be in somebody else's business, when her own is raggedy. I never would have pictured you to be a skank."

She knew she shouldn't have said those last words. However, something inside made her want to reach out and hurt this girl for all the other girls who had hurt her. Guilt immediately pricked her conscious when tears welled up in

Hannah's eyes. Hannah didn't say anything. She just raced in the opposite direction.

Seta wanted to go apologize, but didn't.

Gabe promised Seta nobody around their vicinity would see the pictures. They were all going to some faraway magazine. Seta at first balked at the idea, but she finally swallowed her words for fear that he would leave. *It's okay*, she told herself. *I'll make some money, take care of Poppy and that would be that. Nobody will ever know.*

Then, she would go to college, find a real job and continue to pay the bills. She didn't know what she would do about her grandfather then, but thought maybe she would find an apartment off campus and move him down with her. It would be tough, she knew, still she couldn't let him live alone.

Seta felt ashamed each time she took her clothes off before the camera and posed in ways that would surely make her grandmother turn over in her grave. Although, the knowledge that she was doing it to help support her grandfather made it bearable. Besides, she only had a little while more to do this. She would be graduating from high school in a few short months.

Just hold on, Seta prodded herself as she studied until three A.M. for the fourth straight night. *Just hold on. You can do this. Just a few more months at this pace, and you'll be finished.* She would have her scholarships and she would be a graduate—hopefully, the valedictorian, which was why she worked so hard at her studies. She wanted to be number one.

With pencil in hand, Seta fell asleep at the table.

Seta's eyes widened at the large, red *F* on her paper. She looked up at Mrs. Mack. "Uhm, Mrs. Mack, there must be some mistake."

Mrs. Mack smiled smugly and shook her head. "No mistake. You made an *F.*"

Seta protested. Even at her worst, she had never made an *F* on a paper. "But, Mrs. Mack—"

"No buts," the teacher said, sashaying down the row and handing out the next student's paper.

Seta was aghast. This simply would not do. She stood and tapped her teacher's shoulder to gain her attention. "Mrs. Mack, I need—"

Mrs. Mack whirled around. "Are you threatening me?"

Seta frowned. "No." *This woman is crazy,* Seta thought to herself.

"Well, don't touch me again, or I will be forced to call security," she said and turned back to doing what she was doing. "Now, sit down."

Seta insisted. "Mrs. Mack, this grade—"

Mrs. Mack's eyes narrowed into tiny slits and her voice lowered. "I said sit it down. Park it. Now."

Seta stepped backward and found her seat while her classmates snickered.

Seta lingered after class. "Mrs. Mack, about this grade—"

Mrs. Mack was busying herself with straightening off her desk. "There is no discussion," she said. "The grade is what the grade is."

Seta didn't understand. How could she have made an *F*? It wasn't possible. "But, Mrs. Mack, I have to maintain straight *A*'s. My scholarships—"

"—are not my concern," the teacher spat the words. Seta wondered at the venom in her voice but didn't comment on it.

"Yes, but, can you at least tell me why?" Seta tried to sound respectful. Anger would get her nowhere, she knew.

Mrs. Mack was sanctimonious. "Well, you wrote on the

wrong assignment. I didn't even read your paper. You should follow instructions. Being good on the basketball court may be all you need to pass other classes, but in room two-oh-nine, you need to do your work."

Seta was outdone. "The wrong assignment? What in the world do you mean?"

Mrs. Mack shooed her off. "Look, I answered your question. Now get out of here. It's my break period, and I'm going to the lounge."

Seta followed the teacher out the door. "I didn't do the wrong assignment. I did the one you assigned."

Mrs. Mack wasn't listening. The acid was gone from her tone as she called out to a fellow teacher. "Oh, hi, Coach Allgood! Imagine bumping into you. Are you going to the lounge?"

Seta didn't wait around to hear his response. Angry and confused, she stomped down the hall to the cafeteria.

Seta slammed her backpack down and snatched out her paper. Jessica sat down across from her. "Hey, what has you looking so pissed?" Jessica asked, tearing open a yogurt.

Seta didn't bother responding. Instead, she slid her paper across the table. Jessica whistled. "Whoa! What is that?"

"Like I know," Seta said.

Amy walked up to the table. "Oh, hi guys," said Amy, who was dressed in coveralls and Nikes. It was the 1990s and everybody owned a pair of Nikes. "So nice to see you again, Seta. We never see you these days."

Seta didn't answer. Amy didn't notice. She pulled out a folded sheet of paper. "Hey, I have all the dirt on that Hannah girl. I talked to Karen who talked to Skye who talked to—"

Seta didn't want to hear that. Amy's gossiping was starting to annoy her. Seta cut Amy off. "There is no dirt. Hannah isn't pregnant."

Amy looked disappointed for a moment, then cheered up. "Yes, she is. I have it confirmed."

Seta stood and snatched her paper and backpack up in disgust. She didn't have time for this. She glanced at Jessica. "I'll talk to you later. I don't have time for this mess."

Amy looked offended for a second, but then shrugged. Seta was in one of her moods.

Seta made a decision. She would apologize to Hannah. The girl hadn't said anything to her since that day Seta had said those awful words to her. But Seta knew what it felt like to be falsely accused of something. She found Hannah eating by herself. Seta's mind flashed back to lunchtime years ago when Hannah's eyes had begged for an invite to sit with Seta and her friends.

"Hi," Seta said, as she approached Hannah.

Hannah said nothing. "Mind if I sit here?"

Hannah played with her straw. "Suit yourself."

Seta sat down. "Hey, look, I'm sorry for what I said the other day." Hannah looked up. Seta chewed the inside of her jaw. "I was just angry. It was wrong of me to call you that."

Hannah's eyes were sad. "All I've done since I moved here has been to try to be nice, to you and to everybody. But it's gotten me nowhere. All it's done is made people want to talk about me or make fun of me." Seta looked down at her lap. She was guilty.

"I just try to do the right thing and treat people like I want to be treated," Hannah said. "But it doesn't work. I would have at least thought you would have understood."

"I do, and I'm sorry. Really, I am," Seta said. For the first time, she saw in Hannah a reflection of herself. All her life, she had searched for acceptance from her father and from anybody around here. And here at school, Hannah was searching for the same acceptance from her classmates. Yet, they had offered her none.

"Yeah, I should have understood," Seta said. "I know, I was too busy feeling sorry for myself that I couldn't feel for anybody else," Seta admitted. She had never shared so much of her soul with anyone, even the girls she called her best friends. To share meant to open up to pain. And she already had enough of that, thank you very much.

Hannah smiled. "It's okay."

Seta didn't let the grade situation rest. She had worked too hard to settle for an *F* on any assignment, especially one she didn't feel she deserved. She confided to Coach Allgood, who read the paper and said he could see nothing that would warrant an *F*. He counseled Seta to attempt to talk to her teacher again, and if that didn't work, the principal.

Seta didn't want to go to the principal. She had already had too many bad experiences in the principal's office over the years. In her mind, the principal's office held nothing good. She asked her coach to talk to her teacher for her. Coach Allgood thought it would be better for Seta to try it one more time on her own, but finally agreed to speak to his colleague.

"So, what did she say?" Seta asked Coach Allgood the next day after practice.

"She said you didn't follow instructions. You didn't write on the assigned topic," he said.

"That's a lie," Seta said. "That's what she told me the other day. But I did. I wrote on exactly what she told us to."

Coach Allgood shook his head. "Well, she said that was the day you left class early and she gave a new writing assignment at the end of class."

Seta frowned, then her eyes widened. That day she had

asked to be excused to take her grandfather to the doctor. How was she supposed to know the assignment had been changed?

Seta went to explaining what happened.

"Well, I'm sure that if you explain to her, she'll make some kind of accommodation," he said. "She's a very reasonable woman."

Seta held little hope that Mrs. Mack would see things her way, but she took her coach's advice and went to talk to her. Mrs. Mack seemed to be seething about something. Still, she listened to Seta and, to Seta's amazement, changed the grade to a C. It wasn't the A Seta wanted, but she bit her lip against a protest and thanked her teacher.

Chapter 22

Phillip was spending the day with Augusta, much to Seta's chagrin. She couldn't get around it. Her aunt had insisted on taking her father to lunch and then maybe to a movie. Seta could only pray that Phillip's condition wouldn't become apparent.

Not wanting to sit at home alone, Seta planned to go to Robert's home.

Seta was nervous about going, but had told Robert she would be there. He had called her twice that morning to make sure she was still coming over. Seta understood his anxiety—she had twice told him she would come, then at the last minute, backed out. *This is a major step,* she thought. She would be visiting in the home she hadn't set foot in years, certainly not since he had settled in with his new family.

Robert called Seta on the telephone weekly. Their conversations were never long, which was her doing and not his. She wanted to take things slowly. So, she would allow him to talk to her for a few minutes, before making an excuse to get off the phone. Seta was guarded in her optimism.

She had gone from hungrily seeking out her father to re-
belling against all that was related to him in the face of his
continued rejection. Now, she was ready to think that
maybe—just maybe—they could carve out a relationship.
In the nearly two years of their tentative new relationship,
she had kept him at arm's length. She was angry at the way
he had treated her, but the anger was softening. Her
mother's words danced in her mind. She told herself she
could forgive. Although, even as the anger dissolved, she
had to admit she was afraid. Afraid her father would one
day wake up and remember why he gave her away all
those years before.

She had tried telling herself she was over all that, that it
didn't matter what he thought. But it did. She wanted him
to like her, to love her even. And she was afraid.

Today, however, she promised herself she would stop
being afraid. She would allow her heart to embrace him
again.

Seta pulled up to her father's house in her car—well, actually, her grandparents' car. She had taken it over since her
grandmother's death. Jessica's father had taught her how
to drive, and had taken her for her driving test. After all,
she felt she was no longer a child. She was living the life of
an adult.

Seta took one last look in the rearview mirror and climbed
out of the car. She had pulled her hair back with butterfly
clips. She wore Guess-? jeans and Keds. Seta slipped her lip
balm into her backpack purse.

Before she could raise her hand to knock at the door, it
swung open. A girl stood there, the one Seta recalled from
when she had run into Robert at the grocery store shortly
after her grandmother died. The girl immediately smiled
and tugged at her hand. "Hi, Seta," the girl said, dragging
her inside. "I'm Berrie, and this is Bennie. My daddy said
you're going to spend the day with us."

Seta gritted her teeth against the words *my daddy*, but managed to smile. *I have to be nice,* she reminded herself. It wasn't this girl's fault that she had stolen Seta's daddy.

"Hello, darling," Lola said. If Seta didn't know better, she would have sworn that was a grimace and not a smile on the woman's face.

"Hello," Seta said. She didn't know what she should call the woman. Mrs. Armstrong? Lola?

Robert appeared in the doorway. He removed a barbecue-stained apron. "Hey, baby," he said, reaching to hug her. Seta almost stepped backward but stilled herself. *This is what you want,* she reminded herself.

"Hi, Robert," she said. She felt him stiffen at her words, though he didn't correct her. She knew he wished she would call him Dad, Daddy or something along those lines, but she couldn't, not yet.

"Well, I'm out back. I just threw some things on the grill," he said, turning slowly to go back in the direction from which he had emerged. He seemed to favor one side, but Seta didn't pay much attention to that. "We thought we'd have a cookout to honor the occasion."

It was a touch cool outside, but this was fall in Texas and so the coldness hadn't overtaken the air. Leaves were on the ground and trees were beginning to turn naked.

"Oh, thanks," Seta said, not sure of what she should say. She wished they hadn't gone to any trouble for her. She didn't want the attention—or the pressure.

The woman named Lola strode to her, holding a tray of glasses. "Would you like some tea?"

Seta took one, grateful to have something to do with her hands. She then took an uneasy step toward the porch swing and sat down. The girl, Berrie, was right at her heels. She nestled next to Seta. Seta wanted to brush her away, to tell her to get out of her personal space, but she didn't.

The child touched Seta's hair. "You're so pretty," she whispered.

Seta looked down at her. The girl's eyes were full of admiration and awe. "So, you really are our sister?" Berrie asked.

Seta could see Lola watching her out of the corner of her eye. She pondered her response. The girl waited expectantly. "Yes, I am."

The girl squealed. "Well, that's what Daddy said. So, will you live with us?"

Seta dismissed the request with a grunt. "No, I don't think I can do that."

The girl was insistent. "But why not? Families live together."

Very astute observation, Seta thought. Families were supposed to live together, but not this one. No, hers was a father who had kicked her out when she wasn't even old enough to walk.

"Well, I'm getting ready to go off to college anyway, so I'll be moving," Seta answered the question, not wanting to talk about it any further.

Robert chimed in. "Yeah, you see that Berrie, Bennie? Your sister has big plans to go to college." His chest seemed to expand two inches. "She's smart. She's going to go far. She's going to make her father proud."

The old anger threatened to rise to the surface. However, Seta fought it back. No, this would be a pleasant afternoon.

"So, Seta, what are you going to study?" Lola asked to fill the awkward silence that fell after Seta failed to respond to Robert's obvious pandering. It was like he was trying to overcompensate for years of not telling her he was proud of her.

"Law," was Seta's one-word answer.

"Oh, really?" Lola raised an eyebrow. "That's nice. What type?"

"Family law," Seta paused for effect. "I want to punish deadbeat dads who abandon their children."

The silence was deafening. Robert dropped the hamburger patty he had been turning over on the grill. Lola's eyes widened, then she busied herself with brushing imaginary lint from her dress. Only Beryl seemed oblivious, as she leaned her head on Seta's arm.

Robert managed to clear his throat. "Well, ahem, that's a fine profession. The world needs good attorneys."

All afternoon, they hovered over Seta. Lola never let Seta's glass get lower than half-full before she was refilling it with more tea. Beryl followed wherever Seta moved. Robert prodded her with questions all evening—first about college, then about her grandfather, then about basketball.

By the time she left, Seta was exhausted.

Seta lay in bed with her hands behind her head. She repeated the words of her mother's letter to herself. Just reciting them to herself gave her confidence and faith. Whenever she read her mother's letter, or thought of her words, she felt an immediate calm. And calm was what she needed after her day. She was happy she had gone to her father's house today. Really, she was. But she was mentally drained.

He was trying so hard to make her forget that he had abandoned her all those years. And that girl, Beryl, had seemed glued to Seta's hip. Seta wasn't sure how to take that at first. However, by the end of the evening, she vowed to be the big sister she never had. In Beryl's eyes, she saw a girl in love with the idea of having a big sister. Seta knew what it was like to be in love with an idea.

Seta didn't know what to make of Lola. She wasn't outright mean or even unpleasant. Seta, though, couldn't help but feel like the woman was watching her, and she didn't know why.

"I'll be back," Seta promised the family as she finally escaped.

She was exhausted.

Robert trudged slowly across the crackling grass to the familiar headstone. He had missed several weeks. He knelt and placed the flowers on the cool, gray stone.

"Hello, sweetheart," he said. "I'm sorry I haven't been by to talk to you lately."

He paused and watched a bird fly overhead. "So many things have happened lately." He closed his eyes for a moment and gently rubbed the headstone. "You'd be proud. I've been trying to spend some time with the baby. Well, I say baby, but she's all grown up now," he said. "She's a beautiful girl."

Emotion constricted his throat. Robert had stayed away from the grave these past few months. The anger he had felt toward the girl had finally found its rightful place. "I still don't know why you put yourself at risk like that," he said. "We talked about so many things. We had so many dreams. Then, you just went and did this, on your own. You didn't tell me the truth."

The words brought back the anger that had turned his heart to stone. This time the anger wasn't directed at the child, but at the mother.

"I stayed away because I didn't know what to say to you," he continued. "I've spent years—years—going over that letter in my mind. Wondering how you could love the dream of a child so much that you would give up your life. But I couldn't be angry with you. No, I couldn't be angry at my perfect Rose."

His voice cracked. "Because to be angry at you would be to admit that you weren't perfect. So, instead, I took it out on the girl. I could be angry with her because she had taken you away from me.

"I know now that it wasn't her fault. You sacrificed your life for her. You traded our life together for what you wanted. You made the decision to tear our family apart . . . you."

He slammed his fist down on the headstone. He didn't notice the pain from the impact, or the bruise. Years of anger seemed to crowd into his chest and choke off his airway. He struggled for breath, that came in short, ragged bursts. A woman glanced at him from a few feet away but turned away, embarrassed at the sight of the grown man bawling.

"You always had to have your way," he said. "Always, no matter what, it always had to be Rose's way. Look at what you did. Why did you do it?"

He asked the last question toward the sky. The rustle of the leaves was the only reply to his question.

Robert didn't even bother to wipe the tears that streamed down his face.

These tears had been a long time coming.

"Gabe, I don't want to do this anymore." Seta had managed to muster her courage to tell him how she felt as they lingered over Chinese. In all the months since she had been doing the pictures, she hadn't grown comfortable with her new job.

She hadn't said anything since that dreadful day when Gabe had seemed like he was ready to cut her loose. Now, though, she was afraid of what would happen if the pictures went public. Plus, posing naked made her soul uneasy.

"Do what?" Gabe asked. He glanced at his watch.

"The . . . pictures." Seta held her breath.

Gabe looked up at her. "What do you mean? I thought you were having fun?"

Seta squirmed in her seat. "I am. I mean, I want to. I

mean, I've tried, but . . ." She let her voice trail off at the thought of his disapproval.

Gabe sighed. "Seta, baby, have I been anything but nice to you? I compliment you everyday. I take you to nice restaurants. I don't pressure you for sex. I've never even so much as come on to you. All I've done is asked you to help us both make a living. What's the problem?"

Seta's heart was beating fast. He was right. He hadn't so much as touched her. He did treat her to nice evenings out and in many ways, acted like a boyfriend, but without making her have sex. She had told him she didn't want to, and that had been that. He had been great, had even given her a job. How could she be so ungrateful? "There is no problem," she said. "I'm sorry. Forget I said anything. Let's enjoy our dinner."

Gabe pinched her cheek. "That's more like it."

Seta had to make her declaration of where she would attend college. She had put it off as long as she could, and the schools were antsy. In the last week, she had heard from a rush of strangers representing various universities, each trying to influence her. It felt good to be wanted. Maybe that's why she had dragged it out for as long as she could.

Big, fancy East Coast schools wanted her. So did regional schools, and some on the West Coast. They each told her she would surely add to their basketball programs—and, oh yeah, academic programs too—and how much they wanted her.

She wanted to go to one of the fancy East Coast schools. However, she didn't want to be that far away from her grandfather. So, instead, she accepted a scholarship to a prestigious private university that was only a few hours away.

Her full scholarship also included a stipend. Therefore,

she would have money to send back home. Seta sighed.
Her hard work had paid off.

Things were finally going well for Seta. She and her father had breakfast together on Fridays. She knew she
would be a top graduate. Her scholarship letter was sitting
on the kitchen counter. Her grandfather didn't seem to be
getting any worse. Life was good.

Spring '93 was a frenzy for Seta and her friends. They
had prom, senior pictures, and graduation on tap. Jessica
was voted homecoming queen in the fall and was to receive
a special recognition at graduation. She was excited because she had auditioned for and been accepted as a cheerleader for a professional football team.

Diana had received news of her scholarship as well. She
would play ball at a good university in south Louisiana.
The news relieved a lot of the pressure of waiting, both for
her and for her parents. Now, she could relax and enjoy the
rest of her senior year.

Amy hadn't said too much, though, about what she
would do in the fall.

"What's going on with Amy?" Jessica asked.

Seta had canceled her photo session today and instead,
stopped by Jessica's house. Jessica sat on the floor, sorting a
stack of pictures. Seta lay on her stomach across Jessica's
bed. Diana was looking for a CD to play.

"I don't know," Seta said absently. She hadn't thought
much about Amy lately. Now that they weren't on the same
basketball team, it seemed that they didn't have much in
common. Seta mused. Years ago, she would have thought
Diana would have been the one she would have drifted
away from, not Amy.

"Di, do you know?" Jessica noticed Diana had been unusually quiet.

Diana's eyes went to Jessica and then to Seta.

"Uh, no."

Something about her tone made Seta sit up. "You sure you don't know something you're not telling?"

Diana was uncharacteristically reticent. "I can't say."

Jessica pounced on her. "Oh, no you don't! If you know something, you'd better spill it. We're best friends."

Seta waited expectantly. Diana walked over to Jessica's bedroom door, making sure it was closed.

"Promise you won't tell?" Jessica and Seta looked at each other. Then, they both nodded. "Amy's pregnant."

Jessica gasped. Seta's mouth fell open.

"You are lying," Jessica said in disbelief.

Diana shook her head sadly. "I wish I was."

"How do you know?" Seta asked. She knew how easily rumors got started. Though Amy had been the source of many, Seta didn't want anyone spreading one about her, especially if it was untrue.

Diana slumped to the floor and drew her knees to her chest. "I bumped into her at the store the other week."

"So." Jessica said.

"So, she was buying a pregnancy test."

"Maybe it wasn't for her," Seta said hopefully.

Diana shook her head. "When she saw me, she begged me to come with her while she took the test."

Jessica was no longer interested in the pictures strewn across her floor.

"It was positive," Diana said.

Seta closed her eyes. She could just imagine what Amy must be feeling. She and Amy weren't as close as they once had been, but she still didn't wish anything bad to happen to her.

"Should we go over there? Call her? See if she needs something?" Seta asked.

"Yeah, like an abortion," Diana shot back.

Seta cut her eyes at Diana. "No. Like, I don't know. Maybe she could use some moral support or something."

Diana wasn't sure. "I don't know. She didn't really want anybody to know."

Jessica was already up and dialing Amy's number. "Well, I'm calling her."

"You just promised you wouldn't say anything!" Diana snatched the phone from her hand.

Jessica grabbed the phone back. "Yeah, but that was before I found out what it was."

Diana looked at Seta for help. Seta shrugged. She didn't know what to do either.

Jessica punched the numbers and let the phone ring. On the fifth ring, someone picked up. "Hello?"

Jessica's eyes widened. Now that she had Amy on the line, she didn't know what to say. She squirmed.

"Hello?" Amy asked, a bit more insistently this time.

"Uh, hi, Ames," Jessica said, using the nickname she adopted for her friend. "We were all just sitting around and thought we'd call to see what you were doing."

"Right, y'all were over there talking about me, weren't you?" Amy said. "I knew that Diana couldn't keep a secret."

Jessica tried to deny it. "No, we—"

"Save it," Amy said. "I know y'all. All of you."

"What? What's she saying?" Seta whispered. Jessica quieted her with a look.

"Well, we were just worried, is all," Jessica offered.

"I know y'all are over there talking about me. You're probably laughing at me, saying this is what I get for always talking about people. Now folks will talk about me." Her tone was angry but scared too.

Jessica shook her head, and then realized Amy couldn't

see her. "No, Amy. We're not talking about you. We love you. We're just concerned, that's all. What did your mom say?"

Amy let out a grunt. "Like she has even noticed. You know she's always working. I could be sticking out about to deliver and she wouldn't notice." Resentment inched into her voice.

Seta nudged Jessica. "Ask her if she wants us to come over," she whispered.

Jessica tried to respond to Seta and Amy at the same time. She waved Seta off and held her mouth to the phone. "Well, maybe it won't be so bad when she does find out." She didn't know what else to say. They had all a moment ago been excitedly talking about their futures, and now there was a big question mark over Amy's.

"Yeah, right," Amy said. "Look, I'm tired of talking. I'll catch you later."

Before Jessica could say anything else, the line went dead. Jessica placed the phone in its cradle. Seta and Diana looked at her expectantly. "So?" Diana asked.

Jessica chewed her lip. "It's not good," she said slowly. "She is really out of it."

"I'm sure," Diana said. "But really, it's just so funny how things happen. She was always the one spreading rumors about others being pregnant, and look who turns out to be. You remember when she said that girl Hannah was pregnant?"

Seta did remember. She remembered all too well how Hannah had to walk through the halls with condescending eyes following her.

"Yeah, but that doesn't make it any better for Amy to be pregnant now. Who knew she was even getting down like that?" Seta asked.

"Well, the whole world will know now," Diana said.

Jessica nodded, sadness circling her eyes.

* * *

Seta grabbed her backpack and slowly stepped out of the car. Her Aunt Augusta's car was parked in front of the house. She frowned. What was Augusta doing here in the middle of the afternoon? At the thought that perhaps Augusta would discover her grandfather's secret, Seta hastily slammed the door and raced into the house.

Phillip was sitting in his recliner, coils sagging under the bottom. He wore an absent smile. Seta looked at Augusta.

"Hi, Auntie," Seta said, trying to hide her nervousness. "Hi, Poppy, how are you doing today?"

She kissed Phillip on the forehead. He touched her hand. "Yes, Barbara, I told you I would forgive you. It's all right. I know it wasn't all your fault," he said.

Seta's eyes shifted from her grandfather to her aunt. She lowered her voice. "It's all right, Poppy. It's me, Seta."

"Yes, Lord, Barbara, I don't hold it against you," he said soothingly.

Augusta spoke. "Seta, I think we need to talk. Why don't you sit down?"

Seta's heart beat fast in her chest. She sat on the couch next to her grandfather's chair. "Yes, Auntie?" She tried to sound calm.

Augusta smoothed invisible wrinkles from her navy skirt. She clasped her hands in her lap and looked up at Seta. "Seta, Poppy can't stay here anymore."

Seta felt like someone had ripped out her heart. She jumped to her feet. "Auntie, no!"

Augusta shook her head. "Sweetheart, he can't. He needs to be someplace where people can look after him, where they can take care of him."

Seta was defiant. "I've been taking care of him!"

Augusta spoke in even tones. "I know, and that wasn't fair to you. I'm sorry. I've been so busy that I've not paid attention to what has been going on right under my nose. He's not well. And you can't keep looking after him."

"I won't let him go." Seta stood in front of him. "I won't, Auntie. I won't."

Augusta chose her words carefully. "Seta, you've become a very mature girl, but you're still a girl. You can't take care of him. He's not well, sweetheart. He's not well and he needs to be somewhere else.

"Besides, you're about to go off to college," Augusta reasoned.

Tears spilled from Seta's eyes. Her chest felt heavy and constricted. "You can't take him away! You can't. He's all I have."

"Child, what's wrong with you?" Phillip spoke with clarity Seta hadn't seen in months. "Come sit on Poppy's lap."

Seta sniffled hard. She wiped the tears away with the palm of her hand and smiled. "Oh, Poppy, it's okay. It's going to be okay."

"I told your grandma not to upset you," Phillip said reprovingly.

Augusta's eyes were sad. She stood and placed a hand on Seta's shoulder.

Seta was doing her best to keep her mind off her grandfather's move. Whenever she thought of it, her heart hurt. She was trying to concentrate on her class work when the office aide entered the room and whispered to her teacher. The teacher beckoned her with one finger. "Seta, you're needed at the office."

"Me?" Seta asked with bewilderment.

"Yes."

She left her books at her desk and followed the student. In the principal's office, Coach Allgood stood with his arms folded across his chest. He looked unusually grim. Seta frowned. "Coach, what's going on?"

Coach Allgood looked at the principal, who dismissed the office aide and then pulled out a magazine. He slid it across the desk. Seta gasped. She was staring seductively, with only a towel draped across her body.

Her mouth fell open. "Coach, I—"

Coach Allgood held up his hand. "Seta, what is this?"

Nobody gave her permission to, but Seta sank in the chair in front of the principal's desk. There she was, naked and for all the world to see. Embarrassment burned her face. But if she were honest with herself, she had known this day would come.

Her eyes searched the eyes of her coach, who had been almost like a father to her. Disappointment seemed to drip from his being, from the sagging shoulders to the eyes that scanned her face repeatedly. Shame bowed her head.

"Seta, you've got to tell me something." Coach Allgood touched her chin and forced her to look up.

"I don't know," was all she said.

"You know something," the principal chimed in.

"Seta, why?" Coach Allgood shook his head.

"I—I needed the money." She knew the reason sounded ludicrous, even to her own ears. Coach must think her the worst person in the world.

"Money, Seta? You did this for money?" He looked almost like he wanted to cry. "Tell me it was something else."

"My grandfather . . . I had to take care of my grandfather," she said.

"Look, I don't want to hear the reasons or the excuses right now. I've already heard from the university. They're withdrawing their scholarship."

Seta's eyes widened. "They're taking my scholarship?"

"Yes. They said they have a morality clause and they can't have someone on their basketball team who poses naked in magazines," Coach Allgood said.

"What about the other schools?" Seta asked. She was

crushed. She had to have a scholarship. How else was she going to afford college? She had worked all these years to get here, and now it was being taken away.

"I've already talked to three others. None of them want you."

Seta closed her eyes and let her head fall back. Nobody wanted her. That shouldn't surprise her, not at this point.

Chapter 23

News spread across the school grounds rapidly. Whispers greeted Seta wherever she went. Boys winked at her and girls turned their noses up. Jessica and Diana rushed to her side.

"What's all this about?" Jessica asked.

Seta shrugged. There was no point in lying. "I took a bunch of naked pictures to get some money and now everybody has seen them in a magazine." She waited for the condemnation.

"Well, as long as you were cute," Jessica tried a joke. Seta smiled slightly but not for long.

Diana stepped closer. "Look, there are a lot worse things a girl can do. Don't let it get to you. You know folks are always looking for something to say to tear you down. Forget 'em."

Seta appreciated her friend's words. Still, she knew there was no way she could forget. "I've lost my scholarship. The school said I can't attend there now."

Diana gasped. "Your scholarship? They can't!"

"Apparently, they can," Seta said.

"Oh, I'm so sorry." Diana knew how terrible her friend must feel. She knew she was counting on a scholarship. "Is there anything I can do?"

Seta shook her head. "Nah, but thanks."

The phone was ringing when Seta stepped into the house. She let her backpack fall to the floor and picked up the phone. "You stay right where you are," a stern voice came over the line. "I will be there in ten minutes."

The line went dead. Augusta was on her way.

The silence in the room was loud. Seta's eyes went everywhere, except for her aunt's face. Augusta sat with her arms crossed over her chest. Her chin jutted out and her eyes bore into Seta.

Finally, Augusta broke the silence. "So?" she asked pointedly, her eyebrow raised.

Seta shrugged, and Augusta almost lost it. She stood and paced across the room, clenching and unclenching her fists. She breathed deeply. Finally, she turned back toward the niece she loved like the daughter she never had.

"Nude pictures, Seta?" Shame burned Seta's face at the thought of her photos.

Augusta glanced skyward. "Lord, Jesus, help us. Seta, did we not teach you anything? How did we fail you?"

The pain in Augusta's voice hurt Seta worse than a screaming rage would have. She didn't want quiet dismay. She would much prefer an angry shouting match.

"Seta, why?" Augusta shook her head.

Seta shrugged. "I don't know."

"Girl, you better explain yourself." Augusta's nose flared.

Seta opened her mouth, but her aunt cut her off. "Don't say a word. If you say anything, it might make me lose my religion in here. Go to your room, and we'll talk later."

Seta closed her mouth and did as she was told. She went

to her new room in Augusta's house. Augusta had moved her in after settling Phillip in a neighboring nursing home the other week.

The house still did not feel like home for Seta, especially today. She sat on the edge of the bed that was now hers, feeling like a stranger in this nice, girlish bedroom draped in pastels and flowers.

Seta twiddled her thumbs and pulled lint from her bedspread.

It was a month before graduation and Seta was on suspension. Augusta tried to appeal it, arguing that what her niece had done did not take place on school grounds. Nevertheless, that only succeeded in reducing the suspension time from three days to two.

Seta had already lost her basketball scholarship and knew her high class ranking was in jeopardy. When she returned from suspension, she walked through the halls of school with her head down. Each step felt leaden.

Nobody seemed to want to talk to her—though, they talked plenty *about* her. She stopped in her tracks. A photo torn from one of the magazines was taped to the front of her locker. Her mouth fell open.

Before she could grab it, someone snatched it down. It was Diana. She balled it up and threw it on the floor. "They are so stupid," Diana said in disgust. "So, are you okay?"

"Yeah, I'm fine," Seta said, but Diana didn't believe her.

That night, Seta sat in her bedroom at her aunt's house with the door closed. Her aunt had no alcohol in the house, but Seta needed a drink. That was the only thing that would take the edge off this pain. She would call Jessica and get her to sneak some to her.

Seta picked up the telephone, then hesitated. The dial tone was loud in her ear. She slowly put the receiver back

down. That was what she would have done in the old days.
No, she wouldn't do that now.

"Coach, is there any way you can help me? I'll play ball
anywhere." Seta sat in Coach Allgood's office. The coach's
lips were creased into a thin, straight line.

"Seta, I don't know. I've talked to a lot of schools and
tried to call in some favors. Nobody wants to take you," he
said. "Nobody wants a troublemaker on their team."

"But, Coach, I'm not a troublemaker," Seta said. She re-
strained herself from stomping her foot. She was afraid all
her dreams had seeped away from her, like the quickness of
a flashbulb.

Coach Allgood shook his head. "Well, you have some serious things facing you," he said. "Schools are really exam-
ining you. They're looking into your background and those
troubles you had early on in junior high don't look so good.
Before, they didn't care about it because that was so long
ago. Now, with this latest thing—"

Seta slumped forward, her head in her hands. "Coach,
please help me."

Coach Allgood looked at Seta, then away. He had tried to
get schools to reconsider her, but to no avail. She was one of
his most promising athletes. Better than that, she was a star
student. It made no difference though. No school wanted
her.

Police arrested Gabe for the pictures he had taken of Seta
and, it turned out, lots of other girls. Seta found out from
the newspaper articles that his name was Gabriel Dunbar
and that he was twenty-eight years old. He had a long history of taking advantage of young girls. She was grateful
the newspaper refrained from printing her name, though
all those at her school knew she was the "top-rated high
school athlete" mentioned in the stories.

Seta longed for her grandmother, to have Barbara's calming words to carry her through this, or to have her grandfather's quiet reassurance. She would have none of that. The people she had depended on to shape her life and protect her were both gone. One, buried. The other trapped in his own mind.

Augusta hadn't spoken much to Seta since that initial day. It seemed almost like she didn't know what to say. Augusta knocked softly on the door to Seta's bedroom. Seta quickly shoved the newspaper article under her pillow. "Come in," she said.

Augusta stepped into the room. Her crisp, navy suit made her seem stiff and prim.

"May I sit down?" Augusta asked Seta. Seta scooted over and Augusta slowly lowered herself onto the bed, her legs crossed at the ankles.

"How are you doing?" Augusta asked.

"I'm fine," Seta said.

"Seta, I'm sorry if I've failed you," Augusta said.

Seta looked up in surprise. That certainly was not what she expected to hear.

Augusta played with her hands. "I should have been paying attention. I wasn't. I was too busy with my work and my own immediate family. I ignored what was right in front of me."

Seta touched her aunt's arm. "Auntie, don't. It wasn't your fault. It was mine."

Augusta wasn't listening. "I knew better. I knew I was letting you take on too much responsibility . . . the house, driving, Daddy. But I just made myself believe that you could handle it because I didn't have time to deal with it."

For the first time, Augusta didn't seem like the polished private school principal she always portrayed. She was sad and broken. "And I'm sorry for saddling you with Daddy."

"I didn't feel saddled," Seta said. She would have gladly done anything for her grandfather.

"Well, it wasn't fair to you," Augusta said. "Seta, Daddy has Alzheimer's."

"What?" The word hit Seta hard.

"That's why he sometimes seems to forget things and why he sometimes gets irritable or doesn't want to take a bath," Augusta said. "He's confused and he's scared. And I left you to deal with all of that because I was too busy and scared to face that myself. I didn't want to believe anything was wrong. So, I pretended everything was fine."

Seta read about that disease at one time and knew it didn't sound good. Scenes from the past year or so flashed in her mind . . . the missed work, the going outside with no shoes on, the nakedness.

She thought of something else.

"What about all the references to Grammy? What was he talking about when he said he forgave her?" She didn't know why she had thought of that of all things.

A strange expression crossed Augusta's face. She shook her head. "Oh, that was nothing," she said. Then she paused. "I'm lying. It was something."

Seta held her breath and waited.

Augusta sighed and rubbed imaginary wrinkles from the front of her skirt. "Well, nobody in the family wanted to tell you because it was old business, but I guess you have proven that you are closer to being an adult than a child."

"What is it?" Seta's stomach felt quivery. "What is it that nobody wanted me to know?"

Augusta paused. It seemed almost indecent to discuss this private matter with a child. However, her niece was no ordinary child. And she deserved to know. "Sweetheart, a long time ago, before your mother or I was born, my mother met this man."

Seta groaned inwardly. She knew she wasn't going to like whatever came next. "Uh huh?"

"Well, I don't know the whole story, just the highlights. Basically, Mama got married when she was really young. Daddy was off at the war, working or something like that. Mama was really miserable—she was little more than a child, really.

"Anyway, she always had dreams of doing something big. She was always in awe of those who had achieved—she loved famous people. One day, she met a jazzman from New Orleans."

Augusta paused. She couldn't defame her mother's memory to this child. But Seta would have none of it. She nudged her aunt to continue. "Go on."

Augusta drew a deep breath. "Well, she ran off with him."

Seta bolted up straight. "She did not!"

Seta was angry with her aunt for saying such things about her grandmother. Augusta stayed the girl. "It's true."

Seta shook her head. It wasn't true. Her grandmother would never do anything like that.

"I can't give you all the details, but basically, Daddy had to go get her and bring her back home," Augusta said.

Seta didn't say anything for a long moment. "So, that was it. She came back home and that was that?"

Augusta had said enough. "Well, that's all you need to know. That's all he meant. They patched things up and moved on."

Seta's eyes narrowed. "So, did anything happen while she was in New Orleans with this musician?"

Augusta blinked rapidly. "No, of course not!"

Seta knew she was lying. She grabbed her aunt by the arm. "Auntie, you have to tell me the truth! It's not fair that everybody else knows the truth and I don't, and I lived with them all my life."

Augusta knew she had said too much not to tell the whole truth. "Well, one thing did happen. My mother got pregnant."

Seta's hand flew to her mouth. Realization widened her eyes. "With my mama?"

Augusta nodded.

"So . . . that means that Poppy isn't really my grandfather?"

Augusta gently touched Seta's arm. "Maybe, in one sense, but in the sense that matters most, he will always be your grandfather. He loves you very much."

Seta felt like another person had been stolen from her.

The pressure of the last few weeks weighed on Seta. Her grandfather had been taken away from her—literally and figuratively. She missed him terribly but didn't know how to process the fact that he wasn't really related to her. She still couldn't imagine her grandmother doing something like that. It all made sense to her now though. That's why her mother didn't much resemble her grandfather. She had coloring of one of those people they called Creole down south in New Orleans.

In addition to having to deal with the revelation of her relationship with her grandfather, Seta also mourned the loss of her scholarship. Without it, she knew she wouldn't attend college. She would be like Amy now, facing a life of uncertainty.

Seta locked herself in her bedroom.

Tomorrow was her graduation day. However, if felt more like the end instead of the beginning.

The sun awakened Seta. She lay there for a moment, welcoming the day. Then reality came flooding back. The pain made her cover her head with a pillow. She wouldn't get out of bed.

A light knock came. Augusta stuck her head in the door. "Rise and shine."

Seta groaned and faced the wall. "Go away."

Augusta stepped into the room. "Come on, Seta. It's your graduation day. It's a beautiful day."

"It's not. It's a horrible day. My life is horrible. I just want to lie here," Seta whined. "I want to die."

Augusta removed the pillow from Seta's head. "You are not going to lie here. Today is a beautiful day. You are going to get up, you are going to get dressed, and you are going to proudly walk across that stage to get your diploma."

"Why? I'm not going anywhere after I get it. I can't even go to college," Seta said.

Augusta handed Seta an envelope. Seta looked at it with disinterest.

"Go on, open it," Augusta prompted.

"Why? I don't care what's in it." Seta didn't move.

Augusta smiled. "I think you will care." Augusta pulled the letter from the already opened envelope. She began to read. "Dear Rosetta Love, on behalf of the university, we would like to extend to you this scholarship. . . ."

Seta stared at the letter. "Is this for real?"

Augusta nodded. "Read it." Seta did. The university was granting her a scholarship to play basketball. She looked at the letterhead. It was the university where her father worked.

"How?" Seta asked. It seemed unthinkable that she would now have a scholarship, not after all the pleading she had done. No schools would accept her.

"Your father talked to a few people," Augusta said. "They said they'd love to offer you a scholarship. You should thank him. He came through for you."

Seta was stunned. It hadn't occurred to her to ask Robert to help her get into college. The fact that he had done what no one else seemed to be able to do made her speechless. Her father had salvaged her future.

Seta recalled something her grandmother had told her a long time ago. She had said God may not answer prayers just when we want Him to but He did answer them. "God answers prayers right on time."

Indeed.

Augusta stood. "Now, get up and get dressed so we can go."

Someone picked up the phone in the middle of the third ring. "Hello."

It was Robert.

Words escaped Seta's mind. She didn't know what she wanted to say. She held the receiver.

"Hello?" Robert said again.

Seta found her voice. "Oh, hi."

"Seta," Robert said. Seta could tell he was glad to hear from her.

"Seta!" Seta heard Beryl call in the background. She smiled.

"Tell Berrie I said hi."

"I will," Robert said. "So how are you? Ready to walk across the stage?"

Seta nodded. "Yes. I am."

At that moment, she knew today was about more than walking across the stage to get a diploma. She felt she was ready to walk into a phase of her life with her father. It had taken her a lifetime to get there, but she was finally ready. Maybe she could finally forgive him.

As imperfect as she was and God accepted her, surely she could forgive her father. Yes, he had made mistakes, but like Ms. Nettie said, so does everyone. The angry ice around Seta's heart had finally thawed. *God is love*, Ms. Nettie had said. *And if I am to be like God, then I must show love too.*

"I found out about the scholarship," she said. "Thank you, Daddy."

Robert's voice caught in his throat. For a moment, he said nothing. "You're welcome."

Chapter 24

On either side of Seta, students used their graduation programs to fan, stirring the heavy air. She dabbed absently at her forehead, wiping away beads of sweat as her eyes scanned the crowd for her father. She couldn't find him. Her mind flashed back to a similar occasion when she was in the fifth grade. She recalled sitting in an auditorium—hot like this one—waiting for her father to show up to see her get her recognition.

But he hadn't come.

Seta closed her eyes and breathed deeply. No sadness came this time. She recalled her mother's words: "I want you to always do your best and to always believe in yourself. You are smart, gifted and beautiful. You are precious."

Seta realized that it didn't matter whether Robert came to see her walk across the stage today or not, or whether he liked her or not. Sure, it would be nice if he did, but she knew now that she had spent too much time basing what she did on trying to gain his approval—or acting out when she didn't get it. She realized now, as she stood ready to step into the next part of her life, that she was who she was.

And she forgave him. She finally released all the hurt feelings, anger, and resentment of the past. Scripture her grandmother had often recited came back to her. *God meant it for my good.* Just like Joseph's brothers had worked against him—had cast him away as if he never existed—so had her father. But that hardship turned out to be for the good, as God used the circumstance to create great change. So many bad things had happened, but she knew they all came together now to shape her.

And she knew she had survived and, with God's grace, would continue.

She had everything within herself to be the best person she could be. That's what she told herself, and that's what she believed. She didn't need anyone's approval, not even her father's. It had taken her a long time to accept herself or to even like herself.

And she knew her life wasn't about struggling to be perfect, but it was about working to be the best Seta she could.

Today, she had finally arrived. She was graduating to a whole new self. She opened her eyes. She drew in a deep and steadying breath and smiled widely. She had survived more than most at her age. And it hadn't been easy.

At least she knew something. She was ready for whatever lay ahead. Even if she had to face it on her own. But as she thought of that, another thing crossed her mind. *Even when I feel alone, I'm not. God is right there.*

Seta didn't make valedictorian or salutatorian of her class. Still, she didn't complain about ranking number three. She felt pretty good. She had done her best—well, with a few exceptions—and that's all she could ask for. She knew things could have been a lot worse—especially if she were honest about the decisions she had made chasing love.

She still hadn't seen Robert, but she smiled broadly all

the same. She couldn't let that bother her. A twinge of sadness pierced her consciousness because it would have been nice for her father to be there, but that was all. She wasn't angry.

"Rosetta Love Armstrong."

At the sound of her name being called, Seta approached the stage of Clear Love High School, the place where this had all begun, the place her father had met her mother. The name of the school was different—there were no "colored" high schools these days—but the place was the same. It had been a life-changing place for her mother. And it would be the same for her.

Her eyes swept across the room. She saw her aunt, who gave her a tiny wave and blew her a kiss. Next to her was Phillip, rocking quietly. Relatives crowded onto the bleachers.

Her eyes widened, and then she looked away. Her old basketball buddy, Mike, was there. Out of the corner of her eye, Seta caught a glimpse of someone.

It was Robert.

Her smile grew wider.

Her daddy had come for her. After all these years, and after so many trials and tribulations, he had come. And this was a new beginning.

She was ready.

Epilogue

Spring 2004

"Auntie, I can't believe you're actually retiring!" Seta said. She sat at the kitchen table, manicured hands wrapped around a glass of tea. Her hair was pulled back off her face and hung loosely down her back.

Augusta nodded. "Yes, it's time."

Augusta still looked much the same as she did when Seta was in high school. Her hair was streaked with gray now, though, but it was still perfectly coifed. Tiny pearl earrings decorated her ears.

"Well, I could have retired a while ago, but I just loved that school so much," Augusta said. Fond memories dotted her tenure at Sunnybrook Academy.

"Enough about me, let's talk about you," Augusta said, smiling warmly. "Look at you, the fastest rising hot lawyer on the East Coast."

Seta waved her aunt off. She didn't pay attention to acclaim, but she was happy with where she was in life. She had fulfilled her childhood desire to become an attorney.

She was going into her third year at a prestigious firm. She had snagged a highly competitive internship, which led to a job following law school.

Seta had spent her undergraduate years playing basketball at her father's college before heading off to one of the country's top law schools. She knew she would someday move back home, but for now, her place was in the nation's capital.

Seta had returned home for her aunt's retirement ceremony that week.

"Have you gotten a chance to see any of your old friends since you've been back in town this time?" Augusta asked.

Seta nodded. "Well, I don't much talk to Amy. I did see her at the mall though. She's a manager at a boutique. She seems to be doing okay. She has three children. Jessica is in California. She's been getting work as an extra in some movies and has worked on a couple of commercials. She's still hoping to get her big break."

"What about anybody else?"

"Well, I don't really keep up with anybody all that much, except for Diana." There was someone else from her childhood she talked to, but Seta didn't mention him. "Actually, her team should be on TV tonight."

"Oh, yeah, I saw her on a poster the other day," Augusta said. Diana was playing in the WNBA. "She seems to be doing pretty well."

"Yeah, she is. We're going on vacation somewhere during the off season, when we both have more time."

The two fell silent. The years had brought many changes.

"So, you ready to go to church?" Augusta broke the silence.

Seta nodded. "Yes, I'll drive."

Seta parked her silver Chrysler Sebring at the edge of the church parking lot. She stepped out of the car and sucked in a deep breath, glancing around at the spring, Texas day. The sky was a perfect blue, the air was barely moving.

She stood perfectly still in the foyer of Mount Bethel. Her eyes roamed the sanctuary in appreciation. This was only her second time in the new building. The building fund had finally paid off with the completion of the new church two years ago. Seta nodded. Maybe all her nickels and dimes *had* gone to something good. She could still smell the faint scent of new paint and wood.

She walked with her aunt to a pew near the front of the church. Yes, her grandmother would have loved to see this place. The piano played softly. Someone tapped Seta on the shoulder.

She turned. "Oh, hi!" She stepped into the aisle. A very pregnant Hannah gave her a hug, while a toddler clung to Hannah's leg.

"Wow, I see life has been treating someone well," Seta said with a wink.

Hannah grinned sheepishly. "Yes, the Lord has been good to me," she said. Her wedding ring sparkled in the reflected light as she rubbed her stomach.

A man walked up to her. "Sweetheart, service is about to start. I'm going to go get our seats," he whispered in Hannah's ear.

Hannah looked at Seta. "I have to go. But we must talk after service."

Seta nodded. "Okay."

Seta had finally been able to extricate herself from well-meaning churchgoers who exclaimed at how beautiful she had become and oohed and ahhhed over her career as an attorney.

One told her he had seen her in the newspaper the week before. "They called you Rosetta Love Armstrong. I wouldn't have known it was you if they hadn't had your picture right there big as day," Brother Smith said.

Seta smiled. She had gone back to her birth name professionally and in most circles. It just seemed right that she would go by the name on her birth certificate, not the name that came from her father's angry resentment so long ago. But to the people at home, she would forever be "Seta."

And that was okay with her.

"Seta, hold up!"

She was almost to her car. She looked around to see who had called her name.

She paused. "Hi." The word came out in one breath.

Mike smiled back at her. His suit fell in neat lines. His hair looked freshly trimmed. He was still tall and lanky, though she could tell, even under his suit that he had filled out quite nicely.

"Good to see you," Mike said.

"Likewise," Seta said. She looked at her aunt.

Augusta immediately got the message. She cleared her throat. "Oh, I see someone I need to speak to. I'll be right back," she turned away and called to someone across the way, "Sister Young!"

A moment later, the two were alone. Mike held her hands. "You're looking good, girl."

Seta was suddenly shy. "Thanks. So are you."

"Well, I was glad to get your e-mail that you were coming home. I didn't want to miss you, like last time," Mike said pointedly.

Seta looked at the ground. Her last trip had been a turnaround visit. She and Mike had been scheduled to go out, but she had canceled. "Yeah, I'm sorry about that. I had a lot going on," Seta said.

The truth was that she and Mike had shared confidences over the years, after bumping into each other three years ago on one of her visits to see her grandfather. However, they hadn't taken it much beyond that. Seta had been afraid anything else would ruin their delicate balance. She liked having Mike in her life and didn't want a romance to ruin their friendship.

"Come on, Seta," Mike said. She immediately knew what he was talking about. "Let's just see what happens."

Seta looked around. "We are at church," she hissed.

Mike shrugged. "I'm not doing anything bad. I'm just asking you on a date . . . tonight."

Seta hesitated. Even after all this time, Mike had a special place in her heart. She remembered all the times he had come to her rescue as a child. But what if she messed this thing up? Then she wouldn't have him in her life at all.

"Come on, Seta. I won't bite." He looked at her with puppy dog eyes. His expression turned mischievous. "Well, unless you want me to."

Before she could comment, Augusta returned. "Seta, baby, are you ready?" her aunt said.

Seta's eyes flew to Mike's. He was smiling. She took a deep breath. "Okay, and this time, I will be there."

Mike accompanied Seta to her aunt's retirement party. Augusta reveled in the attention as her husband ushered in guests who paid tribute to her. The room was packed. Seta was happy for her aunt.

Someone handed Seta a plate. She turned to see that it was Robert.

"Hi, Daddy," she said. He kissed her cheek.

"How are you?" Robert asked. His limp was more pronounced these days and he leaned heavily on a wooden cane, but other than that, he looked virtually the same. Well, except for the fact that all his hair was gone.

"I'm fine," Seta said. It felt good to be with her father. She saw Bennie and Berrie approaching from across the room. They were both in college.

Berrie got there first and hugged Seta. "Hi, Sis! I've missed you. When are you coming to visit me at school? And can I come stay with you over the summer?"

Seta laughed and held up her hands, as if to ward off all the questions. "Slow it down, slow it down! I can only answer one question at a time," Seta told her.

Bennie shoved Berrie away from Seta. "Hey, Seta. Are there any cute girls where you live? Maybe you can hook me up with one of your friends," he said.

Seta shook her head in mock sternness. "I don't think so. You just need to focus on your grades."

"I can do both. Focus on girls and focus on grades. I'm multitalented," Bennie laughed.

Seta rolled her eyes in mock disgust.

Lola stood to her side. "So, are you coming over for dinner?" she asked.

Seta looked at Lola. She could tell without asking that things were better between her father and his wife. Each time Seta visited them over the last few years, she had seen a growing closeness. Robert had finally laid her mother to rest.

Seta fingered the locket that hung around her neck. Robert had given it to her upon her graduation from high school eleven years ago. It contained a picture of her mother. She still missed the crucifix she had angrily discarded one day years ago, but she didn't need a piece of jewelry to remind her of her spiritual connection. And this locket seemed like the perfect adornment for a daughter who treasured a mother's memory.

As she touched the locket that cradled her mother's photo, Seta silently said good-bye to the uncertain little girl who had spent so many years searching for love and acceptance wherever she could find it. Her heart was full. She felt truly loved.

Hers hadn't been an easy life and she doubted if it ever

would be. It was a life doctors said she shouldn't have even had. It was a life she had at times hated. It was a life her father had even resented. Still, it was a life God had given her. She had sacrificed many things as she chased the one thing she wanted most—love. As an adult she now knew the love of God could never be taken away from her, no matter what else happened.

She couldn't be sad for the little girl she had been, for that girl's choices had been what shaped the life Seta had today.

This was the life she was meant to live.

And maybe the man at her side was meant to be a part of it. Her eyes locked with Mike's.

He reached out for her hand, and she grabbed his.

THE END

Readers Group Guide

1. How do you feel about Rose and Robert's relationship? Was it healthy or unhealthy?

2. Rose's greatest desire was to have a child. She prayed for this, even bargained with and begged God for this to come to pass. After the disappointment of miscarriages, she wanted to try again. Was this selfless or selfish on her part?

3. Rose went against the counsel of others—her husband, her doctor—and chose to believe, instead, that God was finally answering her prayer and that it was all right for her to become pregnant. Is her action typical or unusual? How so?

4. Rose married a man who was not a strong Christian and who had issues with God. Did she have a responsibility to help lead him to Christ?

5. While no one can tell another how long to grieve, it is unusual for one to grieve so severely for a loss as long as Robert did. He was stuck in a level called dysfunctional grief, which extended for more than a decade. Why do you think Robert grieved so long?

6. Robert did not have a strong relationship with God. How might this have affected how he viewed his wife's death and his grieving process?

7. Robert could not blame Rose for her own death, but instead he placed his blame on the product of her life, the baby. Why do you think this happened?

8. Robert's new wife married him knowing he was still grieving for another woman and that he could not love her fully. Why do you think she still chose to marry him? Is this something that happens in real life—that women get married to men they know don't love them? If so, why?

9. Barbara resented Robert. Why?

10. How do you feel about Barbara and Phillip's relationship?

11. Seta made some choices she knew were not right for her, but she made them anyway based on emotion. How often do we make choices we know aren't good for us, but we do it anyway because of how we feel at the time?

12. How did Seta view God and religion?

13. How did God play a part in Robert's choices—both early on and later in the book?

14. What was the greatest sacrifice each of our key characters (Rose, Robert, Seta, and Barbara) made?

15. Barbara was an active woman in her church. What kind of Christian was she? What do you base your answer on (Her actions toward Robert; Her regular church attendance; Her stern admonishments to Seta, etc.)?

16. What do you believe was the hardest thing about childhood for Seta?

17. Did the faith foundation Barbara gave Seta play a role in allowing Seta to forgive her father and move forward?

18. Was Seta too hard on her father when he finally was ready to reach out to her? Why or why not?

19. How did Seta and Robert grow and change throughout the book? What made them change?

20. Do you feel as though you could have been as forgiving as some of the characters in this book if you were in their shoes?